The Blueprint

Mark Braund is the author of The Possibility of Progress (2005) and co-author, with Ross Ashcroft, of Four Horsemen: The Survival Manual (2012). He has written for The Guardian and The Times Literary Supplement, and is a regular contributor to the Renegade Economist website. The Blueprint is his first novel.

The Blueprint

Mark Braund

MOTHERLODE

First published in 2013 by Motherlode.
Studio 5, St Oswald's Studios, Sedlescombe Road,
London, SW6 1RH, UK.
www.motherlode.org.uk

A CIP catalogue for this book is available
from the British Library.

ISBN 978 0 95639 852 9

Cover design by Nina Riutta at Motherlode

For Mum

Acknowledgments

A number of people read The Blueprint in various drafts and gave helpful feedback. Principal among these was Maggie Carr, whose contribution was such that she really deserves a writing credit. Jeni Braund was meticulous, and as encouraging as ever. Nicola Gregson's comments persuaded me the book was worthy of publication. Thanks also to Karolina Sutton, Anthony Werner, Zach Young and Simon Modery. Megan and Ross Ashcroft at Motherlode were wonderfully supportive throughout. And my wife Henny, without whose encouragement the business of writing would be a struggle, gave it an early stamp of approval which meant so much.

While The Blueprint is a work of fiction, several of the characters featured are real people. I hope these individuals, should they come across the book, will accept their inclusion in the positive spirit in which it is intended. Their presence on these pages connects an imagined world of tomorrow with the real world of today.

As these 'celebrity' appearances comprise only a small number of the characters in the book, I have included a *dramatis personae*, which you will find overleaf.

Principal Characters

The Committee
Helen George, Ireland, Chair
Saeed Jamali, Egypt, Deputy Chair
Kersen Arunatung, Indonesia
Daniel Barenboim, Israel
Safiya Beyene, Eritrea
Rita Correia, Brazil
Ann Margaret Eckhart, Germany
Stefan Lundberg, Sweden
Jay Robertson, Canada
Ajala Sumbramanium, India
Jemma Wiseman, New Zealand
Wen Zhang, China

Intelligence
Mike Dixon, United States
Harry Noble, Great Britain
Oscar Silverman, United States
Yuri Zaytzev, Russia

Politicians
Rachel
Sarah Brightwell, Prime Minister of Great Britain
Takeshi Horomito, President of Japan
Vladimir Kotov, President of Russia
Anna Sianturi, Prime Minister of Indonesia
Hilda Solis, President of the United States

Citizens
Citra Sianturi, Indonesia
Antonella Soares, Brazil
Mbonga Siphosa, Swaziland

One

The opportunity to be involved in planning a new society, virtually from scratch, was not one that Helen George had imagined would come her way. Yet here she was, on a flight from Cape Town to Rio de Janeiro, leading a delegation of a dozen individuals who pretty much held the future of humankind in their hands.

She took a sip of champagne. She rarely drank while working, but the Cape Town meeting had gone unexpectedly well. In any case, they now had two days in Rio to prepare for the next summit.

She pulled up the minutes from Cape Town; it was the first of seven summits on five continents at which the fate of billions of people would be decided. If agreement could be reached on the blueprint for change on which the committee had been working for the last year and a half, there was a good chance of effective action to address the urgent threats to planet and people. Without agreement, the future was bleak.

The record made encouraging reading. All but two African heads of government had turned up. While the continent had most to gain from an agreement, there had been concerns over the reaction of national leaders to the loss of sovereignty implicit in the plan. The blueprint amounted to a global constitution for political governance, and a substantially altered framework for the world economy. It was so radical that even its supporters were surprised it survived intact, four months after publication. Beyond some minor quibbles over wording, the reaction of African leaders had been universally positive.

Helen put down the minutes and pushed back her seat. So much had happened in the seven years since her fortieth birthday, the day in late 2016 when the Republican Party had won back The White House after eight years during which Barack Obama largely failed to hold back the tide of bigotry, ignorance and plain unreason that was consuming large swathes of American society.

Renewed in spirit and ambition after winning re-election, Obama surprised many by returning to some of the issues left on the back burner during his first term. He supported the establishment of the Global Climate Forum, successor body to the Intergovernmental Panel on Climate Change. Helen suspected he also had something to do with her surprise appointment as the forum's rapporteur. That appointment had changed everything. Overnight she went from being a successful businesswoman to a senior diplomat.

But Obama's second-term achievements on the world stage had come at the cost of electoral support at home. His successor as Democratic Party candidate had no chance of securing the presidency, and his replacement by a man cut from quite different cloth had affected Helen badly. After leaving office, Obama withdrew from public life, and it didn't take long for the new president, John Hendricks, to make clear that his administration would actively work to undermine the Forum's work. Helen decided to step down and take a lower profile position at the United Nations.

The post-Obama world proved deeply frustrating for anyone committed to the idea of a more just and sustainable society. With the Americans electing to ignore the overwhelming evidence for the causes of accelerating climate change, the fragile international consensus forged under the previous administration quickly fragmented. While some countries held the line, others were swayed by pressure from the new one. Global efforts to tackle mounting environmental problems stalled as several major energy consumers once again buried their heads in the sand. The US policy shift also had serious economic consequences.

By 2016, mainly due to a contraction in oil production, the renewables sector accounted for nearly a fifth of global economic activity, and almost ninety per cent of year-on-year growth. Thanks to renewables, the world had largely recovered from the 2008 financial crisis. But two years after Hendricks' election, it was plunged into an even more severe recession, this one driven by widespread pessimism, as the number of lives lost to poverty and climate change came to be counted in millions.

The global economy failed to respond to a raft of coordinated policy measures designed to stimulate it. Whatever they tried, politicians were unable to inspire confidence, in themselves or in the prospects for economic improvement. Those fortunate to have jobs saved every penny, convinced their luck would soon run out. This seemed the obvious option to people who would rather trust to common sense than the weasel words of politicians.

There was widespread civil unrest in many of the countries worst affected by climate change. Industrial sabotage became a favoured tactic of eco-terrorists frustrated at the slow pace of reform. Desperate, often starving, people took the law into their own hands, attacking any symbol of the economic system they blamed for their misery.

On the diplomatic stage, the United States disengaged completely. If the new President lacked Obama's moral vision, neither did he possess the gung-ho conviction that characterised the presidency of George W. Bush. Hendricks believed America to be the greatest nation on earth but didn't feel the need to prove it. The country would go its own way. Europe maintained polite diplomatic relations but had no common ground with Hendricks on economic or environmental policy.

But Hendricks remained stubbornly popular at home. He may well have won the 2020 election had it not been for the events of that year's hurricane season. In a six week period from the end of September, three major hurricanes made landfall. All were stronger than Katrina, which caused such devastation in 2005. New Orleans was badly hit again, but thousands of lives were lost in Corpus Christi and Galveston, and hundreds of thousands made homeless. When the pattern of destruction turned out to be almost identical to the predictions of climate scientists, and when it was further revealed that Mexico suffered less loss of life because of simple pre-emptive measures taken by its government, there was widespread civil unrest. It became impossible for Hendricks to campaign in public, and his Democratic opponent was elected with a comfortable majority.

Hilda Solis had served as Labor Secretary in Obama's cabinet, and wasted no time in steering the United States back on to the course he had set. She was instrumental in Helen's promotion to UN Deputy Secretary General, and was also a key player in the establishment of the awkwardly named Committee for the Establishment of a Framework for Global Governance and Economic Reform which Helen now led.

Helen liked and admired Solis; she had overcome serious obstacles to get to the White House: the first female President, and the first latino. She shared Obama's vision for a better world, but brought with it a conviction that was forged as much in her heart as in her head.

Would you like some more champagne, Madam?" The flight attendant brought Helen back to the present.

"Yes, why not?" she replied. "How long until breakfast?"

"About two hours, it's a shorter flight than you think."

Helen nodded and smiled.

It wasn't just in the United States that climate change wrought havoc during the Hendricks' presidency. Across Africa, drought claimed millions of lives; across much of Asia the culprit was unprecedented flooding caused by record monsoon rains combining with rising sea levels. In rich and poor worlds alike, coastal geographies were being radically altered, and large areas of many major cities were either evacuated, or their populations left to fend for themselves, with great loss of life.

By the time the UN General Assembly met in emergency session at the beginning of 2022 it was clear that the world was in urgent need of coordinated action to save both the economy and the planet. Newspaper editorials about the looming threat to civilization, along with globally coordinated mass protests, had finally forced governments to act in concert.

The crisis was too urgent for a drawn out process of negotiation. A clear plan of action was required. While there was near-unanimous agreement on the need for an accelerated version of the pre-Hendricks programme for reductions in carbon emissions to keep global temperatures within two degrees of pre-industrial levels, there was no immediate consensus over the process by which a blueprint for global transformation might emerge. There was some support for the idea of a small panel of eminent people to produce a draft proposal; but how should that panel be constituted?

In the event, the process by which the committee members were selected was completed with surprisingly few arguments. Helen resigned her UN post in order to become a candidate, and hers was among nine names around which there was soon agreement. Negotiations were then deadlocked for a time as the Chinese lobbied for a second Asian in the shape of Wen Zhang, the country's Finance Minister; a respected economist, but a man with little experience on the world stage.

The Chinese eventually prevailed as part of a compromise which saw the controversial Swedish human rights lawyer and former European President, Stefan Lundberg, appointed. As part of that deal, Helen would chair the committee and be given a free pick of the final member. She had twelve hours to make her choice. That night she sought her husband's counsel.

Rudolf Dreyfus knew his wife was exceptional, but he also knew she needed to be reminded of the fact occasionally. After he had coaxed Helen towards the decision he knew she wanted to make, he told her how much he loved her and begged leave to sleep. She had forgotten that he was in Dresden to conduct the world premier of John Adams' much-anticipated new opera, Sacred World. She kept her promise to watch the live broadcast. It was remarkable.

Helen's pick for the final place on the committee was a relatively unknown radical economic philosopher called Jay Robertson. He certainly wasn't on anyone else's list, and was therefore something of a gamble. But she had known him for some time, and was impressed by his intellect, his articulacy and his passion for social justice. At 42 he would be the youngest member of the committee. His almost perfect profile was completed by the fact of his Canadian nationality. Helen loved Canada, and had liked almost every Canadian she had ever met. The final reason for choosing Robertson was that the committee lacked an American. A Canadian based at Yale was the next best thing; his appointment would allay any fears on the part of the Solis administration.

She looked across the cabin to where Robertson was sleeping. He had chosen not to convert his seat into a bed. She never went to bed on a flight, and was pleased to see he shared her reserve. He was a fascinating man: a brilliant mind and a passionate spirit. He might want for a little modesty though. In that respect he didn't compare to her husband.

Stefan Lundberg occupied the seat behind him. He must have been good looking once, now he was rather overweight. He was also something of an enigma. There were several inflated egos on the committee, but his was the only one seemingly untempered by self-awareness. Helen had always found self-effacement to be a useful tool in diplomacy. She had never heard Lundberg make a joke against himself. But then he was a lawyer, not a diplomat.

On the final morning of the General Assembly meeting, it had taken less than an hour to confirm the committee members. There had been some demurring over Robertson, as Helen had expected. Questioned by video link, the Czech President asked him to explain the difference between an economist and an economic philosopher.

"To my mind," Robertson answered, "an economic philosopher examines ways in which the economy, and indeed the discipline of economics, can be revised and re-invented to better serve the interests of all human beings including those yet to be born. Economists, with a few honourable exceptions, spend their time devising new and clever ways for human beings to serve the ends of supposed economic progress as determined by minority vested interests."

Hearing this, Helen had to restrain an urge to thrust her fist into the air. She knew the committee's success would depend on its ability to convince people of the links between minority wealth and privilege, the disenfranchisement of a growing majority, and the economic pressures driving climate change. Robertson's credentials were beyond doubt. And once the Chinese had, rather surprisingly, supported his nomination, and President Solis had signalled her approval, the committee was complete.

It was a good team. Six women and six men; all five continents represented; each major ethnic and religious group with a voice. She had met nine of them previously and worked closely with three. Those she didn't know all had gargantuan reputations in any case. There was Lundberg, Zheng, the Chinese economist, and Ann Margaret Eckhart, the German novelist, playwright and futurologist, whose work Helen admired. Among those she did know, she was most excited by the prospect of working with Daniel Barenboim, the oldest member by some way. Before stepping down to join the committee, Barenboim had, for four years, managed to combine his career as the world's most sought after conductor with his duties as President of Israel.

Four of the committee were on this flight, the others were travelling in two separate groups. Although there was no intelligence to suggest a terrorist threat, Helen had set a limit on the number flying together. And although inconvenient, she and her deputy, the Egyptian theologian Saeed Jamali, never travelled together.

On this flight, along with Robertson and Lundberg, was the Brazilian geneticist and stem cell expert Dr Rita Correia whose clear thinking and political objectivity had proved a considerable asset to the committee's work. Rita was desperately excited to be going home for the first time in nearly two years.

With the skies beginning to lighten, Helen discounted any possibility of sleep. She also began to experience one of her occasional bouts of anxiety. Rationally, she knew the committee's cause was just, and the process in which they were engaged vital, if global catastrophe was to be avoided. But she struggled on two fronts: At times she became immensely frustrated at her failure to persuade opponents of the case for change, at others she was racked with self-doubt: she knew that if the blueprint was implemented but failed to deliver on its promises, she would be held responsible. It was a hefty weight to carry.

And she did have some doubts about the blueprint: Its conclusions were so radical that were they to be adopted, society would be subject to transformation on a scale never before contemplated. The upheaval would be enormous; and the impact on the psyches of billions of people, impossible to predict. The nagging doubt in Helen's mind was summed up in a question frequently asked by opponents: "are things really so bad that we have to turn the world upside down?"

Her usual response was to answer with a question of her own: "just how bad do things have to get?" She would then reel off a list of unarguable statistics to illustrate the frightening extent of suffering and loss of life and the degree to which it had increased over the last decade. If pressed she would get more assertive: "What right," she would ask, "does a tiny minority of well-off individuals have to impose its will on the rest in order to maintain its own privileges through an economic system which denies a decent chance in life to millions around the world, and leaves billions chronically insecure?"

If further challenged, she would state with determined finality that even if you reject the moral argument for a more inclusive economic order, you simply can't ignore the realities of climate change, the impact of which is quite indiscriminate, already claiming many lives in rich countries as well as poor ones.

Confronted with this impenetrable wall, some questioners would change tack: "Okay," they would admit, "let's accept for a moment that the current system is broken, wouldn't it be less of an upheaval just to fix it?"

"That's precisely what we are doing," she would answer, "taking the good bits of the current system, and replacing those parts that cause the whole machine to perform so erratically." Still, she knew from long experience that some people wouldn't be swayed by even the most carefully reasoned argument. Resistance to change seemed to be hard-wired into the character of many people. But Helen had two things on her side: The process she was leading had massive popular support, and the majority of world leaders, the people she and her colleagues had to convince, clearly recognised the need for change, if only, in many cases, because of the consequences of continued inaction for their own electoral prospects.

"Ladies and Gentleman, we will shortly be starting our descent into Antonio Carlos Jobim International Airport. Adverse winds have delayed us slightly en route, but this means we will be landing about 20 minutes after sunrise, so I can promise you a spectacular aerial tour of the world's most beautiful city. The weather at our destination is clear, and the temperature a pleasantly warm seventeen degrees celsius."

Helen tuned out. Rita had told her so much about Rio. She had been to São Paulo several times but had never made it to the *cidade marviliosa*. The first officer had not lied. Flying into Rio at sunrise was spectacular. As the plane banked, one after another Helen spotted each of the landmarks by which this fabled city was identified. The beaches of Ipanema and Copacabana, the Sugar Loaf, the favelas spilling down the hillsides, and the huge brown tranches between surviving favelas where so many had lost their lives in landslides. Then there was that statue, the *Christo Redentador*. Helen had shed her catholic upbringing as a teenager and was now a committed agnostic, but the sight of that immense figure towering over the city set her heart racing. The land below was breathtaking, and not just for its incredible geography. She marvelled at how human beings had been able to create such a city. This beautiful planet, and the civilization it nurtured, had to be saved. Her committee could not afford to fail.

Two

Mbonga Sibhosa opened his eyes. They must have been closed for some time as the sun was now only inches above the horizon. He'd been sitting on the hard ground for several hours, propped up against his favourite green monkey orange tree. He looked up into the dead branches that once bore the fruit which so fascinated visitors. There had been no visitors for nearly a year now.

In better times, nobody would leave the reserve without first learning about the green monkey orange, and, unless they were especially stubborn, without tasting the chocolaty flesh he would offer them after cracking open the hard outer shell. He loved the surprised looks as they tried the unknown fruit and spat out the large flat pips. How easy it had been to impress educated westerners with his knowledge. He sometimes wondered what they might teach him, if ever he had the opportunity to visit their countries.

He was hungry. He hadn't eaten since breakfast, and then only an overripe mango. He had a craving for bread. That would repair the empty feeling in his gut, though probably not the empty feeling in his heart. He looked over at the rhino carcass lying just a few feet away. It was beginning to smell. Maggots were hatching and getting to work in the bloody recess below the animal's eyes where its horn had been gouged out. The bullet wounds suggested it had died before the butchery began. He was grateful for this.

He was pretty sure this was the last rhino in the reserve. Working alone for many months, he had struggled to keep the fences properly maintained. Some animals may have broken through to take their chance in the Swazi countryside, but most of these beautiful creatures would have fallen prey to poachers.

Mbonga felt almost as much pity for the poachers as he did for the lost rhino. They were only slightly less innocent. Most were far hungrier than he was, and desperate for cash to buy food for their families. He doubted that the men who killed this last specimen would get anything like the money they had been promised. There was no longer much of a market for rhino horn. The economic crisis had reduced demand for most non-essentials, including quack medicines and unproven aphrodisiacs. But news of the changed market conditions had failed to make it up the supply chain. The poachers would poach to the last, driven on by desperation and the empty promises of those who controlled the trade.

For all he knew, this rhino might have been the last one anywhere in the world. It was five years since the black rhino had become extinct. He had little faith that the species might one day be resurrected from the DNA samples kept in laboratories. People would have to start caring about each other again before they started caring about animals like the rhino.

The sun had almost gone, but there was nothing waiting for him back at the camp. He reached into his pocket and pulled out a well-thumbed copy of the blueprint. He looked at the image on its cover, the face of a smiling African child. He couldn't tell if it was a girl or a boy.

He had read the blueprint from beginning to end, several times, and he thought he understood most of it. As far as he could tell, it was a pretty good plan for saving civilization, although he failed to see how it could ever actually be implemented. Personal experience had taught him that when things get really bad, human beings tend to turn against their neighbours, rather than working together towards their common survival. On the other hand, it was exceptions to this rule that tended to stick in his mind. And it was the exceptions that provided the best examples of humanity.

He read his favourite passage from the introduction: "The only hope for the survival of human society in a form that can be considered civilized is for the basis of relations between individuals and groups to move away from competition and towards cooperation in all spheres of social activity." He was pleased to see his own thoughts echoed in such an important document, but he wondered why it had taken twelve of the cleverest people on the planet more than a year to articulate what his mother had taught him as a child.

He looked up at the moon, now high in the sky and three quarters full, and remembered her almost identical words: "If Swaziland is to become a truly civilized country, a country where justice reigns and where all people have a decent chance in life, then we must stop trying to get ahead of the next person and instead start working together."

It was from his mother that Mbonga got his brains, and his interest in the wider world. A decade after her death, she would be appalled at the state of her beloved Swaziland. But she would have celebrated the blueprint as a chance for humankind to start over, and an opportunity for ordinary people to take an active role in shaping their own future.

Mbonga felt the same, although he wasn't sure what role he could play in the creation of this brave new world. He was an insignificant figure propped up against a green monkey orange tree under a sky full of stars, some so far away their light had been travelling for millions of years. He smiled as he considered the unimaginable distance of a long dead star, and the similarly remote possibility that the book in his hand might hold the key to a better future.

It was getting cold. He got into the Landrover and turned toward the southern cross, heading back to camp. Twenty minutes later he was checking over the abandoned stone cottages where visitors used to sleep before their early morning game drives. It was a pointless exercise; nobody would have been near the place while he was out, but he couldn't let go of the ritual. He lit a kerosene lamp and then the fire over which he would roast the last of the kudu meat he had saved. He hadn't yet made firm plans, but he had a feeling this would be his last night in the place that had been his second home for nearly sixteen years.

He had done well out of the game reserve, earning several times the average wage in Swaziland. His wife also worked, as a teacher, and between them they had been able to save quite a bit over the years. He hadn't been paid since the reserve closed seven months ago, so they were surviving on his wife's earnings and by dipping into their savings. He calculated they could manage another year like this, but that didn't solve the problem of how he was going to earn a living in the long term. Both of their sons were now teenagers, but he was adamant they would not go out to work before they had completed their education. In any case, there were no jobs to be had, and certainly no free land to farm.

After dinner he lay on a sofa in the bar area and turned, again, to the blueprint. The more he thought about it, the more fascinated he was by the process which had led to its publication. It was not always easy to get information, but there was increasing coverage in the newspapers, and he had seen several news reports on the TV at the shebeen near his house. He knew that an important summit was taking place in Cape Town at which African leaders were meeting to discuss the blueprint. He decided to pack. He would leave early in the morning, make the two hour journey home, and hope to see some coverage of the summit on TV.

He woke shortly after 6am. It was late August but there was little sign of spring. The outdoor bathrooms in the cottages were not much fun on a winter's morning, but marginally better than the options for washing at home. He packed quickly and took a final walk around the camp. On the way out of the reserve, he took care to lock each of the four gates securely and when he reached the main road, turned right towards Manzini. There were few vehicles on the road, a result of chronic fuel shortages. He had loaded the remaining cans of diesel into the back of the Landrover, although he wasn't sure how he was going to keep them safe from theft.

By the time he reached their small house on the outskirts of Manzini the sun was up and it was getting warmer. As he expected, the place was deserted. The boys would be at school on the other side of town, while his wife, Temily, would be at work not a hundred yards away. He hadn't seen her for ten days so he walked over to the school building and looked through the window at the back of her classroom.

She was sitting on a stool reading a story to her class. The children were sat in a semicircle on the floor in front of her. She looked as beautiful as ever. He tried not to attract attention as he knew what would happen, but it was too late. One of the children spotted him at the window, pointed towards him and yelled out his name. The entire class of fifty children leapt to their feet and made for the door. In the thirty seconds it took them to pile through the corridor and out into the yard where he was standing, Temily walked slowly to the window and opened it. She kissed him on the cheek.

"Welcome home," she said.

"Is that all I get?"

"While I'm at work, that's all you get," she said, sternly. He feigned disappointment. "Later, different rules may apply," she added, smiling.

Mbonga disappeared beneath a scrum of five year olds for a full minute before Temily ordered them back into the classroom. As the lesson restarted he headed back to the house. He needed to unload the Landrover and find a suitable hiding place for the fuel.

By the time he'd finished humping jerry cans and changed out of his clothes, which were smelling unpleasantly of diesel, Temily was home. They calculated they had about forty minutes before the children returned. They closed the front door and ran into the bedroom.

"I can't remember the last time we made love in the middle of the day," Mbonga said.

"I can't remember the last time we made love."

He looked hurt. "It hasn't been that long, has it?"

"Long enough." They didn't talk again for half an hour.

"What do you think I should do?" Mbonga asked, finally breaking the silence.

"How do you mean?"

"With my life, with my time, now I have no job, now the reserve is closed."

"Are you not going back then?"

"I can't see any point. I lost the last rhino yesterday. I can't keep the place maintained on my own. There are no supplies left."

"What would you like to do?" she asked.

"I don't know. I need to get a job, our savings will not last forever. But I've been looking for seven months now. Perhaps I should do something completely different."

"Such as?"

"Well, I would like to travel. Could we manage if I didn't bring in any money for a couple more months?"

"As long as we're careful, I don't see why not. But where will you go, and how are we going to pay for it?"

He looked at his wife with a slightly hopeless expression. "I'm not sure really. I have to think about it a bit." The conversation was interrupted by voices outside. It was the boys. Mbonga leapt out of bed and threw on his clothes. Each time he returned home he had to remind himself they weren't really children anymore. He hugged them all the same.

"So, are you both well?" They nodded and smiled. "Too old for a game of football with your dad?" All three were outside in seconds.

After dinner, Mbonga went down to the shebeen to see if there was any coverage of the summit on TV. After exchanging greetings with most of the people there, he sat on a stool with a good view of the screen fixed to the wall. The Cape Town meeting still dominated the news. There were discussions with pundits about the prospects for the blueprint after a meeting which was being hailed as a great success. This was interspersed with re-run footage of key people speaking to the media.

He recognised the tall red-haired woman as Helen George. Nobody seemed to have a bad word to say about her. He recognised a couple of the others but couldn't put names to the faces. Then he saw a black woman standing beside George as she spoke to reporters outside the conference centre. That must be Safiya Beyene, the African representative on the committee. Mbonga knew nothing about her except that she was from Eritrea, a country he knew equally little about.

He couldn't take his eyes off the coverage. After more than a year of meetings behind closed doors, the summit was bringing the whole thing to life. Now, for the first time, he could see the people responsible for drafting the blueprint, and everybody was talking about the little book he had been reading. He watched as the delegates were driven away from the conference centre. Then the TV camera pulled back to reveal hundreds of South Africans singing and dancing behind the security cordon. It was clearly a spontaneous celebration, not stage managed. He'd never seen anything like it.

After a while, the coverage started repeating. He didn't want to buy another beer, so made his way home. The boys were already in bed, but Temily was waiting up for him.

She made some tea and they sat down on either side of the wooden table that stood in the corner of the main room by the sink.

"So, what would you say if I went away for a couple of months?" he asked, slightly fearful of her response.

"To be honest we have become used to not having you around," she answered pointedly.

He knew he was asking a great deal of her, but was set firm on his course. "I was just watching coverage of the Cape Town summit on TV. It was so exciting. People seem very optimistic about the prospects for the blueprint. I wish I could have been there."

"So?"

"I would love to go to one of these summits, you know."

"To do what exactly?"

"Just to be there. To be a part of it; to feel the excitement. So I could tell our grandchildren that I was there when everything changed."

"It's not done and dusted yet, you know?"

"I know. But there's a good chance it will happen. Something tells me I should go."

"So which one are you planning to go to? Your timing is not good, our local summit has just ended."

Mbonga smiled, then sighed. "I can't afford to fly, so I'll have to travel over land"

"Wait a minute. Where are the other summits?"

"Um, Brazil, Indonesia, Japan, America, Georgia and Germany."

"And which of these countries do you think you can travel to by land."

"You're the teacher, you tell me." She gave him a withering look. "Okay, I'm sorry. Theoretically I could get to Georgia or Germany by land. Although I think my best chance is to travel north through Africa and get a boat to Italy or France."

"And do you know how many miles it is to the north coast of Africa?"

"No. How many?" he asked, sheepishly.

She couldn't help but laugh. "Well, I don't know either, but it's a very long way. And how are you going to pay for this great adventure?"

Suddenly Mbonga felt on surer ground. "I've got a full tank of diesel in the Landover, and a further 240 litres in jerry cans I brought back from the reserve. By my reckoning, that's about a thousand US dollars on the black market. I know Walter will give me a good price. With that much money I can easily make it to Berlin."

"Berlin? Is that where you're going then?"

"Yes. With your permission, of course. Berlin is the final summit. It starts in seven weeks. That should give me plenty of time to get there."

"And when do you plan on leaving?"

"I thought Monday. I'd like to spend the weekend with you and the boys first."

She leant across the table, put her hand around the back of his neck and pulled his head towards hers. "Are you sure about this?" she asked, realising for the first time that he was deadly serious.

"I am my love," he kissed her forehead. "I really am."

Three

Helen was thrilled to be eating breakfast on a terrace from which she could see the entire length of Ipanema. For the next two days the committee would have exclusive use of a modest but perfectly located hotel at the Copacabana end of this beautiful beach. She had already enjoyed an invigorating pre-breakfast swim and was now tucking into some of the best papaya she had ever tasted.

After the rest of the committee had arrived the previous afternoon, they had enjoyed two productive sessions either side of dinner. The first was an evaluation of the Cape Town summit, the second focused on how to manage the media coverage, some of which was becoming negative. She rather wished that session had been held over until today, as this morning's news included some information not cleared for release. While she was fairly sure the committee was water-tight, she had to face the possibility that someone was leaking.

"Good morning." It was Lundberg. "May I join you?"

"Of course," she replied.

"Was that you I saw ploughing across the bay earlier?"

"Possibly."

"I had no idea you were such an athlete."

"You should have seen me swim thirty years ago. Olympic trialist, you know?"

"I had no idea. Why did you give up?"

"Injury, and I got tired of going up and down endlessly."

"So you swapped that for a life going round in circles?"

"You forget, I was a successful businesswoman before I became a diplomat."

Lundberg smiled. Despite his own eminence, he routinely failed to acknowledge other people's achievements. Helen rarely spoke of her own record, but with Lundberg a little boastfulness sometimes proved an effective means of puncturing his ego.

"What would you like for breakfast, Sir?" The waiter arrived just in time.

"Cafe con leite, duas ovos fritas, cogumelos, torrada com marmalada, por favor". Helen smiled as Lundberg answered in apparently perfect Portuguese. She caught the waiter's eye; he appeared less impressed.

"You should have poached eggs, you know. Better for the waistline," Helen said, digging into her papaya.

Lundberg looked out onto the beach. There was already a good smattering of people soaking up the sun, and a couple of volleyball games underway. "I do so hate beaches," he said.

Helen had never worked out if Lundberg really did hate nearly everything, as he claimed.

"Is it beaches you hate, or the sight of people relaxing and enjoying themselves?"

"Can I not hate both?" His tone had softened slightly, suggesting that this first little joust of the day was over. Whatever Helen thought of him, she didn't doubt his professional respect for her. Though he was a combatative opponent, he had never tried to undermine her, even if he did have an unappealing tendency to bully any committee member that didn't meet his rigorous standards. His breakfast arrived and they ate without speaking for several minutes.

"Tell me," Helen asked, "If one country or bloc is going to scupper this process, who would you put your money on?"

"I have to say I think the Russians, with the support of those neighbouring regimes they keep in power."

"I think you're right. We're going to have to do some serious politicking before we get to Tbilisi."

Lundberg must not have seen the piece in the Wall Street Journal in which his opinion about the Russians had been echoed, along with some insights into the committee's work which should not have been in the public domain. She had to be careful. It would be hard to prove anything against him, and the last thing they needed now was an internal crisis, but she was concerned that he could be leaking to a hostile news provider.

"Fancy a game of tennis?" she asked, smiling her best beaming smile at him.

"Don't tell me, junior Wimbledon champion?"

He proved to be as out of shape as Helen had suspected, but must have been a decent player once. As it became warmer they agreed to leave it at one set all. She made her excuses and returned to her room as she was expecting a call.

"As far as I can tell, he's not had any dealings with the guy who wrote the piece. But he did spend a year at Stanford at the same time as Veronica Abel."

"Wait a minute, she's married to Victor Weiss, isn't she?" Helen tensed as the pieces fell into place.

"That's right. I'll give you a call if I get anything more."

Gerald Small had first worked for Helen twenty years ago when she appointed him head of public affairs at GeorgeTech. He hadn't been formally employed by her for many years, but insisted on remaining her 'invisible retainer'. Whenever she needed some digging done, she called Gerald.

Victor Weiss was President of the Wall Street Journal Group, and Lundberg knew his wife. If the Swede did have his own agenda and was planning a drip-drip campaign of leaks, he had the perfect outlet. This was not good news.

There was a knock at the door. It was Rita. They kissed on both cheeks, more times than Helen thought necessary in any culture. "Helen, fantastic," she said. What are you doing tonight?"

"Nothing, you told me to keep it free," Helen answered, feigning seriousness.

"Fantastic. My parents have invited you to dinner. They are so excited to meet you. You fancy a walk along the beach? I'll take you to my absolutely favourite coffee shop, in Leblon. You think we have to take those awful spooks with us?"

"Yes, I do think we need a security detail. You are possibly the best known Brazilian woman in the world, and I am probably the best known non-Brazilian woman. If we walk along that beach without some protection, we'll be mobbed."

"Yes, but the Brazilian people love you. You know the committee has a higher approval rating in Brazil than in any other country," Rita continued.

"I know. That's why I'm glad to be here; but that's also why we need some protection."

"You are right, as always." She took Helen's hand and dragged her towards the door.

"Hang on, just a minute." Helen put the papers she had been reading back in her briefcase and locked it before sliding into the sandals she'd abandoned in the middle of the floor.

They went down the stairs rather than waiting for the rather antique looking lift. Rick Spedman, spookmeister-in-chief as Rita called him, was waiting for them at the bottom. He did always seem to know when someone was moving and needed cover, and it was rather spooky, Helen had to admit. Rick had a great sense of humour, though, and was very good at his job.

As they made their way through the restaurant and out onto the terrace, they were joined by two of Rick's team, both women, who kept a discreet distance. Despite their civilian clothes, they still looked like bodyguards. But Helen cared neither what they did, nor what they looked like, just as long as she could do her work, and on this occasion, she and Rita could walk untroubled along the beach until Ipanema became Leblon.

"The city is as beautiful as they say."

"I know." Rita sighed happily.

It hadn't taken Helen long to work out that the Brazilian had three modes of behaviour and only three. She was either an excited puppy; she was wistful and serene; or she was the consummate professional. From the outset, her contribution to the committee's work had been impressive, especially given her lack of diplomatic experience. More than once she had reduced Helen to tears, imploring colleagues to adopt some measure or other in order to tackle poverty in superficially successful countries like her own, while illustrating her argument with heartrending stories of suffering and loss.

"Did you think we would ever get this far?" Helen asked her.

"Not after that first meeting."

"It was a bit of a bumpy start, wasn't it? Not helped by the fact that we were in Baltimore, of all the godforsaken places."

"What do you mean? Baltimore was ideal. Top-notch facilities at Johns Hopkins and a sharp media focus on intractable poverty in the richest country in the world. You said you didn't want the coverage to be all about climate change. The media really went to town on the poverty issue."

"And you were dead right, I just don't like Baltimore."

That first meeting had indeed been fraught. Arranged at short notice just three days after the General Assembly resolution because most of the committee members were already in New York, Helen had needed quickly to establish terms of reference to ensure they didn't talk for weeks without achieving anything concrete. When she and her deputy, Saeed Jamali, had entered the room, ten minutes before the scheduled start, the others were all waiting for them. The atmosphere was calm, but it felt like the first day at a new school, for both teacher and pupils.

"I'm sure you are all aware of the magnitude of the task ahead," Helen began. "It might sound crazy, but we have eighteen months to come up with a plan for global political and economic reorganisation to address the threats of climate change and poverty, and to convince nearly two hundred national governments to accept our recommendations." She paused and looked around the room. Daniel Barenboim caught her eye.

"Not so many years ago," he said, "people told me I was crazy for suggesting that a resolution might be found to the Israel/Palestine problem, but we did it. Today, that historic settlement is threatened by the same factors that threaten the viability of societies the world over. We have no choice."

Helen was pleased to receive Barenboim's unqualified support. His experience and wisdom would be crucial in getting the more pessimistically pragmatic members of the committee on side.

"Perhaps I might continue with a question?" she asked. "To be sure that we are all singing from the same hymn sheet, does anyone believe a solution to the problems facing people and planet is achievable without wholesale changes to global economic and political institutions and structures?" She waited again. She had agreed a strategy for the meeting with Jamali and after a few seconds, he obliged.

"It seems, Helen, that we have passed the first test of unanimity with flying colours. Everybody is agreed: no salvation for humanity without radical political and economic change on a global scale." Jamali paused and then smiled. "Seriously though, I think our first major hurdle will be persuading people that such change is not only essential, but also achievable. Many people struggle to see beyond a politics in which individual nations plot their own course despite a global economic framework over which they have little control. We need to convince people that problems rooted in a competitive and unforgiving economic system can only be addressed by changing the way that system works. As it's a global system, those changes have to be implemented globally, and all nations have to sign up."

"I don't disagree, Saeed," said Lundberg, "but I do think we also need to be clear that we are not advocating a single global government. The world certainly is not ready for that."

"That may be so," Jamali replied," but the outcome must be substantive changes to key aspects of the global economic system. That may be possible without establishing a unified government, but effective institutions of global governance will have to be created if we are to have any chance of success."

"If you ask me," said Jay Robertson, "we need a resurgence of good old fashioned internationalism. We have to move the world economy from relations between nations based on aggressive competition, which serve only the interests of a wealthy elite, to relations based on mutually beneficial cooperation. An economy that requires cooperation between nations will also inspire cooperation within nations, and create conditions in which national governments can do the right thing by their entire populations."

"Yes indeed, Jay," Helen said, which is why, if you'd switch on your readers, I'd like to propose a certain text as the starting point for our discussions."

She waited while they looked at the document on their screens. "As you will see, I suggest we use The 27 Principles to help frame our discussions. I'm not suggesting that the committee adopt it as some kind of credo, nor that our work be bound by it. Only that we use it as a starting point."

Helen knew this was risky. The 27 Principles was a controversial document, as much for its provenance as its content. It had only existed for eight months, having been posted online in response to an article about the social impact of climate change on the website of a Brussels-based think tank.

A lower profile launch would be hard to imagine. Mysteriously, after twelve hours the document was removed, apparently by its original poster.

For reasons nobody quite understood, it had been impossible to establish the identity or location of the author, but in the short time it was online, The 27 Principles became the subject of a hugely successful process of viral distribution. It was copied and pasted from blog to discussion board to social networking site thousands of times over. Within 48 hours, a web search for 'the 27 principles' yielded more than 10 million results. While suspicions over its authorship remained, it was widely accepted that its distribution was spontaneous and unmediated. In unprecedented numbers, people liked what they read and decided to share it.

The 27 Principles was a remarkably concise and persuasive distillation of ideas that had been emerging, mainly from the web, over a period of years. Whoever had been responsible, and most people thought it the work of a single author, it was the clearly the product of an exceptional mind. It quickly became the subject of learned articles and opinion pieces; publicity that further fuelled its spread. Pundits speculated on the reasons for its success. Many concluded that the fact of its anonymous authorship was key. People were sick of politics and the empty promises of politicians. The 27 Principles struck a chord, largely because it wasn't identified with any established political entity. Its anonymity meant the principles could be owned in common by anyone who shared its ideals.

Within days, what became known as '27 clubs' were springing up all over the world. Groups of people would get together to discuss the principles, how they might be used to tackle the mounting economic and climate crises, and how they could be applied at community level. This anonymous document, and the reaction it inspired, had indirectly led to the special session of the General Assembly at which the resolution to establish the committee had been passed.

Helen looked around the table. She already had a pretty good idea who the dissenters would be. To her left was the former Eritrean Foreign Minister, Safiya Beyene. She had started life as a firebrand trade union leader, coming to global prominence after a speech to the UN General Assembly demanding concerted action to save Africa from the ravages of climate change. She would be fine.

Next to Beyene sat Jay Robertson. Helen knew Robertson's views very well and had no concerns. Next was Jemma Wiseman, from New Zealand. An urban planner and architect, she was one of the trailblazers of the sustainable building movement. Helen had known her for many years; she could also be relied upon. Next to Jemma sat the Indian, Ajala Sumbramanium; softly-spoken but fiercely intelligent. Every member of the committee was distinguished in their field but Ajala almost defined the word. She was one of the world's leading climate scientist̩s and possessed a superb ability, when speaking, to combine the science underlying climate change with empathy for those whose lives were destroyed by its effects, while all the time remaining resolutely apolitical. While Helen didn't know where she stood on the principles, she knew that if she did have reservations, they would be politely put and well argued.

Next along was Kersen Atunarung, the Indonesian academic who was expert in two distinct spheres: agronomy and social anthropology. So often had he been asked to explain the connection between his two disciplines that the reverse of his business card was printed with an explanation that he encouraged people to take away and consider. It read: "For 99 per cent of people who have walked the earth, both culture and economics have centred around harvesting and husbanding the fruits of nature. Anthropology and agricultural science are therefore inseparable." Helen knew his views on land rights and the ability of people to feed themselves; he would be supportive.

Seated between Atunarung and Barenboim was Lundberg; he would be the first, and probably most vocal, dissenter. Then came Rita: Helen already had a strong sense of a burgeoning soulmateship with the Brazilian. Next to her was Ann Margaret Eckart, the German writer. Dismissed by her critics as hopelessly utopian, she had been one of the biggest celebrity promoters of The 27 Principles after its publication. Next was Wen Zhang, whom Helen had not met until last week, since when they had exchanged little more than pleasantries. Zhang was widely seen as a guardian of economic orthodoxy, and likely, therefore, to be antagonistic towards the economic radicalism of the principles.

Finally, on Helen's right sat Saeed Jamali. Helen had been allowed no say in the selection of her deputy. She had been amazed, therefore, when he emerged as the consensus candidate. Everybody knew they were close; they had even co-authored articles for the New York Times. So Lundberg and Zheng would be sure to raise some objection, and

Subramanium she wasn't sure off. She was slightly surprised, therefore, when Jemma Wiseman indicated her wish to speak.

"Helen, as you know I'm a great supporter of The 27 Principles; if there is any hope of progress, they will all have to be realised and then some," she began. "My concern is about how we manage the opposition. Despite massive popular support, many people remain deeply opposed to the thrust of the principles. Among business leaders, approval remains below 50 per cent. Part of our brief is to publish regular progress reports so the world can follow our work. My fear is that if the press gets hold of the fact that we are using the principles as our starting point, the objectivity of the committee will be questioned before we have even begun."

"So, don't tell them," Barenboim interrupted. It took several seconds before he realised he would have to elaborate. "Look, all Helen is suggesting is that we use the spirit of this document to help frame our discussions. We are under no obligation to report this private understanding to the outside world. Doubtless our discussions will be also be informed by the wisdom of many celebrated texts, from the Torah to the Koran; from the proverbs of Confucius to the speeches of Martin Luther King. What are we to do? Give the world's media a list of all the books we have each read?" There was laughter.

"I agree with President Barenboim." Helen had to conceal her surprise at this intervention from Wen Zhang. "If the work of this committee is to be effective then yes, of course we have to be transparent, but we certainly should not be airing all our dirty laundry in public. Personally, I have some philosophical problems with five of the principles, but in general I think the document would make an excellent starting point for our discussions; unless anyone has a viable alternative?" Zhang was more wily than Helen had anticipated, for as he asked the question, he looked directly at Lundberg.

"Well," answered the Swede. Helen wondered if the others thought him as slimy as she did. "I have to admit, I don't think I've ever read the document in its entirety, so I may not be qualified to comment. That said, we don't have a great deal of time, and we certainly have to start somewhere. I have no substantive objection to the proposal from the chair, as long as we are all agreed, and as long the decision remains unminuted."

Helen felt her shoulders drop a couple of inches. This was a result. "Jemma," she asked, "is that okay with you?" The New Zealander nodded her agreement.

Rita moved away from Helen in pursuit of a stray volleyball which she expertly returned to the server at the far end of the court they had just passed. "I wonder if we'll have time for a game while we're here?" she panted.

"I doubt it," Helen said. "Did you see this morning's Wall Street Journal?"

"I saw it. I didn't read it though. It's always so dry."

"I know. But they ran an opinion piece which seems to be targeting the committee."

"Well, the Journal has been antagonistic towards us since the start." Rita had flipped into work mode.

"Yes, but the piece contained a rather familiar phrase."

"Go on."

"Certain of the committee's proposals in respect of changes to global economic structures seem to have come, unimproved, from an undergraduate class discussion at a third rate university."

"Third rate university? That's exactly what Lundberg said during his rant in Paris last year."

"Yep. I think we may have sprung a leak."

"Yes. But he was just trying to stamp his authority on proceedings, wasn't he? He's mellowed quite a bit since then."

"He has. But it's hardly a common phrase. It can't be a coincidence that it's now been used twice to describe the committee's work."

"I must say," Rita replied, "I've been surprised how long we've been allowed such an easy a ride by the media."

"Me too. I guess after Cape Town it's beginning to dawn on people how close we are. I think we can expect things to hot up now. I'll make some phone calls this afternoon, make sure nobody's getting cold feet. Are you still seeing Francesca Di Soto this afternoon?"

"Yes, I have to be at the residence for 1.30. Don't worry, I'll make sure our President is on message."

They reached Leblon and crossed the road to the coffee shop. Rita ordered, and they sat facing the sea. She took hold of her friend's hand. "Don't worry," she said, "Lundberg doesn't have enough power to undermine the process."

"I hope you're right," Helen replied. "What was it Zhang said in Cape Town? 'Have no friends not equal to yourself.' In the eyes of many people Lundberg is at least my equal".

"Yes, Helen, but he has few friends."

Four

Antonella Soares looked across the bed at her mother. They had both been looking for a sign of life, but there had been no breath for several minutes. Her mother nodded, and managed a faint smile, before a tear formed in her left eye and ran down her cheek. Antonella walked around the bed and placed both arms around her. She felt her mother's body shake before tears consumed them both. Minutes passed before she unfolded Antonella's arms and turned to face her daughter.

"Thank you," she said, softly.

"For what?" Antonella was unprepared for either conversation or thanks.

"For being here. For loving my mother as much as I did. For being such a wonderful daughter."

Antonella looked at her grandmother's face. More than anything she had not wanted her to suffer. Over the last three months she had taken every hour of overtime she could get to pay for drugs to keep the pain to a minimum. Her grandmother had been conscious until only a few hours ago. Several times yesterday they had enjoyed lucid conversations. Antonella couldn't imagine how life would be now. Her earliest memory was of the three of them together.

Her father had died in a mining accident when she was ten. She and her two younger brothers had grown up with two mothers, a grandmother who looked after them, and a proper mother, who worked. Not that she didn't love her children; she spent every minute she could with them. But she had to work. There was no choice.

"I'll go next door and telephone Sr. Carvalho," her mother said. Antonella had been to the undertaker that morning to advise him that her grandmother would probably not survive the day. As her mother left the room she sat down and took the dead woman's still warm hand. She remembered the story of how she came to be in Brazil. It was remarkable that she had survived her first year of life, never mind into a ninth decade.

Born in March 1943 of Jewish parents, Sophia Ascoli began life fleeing persecution. Had she not been born two weeks early, she would probably have ended up in one of the internment camps from which thousands of Italian Jews were transported to Auschwitz.

Compared with much of Europe, Italy's small Jewish population got off relatively lightly until Mussolini was overthrown and the Germans occupied the north of the country. Sophia was born only days before the German Army entered Genoa, but, with the help of a priest, she and her parents were smuggled around the Riviera to a small village near Aix-en-Provence where they were hidden for several weeks by a French family. Their protectors had contacts with the Brazilian ambassador to the Vichy Government, Luis Martins de Souza Dantas, who, in clear breach of his government's immigration policy, issued them with diplomatic visas to enter Brazil. They eventually made it overland to Cadiz and then onto a boat to South America.

Four

Sophia had arrived in Rio de Janeiro in late 1943 and remained in Brazil for the rest of her life, not leaving the country even for a holiday. While she had been free from persecution in her new home, life had been extremely hard. The child of middle-class Italian parents had raised a family in poverty, a condition from which the subsequent generation was still struggling to free itself. She had begun life as a victim of political persecution at the hands of people who despised her for her ancestry. And she ended it a victim of economic persecution; not hated, but largely ignored by those who set the rules by which everyone has to live.

Sofia was never in any doubt that the holocaust was the greater moral crime; it was premeditated after all. But as she frequently reminded Antonella, more people had died prematurely because human beings had yet to devise an economic system which gave everyone a decent chance in life, than at the hands of the Nazis.

And now she was gone. Antonella looked around the room. She felt an acute sense of injustice that her grandmother's life had been so hard, and her mother's the same. She squeezed the dead woman's hand and promised her things would be different for her own children.

Her mother returned. She'd clearly made a determined effort to stop crying just before entering the house. "Sr. Carvalho is sending someone. They should be here within the hour. He is going to speak with Rabbi Romero. It should be possible for tomorrow."

"Okay," Antonella smiled.

"You'd better to get to work."

"I know, but I really don't feel like it."

"You know what she would have said. You have a good job. You are very lucky. You can't afford to lose it. In any case, they have been very good to you, all the extra overtime."

"Yes. I'll go and change. Will you be alright?"

"Your brothers will be home soon. I'll be fine."

Antonella worked at the São Paolo Hilton. She started out as a chambermaid, but it had taken just six months to impress sufficiently to get transferred to catering. She now spent much of her time working in room service, but she also served behind the foyer bar, and covered tables in the various restaurants. When they were short staffed she moved back to housekeeping, which she didn't enjoy. Having proved herself capable of showing initiative, she was given a considerable amount of responsibility. And with responsibility came a degree of freedom that was not enjoyed by the other junior staff.

On the bus to work she thought about her promise to her grandmother. While she had been confined to bed they had discussed the prospects for the blueprint at length. Initially Sophia had been sceptical: it was just another supposed solution being imposed on poor countries. Why should things be any different this time? But when Antonella pointed out that the committee included as many representatives of poor countries as rich ones, and did not include a single American, her grandmother changed her tune. Antonella didn't know if her uncharacteristic calmness was a symptom of realising her time was nearly up, or if she really was persuaded that the blueprint could make a difference. But she did know that there was little chance of making good on her promise in respect of her own children if the blueprint wasn't implemented.

She walked quickly along Avenida das Nações Unidas and down the alley that led to the staff entrance. Although it was longer, she took a route through the kitchen, the best place to pick up any gossip that might come in useful during the shift. She pushed open the large swing doors and noticed an unusual buzz about the place. There was not a great deal of work being done. Tito, one of the commis chefs, saw her come in. "Hey Antonella," he shouted, "come over here."

"Hi Tito, what's going on?"

"You haven't heard?"

"Heard what?"

"About the summit? The hotel has been chosen to host the summit next week."

"The blueprint summit, you mean? I didn't even know it was going to be in Brazil?"

"Nor did anyone else. They've been keeping the summit locations under wraps. Are you okay?" Tito could see she was distracted.

"I'm fine."

"Well, you'd better go and find Lourdes. She's going to have plenty of overtime for you. How is your grandmother today?" She shook her head. He gave her a hug. "I'm sorry," he whispered.

Five

Harry Noble was three years from retirement. He could have gone earlier; his pension pot was certainly big enough. But his superiors were keen for him to stay on, and he had no idea what would he do with himself at home. As he turned from Page Street into Millbank, he looked up at Jagger's statue of St George high on the facade of Thames House before entering through its glorious arch. He loved everything about this place.

His work had been his life, and he was deeply proud of the service he had given his country and, by extension, the civilised world. If that world still faced many problems, it would be in far worse shape had he and his colleagues not held the line so successfully over the last few decades. Nowadays, he acted more as a political consultant than a senior intelligence officer. The last few years, based in his office, or in various meeting rooms around Whitehall, had suited him down to the ground.

But all was not well in Harry's world. He was still close enough to the centre of things to notice a gradual shift away from the natural political alignment of The Security Service. There had been a change in the culture of the organisation. As new blood replaced old school, different thinking had found its way in, and to quite high levels. Harry thought it threatened the essence of the organisation to which he had devoted his life.

He sat down behind his desk with the coffee he had carried up three flights of stairs. Quite why the coffee produced by an identical machine on the second floor should be of such superior quality to that which flowed from the one on his own corridor was a mystery. He turned on his monitor. There was a message from Oscar Silverman. He'd last seen Silverman on a trip to Washington about eighteen months ago, but had not heard from him since. His old friend had now retired from the CIA. Harry had been impressed at the ease with which the American had managed to cut all ties with his lifelong employer.

"Call me you old bastard," was all the message said. Harry smiled, and dialled.

"Oscar, it's Harry."

"Harry, thanks for getting back. Are we secure?" Harry assured him he was calling on a secure line, but was surprised that Oscar was.

"Listen, Harry, didn't you have some dealings with Helen George a while back?" the American asked.

"I wouldn't say dealings exactly. We spoke at the same conference, and subsequently dined together. It was just after that ghastly man Hendricks got in. She organised the conference, er, Consolidating the Humanitarian Frontier, that's what it was called. I was asked to give our angle on the probability of increased terrorist activity, post Obama. Nothing controversial or classified. Lots of good people there though; especially Helen, I liked her a lot.

"Do you think she remembers you?"

"I should think so. I'm a big fan of her husband. I'm afraid I rather bored her by going on at length about how much I admired him."

"Oh yeah, the conductor guy."

"Culture never was your strong suit, was it Silverman?" Harry maintained a mildly patronising tone towards Americans, even those he considered friends.

"Cut the crap Noble. Remember, your empire collapsed in ruins long before ours did." This made Harry smile.

"What can I do for you Oscar? Presumably it has something to do with Helen and her committee?"

"You busy at the weekend Harry?"

"Yes, actually, but I'm sure you won't let that get in the way of your plans."

"OK, I'll come to you. I'll call when I get into Heathrow."

Dinner with Rita's parents was as intellectually stimulating as it was culinarily impressive. Her mother was a doctor, world-renowned in the treatment of childhood leukaemia; her father, a journalist and a respected campaigner for social justice.

"So Helen, what do you think of the brave new low-carbon world we have created here in Brazil?" Sr. Correia asked.

"I think it provides a great example of how it's possible to combine economic development and sustainability."

"Those who claimed it wasn't possible either had too much invested in traditional methods of energy production or were too narrow-minded to embrace change. Good business people recognise the threat of global warming for what it is: an opportunity to create new industries and to take the Brazilian economy to a different plane."

"But do you think the changes have gone far enough? Has there been a significant impact on poverty at the bottom?" Helen asked.

"No. Living conditions, average life-expectancy at birth, these are as bad as many countries in Africa. We may have proved to the world that economic growth can be driven by moving to a renewables-based economy, but the poorest have seen no improvement. We are repeating the mistakes of the industrial revolution. We have cracked the secret of wealth creation, but done nothing to ensure that the benefits reach those most in need."

"Do you think the state should be taxing corporations and wealthy individuals more heavily to fund social programmes?" Rita asked her father.

"That is one option, but not the best one. Social programmes need funding only because the economy doesn't provide opportunities for all. But what a crazy way to arrange things: allow some to work and tax them to support those denied jobs; it makes no sense. Taxing effort and enterprise disincentivizes entrepreneurs, and leaves companies with less capital for investment. Certainly we need more investment in infrastructure, in law and order, and in education, but if such programmes are going to benefit the poorest, we also need an economy that provides viable employment opportunities for everyone. Redistribution through taxation does not achieve that, and in many otherwise successful countries it has created a culture of dependency."

Rita's mother offered a similar story: "It's the same in respect of health care," she said, "which is a basic economic need, universally shared. Take up of services reflects disparities in wealth and life opportunities. Even where free services exist, many of the poorest are unable to access them because they have no transport, because they don't know they exist, or because they are too afraid to leave their homes."

"And that's another big problem. Lawlessness in the favelas has reached unprecedented levels," added Sr. Correia. "Some neighbourhoods are run as virtual fiefdoms, beyond the reach of the city authorities. They are excluded from the benefits of economic progress and participatory democracy."

"What about in more rural areas?" Helen asked.

"Things are much better outside the cities. That's where most of the new jobs have been created. On the wind farms, the algae lakes and the tidal power stations. Rural poverty has been cut, but more than half of Brazil's population is now urban; and most of the new arrivals end up in the favelas, with little hope of escape."

"So moving the global economy to a renewables base is not sufficient?" Helen knew the answer but wanted to hear it articulated.

"If it could be achieved on a global scale, obviously it would help in preserving the life-sustaining capacity of the planet, but it would do little for the poorest. That is a challenge that predates climate change by centuries. The renewables industry today uses less labour than was employed extracting and processing fossil fuels fifty years ago. It's a technology-driven industry. It will not provide jobs for everyone."

"This is exactly the conclusion we have arrived at," Rita said. "Climate change may pose the most immediate threat to livelihoods and wellbeing, but it's the economic system that encourages unsustainable outcomes and deepening poverty. To address both problems at once we need a completely different kind of economy."

"I think the proposals contained in the blueprint address that point very well," Rita's mother replied. "My only concern is that it lacks the kind of concrete policy proposals that national governments will need quickly to implement."

"I know," Helen agreed, "but we have a tough battle, politically. We are asking national governments to give up many long-established sovereign rights. We've had to avoid being overly prescriptive."

"How have politicians reacted to this potential loss of sovereignty?" Sr. Correia asked.

"Reactions have varied," Helen answered, "largely depending on the politics and interests of individual governments. Many have come to terms with the need for formal global governance, especially in respect of the economy. Most leaders of poorer nations see a positive trade-off between their own loss of sovereignty and curtailment of rich country power. They reckon they'll be better off once rich countries are no longer able to ride roughshod over the economic rights of their citizens."

"That's interesting. It reminds me of something my great friend Sergio Vieira de Mello once said: 'the humanitarian is engaged as much in a struggle to counter the unbridled political power of rich nations, as he is in a struggle to persuade those nations to give more in aid to alleviate poverty.'"

"You knew Vieira de Mello?" Helen asked. "He's one of my heroes."

"Mine too." Sr. Correia replied. "Yes, indeed. We studied together at the Sorbonne. We even stood together at the barricades in '68. I was with him when he got that scar above his right eye, from the baton of a French police officer, you know? He despised the illegitimate use of power against ordinary people, especially the poor. That experience largely framed his humanitarian outlook. I still miss him, all these years later. He would be very proud of what you are doing."

Helen felt the anxieties of the last couple of days ebb away.

"Right," said Rita, "who would like some coffee?"

"Wait," said her father, "I'll fetch some of the special beans from the cellar."

The first leg of Mbonga Sibhosa's journey had gone well. It was never going to be a comfortable trip. His principal means of transport was the ubiquitous bush taxi, which usually meant being squeezed into half a seat in an over-loaded minibus for long periods. He hoped to be able to save some money by hitchhiking, and by travelling overnight or sleeping rough where it was safe to do so. He was travelling light: a sleeping mat and a thick coat for the cold nights were the only luxuries he had allowed himself.

Temily had gone with him to the bus station in Manzini. They had half an hour to wait as the bus had been delayed on its inward journey. They sat on a concrete step, away from the crowds. Neither spoke for several minutes.

"Are you alright?" Mbonga eventually asked, rather meekly.

"No. I'm not alright. I'm frightened half to death. I don't even know if I'll see you again. What if something happens to you? How are we supposed to manage?"

"I don't have to go you know?"

"Do I have any right to stop you?"

"I don't want you to think this is something I am doing lightly. As soon as I get back, I promise I will find work. I won't leave you alone again."

"It's a long time. I don't imagine you'll be able to telephone. I will worry about you."

"You mustn't worry. I can look after myself." He turned to look at her. "I have to do this. I'm not sure why, but I must go."

"I know. And you go with my blessing. Just come back to me. Promise me that."

"I do promise."

He boarded a minibus bound for the border post at Namaacha, quickly putting the pain of parting behind him. Having persuaded a friendly border guard that his visit would only last a few days, he was allowed into Mozambique without a visa, and found a quick connection to Maputo.

He had visited the Mozambican capital on several occasions, but not for some time. Having arranged a seat to Quissico the following morning on a maxibomba – in theory a more comfortable means of transport – he made his way to the central market where he was in time to find a cheap supper among the discarded produce. He had budgeted a dollar a day for food. On this occasion it was sufficient, but he knew it wouldn't always be so easy.

It was a warm evening. As the sun went down he headed for the beach where he hoped to get a peaceful nights sleep. As he made his way up Avenida Patrice Lumumba and then onto Julius Nyerere, he was struck by the growing signs of social breakdown. Despite two decades of political stability, and economic growth among the highest on the continent, more than half the population of Mozambique had experienced no improvement in wellbeing or security, and many of these had made their way to the capital in the hope of finding work.

His memory of Maputo was of a place with symptoms of poverty not so different from those at home. But if things had deteriorated steadily in Swaziland, they had taken a rapid turn for the worse here. He witnessed several fights between street vendors vying for tiny patches of pavement space. It all seemed so futile; there were no buyers for the single cigarettes or tiny paper twists of cashew nuts they were desperate to sell.

He passed the once resplendent Hotel Polana. Restored to its former glory after the civil war had ended in the early 1990s and earning a reputation as one of the finest hotels in southern Africa, it had once again fallen on hard times. It was still open, but judging by its dilapidated state, its rooms were no longer commanding western prices. No matter, it was still way beyond Mbonga's budget. He made his way down to the beach below where he found an area sheltered from the breeze blowing in off Maputo Bay.

He settled into his make shift bed, his head resting on a pillow shaped from the still warm sand. He looked up at the clear skies and reflected on his mad-cap adventure. He had no idea why he was making this journey. It felt like some mysterious force was pushing him on his way. He didn't understand it and it made him uneasy. He just knew he had to get to Berlin.

The sessions in preparation for the São Paulo summit had been positive. Jamali and Barenboim had each, independently, picked up on the Lundberg quote in the Wall Street Journal. Helen planned to keep it under wraps for the time being but was pleased they knew of her suspicions. For his part, Lundberg now seemed on especially good behaviour.

With the experience of Cape Town under their belts, pre-summit preparations began to take on a life of their own. On paper, this was one of the easier ones. The Brazilian government was strongly supportive, and Argentina was also onside. There was a new regime in Colombia which was playing its cards close, and Paraguay had yet to make a public statement on the blueprint.

They travelled to São Paulo by train. Although opportunities were limited, the committee tried to avoid air travel where possible. While many airlines' fleets included new aircraft fuelled by algae-produced biofuel, the sheer quantities required meant that commercial aviation was still a major contributor to global warming. Carbon-neutral biofuels were not yet produced in sufficient quantities to enable the total abandonment of fossil fuels, and replacement engines that ran on biofuels were not being manufactured quickly enough. Under the blueprint, fossil-fuelled air travel would end within five years. In the meantime, overconsumption by the aviation industry meant less biofuels for other activities still dependent on power by internal combustion. Despite the great progress made, flying was still the least climate-friendly way of getting round, so it was good PR to travel the 350km to São Paulo on the fast and clean *Trem de alto Velocidade.*

Helen sat next to Jay Robertson on the eighty minute journey. He was in unusually bullish mood. He generally took every opportunity to browbeat Helen for allowing too many compromises in the final wording of the blueprint. He hated vagueness and refused to accept her argument that, assuming it was adopted, the measures outlined would be naturally binding. She was adamant they must not dictate policy to sovereign nations. In any case, the tribunal for adjudicating complaints against any nation's failure to adhere to the substance of the blueprint would discourage defaulters. And if that didn't work, the withdrawal of cooperation by the majority under new economic arrangements which made economic success dependent on nations working together would act as a strong disincentive not to break the rules.

Security in São Paulo was inevitably high, even at the railway station where their train was the only one carrying delegates to the summit. All twelve heads of government were expected, each with a sizeable entourage of advisors. The two day summit was the largest diplomatic meeting in the region since the abortive G20 summit six years earlier, when President Hendricks had announced his country's effective withdrawal from the international stage, and the world had been plunged into the crisis from which it was now struggling to emerge.

Five

The only document on the table at the summit was the blueprint. Delegates had also been provided with copies of the minutes from Cape Town, and a copy of the communiqué issued there. The objective was to get each government to sign up to the blueprint, and put in place a ratification process which could be quickly completed once the summit round was over.

The opening plenary went smoothly enough. President Di Soto's remarks were, if anything, a little too effusive. She nonetheless won a sustained round of applause, although Helen rather wished the President had waited for the closing session before taking her hand and raising it aloft.

Each head of government spoke refreshingly briefly. Only the newly elected President of Colombia went on too long. He reminded delegates that modernity had been founded on the common recognition of the sovereign powers of nation states. He warned them that any agreement that threatened national sovereignty could have unforeseen consequences. He sat down to murmurs: half the room wished he had elaborated his concerns further; the other half was glad he hadn't.

Then it was off to the working groups. Helen would have private time with each government head over the next two days, but the schedule for these sessions was drawn up in response to requests made ahead of the summit. Her first meeting was with a joint delegation from Peru, Chile and Paraguay. She would be accompanied by Ann Margaret Eckart, whom she used a lot in meetings.

They were surprised to find the leaders of all three countries present from the start. President Carrasco of Chile began, speaking through an interpreter.

"Thank you for agreeing to meet us. As you may know, the three of us are very close, politically and personally. Since the General Assembly resolution was passed, we have followed the work of the committee with great interest. And since publication of the blueprint, we have met privately on two occasions to discuss its provisions. First I would like to say that we find much to commend in your proposals. We are particularly interested to discuss with you the manner of their implementation, assuming, of course, that the blueprint wins the support of all nations at the Berlin summit." He looked at President Ramirez of Peru, who continued in English.

"We are especially interested in your thoughts on the changes required in the behaviour of individuals, if your proposals to transform the economy are to be viable. Even if all governments succeed in passing the necessary legislation, it seems to us that the perceptions and motivations of ordinary people are going to have to change very quickly. The changes you are proposing are as much cultural and psychological as they are political and economic." He gave way to President Baez of Paraguay.

"I suppose the big question is: can you be sure that ordinary people are capable of making the changes in themselves that will be necessary for the project to succeed? It is one thing for seventy-five per cent to say they strongly support the blueprint, but will they be able to cope with the inevitable disruption to their lives."

"And then of course," concluded President Ramirez, "there is the question of the twenty-five per cent who are opposed to change. Where do they fit into this brave new world?"

Helen looked at Ann Margaret, who took a deep breath. "Can we be sure that people are ready for this scale of change?" the German echoed. "Of course, we cannot be sure. But we have discussed the matter at length, and taken evidence from a number of experts on cultural change, as well as psychologists. We have concluded that, while people do not have the capacity to fully imagine the impact on their lives or consciously plan for it, most will cope. There is much evidence for people's ability to adapt quickly to changed circumstances. We also believe that people are supporting change because they need it. Levels of unhappiness, clinical depression and fear of the future have been rising steadily for many years. We believe the demands that implementation will place on individuals will encourage renewed community spirit. It will be something everybody can identify with and be a part of. Not only will people be encouraged to forge stronger ties with their neighbours, they will also feel solidarity with people on the other side of the world. These changes hold the promise of a genuine global community of human beings, all working towards a collective goal," she paused for breath.

"Of course," Helen took over, "we hope that politicians will lead by example. The message you need to get across to your people is that this new international order gives each of your countries the opportunity to achieve anything it wants. People need to be persuaded that change will benefit them directly. You need to inspire them to have the confidence to take control of their lives, and to take advantage of the new opportunities that come their way."

"I'm more than happy to go out and sell your proposals, Helen," said President Baez. "What I'm not sure of is how people are going to be incentivized in a world in which competition is officially frowned upon."

"I've always thought it strange that we bring up children to be mindful of the feelings of others and then release them into a world which rewards competitive behaviour. The more ruthless the behaviour, the higher the rewards. In my experience, most people don't enjoy having to compete with others to achieve economic security. Once people grow accustomed to the changed context of their interaction with others, I think most will find the new way of doing things fits more comfortably with their own preferences."

"But do we know that humankind is ready to transform itself from an essentially competitive species into one that is primarily cooperative in outlook?" asked President Ramirez.

"If you look back through history," Ann Margaret answered, "you will find that in both biological and cultural terms, every great leap forward has resulted from new levels of cooperation between previously competing groups. We hope to create an environment in which cooperation can be taken to the ultimate level: cooperation between all human beings, working to satisfy their common aspiration for security and fulfilment."

"But creating that context does not guarantee that individuals will be able to make the necessary psychological leap," pressed President Baez.

"No it doesn't, but many thinkers believe that the future of our species, and of the planet as a viable home to sentient life, is dependent on human beings developing a psychology that will enable us to be self-evolving. There is no doubt that many individuals have already achieved this. And there are clear signs that many others could follow, given a conducive environment and the right incentives."

"And what about the twenty-five per cent that really don't like the idea of change, or at least the kind of changes that you are proposing" asked President Carrasco.

"That's the 64 dollar question," Helen replied. "We are selling this plan as the ultimate achievement of democracy. For the first time in history each nation will be governed in the clear interests of a majority of its citizens, within a global context that doesn't force countries to compromise on the values of democracy. Those who oppose the blueprint are going against the democratic wishes of the vast majority. We have to try to win them over through reasoned debate. At the same time, assuming the blueprint is adopted, legislative revisions will be needed to ensure compliance, for example, in respect of acceptable business practices."

"So you think coercion will still be necessary?" asked President Baez.

"I hope it won't be necessary. Once people come to see that new economic arrangements work in the interests of all citizens, and that by opening up the economy, more opportunities are created for everyone, then legislation will quickly become redundant. Quite frankly, the only grounds for opposing such change would be the desire of certain individuals to set themselves apart through exceptional wealth and by wielding economic power over others; an aspiration that runs counter to the demands of democracy."

"But whether they be democratic or not, is it not these competitive instincts have driven economic expansion since the industrial revolution?" asked President Ramirez.

"Yes and no," answered Ann Margaret. "We believe that economic advance under the established capitalist model would not have been possible without the emergence of strong government to set a regulatory framework, to periodically bale out capitalism when it overreaches itself, and to provide a safety net for those for whom the economy does not provide opportunities."

"And the qualities that drive economic progress, not just the desire to compete but also creativity and entrepreneurship, are present in many who eschew established business models," Helen continued. "People who choose to work in the not-for-profit sector; those who go into teaching, or those who run small businesses and would happily keep things small were it not for the pressures to compete and grow, and the fact that investment capital is often only available at the cost of losing control. I have met so many creative people whose ambitions are thwarted by business pressures which are not inevitable, but are a function of the way the economy is configured."

"So you think your proposals could release a pool of untapped potential?" asked President Baez.

"Exactly. In terms of wealth creation, I think we can expect a considerable increase in economic growth, only it will be growth in output of more of the things that people need. More people will be involved in production. And as for incentive, more people will find motivation not from the possibility of outdoing their neighbours, but from the knowledge that they have an equal stake in an economy which rewards everyone fairly."

"That's an interesting point," said President Carrasco. "Do you not think that some people are just plain lazy; so lazy in fact that they will not be bothered to take advantage of the opportunities on offer?"

"I think some people are as you describe, and a few probably irredeemably so," answered Helen. "But in many cases that laziness, that unwillingness to take advantage of opportunities, is a consequence of the frustration felt my many at an economic system which sets strict limits on the number of people who can be successful."

"And the only way to test how many people are innately lazy or unwilling to contribute to their own wellbeing," added Ann Margaret, "is to create a truly level playing field, and see how many still refuse to play by universally accepted rules."

The conversation appeared to have come to a natural end. President Ramirez thanked them for their time. Helen thought the meeting had gone well. These three were conventional politicians, but would all count themselves on the left of the political spectrum. And while the blueprint tried to transcend the left-right paradigm that had framed politics for so long, they were well aware that it contained a set of reforms that were already very popular among voters.

•

Six

The second day of the summit passed without problem. The closing plenary lacked the celebratory atmosphere of Cape Town, but Helen put that down to cultural differences. Rita had organised what she insisted on calling a 'mystery magical tour' for the two of them, the following day. Then it was back to Rio, a flight home to Geneva, and the rare prospect of four days and nights with her husband; much needed respite before heading to Jakarta for the next summit. All Helen had to do now was survive the end of summit dinner.

She could have done without another lengthy social engagement, partly because she only had two pairs of shoes, both of which were giving her trouble. She decided to try them out before getting dressed and had just managed to get into the left shoe of the more comfortable pair without dislodging a discretely placed plaster, when there was a knock on the door. She got up from the bed and walked over to open it, but as she leant forward to turn the handle, inexplicably she fell, banging her head on the door as she did so. She lay, slightly dazed, for a moment.

"Miss George," she heard a voice from the other side of the door, "are you alright?"

She hauled herself into a kneeling position and reached again for the knob, pulling the door open. She looked up to see a young woman from housekeeping who was returning the evening dress which she had sent to be pressed.

"Oh my goodness, here, let me help you." She walked quickly past Helen and laid the dress on the bed before returning and helping her to her feet.

"Are you okay? What happened?"

"I'm not really sure," Helen answered, rubbing her head, before realising her left leg was a good two inches shorter than the right.

"Looks like I broke a heel."

"Come and sit down. Let me take that shoe off for you."

"Thank you."

Helen wasn't used to being given instructions, neither was she used to being looked after; she rather liked it. Once both shoes had been removed, the young woman stood up and looked at her.

"How is your head? It sounded like you hit the door quite hard."

"I did, but it's okay, I think. Thank you."

"No problem." The young woman held out her hand. "Antonella Soares, pleased to meet you."

"Helen George, pleased to meet you too."

"You really don't have to introduce yourself. I have been hoping to meet you ever since I heard the summit was going to be held here."

"I bet you didn't expect to have to pick me up off the floor."

"No," she laughed, "that's a bonus. But don't worry, I won't tell anyone." She sat down on the bed beside Helen.

"You know, I had rehearsed exactly what I was going to say to you when you opened the door."

"Really? Go on then."

"I think it would sound a bit strange if I said it now, now that we've already met."

"Don't worry, I won't tell anyone," Helen said, smiling.

"Okay," Antonella laughed again. "I was going to say that my family wish you and the committee every success. We think you could make a big difference to our lives and to the lives of millions of poor people in Brazil, and in other countries, of course."

Helen was momentarily lost for words. "Thank you," she said eventually, "that means a great deal to me."

Antonella looked at her and smiled, before suddenly looking appalled.

"What is it?" Helen asked.

"There, just above your right eye, there's a red mark. You'll have a bruise if we're not careful." She jumped up and skipped into the bathroom, returning seconds later with a cold compress which she applied to Helen's forehead.

"Right, hold it there for at least a minute. It should stop the bruising. You can't go to the reception with a black eye can you? It would show my country in a very bad light."

Helen tried not to laugh and did what she was told, while Antonella stood guard over her.

"Antonella's an Italian name isn't it?" she asked, careful not to let the compress slip.

"It is, my grandmother, she was Italian."

"Is she no longer alive then?"

"No, she died, just last week in fact."

"I'm sorry. Were you very close?"

"We were. I miss her very much. But she was ninety years old."

"And how old are you, if you don't mind me asking?"

"I'm nineteen."

"And how long have you been working in this hotel?"

"In this one? About eight months. Before that I worked in a different hotel for two years, but this one is much nicer."

"I hope you don't mind me saying, but you seem a very articulate and intelligent young woman. Do you have ambitions to get out of the hotel trade?"

Antonella smiled and blushed slightly. "I have ambitions, but not to get out of the hotel trade. One day I plan to own a hotel like this one. That is why I am studying for a degree."

"So you only work part-time?"

"No. I work here full time, fifty hours a week, and I take as many extra shifts as I can, usually up to about 70 hours. It's the only way I can pay the fees for my course, and help support my family. But I have to refuse shifts if they clash with my lectures."

"So when are your lectures?"

"Usually in the evenings, quite late sometimes."

Helen couldn't think of anything else to ask. She felt deprived of the company of ordinary people. "What time is it?"

"It's nearly seven thirty," Antonella replied, looking at the clock on bedside table behind Helen.

"Goodness. I'd better get moving. I'm expected down-stairs."

"Just a minute. Let's have a look under there." She lifted Helen's hand and removed the compress.

"Perfect," she said, "you can go to the ball. I'd better go too or I'll be in trouble."

Helen stood up. She was about to offer Antonella her hand, but instead kissed her on both cheeks. "Thank you, really," she said.

"No problem. Oh my god, do you have another pair of shoes?"

"I do, though they're even less comfortable than the ones I just broke."

"It's tough being a woman, don't you think?"

They both laughed before Antonella turned on her heels and left the room. Helen had soon forgotten about the bang on the head, but as she made her way downstairs, she couldn't stop thinking about the impressive young woman she had just met.

She dreaded these occasions, mainly because they were anything but social. She would have to remain at maximum diplomatic guardedness which meant refusing all offers of champagne. As she approached the ballroom she could hear the buzz of conversation over live music. She pushed open the double doors and found herself atop a sweeping staircase. It seemed as if the whole room turned to look at her, although the applause that followed appeared spontaneous. Then she was handed a microphone. She smiled and turned to the room, hiding her annoyance that no one had briefed her about having to speak.

She said a very few words, reminding her audience how close they were to their goal, urging the decision makers among them not to waiver in their resolve, and hoping that everyone would have a good time this evening.

She descended the stairs in her best supermodel glide. Saeed Jamali caught her eye; he always knew when she was taking the piss. She joined the first group she spotted that contained someone whose name she could remember and was immediately complimented on her appearance. She resisted the temptation to reciprocate by drawing comparisons between the dinner jackets now bearing down on her, more than one of which was poorly fitting. After an interminable five minutes she was rescued by Jamali. At least she thought she was being rescued.

"Something's come up, we need to talk. Meet me on the balcony, third window from the left, in two minutes. Mike Dixon will be joining us."

Helen had almost forgotten about Mike Dixon. He was the committee's intelligence liaison. For the last year and half he had been the most underworked of the committee's small supporting staff. This was the first time she had been called at short notice to speak to him, so it had to be something serious.

She made her way to the balcony. She had become rather expert at crossing a room full of people, all desperate to speak to her, acknowledging everyone, while making it clear that she was not stopping.

"Hi Helen," Mike was waiting for her. He was possibly the most accomplished individual she had ever met: Harvard, Cambridge, a stint in the US Navy before joining the FBI, secondment to MI5, then the UN Intelligence Agency and now a key role with the committee. But despite his institutional pedigree, he remained fiercely independent of mind. Privately, he was critical of an intelligence community that refused to see beyond a world of competing national interests, but he still maintained excellent contacts in all the key agencies.

"Mike, how are you? I'd thank you for rescuing me from the vultures in there, but I know you don't do helpful things like that."

"Harry Noble," he said, smiling. It was more of an agenda item than a question. Helen knew what he wanted.

"I met him two and a half years ago at a UN conference I organised. He spoke at one of the sessions and we had dinner afterwards. I liked him; rather human for a spy; not unlike you in that respect. Though if I remember correctly, he accepted the invitation to speak not because it was my conference, but because he wanted to meet the wife of Rudolf Dreyfus."

"So it was before the committee was established?" Mike asked.

"Yes, almost a year before. Why, what's up?"

"Your name was mentioned in a conversation he had with an ex-CIA agent, Oscar Silverman."

"They were speaking over a secure line, then?" Saeed had joined them.

"They were," Mike confirmed, "but we don't know why. What we do know is that Noble and Silverman go back a long way. We also know that Silverman initiated contact, that he's just landed at Heathrow and is headed for Henley, presumably to spend the weekend with your friend Harry Noble."

"To talk about me?" Helen asked, feigning flattery.

"Looks like it. It's not going to be easy to get close to them, but we have some good people in London." Mike left them alone on the balcony.

"Do you think we need to worry?' Helen asked Saeed.

"Frankly, I'm surprised it's taken this long for such a conspiracy, if that's what it is, to come to light. What did you make of Harry Noble? Would you say he is the conspiratorial type?"

"Possibly," Helen replied. "He's certainly old school. I'd guess he's a classic change resister: bright, successful, but deeply conservative."

Mbonga was making steady progress. With a minimum of difficulty he'd made his way north through Mozambique to the small town of Caia on the banks of the great Zambezi river, where he was thrilled to find hippos still resident, even if he couldn't find anyone locally who shared his excitement.

From Caia he had hoped to find a direct route into Malawi, but was soon advised that despite it being only about 70 kilometres to the border, there was no proper road. He would have to make a diversion via the city of Tete which was, itself, only reachable via a circuitous route. This diversion cost Mbonga a couple of days travelling time. On the other hand, he was able to make it all the way to Tete without spending anything on transport. With some of the cash he'd saved he bought himself a good meal, which he ate on the dilapidated veranda of the Hotel Zambeze. What the dish lacked in quality it made up for in quantity.

The oppressive humidity of the Zambezi valley made him wish he didn't have to spend the night here, but there was no way out of Tete until morning. He treated himself to a couple of beers which, with some careful nursing, he made last most of the evening. He watched the traffic lights up from the hotel change repeatedly from red to green and back again, as not a single vehicle crossed the junction in more than two hours.

After a restless night he was up early for a passable breakfast of strips of omelettized egg before heading down to the bus station. Passing a rubbish dump disconcertingly close to the centre of town, he saw dozens of hungry children scouring the site for anything of value that may have been left overnight. The further north he travelled, the more evidence he saw of the economic turmoil that was overtaking the continent. And this part of Mozambique had been relatively lucky. The rainy season had held to established patterns for the last three years which meant harvests had been good. But there was still not enough food to go round. Since the country had embraced the free market, steadily more productive land had been bought up by commercial landowners and turned over to cash crops for export. There was little profit to be made producing food for sale into local markets.

Mbonga enjoyed the ride to Zobue on the border with Malawi. He shared the cab of a three ton truck, converted for use as a bus, with the driver – a white Mozambican named Francisco – and two heavily pregnant women. Neither spoke any English, but he gathered via Francisco's translation that they were headed to Mwanza, on the Malawian side of the border, where they had distant relatives and hoped to find better medical care for the birth of their children than they might at home. Although Francisco was careful not to disabuse them of this notion, he told Mbonga that he thought they'd be much better off at home in Tete, where at least they would have their loved ones close at hand.

As they approached the border, the two women became rather agitated as Francisco tried to explain something to them. Although Mbonga had a few words of Portuguese, he couldn't work out what the rumpus was about. The truck pulled up on some wasteland within view of the border post and the two women climbed out, apparently throwing insults back into the cab. Mbonga asked Francisco what had gone on.

"I suppose I should tell you too," he laughed. "You see the border post over there?" Mbonga nodded. "Well, that's where you leave Mozambique. Unfortunately, you don't reach the border post on the Malawian side for a further three miles," by now he was laughing uproariously.

Mbonga saw the funny side. "So, there's three miles of no man's land between here and the next bus stop?"

"Exactly," Francisco replied. "No transport, no shops, nothing. You might be lucky and get a lift, but there doesn't seem to be much traffic crossing the border this morning. There is some good news though."

"Go on," Mbonga said.

"It is downhill all the way."

They both laughed. Mbonga thanked his guide, jumped out of the cab and caught his rucksack as it was thrown down to him. As he walked towards the border post, he saw the two women sitting sulkily by the roadside. Once through, he looked back to see them again in conversation with Francisco, who had got down from the cab. Mbonga presumed he was trying to persuade them to return to Tete with him.

The view down the valley into Malawi was spectacular, and Mbonga would have looked forward to the hike had it not been so humid.

As he set off he was approached by two boys, both around twelve years old, riding bikes. Within seconds the deal was done. For 500 meticais each, he was given use of one of the bikes, while the boys shared the other. Together they free-wheeled down the valley – at times reaching quite exhila-rating speeds – until they arrived at the Malawian border post. The trip took little more than five minutes. Mbonga handed back the bike, shook hands with each of the boys and headed into the ramshackle building by the side of the road to get his passport stamped.

Oscar Silverman was due any time. They would go out for dinner, but first Harry would impress his friend with something special from the cellar. Silverman was a philistine, but he liked his wine. Harry had three bottles remaining of the 2005 Clos de Vougeot, and it was a year since he'd last had one. He opened a bottle and placed it on the mantel-piece above the unlit fire. He was looking forward to having company for the weekend, but slightly concerned about the reason for the visit.

He heard the taxi come up the drive, and the booming American voice send off the driver, no doubt with an absurdly large tip. He opened the door and the two men shook hands warmly. Harry took his guest's bag and placed it at the foot of the stairs before waving him through to the sitting room.

Six

"There are a lot of worried heads, back home," Silverman began. "Your friend Helen George and her committee are ruffling feathers."

"But it's nearly two years since the committee was set up. Why has it taken so long for the grumbles to start?"

"I guess we never really expected it to get this far. An informal group has been monitoring the situation all along. We decided to wait for the committee's recommendations to be published, and assess the reaction before activating the operation."

"So there's an operation, then?" Harry asked, surprised.

"Since the Cape Town meeting. And it looks like São Paulo is going the same way. She must be some diplomat."

"She certainly is an impressive and capable woman. I'm not sure there's much I can tell you about her though. There's nothing in her background that isn't available on the net. GeorgeTech was lauded for its transparency. They published every expense claim online, as well as remuneration details and any perks enjoyed by their execs. They were squeaky clean. And I'll wager she still is. And she is totally devoted to her husband, though god knows how they ever manage to see each other."

"We certainly can't find anything on her. We went into her husband's background and drew a complete blank. There was something about a daughter by his first marriage being involved with drugs, but she was living with her mother at the time."

"So how do you think I may be able to help you?"

"I want you to join us Harry: a group of right-minded people determined to ensure the failure of Helen George and her committee by whatever means necessary," Silverman's tone was grave; Harry knew he was serious.

"Any means necessary. Are you sure?"

"There's a strong consensus within the group that if the committee succeeds in its objectives, the core values of western society will be discarded. It'll be a free for all. The idea of national sovereignty will become a historical curiosity. The world will change beyond recognition. Yes, we are prepared to do whatever it takes."

Harry thought for a moment. "Presumably you want me on board because I have access to Helen George?"

"Partly. But also because you're a influential MI5 insider."

"Are you struggling to find support on the inside?"

"I wouldn't say struggling, but we could do with a few more. We have been surprised by how many in the intelligence community appear to have thrown in their lot with the new order."

"I've been thinking the same." Harry thought for a moment. "Who's running the show?"

"Howard Dawkins." Silverman answered.

Dawkins was a former deputy director of the CIA, and well connected with both political parties in the United States.

"Alright, count me in." Harry smiled as he poured some more wine.

Helen was dozing in the passenger seat of the car they had hired. Rita had managed to escape the party at a reasonable hour. Helen hadn't made it to bed until 2.30.

"You okay?" Rita asked.

"Fine. How far is it, this place you're taking me?"

"About an hour more," Rita said.

"And you won't tell me what it's called?"

"Okay I'll tell you. It called Parati. It's on the coast, about two hours south of Rio. It's a small town but has some of the finest colonial architecture in the country."

Parati turned out to be worth the trip; it was a gem. As they entered the Capela de Santa Rita, one of four exquisite baroque churches in the small town, Rita pointed out the damage to the foundations caused by flooding. This beautiful building had survived three hundred years, cared for first by Portuguese settlers, then by local people once the Portuguese had left. It would not survive another thirty unless rising sea-levels could be reversed. Rita was clearly in love with place.

"I know it's not a proper thing to say, but our work is not just about saving lives, or reducing suffering, you know, it is also about preserving things like this church, things which mean something to people, for whatever reason."

Helen nodded in agreement.

"And it's not just churches; all manner of architecture and ancient monuments. Historical cityscapes from which we can learn so much about our ancestors and their societies. And that's just the stuff we have created. We are also destroying so much of the natural environment. What will happen to our capacity to appreciate beauty in nature if much of that beauty is destroyed? The thought of it is too much to bear sometimes."

"You know, I have a good feeling. We're not there yet, but if we can get this plan agreed we might just save this beautiful church, and others like it." Helen knew that Rita was a regular churchgoer. She took her arm. "Come on," she said, "let's pray together. You never know, someone might be listening."

In the car on the way back to Rio, Helen told Rita about the conversation with Mike Dixon.

"Do you think these mad people could cause problems to the work of the committee?" Rita asked, "I mean, do they have that much power?"

"It would depend how much support they have, and how well connected they are. If there are enough of them, and if they have good contacts at senior levels within wavering governments, it's certainly possible."

"But do they really think the world has any option but to change?" Rita was exasperated.

"I don't know. People act for a whole range of motives. Most of those who work for the security agencies score high for resistance to change. They have a rigid world view virtually bred into them: they think a world divided into vigorously competing nation states constitutes the natural order. National sovereignty, at least that of their own country, is paramount."

"It must be strange to feel and think that way. I can more easily understand someone who defends the status quo in order to protect their wealth, especially in an insecure world, but to put your life on the line for the sake of a principle? These spooks must be a little crazy in the head, no?" Helen laughed. "I guess it gives them a feeling of power," Rita concluded.

"I suppose so, but Harry Noble didn't exactly strike me as a megalomaniac. Many of his values were not far off mine or yours."

"Do you think he would try to undermine the project?"

"I don't know him well enough to say. But I wouldn't entirely trust someone who has survived nearly four decades in MI5." Helen was as serious as Rita had seen her. They spent the rest of the journey in silence.

The eleven hour flight to Geneva went quickly; Helen had some sleep to catch up on. She hadn't seen Rudolf for nearly three weeks, and while they had become used to long separations, she never felt as well as when she was with him. They would have a long weekend together at their home outside Thonon, before travelling to London where he had a concert on Tuesday evening. The following day she would fly to Jakarta. But as she walked through the diplomatic channel at Geneva airport, that felt like weeks away.

As her taxi pulled up, she could see Rudolf working in the garden. It was a beautiful autumn day on the shore of Lac Leman, and a refreshing ten degrees cooler than Brazil. The taxi driver looked on as she ran towards her husband and threw herself into his arms. He spun her round several times, feet off the ground. On their third revolution she noticed the driver waiting patiently, and whispered in Rudolph's ear that perhaps he ought to pay the man.

"You look very well," he said, "for a woman with the fate of the world on her shoulders."

"It's really out of my hands now. The blueprint has massive popular support. The world is with us. If we don't make it now, it'll be because the politicians fuck it up."

After a long, delicious lunch – he was the better cook – they bathed together and spent much of the afternoon in bed. She hadn't made love with another man for 18 years, and had never wanted to. She longed for the day when they could spend more time together.

They caught up with three weeks of each other's news. Rudolf was intrigued by the possibility of a conspiracy against the committee, especially as one of the key conspirators was a fan of his.

"It really wouldn't surprise me if there were large numbers of arch-conservatives lurking in the corridors of power, keeping their powder dry," he said. "And don't forget, while there's overwhelming support in the opinion polls, in most countries this sea-change in popular thinking has yet to be reflected through the ballot box. Most of those in power still represent the old guard."

"That's true," Helen replied. "We've spent many a long evening wondering how, assuming the blueprint is adopted, the dinosaurs still running things at national level will manage to implement it."

"They'll have to, or else risk ejection from power at the first opportunity. In any case, presumably most of the structural changes will be facilitated by the new global governance body?"

"That's true, the global authority will define and manage the framework, but the revision of domestic statutes will be left to national governments. It could still get very messy."

"Once the blueprint is ratified," he said, "I imagine things will have to move very quickly in order to capitalise on the popular enthusiasm for change. It would be dreadful if people became cynical about the new order before it was properly established. Are you sure you will have the right people in place in time?"

"That will be somebody else's problem. I'm making recommendations regarding key appointments, but after Berlin I shall be coming home to spend time with you."

"That reminds me, the Germans are planning a gala concert to mark the end of the Berlin summit. The Staatskapelle has already committed, and guess who's been invited to conduct?"

"That's fantastic. How wonderful."

"Of course I was offered this commission purely on the basis of my being one of the world's leading conductors."

Seven

The weekend was everything Helen had hoped for, except that it was over too quickly. At least she had the Barbican concert to look forward to. After the taxi dropped them off in Silk Street, she went with Rudolf to his dressing room and, once he was settled, left him to his work.

"I'll see you afterwards," she said, kissing him. He just about managed a smile. He suffered dreadfully from pre-concert nerves. Fortunately, the afternoon would be taken up with rehearsals, but then he would have to endure a tortuous two hours in his dressing room. She felt enormous sympathy for him but knew there was nothing she could do.

It was Helen's first visit to The Barbican since the terrorist attack four years earlier. A van packed with explosives had been detonated by a suicide bomber in the road tunnel under the complex. Remarkably, given that both the concert hall and the theatre had been full at the time, only twenty people had died. The reinforced concrete construction of the 1970s built edifice saved hundreds. Although no group had claimed responsibility, and the authorities failed to apprehend the culprits, the Barbican bomb was a turning point. It was the eighth attack on a western target in as many months. And, while it would take the ejection from power of the Hendricks' administration to set the ball rolling towards a new world order, the event had become highly symbolic, not least because President Barenboim had been conducting the

London Symphony Orchestra at the time of the explosion. Once the dust had begun to settle, Barenboim had hauled himself to his feet, turned calmly to the audience, and asked them to make their way slowly out of the auditorium by the rear doors.

The Barbican Centre and one of the fifteen storey towers nearby had to be demolished, so the building which Helen now found herself exploring was quite different from the one she had frequented as a student. She was amused, however, to discover that the architects had made one concession to the previous building: this one was just as difficult to find your way round.

She bought herself lunch and found a table on the terrace in view of the ancient church of St Giles. She remembered her conversation with Rita in Parati. St Giles had survived the Great Fire, the Blitz and now the efforts of a suicide bomber. Nothing, it seemed, could bring down this 14th century gothic wonder.

"Well, what a pleasant surprise."

The voice was behind her. She turned around and struggled to maintain her composure as she recognised Harry Noble.

"Don't tell me you don't remember me," he goaded her in the helplessly patronising manner of a 20th century-schooled English gent.

Helen decided to feign ignorance. "Recognise the face," she said, "but can't put a name to it."

"Harry Noble," he said, "we met at your Sunningdale conference a few years ago."

"Of course. Harry, how lovely to see you. And I bet I know why you're here."

"Well, I've never seen your husband conduct Paart. It was simply too good an opportunity to pass up."

"You're rather early aren't you? It's only three."

"I decided to take the afternoon off and come here for a bite to eat. I may take a stroll later. What are you doing for the rest of the afternoon? Perhaps you'd like to join me?"

"Perhaps, but first why don't you sit down and have some tea?"

He did as she suggested. She was aware of her security detail only yards away. But she also reckoned he would have no idea of the connection with Noble, nor be drawing any conclusions from his sudden appearance. She was on her own.

"How long are you in London?" he asked.

"Just until tomorrow," she replied breezily, "then it's back on another aeroplane."

"Oh yes, the next summit's in Jakarta, isn't it?"

"That's right."

"Lovely city Jakarta, it has the most wonderful 17th century Dutch colonial drawbridge. Doesn't work any more of course, but a beautifully preserved example. Unique in the world as far as I know. You must try to make time for a visit."

"I'll do my best," Helen replied, trying to sound grateful for the tip. There was a moment's silence while they both sipped tea. Helen sensed that Noble was plotting his next move. She decided to direct the conversation.

"How are things at MI5? I guess I must be putting a few people's backs up."

"I wouldn't say that. You might be surprised how many of my colleagues support the work of your committee."

"How about you Harry, the last couple of years must have come as a bit of a shock to an old hand like you?"

"I've certainly been surprised at how easily you've been able to persuade the world to embrace the possibility of change," he said calmly.

"To be honest, people haven't required much persuading. Once they become aware that there is a viable alternative to the established order, they seem to line up behind us pretty quickly. It's real democracy." She smiled.

"Ah yes, democracy." He didn't bother to disguise his cynicism.

"But surely you were a great defender of democracy when it was under threat from Soviet communism or from Islamic fundamentalists?" Helen asked.

"Indeed I was, but as we both know, the form of democracy that protected us so well from extremism was quite different from the kind you are now advocating."

"Absolutely. What's on offer now is a more evolved version. Your democracy was always so, well, undemocratic, certainly in respect of the balance of power in society." Helen felt a spurt of adrenalin.

Noble looked slightly irritated. "You're not going to give me the elite power lecture are you?"

"It would be wasted on you."

They returned to their tea. Eventually, and seemingly changing the subject, Noble revived the conversation. "Tell me, what's Barenboim like? He's always fascinated me. A great man of art and humanity."

"He has a good sense of humour. And he's very calm. Rational, though obviously not without feeling. I knew him long before we both joined the committee. Rudolf was studying under him when we first met."

"Does he have any more plans to conduct, do you know?" Noble was much more likeable when enthusing over his passion for music.

"I don't think so. He is 81."

"But he's in good health, isn't he?"

"Amazingly good health, as far as I can tell. I'll be seeing him tomorrow. I'll mention our conversation and see what he says. Now, what about that walk?"

They got up from the table, and Helen indicated that they should head west towards Aldersgate street. As they made their way past the Museum of London, Noble asked if they were going anywhere in particular.

"Yes," Helen replied cryptically, and shortly they turned right through a small gate next to a rather nondescript church.

"Do you know this place? " Helen asked.

"Can't say I do", Noble replied. "What's it called?"

"Postman's Park. It's one of my favourite places in London," she told him, slightly distracted.

"And does it's name mean anything?"

"Yes, the old General Post Office had it's headquarters in that building there. The postmen used to take their breaks here." She pointed to an unfussy late Victorian office building which made up the southern boundary of the park.

"I know that building. Yes, it's a Henry Tanner. Most of his stuff was remarkably dull considering the period in which he worked, but this one has some rather exceptional sculptures in the spandrels around the windows. Glad I've finally found it. And this park," he added, looking around, "it's very nice, but that can't be why you've brought me here."

"You're very astute, Harry. Let's go and sit down over there." She pointed towards a bench facing a well-preserved loggia that had already caught Noble's eye. As they sat down he noticed that the wall beneath the loggia was decorated with ceramic tiles, each of which bore the name of an individual above a description of the manner of their death.

"This is the Memorial to Heroic Self Sacrifice. It was established in 1900 to honour the lives of ordinary people who died saving others."

"Yes, yes, I've heard of it. Fascinating. I never knew it was here though." His interest was genuine, and he was clearly moved by the stories he read.

"I used to come here a lot," Helen said after allowing him time to read a few more of the heartrending accounts, "especially when my faith in human nature needed reviving."

"I would have though the world you inhabit was full of selfless people. The renewables business, the UN. Right-minded individuals doing their bit to save the world, surely?"

"Oh, you'd be surprised. Lot's of big egos, I can assure you."

"Well, it's a complicated thing, motivation. Wouldn't you agree?"

Helen sensed he was letting his guard down. "Tell me about your motivation, Harry. Why did you make a career in The Security Service?"

"I joined the service because I felt certain values, values important to me, were being eroded. I decided those values were worth defending, and I concluded that I would devote my life to their defence. Almost a calling really. I could certainly have made more money had I followed my father into banking. But there are more important things in life than money."

"So what are the values you work to defend?" Helen asked.

"Well, it's a way of life, isn't it," he replied, rather vaguely.

"Go on," she urged.

"I believe that people should be free to live as they desire without being subject to constraints imposed by some centralised, bureaucratic authority. That is why this country fought wars of different kinds against fascism and communism."

"That's very noble, Harry," she struggled to stifle a giggle as she realised what she'd said. "But what if, in exercising that freedom, some individuals deny the same freedom to others?"

"Well, nobody's pretending the world's perfect. Freedom doesn't come cheap. There will always be a price to be paid. In a competitive society there are bound to be winners and losers."

"But right now, even by the most conservative estimates, a good third of the world's people are on the losing side: living in abject poverty, lacking food security, with little or no access to healthcare and sanitation; no schools for their kids. Freedom hasn't done them much good."

"Yes, but then it's a question of development. Freedom, particularly economic freedom, is a prerequisite to the kind of development that will help these people pull themselves out of poverty."

"And how long, would you say, has this country enjoyed the kind of freedom you describe?'

"Well, allowing for the tendency of politicians of all parties to trample on our hard-won freedoms, I would say Britain has enjoyed a free society for nearly two centuries. If I had to put a date on it, I'd say 1834." He looked at her for a sign that she knew what he was talking about.

"The Poor Law Amendment Act?"

"Very impressive. You clearly know your history."

"We both know our history. What matters is how events are interpreted, in terms of their motivation, and their consequences. You think poor law reform was a benevolent piece of legislation enacted by visionary politicians with honourable intentions. I think those politicians failed to think through the consequences, or deliberately chose to ignore them. Either way, the upshot was to remove from the poor their only protection from starvation."

"But Helen, that single piece of legislation established the free market economy which has driven two centuries of progress. By finally allowing labour to be fully subject to market forces, the modern economy was born."

"Bringing with it an end to the subsistence farming by which most people had fed themselves for centuries. And with the removal of the rudimentary welfare provisions which had saved thousands of lives over the preceding two hundred years, the poor were thrown upon the mercy of a labour market that often paid wages below subsistence levels.

The majority of Britons were plunged into a poverty deeper than anything experienced by their immediate ancestors."

"But my dear Helen, there will always be a trade-off between individual freedom and social justice. Certainly, you can have equality. The state can take charge of the economy, shut down the market and ensure everyone is equally poor. Or, the state can keep its nose out, allow people their legitimate freedoms and let the market do its work. People may not be equal, but everyone will be free to make the most of their abilities."

"And you believe that under current arrangements everybody is equally free to make the most if their abilities? Do you think everybody enjoys a secure, nurturing upbringing and access to a decent education. And do you think economic arrangements have no impact on people's ability to make the most of their talents?"

"I suppose the economy may have some impact, but character is far more important. Most of those at the bottom of society simply don't have the mettle to make the most of the opportunities presented them."

"And that mettle, or lack of it, is a consequence of bad genes, is it?

"Largely, I would say," he replied, apparently in earnest.

Helen considered her response. "Well, I guess we disagree on some of the fundamentals. With respect, your argument sounds not so different to those of the eugenicists, a century ago. And you know what that kind of thinking led to."

"I can assure you I'm no eugenicist, Helen." He sounded offended.

"Well, perhaps not. But surely the only way to discover the extent to which ability and potential are determined by individual circumstance is to arrange things so that everyone gets an equal chance in life. I think that's an experiment worth conducting."

"Perhaps, but you still have the problem of trying to reconcile two absolute opposites. How are you going to protect individual freedoms and create an economic context in which everyone can make the most of their abilities?"

"By changing the rules of the economic game, Harry. You've read the blueprint, I assume? You know there are changes to economic arrangements which, while they may restrict the freedom of a small number to amass huge personal fortunes, will deliver the freedoms that you and I take for granted to millions of people, for the first time."

"It'll never happen," he replied defiantly.

"But it could Harry, it could."

Noble offered no response, though Helen knew this was no admission of defeat.

"Look at that one," he said after a moment, pointing towards one of the tiles. "Henry James Bristow. Saved his little sister's life by tearing off her clothes but caught fire himself and died of burns and shock. Eight years old. It certainly makes you think. I am grateful to you for bringing me here," he said.

"I'm afraid I have to make some phone calls, but we could have a bite to eat before the concert if you don't have any plans?"

"That would be lovely, where do you suggest?"

"There's a new place on West Smithfield that's supposed to be very good. Day for Night I think it's called. Why don't we meet there in half an hour or so?"

"Sounds perfect. I'll see you there." He stood up and headed back towards the park entrance.

Helen sat for a moment. She didn't know what to think. This couldn't be a coincidence. But then how would Noble have known where to find her? Unless he already had her under surveillance. And assuming he was tracking her, what was his plan? Apart from the question about Barenboim, he hadn't got close to asking about the committee's work. Her phone rang. It was Mike.

"Mike, you'll never believe"

"I will," he interrupted, "I've been listening for the last hour."

"How, you haven't bugged me?" Helen was indignant.

"Of course not, Helen. We bugged him."

"Jesus, how?"

"Well, as he said, certain of his colleagues are rather sympathetic to our cause. Let's just say we have people on the inside."

"But what about the device. He's a spy, he'll find it, won't he?" Helen knew she wasn't cut out for espionage.

"Not unless he's in the habit of inspecting his stools."

Helen laughed. "So what's the story? How did he find me?"

"He got lucky really. He accessed the Eurostar passenger lists yesterday. That's how he knew you were in London. Beyond that he just put two and two together."

"Should I be worried?" she asked, trying not to sound worried.

"Helen, he isn't going to kidnap you, and he's certainly not going to poison you."

"So what should I do?" she asked

"Enjoy dinner. Enjoy the concert. We'll discuss it at the airport in the morning. Saeed and I think we should constitute an ad-hoc group to meet regularly to keep tabs on Noble and his friends. You, me, Saeed and Daniel. Is that okay with you?"

"Fine. Thanks Mike. See you tomorrow."

She called up Rudolf's number and dialled.

"Hello my love," he answered almost immediately.

"Hi, how was the rehearsal?"

"It went exceptionally well, thank you." He was always strangely formal when talking about his work.

"And how are you feeling?" she asked tentatively.

"Fine, honestly fine. The rehearsal went very well. I'm surrounded by friends and looking forward to the concert."

"You'll never guess who I just ran into: your number one fan."

"Harry Noble? That can't be a coincidence, can it?"

"Somehow I doubt it. I'll tell you all about it after the concert."

"Okay darling. Bye now."

She got up and walked towards the memorial wall. She traced the names on several of the tiles with her finger and tried to imagine what these brave souls must have felt in the moments before they died. Then she headed back towards Aldersgate Street. She would take the long way to Smithfield;

she wasn't ready for another session with Harry Noble quite yet.

Antonella Soares had been unable to put the meeting with Helen George out of her mind. Apart from the honour of having met possibly the most important person in the world – someone who was an inspiration to women everywhere – she had a strange sense that the episode meant something. She was not a superstitious person. She had spent many hours arguing with her grandmother over whether there was a place for superstitious beliefs in the modern world. To her mind, such beliefs only served to hold back development in countries like Brazil. The arguments with her grandmother had frequently ended in tears, but they helped deepen the respect they held for each other. Had she still been alive, she would certainly have had something to say about the chance encounter and its meaning.

After the meeting she had felt euphoric. She had come across a couple of minor celebrities through her work in the hotel, but none had even bothered to acknowledge her. Not only did George do that, she took a genuine interest. She had returned home very excited, bursting to tell her mother all about it. But when the time came she found herself unable to do so.

On her way to work she wondered what Helen George would be doing now. She had been following news about the committee's progress with great interest. There was speculation in the media that George had taken advantage of a break in the summit schedule to return to her home in France. She didn't know why she lived there. She had assumed she was

British, but when she spoke to her, she realised her accent was wrong. She would have to do some research.

She looked out the window of the bus and winced as she saw a policeman handcuffing a man spreadeagled on the ground and held down by the boot of a colleague. It looked like a drug bust. Antonella's route to work was particularly good for spotting criminals and the excessive but ultimately hopeless efforts of the police to curb the drugs trade.

While the bus waited at a red light she looked at the face of the young man, squashed painfully against the pavement. He looked no more than seventeen. She wondered how he'd ended up dealing drugs and whether he was any good at it. She smiled as it occurred to her that he probably wasn't given his current predicament.

As the bus pulled away, the policeman dragged the suspect to his feet and she saw his face for the first time. Through the blood and bruises she noticed his expression: he wasn't angry or defiant, instead he looked desperate and utterly defeated.

"Hello Oscar, it's Harry." Noble had calculated he still had a few minutes before Helen joined him in the restaurant.

"Harry, how's it going?"

"Surprisingly well, actually. I just spent the afternoon with Helen George, and she invited me to dine with her."

"Great work Harry. Now, how easy is she going to be?" he asked, suddenly serious.

"I've already told you; there's no way I'm going to turn her. If I can get her to trust me, then I may be able to get some information that may be of use. But that's likely to be the extent of it." He heard Silverman breathing. This was a man used to getting his own way.

Eventually he spoke. "Okay Harry, there are plenty of ways to skin a cat. You keep in touch."

"Will do. Goodbye Oscar."

Harry felt under pressure. He didn't want to let Silverman down, but he had a problem. Helen knew he worked for MI5. The moment he showed an interest in her work she would get suspicious. He wanted to do everything he could to derail the project, but he wasn't sure how much power he had, nor what his strategy should be. He decided he would have to be more direct.

He was staring into his glass as Helen approached the table.

"You found it then?"

"Yes, no problem. What would you like to drink?"

"I'll have some of that, if I may," she said, pointing to the open bottle of wine on the table.

He poured her a glass.

"Helen," he began, rather more guardedly. "Would you mind if I asked you about the work of your committee?"

"Not at all," she said breezily, "fire away."

"I guess I'm most interested in whether you really think the blueprint will be ratified by all nations at the end of the summit process."

"I think there's a very good chance, but I wouldn't bet my house on it," she replied.

"Presumably, success depends on securing support from every government?"

"Not necessarily, one or two dissenters among the rich nations would probably scupper the whole thing. But it would need a larger block of developing nations." She wondered about his line of questioning. So far she didn't feel any need to censor herself.

"But you don't know if any such dissenting group or block is planning to vote against?" he asked.

"If I did, do you think I'd tell a senior MI5 officer who has made little secret of his own distaste for the committee's proposals?"

"I suppose not. But if I may say so, you seem very convinced by the righteousness of your cause."

"I am. Look at the polls. There's huge popular support for the blueprint among ordinary people in every country, and across all cultures. That's why I'm convinced. We put a document into the public domain just four months ago. It's been digested and regurgitated by pundits and politicians, yet it still has the support of more than three quarters of people questioned. How could anyone committed to the principle of democracy not support it?"

Harry looked glum. He'd never had much time for democracy. He didn't believe most people were competent to make decisions about how society should be run. He had no problem with a system that gave people the impression they had control over their lives. He did occasionally feel uncomfortable with the idea of an elite exercising power over a population kept largely in ignorance, but he was a pragmatist. There were limits on the extent to which power could be devolved: give too much too quickly and the result would be anarchy.

"Do you think the masses are ready for the kind of power your vision for democracy would grant them?" he asked.

"We're not proposing a referendum on every last policy detail. In fact, you could argue that this is an exercise in ultra-elitism. Twelve unelected people telling the world how it must change in order to survive. It's not so different from how things have always been run, is it?" she smiled.

"No, I suppose not." He was getting frustrated. He decided to move the conversation on. "Tell me, what do you suppose will happen to the arts in this brave new world of yours?"

"I hope that over time they will be opened up to a far wider audience." Helen answered.

"But if you attempt to popularise art, then standards will fall."

"If you did nothing to extend access to education and culture, I would agree. But that's an integral part of the blueprint, not only to create conditions where more people can take responsibility for their own economic well being, but to also allow them access to the kind of cultural privileges that you and I grew up with."

"But not everyone has the innate capacity to appreciate the finer aspects of art."

"I agree that not everyone has that capacity, but I'd like to see evidence to back your assumption that differences in sensibility are innate. There is none. Your claim is based on the same prejudice that persuades you that many people are incapable of providing for themselves economically, thus justifying a system under which they are expected to be grateful for what they get."

"That's all very well," he sounded agitated, "but how are you going to pay for this massive expansion in the arts?"

"By creating demand: by getting more people interested, and by creating an economy where everybody has the option to support the arts if that's their thing. I agree, there's not enough money to fund the arts at present, but that's because interest is restricted to an elite, which, despite the wealth of its members, is often unwilling to match its aspirations with hard cash."

"I have to agree with you there."

"And it's not just about bringing 'high' art to a wider audience, Harry. It's also about consolidating and extending the democratisation of art that has taken place over the last few decades."

"I'm not really sure what you mean."

"Well, encouraging greater participation in the creative arts; enabling more people to become creators, or purveyors, of art, rather than just passive consumers; expanding the boundaries of art beyond the classical. Enabling anyone who wants to, to make a contribution to shaping and developing culture through art."

"What, street art, that kind of thing, you mean?"

"That's one example. There's a huge pool of untapped creative talent out there, Harry. It has the potential to reshape both the economy and the arts once each of those spheres is opened up."

"It all sounds very inclusive Helen, but I'm not sure I get it. And I certainly can't see it happening, not in any meaningful way."

"Do you like jazz, Harry?"

"Yes, enormously. How did you know?"

"I just guessed."

"And your point?"

"If we'd been having this conversation a century ago, you'd be telling me that jazz isn't proper music; that negroes who never learned to read music couldn't possibly create real art. Yet a century later you consider it legitimate."

Harry looked pensive. "Actually, I think it's possibly the highest form of art yet created." He sighed. "Perhaps you do have a point. I just can't see a place for graffiti in the National Gallery, that's all."

"You should check out some of the less prestigious galleries. You might be surprised by what you find."

"What's your husband's take on this?"

"He broadly agrees. Like us, his taste is more traditional, but he accepts that's largely down to the way he was brought up. And he's heartily sick of having to pander to people who have no real interest in his work but attach themselves to it because of the kudos it brings."

"I can quite imagine how he feels." Harry sighed again.

"Talking of my husband. If we don't order soon, we'll be late for the concert."

Eight

Helen handed her carry-on to the flight attendant and collapsed into her seat. She was pleased to be travelling alone. After a good rest at home, London had been draining.

The concert had gone very well: she'd been able to get backstage while Rudolf was taking his second bow, and greet him as he came off. She loved these moments, when he was on top of the world. She accompanied him back to his dressing room and told him about her afternoon.

"It's all getting rather 007, isn't it. Is he still here?" he asked.

"I think so, he was rather hoping to meet you."

"I tell you what," he said. "I've not got anything much to do here. I'll get changed and I'll meet you both in The Two Brewers in half an hour."

"The Two Brewers? Is it still there?"

"It is. I asked one of the people here this afternoon."

She left to find Noble hovering hopefully by the stalls bar as instructed.

"There you are Harry. Did you enjoy the concert?"

"Yes, it was marvellous," he said, with genuine feeling.

"Good. Right, follow me. We're going to meet Rudolf for a drink."

Noble's eyes lit up like a child's on Christmas morning. He tried to say something, but Helen had already started walking towards the exit.

The Two Brewers was a pub on Whitecross Street which had been their local when they were first married and had lived near the Barbican. Helen was pleased to find it largely unchanged. It was a proper London pub, and too few of those remained. She watched Noble for a reaction. Probably not the kind of establishment he was used to frequenting, she thought.

They both went to the bar. By the time they had their drinks, Rudolf had arrived. He held out his hand to Harry.

"It's great pleasure to meet you," Noble said.

"You too Harry, Did you enjoy the concert?"

"Yes indeed, especially the three Fratres, they're so rarely played these days."

"They are wonderful, aren't they. If I had my way, I'd have played them all, but I'm told such indulgence is not commercially viable."

They found a table and sat down.

"So Harry, Helen tells me you're a spy. How exciting."

"I have to admit I do work for the government. But I was hoping we might talk about your work, rather than mine."

"Of course," Rudolf said, "how dull of me."

For the next forty minutes they talked about music, about Barenboim, and about the future of the arts. All the while, Helen watched Noble intently. She wanted to learn as much as she could.

From the border crossing at Mwanza, Mbonga had made his way to the Malawian capital, Lilongwe. This turned out to be a rather soulless place, much of it having been built to provide a new capital after independence in 1964. His objective from here was to make his way into Tanzania, if possible taking a route that followed the western shore of Lake Malawi. He had read about Africa's third largest lake, and hoped to be able travel north by boat.

At the bus station he struggled to find any information about itineraries that might include a scenic boat trip, so he opted for a cup of tea in the café across the road. There, he got talking to the owner, who happened also to run a nearby travel agency. This rather impressive woman had taken on the cafe after the travel agency had fallen on hard times. So she was thrilled to find a real life tourist to advise.

"I wouldn't exactly call myself a tourist." Mbonga laughed as she sat down opposite him.

"You wish to see the sunset over our beautiful lake; that makes you a tourist in my book," she said unfurling a tightly rolled map of the country.

"Now, we are we?" she asked herself, squinting at the map through middle-aged eyes.

"Ah yes, Lilongwe. Right. From here you can catch a quite reliable bus all the way to Nkhata Bay," she surveyed the map again. "Here," she said, locating the town and placing her finger on the map. "Nkhata is quite a nice town. When I was a girl it was one of the busiest resorts on the lake. But there's not so much going on now."

"Is it a good place to see the sunset?" Mbonga asked, deciding to humour the woman.

"Not really, it faces east, you see. Nkhata Bay is one of the stopping off points for the Illala." She made this statement with some pride, emphasising the middle syllable as if everyone would have heard of the Illala. Mbonga looked at her blankly. "The Illala is one of the most famous ships in all of Africa," she continued, "I'm surprised you haven't heard of it."

"There isn't much call for ships in my country," he explained.

She gave him a funny look. "Anyway, the Illala has been sailing up and down the lake for as long as anyone can remember. It takes about 36 hours to make the voyage from Nkhata to Itungi."

"And Itungi is in Tanzania?"

"It is indeed. And by the time you arrive you will have experienced not one, but two of the most spectacular sunsets you have ever seen," she sat back in her chair and waited for his response.

"Well, that's perfect. Thank you." He wasn't sure what else to say.

"My very great pleasure. Now tell me, why are you going to Tanzania?"

"I'm going to visit a friend," he said, which wasn't completely untrue.

On arrival in Jakarta, Helen was met by Mike who took her to a quiet coffee shop where Jamali and Barenboim were waiting for them.

"Hi guys," she greeted them, resurrecting her diluted Irish brogue for effect.

Barenboim looked tired, but managed a smile. Helen leant over and kissed him on the cheek.

"How is Rudolf?" he asked.

"Well. He sends his love. And I've also got a message from another admirer of yours."

"Yes," replied Barenboim, "I've been hearing all about Mr Noble."

"So Mike, what's the latest?" Helen asked.

"The transmitter gave out about halfway through the concert. But we do know he spoke to Silverman while he was waiting for you to arrive at the restaurant. You did well, Helen. Noble has a problem. He doesn't know how to deliver the goods to his master. I'm not sure there's much more he can do. I worry about Silverman though. He has a reputation for ruthlessness."

"Do you think they are planning some kind of physical assault?" Jamali asked.

"It's possible," Mike answered. "The whole world knows our itinerary for the next few weeks. We can't get security as tight as we would like."

"But surely," Barenboim said, "an attack on the committee, or any of its members, would only serve to strengthen our position?"

"Unless they managed to wipe us out completely." Helen was surprised at how calm she was.

"I think," Mike said, "a political move is more likely, assuming they have high level contacts in governments yet to make up their mind. Or else a classic sting."

"Blackmail, you mean?" Helen asked.

"It's possible. It might be an idea to talk to the others."

"I'll mention it this afternoon. Is everybody here?"

"Rita's flight was delayed, but she should be landing about now."

"Good. I'll wait for her."

"There's one other thing." Mike sounded even more serious. "We think we know who's heading up Silverman's operation."

"Go on," Helen said.

"Howard Dawkins."

"The little shit." She immediately saw they were shocked at her reaction.

"I'll tell you about it one day," she offered by way of explanation.

"Can you talk to President Solis?" Jamali asked.

"I'll try, but she won't be able to do much about Dawkins. So now we're fighting on two fronts: Noble and Lundberg. I must call Gerald, see if he's got anything else on the Wall Street Journal connection."

"I spoke to him yesterday," Mike said. "There have been three more articles, the source for which could be Lundberg. None as obvious as the first, but suspicious all the same. Oh, and there's a file at Langley which suggests that Lundberg was romantically involved with Veronica Abel."

"While they were at Stanford?" Jamali asked.

"Yes. But also for several, well, many years afterwards."

"How many years?" Helen asked, intrigued.

"Right up until 2016, it seems. Looks like they decided to cool it when Lundberg became European President."

"Wow, how did they manage that?"

"It certainly makes him a potential blackmail target," Barenboim said.

"It does." Mike affirmed.

"But aren't we working on the assumption that he's batting for the other side?" Jamali asked.

"Jesus, I hope it doesn't get any more complicated." Helen stood up. "Right, I'm off to find Rita."

Oscar Silverman was back in Washington; his first visit since retirement. Howard Dawkins had arranged a secure hotel room for their meeting, and he opened the door himself.

"Come in Oscar. How was London?"

"I think we've made a reasonable start."

"Harry Noble come up with anything?"

"He's got pretty close to Helen George. But she's a tough bitch. Noble will help us, but we need a plan that doesn't involve George."

"Any ideas?"

"Well, I don't think we should rule out force. We know where they're going to be. And we have well-placed people who can be trusted. There are still plenty of bomb-wielding maniacs out there. They'd never trace it back to us."

"I've thought about it Oscar, but it's too risky. You know how much support these people have. If we went after them there could be a massive backlash. I think we need to be more subtle. I know you prefer a more direct approach but we have to get the right result here."

"I guess you're right. But how are we going to get close enough?"

"Come on Oscar, you remember the training manual: we identify their weakest link and test its resilience to breaking point."

Helen had arranged to meet Kersen Atunarang for a briefing, and a whistle stop tour of Jakarta. Although she didn't know him as well as her old friend Saeed, he was clearly cut from the same cloth. He had great experience of life, was calm and wise: the kind of man she was able to get along with without effort. When she mentioned Harry Noble's drawbridge, he politely suggested that there were several equally impressive indigenous artefacts close to the centre of Jakarta that she might prefer to visit, and she was happy to follow his recommendation.

Kersen had positive news ahead of the summit. The Indonesian Prime Minister, who wielded considerable influence in the region, and whose government had been elected only a year earlier on a platform strongly supportive of the committee's work, had invited Helen and Jay Robertson to dinner that evening. Helen had heard much about Anna Sianturi, and it was all good. She looked forward to their meeting.

Mbonga had never been on a boat before, nor had he ever learned to swim. He was therefore a little nervous as he boarded the MV Illala shortly after watching the impressively large steamer dock at Nkhata Bay. It was possible to book cabins for the overnight trip at no extra cost, but the ticket agent suggested he would be more comfortable bedding down in one of the steamer's two passenger lounges. They were still cleaned periodically, unlike the rarely used private accommodation.

He walked down the narrow metal staircase and into the starboard lounge. He tried to imagine what the boat, and its clientele, might have looked like in colonial times.

Attached to the wall beside the bar, which seemed not to be holding any stock, was a glass display case containing a history of the MV Illala including some badly foxed press cuttings. He learned that the ship had been built in Glasgow in 1949 and transported in pieces to Malawi where it was put together. It had been making the trip up and down the lake ever since. So it was old. On the other hand, it was still going, 74 years after it was built. Mbonga felt reassured.

As he hadn't slept well the previous night, he claimed a row of seats next to a window and settled down for a snooze. Before long he was disturbed by a man in uniform asking to see his ticket. Everything being in order and having been shown a rather formal looking menu, he asked the steward to wake him before dinner, and was asleep in minutes.

Helen detected some weariness among her colleagues as they gathered on the eve of the Jakarta summit. "Here we are again then," seemed to be the stock greeting. This remarkable group of people had been together for nearly two years, with few breaks as long as the one they had just enjoyed. It was understandable they were getting tired of each other's company. Today the troops were in need of rallying and it was her job to rally them.

"Good to see you all again, after such a long time apart," she joked as the meeting began. There was some laughter, but mostly from Rita who was under instructions to be as upbeat as possible.

"As you can see, I've asked Mike Dixon to join us for the first part of the meeting. Unfortunately, though perhaps not unexpectedly, Mike has uncovered what looks like a plot to derail the process, presumably prior to our arrival in Berlin in five weeks time. We don't know how or when the conspirators are likely to strike, but we do know they include some high-ranking and well-connected individuals from the security services of more than one country. Mike?"

"Thanks Helen. I'd just like to reiterate what I've said previously. Please continue to be vigilant. We are stepping up physical security around you all. Don't go anywhere without your security detail. We're also increasing protection for close family members. Next time you speak to your loved ones you might want to stress that these measures are purely precautionary. We have absolutely no indication that any terrorist attack is being planned, although we cannot completely rule out the possibility."

"Thanks Mike," Helen continued. "There are, of course, two other options the conspirators may pursue. They could directly approach key people close to decision makers in key governments; there's little we can do about that, except double our efforts in respect of any governments so targeted. Or, they could try to compromise members of the committee. I know I don't need to say this, but I have to ask you to be careful of any unplanned contacts with people not already known to you. We can't afford any slip-ups at this stage. Parts of the media are already ramping up their efforts to discredit us; revelations of any indiscretion, however minor, could be extremely damaging."

"Helen, do you have any idea how serious these people are?" asked Jemma.

"They are likely to be very determined," Mike answered.

"But the most important thing," Helen interrupted him, "is that we are not distracted from our work. Don't worry guys, we're going to make it. I know you're each as committed to this process as I am. I couldn't have a better team."

At this Rita began to clap excitedly. Most of the others joined in enthusiastically until the applause degenerated into laughter. It was just what was needed to break the tension. With a new common enemy to unite a sometimes fragmenting group, the rest of the meeting went well.

Harry Noble had been back in his office for two days. He had been feeling rather out of the loop; now he was back in the thick of it, even if, to his mild bewilderment, he was engaged in an operation whose objective was diametrically opposed to the policy of the government by which he was putatively employed.

The British were not waiting for the Berlin summit to declare their hand. Working with the Spanish and the French, they had corralled the rest of the European Union into signalling its intent to support the blueprint before the summit round had begun. All but three of the twenty-five member states had signed the declaration, along with most of the other non-EU European nations, including Switzerland.

In Harry's opinion, The Liberal/Green coalition that had come to power in 2018 was not working in Britain's interest. He had always considered himself a classical liberal in the tradition of Locke and Mill. But the present government, especially in its embrace of so-called cooperative internationalism, bore no comparison to the ideals of these great Enlightenment thinkers.

Now, perhaps, he could make a difference. He had instructions from Silverman to get close to the Russians. His contacts with Moscow were still good. He was to identify key people in the Russian hierarchy likely to be opposed to the blueprint, with a view to forming an ad-hoc group of influential rebels who could bring pressure to bear on President Kotov. But Harry reckoned he could do better than that. He intended to be at the Tbilisi summit, the last one before Berlin, in person. He was glad to have a diplomatic role; his appetite for subterfuge had diminished over the years. And he was uncomfortable with the idea of Silverman's victory at any cost. If he was going to engage Helen George in battle, he wanted to win openly and fairly.

Mbonga's travel agent had not lied about the sunsets. From the upper deck of the Illala he witnessed nature at its most spectacular. On his way back down to the lounge he passed an older man leaning over the railing, smoking a pipe. Mbonga caught his eye, smiled and nodded a tentative greeting. The man stood up and turned towards him. Mbonga saw from his uniform that he was a member of the crew.

"Lovely sight, isn't it?" he said.

"It certainly is," Mbonga replied

"Where are you from? I don't recognise your accent."

"I'm from Swaziland."

"You're a long way from home. What brings you to Malawi?

"Well I suppose I'm on holiday," Mbonga replied

"Really?" the old man gave him a quizzical look

"So where you heading?"

"To Tanzania, to visit a friend." Mbonga felt bad about lying. He had already calculated the man warranted more respect.

"And from there to Berlin," he said, assertively.

"Berlin eh? You know this boat don't go that far?" Mbonga laughed. "You going to the summit?" the man asked.

"I am. How did you know?

"Why else would be somebody be travelling overland from Swaziland to Berlin at the present time?"

"So you don't think I'm crazy?"

"I don't know you well enough to answer that question. Why don't you come up to the bridge? I might be able to find something for us to drink. You can tell me all about your trip to Berlin."

Without waiting for an answer the man turned and headed towards a doorway, leaving Mbonga no option but to follow. As they approached the bridge, he got out a large ring of keys and opened the metal door. "Come into my office," he said, smiling. As he used another key to open a cabinet built into the wall underneath the ship's wheel, it occurred to Mbonga that he must be the captain. He poured two generous glasses of Jameson's whiskey and handed one to Mbonga. "Here's to Berlin, and a successful summit," he said, holding his glass aloft in Mbonga's direction.

"Have you been following the summit process?" Mbonga asked, trying not to choke on his whiskey.

"As much as I can. It's not always easy, especially when you spend as much time on this boat as I do."

"I suppose it's a full-time job?"

"Six days and nights every week. I'm supposed to have every third week off, but that hasn't happened for a long time now."

"At least you have a job."

"Not for much longer."

"Really?"

"The Illala makes her last voyage next month. The government says it can no longer subsidise a service that attracts so few passengers."

"It's the same everywhere. I was employed as a ranger on a game reserve until the visitors stopped coming."

"I'm sorry."

"No, no. I'm much more fortunate than most people."

"It's funny, isn't it," the captain paused, "the economy has ground to halt, but somehow society continues. People muddle through. We help each other out where we can."

"That's true. But thousands of children have been orphaned by aids, and rates of malnutrition and child mortality have shot up. Many people have already paid with their lives."

The Captain refilled his pipe and lit it. "Do you have confidence in the blueprint to sort all this out?"

"I don't know if the blueprint will make a difference in my country, or in yours. I don't know if this ship will ever be back in service with a full passenger list. But I do believe the blueprint is our only hope."

"Well, I'll drink to that."

Nine

Helen, Kersen and Jay travelled together to the Prime Minister's residence where they were joined by the Minister for Economic Development. They enjoyed an excellent meal, prepared, to Helen's surprise, by the Prime Minister's daughter, and served by her husband.

"I hope you don't mind," the Prime Minister asked as coffee was served, "but I wonder if my daughter might sit in on the rest of our meeting. She is currently completing her doctoral thesis, and when I told her that you were coming, she asked if she might join us."

Helen was delighted at the informality of it all. She looked at Jay, who indicated he had no problem. Kersen just sat there with a big smile on his face.

"Of course," Helen answered. The Prime Minister's husband left the room and a few seconds later a woman in her mid-twenties came in. She was strikingly beautiful, and introduced herself in impeccable English, first to Helen, then to Kersen and finally to Jay, for whom she appeared to have rehearsed a personal greeting.

"Professor Robertson. It is a great pleasure to meet you. I am a devoted follower of your work, and I am thrilled to have this opportunity to spend time with you." She acknowledged the Minister for Economic Development before sitting down on a chair which her mother had pulled rather noisily to the table.

It was quite an entrance. Not only was she gorgeous, she was articulate and confident, and showed no signs of being overawed by the company. Helen supposed this to be a result of growing up in a successful political family. Still, she did seem exceptionally accomplished.

Jay couldn't take his eyes of her. "Citra, what an interesting name," he said as she introduced herself.

Helen looked at Kersen who raised an eyebrow. "I understand you're doing a Phd?" she said, before Jay could embarrass himself further.

"Yes. It's entitled The Implications of Land Tenure Arrangements for Rural Development in Poor Countries" she replied, throwing a smile in Jay's direction.

"How interesting," Helen replied, "it'll be good to get the opinion of another expert on the subject."

"Well," said the Prime Minister, "that's the introductions out of the way, let's get down to business." She indicated to her colleague to begin.

The Minister for Economic Development had said little over dinner. He wore a cheap suit and looked like a career bureaucrat. When he did speak it was in grave tones. "Our government has some concerns about the proposals set out in section 14 of the blueprint, on the question of land." Jay shuffled in his chair. "We accept your assertion that all citizens need access to land in order to work and, of course, to make a home for themselves and their families. We also accept that the sustainable management of land and natural resources is essential if the environment is to be protected for future generations. Our main concern is over the provisions regarding land ownership. The evidence of history suggests that the private ownership of property, most especially land, is an essential prerequisite to economic development. It is hard to imagine how the great industrialised nations could have come to dominate the world economy had they not permitted private property in land. Your proposals appear to deny less-developed countries that same path to development. This being the case, how do you expect poorer countries to pull themselves out of poverty?"

Helen could sense Jay champing at the bit. "Minister, this question has been discussed at length by the committee. Perhaps you would allow my colleague Professor Robertson to answer?"

As Jay began to make his case, Helen remembered the first time they had discussed the topic, at their first proper session together, in Paris, two weeks after the Baltimore meeting. The second afternoon and evening were given over to the land question, from the starting point of the fourth principle, which put much of the blame for historic and contemporary injustice on the conventional view of the entitlements of land ownership. While the principle acknowledged Minister Suparno's point about the role of private land ownership in economic development, it also argued that the established rights of land ownership placed strict limits on economic justice, as well as influencing the shape of society, and perceptions of the causes of poverty.

The Paris meeting had seen the first of several run-ins between Robertson and Lundberg. Helen had opened the session by reading a quote from a little-known 19th century

American economist with whom she happened to share a name.

"For as labour cannot produce without the use of land," she read, "the denial of the equal right to use of land is necessarily the denial of the right of labour to its own produce." She let them think about it for a few seconds, before continuing. "Okay, let's bring the language up to date: when a person has no choice but to work on land owned by others, then some of the product of his or her effort is inevitably retained by the landowner. The wage received by the labourer always falls short of the true value of his effort. The difference is pocketed by his employer, in most cases the landowner." She paused.

"There is a disconnect between land ownership and the need of all people for access to land in order to survive. Why do people go hungry in poor countries? Because they have no land to farm. Why are people unemployed in rich countries? Because they have no land from which they can run a business. Why are people homeless the world over? Because they have no land on which they can build a house. If most of the usable land is owned by a small number of people, and they can charge for its use, then the majority immediately become second class citizens."

Lundberg snorted, apparently in derision. "I'm sorry Helen, but you are addressing some of the most accomplished people on the planet, yet you start with a radical, student-like appeal to our emotions."

"So you think the plight of the hungry, the unemployed and the homeless; billions of people worldwide, is not worthy of our consideration?" Helen shot back.

"Of course they are worthy," Lundberg was a little defensive, "but we need a discussion based on reason, not emotion."

"I have to disagree with you," interrupted Ann Margaret Eckart. "It seems to me that western civilization finds itself at an impasse precisely because, for the last two centuries, it has allowed its decision-making processes to be influenced solely by rationality, and has neglected the very valuable role of emotion and empathy. If you want an example, just look at the history of my own country, Germany. Reason can be applied in the pursuit of any end. Only if the underlying values are right can it help to create a positive moral outcome. For those values we have to look as much to emotion, especially the capacity to empathise with the less fortunate."

Helen adored Eckart's use of language. Nobody else could have made an appeal not to exclude emotion from debate in such a rational way.

"In respect of the land question," the German continued, "what Helen said is self-evidently true; or do you think the problems of hunger, unemployment and homelessness have no connection with the way land and natural resources are allocated under the current system?"

"I think," replied Lundberg, calmly, "that if you want to base a blueprint for economic transformation on changing rules of land ownership that have prevailed for ten thousand years, then you are going to have a fight on your hands. And you should probably keep your Henry George quotes to yourself."

"I hadn't realised that you were a student of Henry George," Helen said, looking at Lundberg.

"Actually, I'm a great admirer of his work, especially his efforts to call economists to account for their failure to consider questions of social justice. But many economists consider him an amateur, and a discredited one at that."

"But Stefan," Robertson said, "you must be aware of the campaign by vested interests to discredit George? Sure, the establishment always had a problem with land reform, but that's because it targets the foundations of minority wealth and privilege. I don't support an economy built exclusively on Georgist principles, but in respect of the land question his analysis was pretty damn good."

"Perhaps, Jay, for those of us who have not read Henry George, you could sum up his thinking, at least those parts which are relevant to our work," suggested Jamali.

"Certainly. George set out to identify the cause of deepening poverty in the midst of the great increase in wealth creation in 19th century America. It struck him that as the country underwent rapid economic development, the poorest were getting poorer. He concluded that to be poor in an advanced economy, where all land had become subject to private ownership, leaves one with no option but to sell your labour to those who own land. The land owning minority are thus able to set wages at the lowest level at which they can attract the necessary workforce."

"Thus works the labour market," muttered Lundberg.

Robertson ignored him. "If there is a pool of unemployed labour, the wage level need only be at subsistence. Henry George believed this was unjust. He believed that all citizens had an equal right of access to land or at least a fair share of its product. As a solution to the unjust distribution of land

and natural resources, George believed that the state should tax what, in his day, was called the unearned increment of land; that is to say increases in the value of land that do not result from the efforts of the landowner."

"But surely all increases in the value of a piece of land are the consequence of its owner's effort?" Barenboim asked.

"Not really," Jay replied. "If you had bought a parcel of derelict land in the centre of Paris ten years ago for ten million new francs and you had done nothing with it, how much do you think it would sell for today? A lot more than ten million, right? And this was George's point. When all land comes under private ownership, because it is limited in supply, its value automatically rises, not as a result of the efforts of landowners, but as a natural consequence of economic advance."

"So how much would landowners have to pay?" asked Jamali.

"George argued that land be taxed each year at 100 per cent of its value, though today, advocates of land value tax, or LVT, generally suggest the tax be levied on the annual rental value of the plot, or a percentage of any increase in value over the course of the year."

"But what," Barenboim interrupted, "if I had built a four thousand seat concert hall on my plot of land, the finest in all of Europe. I would attract the greatest musicians to play. Every night would be a sell out. We would make enormous profits and the value of my land would increase tremendously. Would I be expected to hand it all that over to the government?"

"No, you wouldn't," Robertson answered. "The profits you generate from your concert hall would be a consequence of your application of capital and labour to the land. For taxation purposes they would be treated differently. The value of the underlying land would have increased in line with the value of neighbouring land. Part of that increase would be a result of your attracting more visitors to the area, and part as a consequence of other developments. The value of your neighbours' land would be taxed at the same level as yours."

"But would the Maestro be expected to pay tax on the value of his land, and on the operating profits of his concert hall?" Jamali enquired.

"Not in Henry George's scheme." Jay replied. "George argued that a tax on land values could ultimately replace taxes on incomes and profits as the principle source of public revenue."

"The famous single tax", sighed Lundberg.

"Yes, but as you know Stefan, I am not an advocate of the single tax." Robertson was slightly rattled by the Swede's constant niggling. "Nonetheless, George's arguments for taxing land values are very persuasive. The main benefits are: first, to curtail the enjoyment of unearned income by the landowning minority; second, to provide an alternative stream of public revenue and thus enable a reduction in other taxes which discourage investment and entrepreneurship; third, to bring about a more equitable distribution of land over the long term; and fourth, to create a context in which everyone receives a just and fair reward for their work. Finally, once the mere fact of landownership has a cost, and ownership becomes worthwhile only if land is put to productive use, then there would be no point in hoarding land, as happens at present."

"I think that was a great summary Jay, but may I add one more point?" asked Jemma Wiseman.

"Of course Jemma, please go ahead," Helen said.

"There is another factor contributing to rises in land values: public investment in economic infrastructure. If the state uses tax revenues to improve public transport provision for example, perhaps making it easier for people to attend Daniel's concerts, then the value of nearby land increases. With most land privately owned, often by large corporations, this has the effect of transferring tax revenues, the burden of which falls most heavily on the poor, onto the balance sheets of wealthy corporations, and ultimately into the bank accounts of their shareholders. Taxing land values ensures that at least some of the return on such investments is returned to the public purse which funded it."

Jay nodded in agreement.

In the year and a half since that Paris meeting, Robertson had rehearsed his argument so many times that the version he delivered this evening was extremely persuasive. Helen watched as he concluded:

"To sum up, the land reform proposals outlined in the blueprint are intended to bring access to the benefits of a dynamic economy to all citizens, instead of leaving many to collect crumbs from the tables of the wealthy."

Helen looked at the Prime Minister, who had been listening intently.

"Thank you Professor Robertson," she said, "that was most illuminating. I hadn't realised the idea of land reform had such a rich and intriguing history. Now, I'm sure Minister Suparno has some questions?"

"Thank you Prime Minister," he began rather solemnly. "Professor Robertson, assuming for a moment that a tax on land values would bring the benefits you suggest, what if countries were to tax land at different rates? This would attract capital and labour across borders and lead to greater inequality. Governments can compete on tax, whether they be taxes on land values, or more conventional forms."

"That's where the principle of simultaneity comes in," Jay answered. "The provisions on land policy, like many of the provisions in the blueprint, will only succeed if they are implemented simultaneously in all countries. This is why all nations have to sign up to the blueprint and agree to implement its recommendations according to a set timetable."

"What about compensating landowners for this change in the entitlements of their land ownership?" asked the Prime Minister.

"We have concluded that as land ownership constitutes an advantage to those that enjoy it, no compensation should be paid. As the tax regime changes, those who own land should have nothing to fear as long as they are prepared to work. If they are not, they will have to sell their land. The proceeds from such sales should be compensation enough." Helen answered this time.

"Also," the Prime Minister's daughter urged, "you have to remember how the current distribution of land was arrived at. It is largely a product of historical injustices: land was carved up as a result of victory in battle, or on the basis of patronage. This initial, unjust distribution of land has been compounded by an economic system weighted in favour of the already wealthy. As well as giving more people a stake in the economy, taxing land values would also address those historical wrongs. It is not landowners who should be compensated, it is those who have been denied their legitimate share of the advantages of land ownership."

Helen was watching Jay. He was listening with his mouth slightly open.

"One final question, if I may?" asked Minister Suparno. "Allow me to play devil's advocate, Ms George. What in your opinion, would be the prospects for my country if we did not sign up to the blueprint?"

"Well that would depend, Minister. If Indonesia was the only country to opt out, I'm afraid it would find itself at a major disadvantage economically. I can see no reason, for example, for other nations to trade with a country that had not signed up to a set of rules by which everyone else had agreed to be bound. There would also be political ramifications. As poverty began to reduce in other countries, the poor in your own country would begin to wonder why they were being denied the benefits enjoyed by people elsewhere."

The Minister nodded in acknowledgement. He looked thoughtful, but content.

"Well, thank you so much. This has been a most enlightening discussion," the Prime Minister said.

In the hall on the way out, Helen chatted to the Prime Minister, while Kersen spoke animatedly with Minister

Suparno who was now much more relaxed. After five minutes, Helen signalled to Kersen to go and find Robertson, who had not yet emerged from the dining room.

"Did you enjoy dinner?" Helen asked him, as they travelled back to the hotel.

Ten

Harry Noble was a member at three London clubs: The Carlton, where much of his business was done, The Arts, where he went to be on his own, and The Reform Club, probably his favourite, where he sat this evening in the splendid oak-panelled library. He was meeting an old friend from the Russian Embassy who, as an undergraduate, had studied with President Kotov.

A steward came into to the room closely followed by Oleg Kandinsky.

"Oleg, how lovely to see you. Now, what would you like to drink?"

"I'll have a scotch, thank you." Harry nodded to the steward, who departed.

"So Harry, what can I do for you?" he asked.

"In a nutshell, I want to meet your President," Harry answered with all the assertiveness he could muster.

"Go on," Kandinsky said, smiling.

"I've been having some dealings with Helen George." The Russian looked surprised and impressed. "She and I go back a long way," he fibbed by way of explanation, "though as you can probably imagine, we don't see eye to eye on her current project."

"I can assure you, Harry, there are plenty of sceptics on our side too. I'm not sure humankind is ready for this wonderful new world Ms George has planned for us."

"Exactly." Harry was growing in confidence. "Now, it's only four weeks until the Tbilisi summit at which your government must decide whether to support the blueprint. It strikes me that a Russian veto is our best way to kill this process stone dead. I don't suppose you have any idea what President Kotov is thinking?"

"From what I hear, he has yet to make up his mind. As you know he is man of great integrity and intellect. He is also a progressive, and something of a maverick. Rather like Gorbachev he appears little concerned with his own position, and genuinely committed to steering Russia towards the best possible outcome for its people, all of them. Knowing him as I do, I think he will be supportive of the blueprint in principle, but unsure if it is in the best interests of the Russian people, at least for the time being. Also, he will be coming under tremendous pressure from the Putinistas. They are still considerable in number, and have great influence in The Kremlin."

"It sounds to me like he's in need of some objective advice, perhaps from someone outside his own coterie, even someone who is close to Helen George."

Kandinsky smiled. "I'll see what I can do, Harry. Kotov is rather impulsive you know. If he likes the idea, he may want to see you at short notice."

The opening session of the Jakarta summit was due to start at 2pm. Saeed was chairing a final meeting at 11am to run over who was doing what in the face to face sessions. Robertson had arrived fifteen minutes late, apologising profusely. He said he'd gone for a run and become lost. He had a history of arriving late for meetings. Helen had been surprised at how disorganised he was. She suspected academia was more forgiving of otherwise brilliant people than the real world.

After the meeting, Mike was waiting to speak to her. Without being asked, he told her that Robertson had indeed gone running that morning, leaving the hotel without his security detail at 6am. Rick Spedman had followed him to the Prime Minister's residence where he was joined by a young woman. They jogged around the botanical gardens for half an hour before returning to the Prime Minister's residence at around 7am. Jay remained inside until 10.30 before leaving, still in his running gear, at which point one of Spedman's men picked him up and brought him back to the hotel.

Helen was furious. She noticed Saeed and Kersen were still in the ante-room, she asked them to come back in.

"How could he be so stupid, after what you said yesterday?" Saeed said, as close to angry as he got.

"It was obvious that he was impressed by her," said Kersen, "but really, had I known he would do this, I would have advised you not to bring him."

"I was impressed by her," Helen fumed, "but I wasn't knocking on her door at 6am dressed in my bloody gym shorts. What are we going to do about it?" she demanded, as if their gender made them complicit in Robertson's misdemeanour. "Is she a risk? Is he a risk?"

"I doubt very much that she's a risk," answered Mike, "but I'll have someone look into it. The real problem will come if it gets out. Robertson is married with a four year old daughter. The media would have a field day."

"Right. I'll talk to him. Mike, I want to know his every movement over the next two days."

Helen took the unusual step of sending for Robertson, rather than calling him herself. She had him return to the meeting room.

"Jay," she began, trying to maintain her composure. "As you would know if you had half a brain, you were followed by our security team when you left the hotel this morning. You were seen jogging in a public park with the Prime Minister's daughter, and then returning to the residence with her, not leaving again for almost four hours. What on earth were you thinking of?"

For a moment he looked uncomfortable, but his demeanour suddenly changed. "What the hell business is it of yours Helen?"

"Jay, you were at the meeting yesterday afternoon? Does it not occur to you that your actions this morning could expose you to precisely the kind of press coverage that could wreck this entire process?"

"Oh, come off it Helen, we were careful. Nobody saw us."

"Rick Spedman saw you. And our opponents employ people just like him to uncover dirt."

"Helen, we're all adults here. You can't keep us locked in our rooms like children."

"We shouldn't need to keep you locked up. I would have hoped you would have some sense of responsibility to your colleagues."

"I'm sorry Helen, but I'm not taking a lecture. I'll be careful, don't worry. I'm not going to do anything to undermine the work of your precious committee. But I'd be grateful if you'd allow me to have a life. And keep your damn spooks off my back." He stood up and left the room.

Helen called Mike. "Meet me in the bar," she said, "and bring Saeed and Daniel."

As she made her way down the stairs, she wondered if she'd handled the situation as well as she might. She hadn't been prepared for Robertson's reaction. She was used to his argumentative style, but she'd never had cause to question his commitment. There was no procedure for disciplining committee members, and she certainly had no power to stop him seeing the woman. The others agreed it would be precipitous to challenge Robertson further. He would be kept under surveillance, and hopefully he would come to his senses.

The opening session was more formal than those in Cape Town and São Paulo. Prime Minister Sianturi spoke strongly in support of the blueprint, but seemed less comfortable with Helen than she had the previous evening. Robertson arrived on time and as far as Helen could tell was doing exactly what was required of him. When the Burmese Prime Minister asked for an introduction he betrayed no hint of their falling out. Helen presumed that as far as the summit was concerned, he could be relied upon.

She only had one meeting this afternoon, with the Australian Prime Minister and some of his colleagues. They would be discussing the provisions for corporate ownership, along with Safiya Beyene. Safiya was another of the exceptional women on the committee, and Helen hadn't spent enough time with her over the last year and a half, in part because Safiya had been absent for a period, after returning to Eritrea when her country seemed on the brink of civil war.

Safiya's life story was a source of endless fascination to Helen. Her parents were both nurses in what was then the Ethiopian provincial capital of Asmara. Three weeks before she was born, her father left to fight with the Eritrean People's Liberation Front in their struggle for independence. By the time Safiya finally met him, fourteen years later, she was as politically-engaged as any teenager could be. Her father helped complete her education, and she graduated from Asmara University a month after Eritrea won independence in 1993.

She had studied geology, one of the few disciplines to survive after the Ethiopian government starved the university of funds in the years before independence. It had seemed logical, therefore, that she should take a job in the fledgling mining industry. But things didn't turn out quite as she planned. After two years working on mineral prospecting projects she became so incensed at the treatment of workers that she helped to establish the first trade union to defend the mineworkers interests. That signalled the start of a lifelong involvement in politics which culminated in her becoming her country's senior diplomat.

Safiya's inclusion had helped quell concerns that the committee was made up entirely of elite-educated academics with impeccable liberal credentials but little experience of the real world. She had plenty of such experience, and, unlike several committee members who would describe themselves as socialists only among friends, was quite happy to wear the badge publicly.

Ten

The committee's early informal debates about capitalism and socialism had proved useful to subsequent discussions on specific policy issues. By the time she was called away, Safiya had stamped her personality on the committee through a series of robust exchanges. She was exceptionally determined and articulate, even in a room full of determined and articulate people. Helen had enjoyed those discussions, not least because Safiya's views were very close to her own. As chair, she was often reluctant to take a polemical position. But it was permissible to lend support where Safiya led.

"What politicians and economists so often fail to grasp," she had argued at a workshop in Montreux the previous summer, "is that economic justice is a question of ownership and capacity: the ownership of resources and the capacity to exploit them. If people are to have a viable stake in the economy, and therefore an equal place in society, they must possess both a worthwhile share in the ownership of the factors of production, and the capacity to do something with them."

"But Safiya," Wen Zhang was always quick to challenge the assumptions of a non-economist, "you tell us that you are a socialist. I'm not sure how socialism enables the equitable distribution of resource ownership you support. It certainly did not in my country as we struggled under the weighty yoke of socialism for many decades."

"Well, it depends on your definition of socialism," she replied. "Unfortunately, whether it be in China, the Soviet bloc, or even the mixed economies of post-war western Europe, socialism has generally been pursued via the state taking control of certain industries. There is plenty of evidence to suggest that, except perhaps during times of war, this is not always the best way to run things."

"I think the failures of socialism stem from a misunderstanding of the shortcomings of capitalism," Robertson joined in the debate. "Socialists look at the failure of capitalism to address poverty and conclude that it's because economic resources are generally subject to private ownership. Their response is to place all or part of the economy under state ownership, but that creates an even bigger set of problems. Opponents of capitalism should try instead to identify what it is about the nature of private ownership that causes capitalism to fail so many people."

"Exactly," Safiya almost shouted, "the problem is not private ownership per se. It's a question of private ownership by whom, or more to the point, private ownership by how many. If the ownership of economic resources is the privilege of a small minority, then there's no chance of economic justice."

"But ownership also becomes the privilege of a minority under socialism: a motley collection of party apparatchiks and technocrats, purportedly acting on behalf of all citizens, but usually feathering their own nests," said Zhang.

"I agree," Safiya replied, "that Soviet-style socialism led to massive abuses of power. And those abuses caused far greater suffering than the injustices wrought by the economic elite under capitalism. But we mustn't throw out the baby with the bathwater; socialism has a moral ambition which capitalism lacks. Capitalists believe their system is the best we can aspire to given the supposed limits of human nature. I think we should be more ambitious. Human nature is flexible.

We should not focus exclusively on our genetic inheritance, but also on the environmental factors that enable people to escape their selfish and competitive drives and develop the capacity for empathy with others."

"Perhaps it might aid our discussion if we were to consider the mechanisms by which the ownership of economic resources has become so concentrated," suggested Saeed, who was chairing the session.

Barenboim joined the discussion. "I would suggest that historical injustices, resulting from war, imperial conquest and patronage play a key role; not just because power and privilege are passed down through the generations, but also because an assumption that minority power is inevitable becomes entrenched in culture."

"But five hundred years ago, wars of conquest were part and parcel of the natural order," Zhang continued.

"Indeed they were, but should we not address the modern-day consequences of the way our ancestors behaved? We need not condemn them; after all their actions were in keeping with the moral precepts of their time. But civilization has moved on; we should take steps to redress accumulated injustices."

"And the best way to do that," Safiya was animated once again, "is to create a level playing field for people today."

"So, you wouldn't support the idea of reparations for slavery, for example?" Jamali asked her.

"It's true that Africa's economic development was strangled by the forced abduction of hundreds of thousands of young men and women for the slave trade. But if I had a choice between an economy based on equitable access and fair trade between nations, and reparations for past injustices, I would take the former. Africa must learn to stand on its own two feet. I believe it will if given a fair chance."

"Another problem with capitalism is the way it heaps further rewards on those who begin with an advantage," Jay continued. "If you start out owning land, or have access to capital which others don't, then obviously you are much better placed than those who start with nothing. There are occasional rags to riches stories: people who have a brilliant idea or prove unusually resourceful, but they are the exception. Such success stories might appear to suggest a system that rewards talent and hard work, but by its very nature, capitalism limits the number of such stories."

"I don't disagree," said Barenboim, "but if that's the case, how do you account for the massive growth in the professional middle class in many nations after 1945?"

Jay smiled. "Actually," he said, "I put it down to the socialist policies implemented before and after World War Two. It was President Roosevelt's New Deal that set up the American century with a massive programme of public investment. This example was followed across the western world, and in Japan of course, after the war, and Korea a little later. It may not have been sustainable in the long term, if only for political reasons, but there is a misconception that global economic growth accelerated after the deregulation of the global economy from the 1970s onwards. In fact, the greatest period of sustained growth was prior to deregulation. This was because state intervention in the economy added value and improved the conditions for economic expansion, with redistribution through taxation creating unprecedented opportunities. Without the special circumstances of the post-war period, and the socialist-inspired policies they demanded, the market liberalisation that followed would have stalled for lack of prior investment in infrastructure."

"So in short," said Jamali, "the economic gains of the twentieth century would have been impossible had capitalism been left to its own, unregulated, devices."

"But also," added Safiya, "whereas the post-war phase coincided with the divesting of colonies and steady economic progress in many of the poorest nations, a key aspect of the neo-liberal period was the suppression of developing economies under structural adjustment polices that reversed many of the earlier gains."

"Which allowed an economic recolonisation of large parts of the developing world by capital-rich multinational corporations," added Jay.

"There's another point I think we should note," said Safiya. "The demands of capital accumulation and the benefits of economies of scale encourage ever greater scale in enterprise. Generally, this is not a good thing for the majority. With advances in technology, large-scale enterprises are able to increase both output and profits while reducing staff numbers. Increased productivity enables them to scale-up further through acquisition. This means that ownership of economic resources is further concentrated among a small number of multinational corporations whose payrolls are steadily shrinking. A few decades ago, people with no direct access to the factors of production could at least find jobs. Before long most will be denied even this option."

"But everyone has the opportunity to acquire shares in these corporations, do they not?" Saeed asked.

"In theory, of course they do," said Jay, rising to the bait, "but Saeed, do you know what proportion of the global population has sufficient surplus wealth to invest in stocks and shares? Less than two per cent."

"And that includes those investments managed by private pension funds on behalf of wealthier individuals, doesn't it Jay?" Helen asked.

"It does."

"It gets worse," Safiya said. "So desperate are those shareholders to line their pockets, that demand for year-on-year profits growth is unquenchable. The only way such demands can be satisfied is for enterprises to further consolidate, to further colonise the untapped economic resources of less-developed countries, and to employ fewer people, forcing a rapid race to the bottom"

"So," asked Saeed, "the argument that as long as economic growth is maintained, some of the additional wealth generated will trickle down to those at the bottom has little basis in fact?"

Safiya and Jay both made to answer at once, before Safiya gave way. "I've spent twenty-four years searching for a serious academic proof of trickle-down theory," Jay sighed. "And you know what? There isn't a single one."

Helen decided it was time to extract specific conclusions from the discussion: "It sounds as if we are all agreed that full employment is non-negotiable. Economic arrangements which do not promote full employment will not deliver a just society. We also agree that neither deregulated free markets or state socialism achieve that objective in a sustainable way."

"Nor, for that matter, does the kind of middle-way social democracy that has been widely practised since 1945," Jay interrupted.

"Okay, so what are the conditions for achieving full employment?"

"All you need," Safiya answered, "is a workforce able and willing to work, with access to land and resources, and a line of credit with which to acquire capital. The key is how you combine labour with land and capital. The established economic framework prioritises returns to land and capital at the expense of labour. Given that the majority of human beings own no land or capital, only one outcome is possible. We must create a new economic framework which properly rewards all labour."

Antonella was exhausted, and relieved to be nearing the end of her shift. For the second day running she'd been asked to cover for an absent chambermaid. She hated making beds and cleaning rooms, not just because of the disgusting mess left by many guests, and certainly not because she considered it beneath her. It was just hard, back-breaking work. Room service was tough too, but there wasn't the continual bending, and there were tips, and occasionally an interesting conversation with a guest.

After clocking off, she decided to flout the rules and walk out through the lobby. She turned right onto Avenida Marginal de Pinteiros and went into the tobacconist on the corner. She bought a lottery ticket from the shop owner whose kindly face reminded her of her father. Then she crossed the road and took a seat near a coffee stand overlooking the river and ordered an Americano. This was a rare treat. Three conditions had to be satisfied before Antonella would blow two hours wages on a cup of coffee: the weather had to be perfect, the river had to be in full flood so she could see the water while sitting, and she had to want to be alone with her thoughts.

Those thoughts were beginning to make her paranoid, dominated as they were by the news of Helen George and her committee. She couldn't believe that only a week had passed since their meeting, and that Helen was now in Indonesia.

She thought about their conversation and of her ambition to own her own hotel. She couldn't begin to imagine how that dream might be realised. Even if she studied hard and came out with a good degree, the best she could hope for was a position as a graduate trainee with Hilton. But there was huge competition for those places, and many well-qualified candidates. Even if she made it, it would only push her a couple of rungs up the ladder. She had spoken to colleagues who had completed the scheme only to find that there were too few management jobs to go round.

She took a sip of coffee. She told herself not to be so pessimistic. She was only 19; she couldn't expect miracles. She looked at the lottery ticket which was still in her hand. She'd been playing the same set of numbers for several months now. They didn't look lucky. Absent-mindedly she turned the ticket over. Sometimes the reverse contained a promotional offer which might make the ticket worth something. There was no offer on this ticket, just information to the effect that every ticket purchased this week would also be entered into an additional draw for a special, one-off prize. The possibility of winning some unspecified prize cheered her up, a little.

The discussion with Prime Minister Kendall of Australia and his team was very lively. Kendall was old school, head of a Labor government that had won a second term only because few Australians could bear the thought of voting Liberal. He was excited at the prospect of change, but struggled with the loss of sovereignty that his comparatively young and isolated country would inevitably suffer. They talked at length about the prospects for Australia's aboriginal population under the blueprint. As all previous attempts to tackle the uncomfortable legacy of the nation's colonial heritage had failed, Kendall wasn't sure a new economic regime would make any difference.

Helen and Safiya explained why they thought the creation of a level economic playing field was an essential first step. Doubtless other policy initiatives would be required, ones specific to Australia's particular situation; but until they got the economy right, there was no hope of ancient and modern cultures surviving intact and transforming themselves together.

But there were other things on the Australian's mind. "One of the things that has concerned me most over the last couple of decades," Prime Minister Kendall said, "is the way in which work has been devalued. Obviously there are fewer jobs in general, and it amazes me how few economists or politicians seem to think full employment is an objective worth striving for. But for the most part, the jobs that remain are stultifying; they provide little in the way of job satisfaction, yet they are the only jobs on offer."

"I agree," Helen answered. "And the upshot is the creation of new class divisions: A professional class consisting of people who are paid well, live well, and generally enjoy their work. An struggling middle class who have to take whatever work they can get, but live with chronic insecurity. And an underclass which, to all intents and purposes, is invisible to the economy."

"But for so long economists have claimed there is no alternative," Kendall said.

"I fear too many economists have very little vision; few are able to think outside the box. They argue that things are better than they were a century or two ago, as if that justifies their complacency. The question is not whether things are better than they were, but how much better they could be with a little more ambition."

The Australians also raised the question of scale. "Do you really think the global economy can be as productive and efficient if enterprise is broken down into smaller units?" the Finance Minister asked.

"In terms of productivity, yes," Helen answered. "Under current arrangements, there are a number of problems with productivity: We are producing too many luxuries and non-essentials at the expense of necessities. We are producing things in the wrong place: surplus food in countries where people eat too much already, and too little where they are hungry. We are involving too few people in the process of production in both rich countries and poor. And, of course,

our methods of production are still not sufficiently environ-
mentally sustainable. We believe that by gradually downsizing
the scale of productive units, and ensuring the ownership of
firms remains close to the markets into which they sell, each
of these problems can be addressed."

"So you see a link between the environmental problem
and the question of scale in production?" Kendall asked.

Helen nodded towards Safiya.

"Most certainly we do. In two respects: firstly, smaller scale
operations are better able to adapt their activities to new
low- or no-carbon energy sources, as these become available.
Second, it is much easier to monitor the carbon emissions of
small firms, and therefore ensure that targets are hit."

"And efficiency?" pressed Kendall.

"There are various definitions of efficiency. Currently
we assess efficiency against the cost per unit of output. A
large element of those costs are labour costs. In effect we
define efficiency as output per unit of labour employed.
Today, running a successful business requires an enterprise
constantly to reduce its labour costs which means employing
fewer people. The human cost, like the environmental cost,
of running an economy on this basis is never counted. We
think it should be. Under the blueprint, these additional
measures of value will be incorporated into assessments of
efficiency."

"But might this not lead to firms employing more people
than they need simply in order to meet government targets
to avoid unemployment?" asked another member of the
delegation.

"Employers will still be under a market-imposed obligation at least to break even. As long as each worker is effectively engaged in producing something that has exchange value in the marketplace, then there is no question of over-staffing or inefficiency," Helen answered. "We believe the structural reforms outlined elsewhere in the blueprint will create an economic framework in which the optimal size of businesses will reduce in response to the demands of the market, not government imposed targets."

"You make an impressive case, Ms George," Kendall admitted. "I suppose you've read this." He opened his case, and pulled out a well-thumbed copy of E.F. Schumacher's Small is Beautiful.

Helen smiled. "Required reading for committee members," she said.

"I first read it as an undergraduate, many years ago. Tell me, why do you think it has taken so long for Schumacher's ideas to be taken seriously. After all, the book was a bestseller back in the 1970s?"

"I think until now the world got by just about well enough without Schumacher, so his ideas remained at the margin. In recent times more people have come to share his disgust at the disregard of the economic system for human lives. And more people have come to believe in the possibility of an alternative, especially in the face of growing environmental problems. These were still distant threats when Schumacher was alive."

"Also," Safiya said, "there has been a subtle change in the balance of power in the world. The wealthy elite have lost their ability to pull the wool over the eyes of the rest of us.

The people have spoken, and our modest committee finally gives them a voice."

"Apart from his arguments for the efficacy of smaller scale enterprises, I remember being particularly impressed by Schumacher's discussion of the benefits of more participatory forms of ownership among firms. And I notice the blueprint discusses the options at some length."

"That's right," Safiya said. "While we didn't feel it necessary to legislate against the traditional joint stock form of business ownership, we are convinced that under the proposed economic framework, other forms of ownership will naturally come to the fore. Even in Schumacher's time there were many examples of successful businesses run as mutuals, or as cooperatives, or where ownership via shareholding was restricted to employees and retired former employees."

"And in the decades since Schumacher wrote this," Helen added, holding up the book, "a great many further successes have been achieved."

She was relieved when Kendall suggested a break for refreshments; her phone had been vibrating in her pocket intermittently for several minutes. As soon as she was able, she took it out and read the message: "Robertson has left the building, heading uptown."

The Canadian had a light schedule, so he wasn't exactly absent without leave, but he had clearly failed to heed Helen's warning. Another message, again from Mike: "I'm outside now." She made her excuses and moved towards the door. Mike looked very serious. She couldn't help but smile.

"He's just entered the Prime Minister's residence. I've got two men on him and another keeping tabs on anyone else who might be following him."

He was obviously feeling the pressure. Helen had already moved this subject from the crisis tray to the large file marked 'problems that have to be dealt with rationally and calmly'.

"Don't worry Mike, we'll sort it," she said. He managed a smile.

Helen returned to the room to find Safiya and the Australian delegation in stitches. At least the Australians were in the bag.

Eleven

Vladimir Kotov was in a foul mood. How could a country with so rich a cultural heritage be reduced to this? Forty per cent unemployment, thousands dying from malnutrition, whole regions falling into virtual lawlessness. His beloved Russia was an unholy mess and he was seemingly powerless to do anything about it. And he was surrounded by idiots. None of his advisors were able to tell him anything he hadn't already worked out for himself. Half of them insisted on telling him things he knew to be untrue, either because they were stupid or because they had their own agendas. He got better advice from his thirteen year old son.

And now he was seeing a British spy. He'd only taken the meeting as a favour to his old friend Kandinsky, although he was mildly interested in what this 'close personal friend' of Helen George had to say, and intrigued that George had friends in the British security service.

The intercom buzzed. "Mr President, Mr Noble is here to see you."

"Show him in," Kotov replied. He had decided to keep an open mind as long as possible.

"Mr Noble," he held out his hand. "How very good to meet you. Our mutual friend Mr Kandinsky speaks very highly of you."

Harry thanked him and sat down in one of two chairs positioned at an angle in front of the President's desk. Kotov sat in the other and noticed Harry looking at the impressive piece of furniture. He ran his fingers along its inlaid mahogany border.

"A fine piece of craftsmanship, wouldn't you agree?"

"And a fine piece of history, I should think." Harry replied, still nervous.

"Indeed. It was Stalin's desk. I believe he rescued it from the bowels of some post-revolutionary storage facility. I remembered it from photographs but when I arrived here I was disappointed to find it had been returned to the warehouse. Putin had wanted something more modern, apparently."

Harry smiled, unsure if he should say something.

"You must be surprised at how easy it was to get time with the President of Russia, or do your contacts always open doors so quickly," Kotov continued.

"Absolutely not Mr President, I think I just got lucky this time."

"Well, let's hope I too have got lucky. I have to tell you, its not been a good day. So, what can I do for you?"

Harry knew Kandinsky would have briefed Kotov; he also knew that Kotov would have made his own enquiries before taking the meeting. He would have to be at the very top of his game.

"I imagine, Mr President, that some of your current frustrations may be connected to decisions you have to make in advance of the Tbilisi summit?" Kotov was giving nothing away. "With the blueprint winning unanimous support from delegates at the first three summits, with the European Union having announced its position in advance, and with the Chinese making positive noises ahead of this week's meeting in Yokohama, your government would appear to be holding all the cards."

"Now tell me something I don't know," Kotov said, smiling.

"Mr President. You need to make the right decision for the Russian people, and for the world beyond your country's borders."

"No pressure then?" He paused. "Tell me Mr Noble, do you think the right decision for the Russian people necessarily coincides with the best decision for the wider world?"

"I do, Sir. I believe that despite the best intentions of those responsible for drawing it up, implementation of the blueprint is bound to fail."

"Go on," Kotov sipped at the coffee that had been placed on the desk in front of them.

"First, I think the principles underlying the proposed global economic framework are unsound and unproven. They are highly theoretical, and if even correct, nobody has any experience of managing societies under such arrangements. For many reasons - political, cultural and psychological - there is every likelihood it will accelerate economic collapse, rather than lead to the hoped-for rebirth."

"So you accept there are fundamental problems with the current set up?" Kotov asked, finally engaging.

"I do, but I see these as problems of poor management and a lack of international coordination. I believe the underlying economics to be basically sound, and best suited to the needs and possibilities of society at its current stage of development."

"But there is considerable evidence that the economic system is unable to respond to the very pressing need for change. I have some sympathy with the argument that it is the system itself which has brought us to this sorry position." Kotov paused again. "You say there are political, cultural and psychological reasons why the blueprint cannot possibly work. But surely it is the economic system that has corrupted politics, culture and even the pysches of many individuals?"

"I certainly agree that for the last several decades the economy has encouraged the baser human appetites. It has given licence to greed and selfishness, and has shaped our collective perceptions of what is right and what is possible. But the remedy is a matter of fine-tuning; of reigning in some of the ideological indulgences of recent years, not discarding the economic fundamentals that have sustained progress for centuries." Harry felt he was getting into his stride, and Kotov seemed to be taking him seriously.

"We certainly know about the perils of ideology in this country," Kotov said. "But the blueprint seems refreshingly free of ideology. Each of its proposals is backed by clear, reasoned argument. I agree these ideas are untested in the real world, so yes, implementation carries risks, but the world is hurtling toward the point of no return. We've had plenty of time to make the necessary adjustments and have failed to do so. I have to say I am inclined to support the blueprint."

Harry was not sure where to go next but Kotov threw him a lifeline. "Mr Noble, I have another appointment in a few minutes, but if you are free tonight for dinner, I would be delighted if you would join me."

"Thank you very much, Sir," Harry answered, surprised.

"Good, I'll have someone contact you to make the necessary arrangements."

Both men stood and Kotov showed Harry to the door.

Mbonga was exhausted. Having made great progress at the beginning of his trip, it had taken him a week to get from Itungi at the northern tip of Lake Malawi to Seronera in the heart of the Serengeti National Park. He had travelled 800 miles, but in eleven different vehicles, and at the cost of two nights in overpriced hostels in small towns where it had been too dangerous to sleep out.

He had visited the Serengeti before, five years ago, as part of an exchange programme with rangers from the Tanzanian Park Service. He had made a very good friend with whom he had kept in regular contact until about six months ago when he stopped getting replies to his emails. So here he was, in the middle of a deserted game reserve, hoping to find information that might lead him to his lost friend.

It was about an hour until sundown. Mbonga had been dropped at the side of the road by a truck driver concerned about leaving him in the middle of a game reserve. He had been too tired to explain to the man that he could look after himself.

He had with him a map of the area from his previous visit, so he set off in the direction of the Seronera Lodge Hotel, which he calculated to be less than a mile away. He quickly found the lodge but it appeared to have been abandoned; the main doors had been forced. As he entered he saw that most of the furniture had been vandalised although none appeared to have been stolen. He soon realised that the hotel had been visited not by hungry humans set on theft, but by bored animals intent on fun. His suspicion was confirmed when he found some fresh hyena droppings behind the bar.

He went through a door to one side of the bar to find a room untouched by the visiting animals in the middle of which stood a snooker table. Mbonga enjoyed playing pool whenever he had the chance, but had never played snooker on a full-sized table. He was pleased to find a full set balls, a selection of cues in good condition, and even a cube of chalk. But before he could enjoy a frame or two, he had to find some food, and a safe place to bed down for the night.

The Jakarta summit had gone well, despite the problems with Robertson. His second rendezvous with Citra proved to be the last. He was booked on a late flight to Tokyo with Jamali, Barenboim and Zhang. The others remained in Jakarta for what proved to be a pleasantly low key end-of-summit dinner hosted by Prime Minister Sianturi. Her daughter did not attend. The Prime Minister apologised to Helen for any difficulty caused by her daughter's behaviour. It was clear that she did not approve and that she held Citra solely responsible. Helen got the impression this wasn't the first time her daughter had embarrassed her.

The rest of the committee would fly to Japan the following morning in readiness for the next summit, in Yokohama, scheduled for Wednesday. This one would be something of an oddity, with just six delegate countries participating. Along with the hosts, there was China, Mongolia, Tibet, Korea and Taiwan; but this group included three of the world's ten largest economies.

The region had seen significant change of late with the reunification of Korea and its unexpected economic resurgence: it had been the only country to avoid recession after the crash of 2018. And with China's more benevolent line over Tibet culminating in regional autonomy being granted to Lhasa in 2020, the only unresolved regional dispute was that between China and Taiwan.

When the summit schedule had been drawn up, it had been decided that this mini-summit could be squeezed in between Jakarta and the European Union meeting in Stockholm the following Sunday. But as she tried to work on the plane, Helen was beginning to regret that decision. It would be full on now until she got to Vienna at the end of next week for her stepdaughter's wedding, and she couldn't put the Robertson situation out of her mind. She supposed there was a chance it would blow over without serious ramifications. There was certainly no chance of him spending further time with Citra, his schedule wouldn't permit it. She knew he planned to spend time with his family in Canada while she was in Vienna. But still she was uneasy; it didn't feel as if this episode was over.

"Helen, may I join you?"

She looked up. "Of course, please, sit down." Helen hadn't spoken to Ajala Subramanium at all in Jakarta, and felt guilty for neglecting her.

"I'm sorry we haven't had chance to talk, Ajala, but I got a very positive report back from Prime Minister Tagore. He said he and his team were very well looked after. Thank you for taking that on."

"It was a pleasure, Helen. As you know he and I go back a long way. It was good to be able to catch up. And you know my sister was part of the Indian delegation? It was just like old times."

"So everything went well then? India doesn't feel bounced into supporting the blueprint?" Helen asked.

"Poor India has no choice in matter. As you know its economy is very weak, even by current standards. Poverty has returned to pre-colonial levels and communal violence is out of control in many areas. Our economic miracle was tragically short-lived. In fact, this is partly what I wanted to talk to you about."

"Go on, we have plenty of time."

"I am worried for my country. God knows it has no chance unless the blueprint is implemented, but I also fear that compared with many nations, it will be at a distinct disadvantage given its recent history."

"And presumably the Indian Government feels the same?"

"Yes indeed. While it strongly supports the proposals for economic reform, Mr Tagore fears that India will be starting way behind many other countries because of the problems of the last few years."

"It certainly won't be easy, but there are measures in the blueprint to ensure more vulnerable nations cannot be taken advantage of. Trade on genuinely fair terms should make it much easier for India to catch up with Korea, for example."

"I did suggest this to Prime Minister Tagore. And he understood. But he's struggling to get his head round what it will mean on a practical basis. After all, once we have finished our work it will be down to national politicians to implement the policies by which the blueprint is judged."

"Perhaps we shouldn't expect too much. The blueprint won't solve all the world's problems overnight. But I'm sure that the prospects for India, and especially the most vulnerable of its people, will be improved. These improvements may not be felt by all Indians for a generation or two, but at the very least things should stop getting worse. That in itself will be an achievement."

"I am sure you are right Helen, and as you know, I am one hundred per cent behind the blueprint. But even I find it difficult to visualise exactly how the future will unfold. I'm not surprised the Indian government is nervous."

"I know, but countries like India will not be left entirely to their own devices. Non-exploitative partnerships between nations at different levels of development will soon become the norm. And while a greater proportion of production will be sold into local markets, trade between nations could come to exceed volumes achieved under the current system as new markets are created in the world's most populous countries."

"That's exactly what I told the Indian delegation. I urged them to think about the world in terms of a single global economy in which the interests of each nation is best served by cooperation. I think they got the message. But like all politicians, they have one eye on the electoral cycle."

"And in that respect, nothing changes. The blueprint cannot guarantee good government; but it will give governments the chance to prove themselves to their electorates. And India's general election isn't due for a couple of years, is it?"

"That's quite true, I reminded the Prime Minister of that as well."

They sat in silence for a couple of minutes.

"Have you thought about what you might do once the committee's work is complete, Ajala?"

"Am I considering a move into domestic politics, do you mean?" she asked, smiling.

"Women play such an important role in Indian society. Perhaps it's time the country was led by a woman once again?"

Ajala was caught slightly off guard by the suggestion. "Who knows what the future holds?" she answered evasively. "What about you Helen? Surely you won't be withdrawing from public life entirely, you're still so young?"

"I certainly won't be going into national politics. Anyway, I don't really have a home anymore. It's nearly thirty years since I left Ireland. Most people think I'm American, yet I've spent more time in London than New York, and now I live in France. No. I'm rather looking forward to following my husband wherever his work takes him, and hopefully to the two of us spending some time at home."

Helen saw Mike walking up the gangway towards her. "Can I have a quick word?" he asked.

"Of course, I'll come down." She turned to Ajala. "Stay there, I won't be long."

"Hello Mike. How are you?" She asked as she slid into the seat beside him. "Ajala and I were just talking about what we both might do once all this is over. Do you have any plans?" She turned to look at him as she asked the question. For a moment he looked rather irritated, then he realised that

Helen was trying to distract him. Perhaps he was starting to take it all a little too seriously.

"About two years ago I invested in a dive school down in the Florida Keys. Somebody's running it for me right now, but it was always my plan to take it on myself. You ever scuba dived, Helen?"

She shook her head. He said nothing more. Helen looked at him for a moment. Relationships with her close colleagues were so frustrating. They lived in each others pockets, yet she knew so little about these people, even the ones she had become close to professionally. It was pleasing to learn something new and entirely unexpected about Mike. She didn't have him down as a beach bum.

"Anyway," he said after a moment, "some frankly bemusing intelligence has just come through from a contact in Moscow."

"Moscow? Go on."

"Guess who President Kotov met with this afternoon?"

"Right now I'd believe anything you say Mike."

"No, go on guess."

Helen had no idea, but she was up for the challenge. Suddenly it came to her. "Fuck," she said, "not Harry Noble?"

Mike nodded and smiled.

"He's not going to leave us alone, is he? How the hell does somebody like Noble get a meeting with the President of Russia for Christ's sake? And Kotov's supposed to be a good guy isn't he?"

"Look on the bright side Helen. If he's using diplomatic channels, then he's unlikely to be putting together a terrorist plot to take you out."

"At least a terrorist plot would be your problem. Noble talking to Kotov is mine. And I was having such a pleasant conversation with Ajala." She got up and moved back to her seat.

Mbonga was woken early by the sun streaming through the uncurtained window. The previous evening, after a couple of frames of snooker which had proved infuriatingly difficult, he had decided to allow himself 24 hours to track down his friend. Should he find him, he would stay on for another day, otherwise he would continue his journey.

After a welcome hot shower courtesy of the hotel's solar panels, he made his way down to the kitchen where he opened another of the cans of peaches on which he had dined the previous evening. He took out his map and worked out an itinerary that would take him to the other lodges in the area and also give him time on the main road through the park. His only strategy was to ask anyone he met if they knew the whereabouts of Julius Alamisi.

The morning proved fruitless. The three lodges he visited were all in a similar state with no sign of recent human occupation. He decided to make his way back to the main road and head north. If he had no joy, there was little point in returning to the lodge tonight. He may as well take advantage of a lift out of the park.

Shortly before reaching the road, he spotted someone dressed in rangers' khaki. He made his way towards the man, who was carrying a rifle, and walking away from him. From thirty metres away he called out, so as not to cause alarm. The man turned round and looked him up and down, before walking towards him. Mbonga introduced himself and quickly explained his mission.

As soon as he mentioned the name of Julius Alamisi, the man's face dropped. He knew Julius, but he had bad news: Julius' wife had died five months ago, and Julius had returned to Karatu to look after his four young children. Karatu was outside the park boundary, but heading south. Under the circumstances, Mbonga decided he would track back.

It was less than an hour before a truck came by heading in the right direction. Before long he was in Karatu and asking directions to Julius's home, which proved easy to find. His friend had clearly fallen on hard times. The house was a ramshackle construction of corrugated iron, re-deployed fence posts and plastic sheeting. There was a doorway of sorts through which Mbonga put his head. The place was empty, but very tidy. There was little furniture beyond a table in one corner and a couple of mattresses on the floor. At least it seemed weatherproof. Mbonga picked up a small stool and took it outside to sit and wait.

It wasn't long before he saw Julius approaching, four children in tow. He couldn't remember their ages, but they seemed evenly spaced, in terms both of height and age; the eldest probably thirteen, the youngest about four. All looked thinner than was healthy.

Julius spotted him as they approached the shack and recognised him immediately. He let go of his youngest daughter's hand and ran towards Mbonga. "My god, what are you doing here my friend? How wonderful to see you."

Mbonga stood up and they hugged. "I was worried about you." he said. "You stopped replying to my emails. I thought I'd come and see how you are."

"You are joking me. All the way from Swaziland, I don't believe it. Come inside and tell me what you are really doing here, oh and bring that stool. As you might have noticed, we are a bit short of furniture."

The children settled down quickly on one of the mattresses, the older two taking it in turns to read to the younger.

"They are lovely, your children," Mbonga said, "and very well behaved."

Julius nodded.

"I heard about your wife. It must be very difficult?"

"Yes. They miss her very much, and so do I".

"What happened?"

"She had AIDS. Not long after Julie was born," he pointed to his youngest daughter, "there was some trouble here. She was among a number of women in the village who were raped by a gang of bandits. She told me about it next time I was home on leave. She coped with the trauma very well, but she became ill after about six months." His voice trailed off.

"Were you not able to afford drugs?"

"That's what is so maddening. I could afford the drugs, and they were working. But about 18 months ago, there were no more drugs to be found. She became gradually more ill until six months ago, when she went downhill very fast. I came back to look after her and the children, but she only lived another few weeks."

Mbonga saw tears in his friends eyes. He reached across the table and held his hand.

Eleven

"How are you managing?"

"Not too badly. I have a job."

"Are you still with the park service?"

"No, no. There are very few jobs left with the park service. We still have plenty of animals on the reserve, but no visitors. It must be the same in Swaziland?" Mbonga nodded. "No, I'm working at the hospital at Oldeani, looking after people dying of AIDS. The money is not good but it's better than nothing."

"It must be grim, being in that environment every day."

"It's not very nice. But it's a job. I can put food on the table, and I can pay the school fees. That's all I care about. I'm a lot better off than most people around here." There was a moment's silence while they both looked at the children who were now playing. "But enough about me. Tell me, what you are doing so far from home?"

Mbonga told him about how he had been inspired by TV coverage of the Cape Town summit, and how, while he still couldn't explain the reason for his trip, he had decided to travel overland to be in Berlin for the final summit. "I hope to be witness to a piece of history," he concluded.

"Ah my friend, what a marvellous adventure. How I wish I could come with you. I can't imagine what it is like in Europe. But will you be safe? How are you going to get into Germany. Don't they have strict controls on immigration?"

"I believe they do. But if I make it that far, nothing is going to stop me getting to Berlin. Don't worry, I'll be okay."

Oscar Silverman's phone rang. He didn't move. He wasn't sure how long he'd been drinking, but he was still sober

157

enough to know that what started out as a couple of shots to calm down had crossed the line that too often signalled a spiral into morbid depression. But he wasn't quite there yet. He picked up the phone.

"Oscar, it's Harry."

"Harry, how are you?" he asked, overcompensating for probable slurring.

"I'm fine, thank you," replied Noble. "I'm in Moscow. In fact, I met with Kotov this afternoon."

"That sure is fast work Harry. I'm impressed. How'd it go?"

"Very well. I'm dining with him this evening. He certainly seems to be keeping an open mind. How are things there?"

"Not much happening to be honest. It seems that this mission is to be pursued by diplomatic means only."

"Don't worry Oscar. I have a good feeling about this. I'll keep you in the loop."

Silverman dropped the phone on the floor. He liked Harry, but he didn't have a great deal of faith in his ability to influence the Russian President. Everybody knew Kotov was his own man, and in so far has he has given any indications, he was sympathetic to the blueprint. Harry Noble was not going to save the world. He reached down, picked up the phone again and dialled.

"Howard, it's Oscar," he said, as Dawkins answered. "Noble's made contact with Kotov. He sounds optimistic, but I'm not so sure."

"Listen Oscar. No details, but Noble isn't the only man in play. You get what I'm saying. Sit tight, and keep an eye on the news channels. And stop drinking Oscar. It makes you unpleasant." Dawkins hung up. Silverman poured himself another whiskey.

On landing in Tokyo, Helen and Mike left the others at the airport and headed straight for the hotel where Saeed and Daniel were waiting for them.

"I had no idea your friend Mr Noble was so well connected," Barenboim said as she greeted him.

"Well we don't want things getting too dull now, do we?" They both smiled. "I spoke to Gerald from the plane. Apparently Noble is matey with an old friend of Kotov's from student days. That's probably how he got the meeting."

"Still," said Jamali, "it's quite a coup for someone like Noble."

"It is, but I think we can learn something from it. First, as I thought, Noble is an honourable man. He has decided to oppose us through diplomatic means. And good luck to him. It just means our preparation for Tbilisi has to be even better. We should try to get a meeting with Kotov in Moscow before we go to Houston. Saeed, perhaps you should come with me?" Jamali nodded.

"And the second thing?" Barenboim asked.

"We now know for sure that Kotov has yet to make up his mind. The glass is still half full. We didn't know that until this morning."

Nobody said anything for a moment, then Barenboim changed the subject. "Right, next item of crisis management: I had a long chat with Robertson on the plane. He's not in a good place I'm afraid. He feels guilty about what happened in

Jakarta, but is ambivalent about the committee and worried about his marriage, which is obviously in difficulty."

"He's due to go home in a couple of weeks isn't he," asked Jamali.

"Yes, but he's not looking forward to that very much," Barenboim replied.

"Well, I guess we need to look after him as best we can. Thankfully Miss Sianturi is out of the picture. Let's hope he knuckles down and keeps out of trouble. And at least Lundberg seems to be keeping below the radar. Gerald reports no sign of further adverse press coverage," Helen said.

"Perhaps the Wall Street Journal episode was not part of any conspiracy," Jamali suggested. "May be he just let something slip to Veronica who passed it on, in all innocence."

"I'm not sure anything happens innocently at the Journal, but at least things are quiet on one front. What time are we leaving for Yokohama?"

Mike looked at his watch. "About an hour," he said.

"I'll see you all in a hour then." She turned and headed towards the elevator with the room key Mike had given her.

Harry had received instructions to wait in the lobby of his hotel to be collected by one of Kotov's drivers. A smartly uniformed man appeared at the specified time and apparently had no problem identifying him. They headed west, towards Kroylatskoye, Harry suspected, the location of the President's official residence. On arrival, electronic gates opened and they drove into an underground car park where he caught sight of a man who looked like Kotov polishing the bonnet of a sports car. The driver opened his door, and ushered him towards the car.

"Ah Harry," Kotov said, standing up from his work. "Look at her, isn't she beautiful?"

"She's, er, very nice." Harry said. "How long have you been together?"

Kotov roared with laughter. "You will get on very well with my wife," he said. "She doesn't get cars either."

He looked back at the vehicle which, Harry ascertained from the animal perched at the end of its bonnet, was a Jaguar.

"It's the only one I own you know. I used to have a little Honda for getting around town, and this beautiful creature for weekends. Now they won't let me drive it."

"I'm glad to see you own a British car," Harry said.

"Series 1 E-Type, made in Coventry, 1964.

"What an interesting coincidence," Harry said. "I was made in Coventry in 1964."

Once again Kotov roared with laughter. He put his arm around Harry and guided him towards a spiral staircase. They entered an elegantly furnished but rather untidy sitting room where Kotov offered Harry a drink: "I have sherry, you know." Harry wasn't sure if Kotov was winding him up; in any case he needed something stronger.

"Scotch please, no ice."

"I think I'll join you," Kotov said, awkwardly pulling a slightly dusty unopened bottle from behind several others.

"So Harry, they no longer make Jaguars in the city of your birth?"

"I believe not," he replied, annoyed at his inability to speak knowledgeably.

"Absolutely not, in fact not for nearly twenty years. And do you know where they are made now?"

"India?" Harry offered speculatively.

"Good effort, but no. The Gujarat plant closed down two years ago when Tata went bust. There are no Jaguars manufactured anywhere in the world today. Hyundai bought the name and has promised to start production in Pyongyang by the end of this year. But they haven't even built the factory yet."

Harry could think of nothing to say.

"So what does the plight of a once great British car company have to do with anything?" Kotov asked. "I'll tell you. It is the supreme metaphor for the global economy over the last 50 years: The total victory of international capital over local interests. We live in a world where nothing is built to last, because we accept an economy in which everything is transient. It's no way to run the world, Harry. That's why I'm inclined to support the blueprint. I agree with you that its proposals for the economy are untested, but things have got so bad."

"Mr President, I accept that the situation is serious. I accept the need for change. I even accept that some of the arguments for economic reform in the blueprint are well founded. But do you think the Russian people really understand the implications of Russia giving up so much sovereignty. If you sign up to the blueprint your government's hands will be tied in so many respects."

"So give me an alternative. My country is dying on its feet. In rural areas the shops are nearly as empty as they were during the dark days of communism. Millions of people have returned to the land, but most have no idea how to work it, so they drink themselves to an early grave. It's pitiful."

"I don't have an alternative blueprint, Mr President. But I can offer you a strategy based on a different ordering of principles. Your point about Jaguar is a good one. It demonstrates the failings of economic globalisation: it's a process that moves jobs to where labour is cheapest, and at the same time accelerates the business cycle so that economic miracles, like that of India, turn out to be depressingly short-lived. But I believe a process of political globalisation would be even more disastrous. In economic terms, people everywhere at least have largely similar aspirations: they seek security and they are prepared to work to achieve it. In terms of politics and culture there is no such homogeneity. Human beings have always identified themselves primarily with the tribe to which they belong. Tribal identity may have been replaced by national identity, but the effect is the same. People need to belong, and they need to belong to something smaller and more meaningful than a collective that comprises the entire human race. Look what happened here when the Soviet Union tried to forge just fifteen disparate nations into a single state under a rigid economic framework."

"But it was the economic framework, and the shortcomings of the political elite, that brought the USSR to its knees. I don't see too many parallels between Helen George and Comrade Stalin. And under capitalism, it is the failure of the economy to deliver a cohesive society that has driven many people to seek refuge in long-forgotten tribal identities," Kotov said.

"That may be true, but most people are not ready to give up their those identities altogether: it's a question of personal sovereignty as much as national sovereignty, and a complex question of individual psychology."

"Yes, but individual psychology can change very quickly, perhaps within a couple of generations."

"Then let us spend a couple of generations getting it right. If Helen George has her way the blueprint will come into effect at midnight on 1st May next year. Are you sure the Russian people will be ready in eight months time."

"I am not sure, but according to the opinion polls there is clear support for the blueprint."

"Mr President, I believe there are times when the democratic will should not be our exclusive guide."

Kotov was silent. Harry thought quickly.

"Mr President, you may well be right. The blueprint may be the best option for our troubled world, but it is not the last, or the only option. In my opinion there is a strong possibility that its introduction will have precisely the opposite impact to that which its architects intend. Your people have suffered too much already; as their President you have a responsibility not to expose them to further risk."

Kotov looked at him. "Harry," he said, "you give me food for thought. Now, let's have some more whisky."

Twelve

Most of the committee were waiting outside the hotel for cars to take them to Yokohama. There was always great confusion on such occasions, mainly, Helen had concluded, because this otherwise exceptional group of people were incapable of completing a simple task like organising themselves into half a dozen cars. She had come to enjoy the spectacle as first one and then another of her esteemed colleagues attempted to create order out of chaos; none had yet succeeded. This time it was Jemma Wiseman's turn, though despite being responsible for some of the most innovative traffic management systems in the world, she was fairing no better.

"Hey, surf boy, why don't you ride with me?" Helen shouted across the forecourt. That got everyone's attention, especially when Mike made his way sheepishly towards her.

"I had hoped that information would remain private," he admonished Helen.

"Sorry Mike, couldn't resist. Not another word, I promise." They climbed into the back seat of one of the rather small cars. "How far is Yokohama anyway?" she asked as they pulled away.

"About half an hour – it's pretty much a suburb of Tokyo, although technically it's Japan's most populous city in its own right."

"Do you know Japan at all?" Helen asked.

"One trip, about ten years ago."

"I have to admit I've never quite got it. I don't know why. There's nothing normal about it. In most countries you find something you can relate too. Something that reminds you of the degree of uniformity that exists among different cultures. But I don't get that here." Mike was silent. "Gerald really likes it here, you know."

"Well that shouldn't really surprise you Helen. Let's face it, there's not much normal about Gerald," Mike said sarcastically.

"You're just jealous because he has a more reliable network of informants than you do."

"Network of informants? He knows a lot of gossip columnists."

"And people talk to gossip columnists, they don't talk to spies." They both laughed. "Seriously, Mike. I'm really grateful for all you've done the last couple of weeks. I had no idea things would get so fraught."

"Changing the world in two years was never going to be straightforward."

"Do you think they can stop us?"

"It depends who they are, and how they go about it. To be honest, I think Harry Noble is your biggest problem. As far as we know he's still in Moscow. He must have a reason for staying, Kotov must be listening to him."

"We need to do some homework before Saeed and I go to Moscow."

"Do you want me to come with you?"

"I don't think so. I was wondering about asking you to go Vancouver to keep an eye on Robertson."

"I'll send Rick, discrete surveillance is his forté."

"Okay." Helen thought for a moment. "Do you remember when Saeed and I interviewed you for this job, in New York, the day after the UN resolution?"

"Shortlist of one, wasn't it?"

"And I asked you why you wanted the job. And you said because you wanted to travel." Mike nodded and smiled. "Do you believe in the process, or is it just a job, an opportunity to travel?"

"I can't admit to understanding much of the economics, but sure, I support the outcomes. I trust that you guys know what you're doing. And from what I can see, each strand of the blueprint is motivated by the right principles. If it fails, it won't be because your approach was wrong."

"But you think it could fail, even if we get it adopted in Berlin?"

"I worry that the world might not be ready, but I accept that we have no choice. Where are we now? 230 million early deaths directly attributable to climate change in twelve years. And nobody dares contest the figures anymore. What kind of a civilization would sit by and do nothing?"

They sat in silence for a few minutes as the car sped along a fast road that had been cleared for the convoy. Helen and Mike were in the front car, just behind the escort vehicle. In the final car, Saeed was seated next to Stefan Lundberg, who had said nothing for several minutes, but seemed uncomfortable.

"Saeed," he said eventually. "May I speak to you in absolute confidence?"

"Of course you may, please," Jamali said, sensing something important was about to happen.

Lundberg tensed, and for a moment looked close to tears. "It's rather difficult, I'm afraid."

Jamali hadn't seen him like this before. People were always telling him what a good listener he was, but he didn't fancy himself as a therapist, not to Lundberg at any rate.

"It's okay, take your time," he said softly.

"I think I may have inadvertently caused the work of the committee to be compromised, and I fear it could become very serious," he broke down completely.

In other circumstances, Jamali thought, he might have placed a fatherly arm around the man's shoulder. But seated as they were, next to each other in the back of a modestly-sized car, such a gesture would inevitably end up with him grabbing the Swede in an unseemly manner, so he decided to keep his hands to himself.

"What is it, Stefan?" he asked, hoping to stem the near flood of tears.

"You are happily married, aren't you Saeed?" He didn't allow time for Jamali to answer. "I am rather envious of you. You see I didn't marry the woman I loved when I had the chance, and she married someone else. Now we are both miserable, except on the odd occasion we can steal some time together. Since I became European President, those times have been few and far between."

Jamali decided there was no need to tell Lundberg he knew about his relationship with Veronica Abel. "So what's happened?" he asked, in his most sympathetic voice.

"I talk to her - oh I may as well tell you - she is Veronica Abel, she's married to Victor Weiss. She's the only person I talk to about work, about anything actually. I have been taking her into my confidence for years, and there has never been a problem. She has always been fiercely loyal to me, despite having married that idiot. Anyway, just recently there have been reports in the Wall Street Journal that could only have been written by someone who was privy to our conversations. I know she hasn't passed on any information to her husband; they have virtually no relationship."

"So she's being bugged?" Jamali asked.

"It appears so. She has no idea by whom, or how long it's been going on. She suspects the CIA knows of our relationship, but she's not been able to find out anymore."

Jamali decided to come clean. "Stefan, we know about the stories in the Journal. Helen spotted the first one when we were in Brazil. We also know about your relationship with Veronica, and I can confirm that the CIA has a file on the two of you."

"I thought Helen suspected, and I'm not surprised the CIA knows. To be honest, it's a relief to have it out in the open. You don't know who's responsible for leaking the stories then?"

"No." He decided it wouldn't be appropriate to let Lundberg in on what they knew about Howard Dawkins, although it seemed likely he would be involved.

"Do you think they are planning to blackmail me? I'm not sure I could cope if all this got out. It would destroy Veronica." Lundberg's head was back in his hands.

"I don't know Stefan. It could be that they are simply trying to discredit the work of the committee through you. Helen, Mike, Daniel and I are meeting regularly to discuss security concerns, including this one. With your permission, I'll tell them what you've told me. We can then decide how to proceed. Have you given up all hope of ever having a normal relationship with Veronica?"

Lundberg didn't know whether to laugh or cry. "That's just the thing, we have it all planned. After Berlin, I was going to lie low for a few months while she negotiated a divorce. Then, with us both out of the spotlight, we would make a new life together, probably back in Sweden."

"It could still happen, my friend," Jamali found himself saying.

"I don't know. If the CIA knows about us, surely Weiss will also know. What if he won't give her a divorce? I'm not sure which would be worse. Being responsible for the failure of this process or not being able to be with Veronica. Both are too dreadful to imagine."

They were entering the conference complex in Yokohama. Saeed realised he had to bring the conversation to an end.

"Okay Stefan, while it's fascinating to see this different side of you, right now we need the old you back. I want you to get out of the car and tell the first TV camera you see how pleased you are to be in Japan and how excited you are at the prospect of another successful summit."

The car pulled up and the door was opened on Lundberg's side. As he moved to get out, he squeezed Saeed's upper arm and took a deep breath. Saeed saw the Swede's face change; it was as if he'd put on a mask. By the time he had hauled himself out the car, Lundberg was addressing an array of journalists. Within seconds he had them all laughing.

Jamali looked ahead and saw Helen. She gave him a quizzical look. She had been wanting Lundberg to take more of a lead with the media; he was probably their best performer. Saeed raised an eyebrow and smiled; it was a look that reminded Helen of her father.

She knew something seismic must have happened in the car, and was desperate to discover the details. But before she could get near him, the media scrum caught sight of her. Rather than stop and take questions, she walked determinedly through them to where Lundberg was standing.

"Don't stop," she said to him. "This is where we start our final push to Berlin."

Harry was struggling with his bacon and eggs. He had toyed with the idea of ordering the Bloody Mary off the breakfast menu, but instead went for the coffee and orange juice cure. He was unaccustomed to hangovers. He never drank more than a bottle of Burgundy these days and rarely less than a premier cru. Kotov's single malt had come as a bit of a shock to the system. It was a price worth paying though. The evening had gone very well. The Russian had a fine mind and much experience of the world. He knew that in the great decisions of state there was rarely a correct answer. And however much he considered himself an internationalist, he knew his duty was to the Russian people first. Harry had sewn a seed of doubt about the blueprint and over the coming days he would be nurturing it assiduously.

The waiter came to his table and handed him an envelope before topping up his coffee. It was a note from Kotov written in his own hand. "I'm away for two days, but stay in Moscow. I'll call you when I get back."

He finished his breakfast and found a comfortable chair in the lobby in view of a large but silent TV screen. He saw Helen and Lundberg addressing the press outside the conference hall in Yokohama. He thought she looked radiant. He didn't know Lundberg, but he suspected the two of them didn't get on. He was surprised, therefore, to see them working the media so well together.

Security officials were struggling to bring the impromptu press conference to an end. Harry read the commentary subtitles. Apparently the summit was to begin with a reception at which all the delegates would be present. It seemed to have been carefully stage-managed to promote a positive image of the committee and the summit process. TV cameras would be allowed into the venue before the delegates and committee members got down to business.

He saw Helen move towards the entrance, the camera following. Coverage then switched to the interior of the conference centre where a camera was surveying the gathered dignitaries. Harry caught sight of the red and orange robe of the Dalai Lama, and, as the camera focussed in on him, he realised that he was engaged in animated conversation with the President of China. He marvelled at the continued youthfulness of the Dalai Lama who, at 88, seemed as lively as ever.

Ironically, having been exiled and smeared by the Chinese authorities nearly all his life, a condition of Tibet being granted political autonomy was that the Dalai Lama serve as President for a five year term, during which the subject of full independence would be considered. He frequently joked that he first tried to retire from politics in 2007 in order to pursue a monastic life in his final years. Since then he had been in the spotlight almost continuously. Harry had been a supporter of Tibetan independence for as long as he could remember. He was something of a closet Buddhist.

The camera panned around as Helen walked into the room flanked by Lundberg and the Chinese economist whose name Harry had forgotten.

She stopped and surveyed the scene. Everyone appeared to be present, and an encouraging degree of mingling was evident. The Taiwanese delegation were as far from the Chinese as the circular shape of the hall would allow, but that was only to be expected. She saw that Zhang was standing beside her. She took his arm.

"Introduce me to your President," she said, and they moved towards the Chinese delegation.

The Dalai Lama saw them approach and broke off his conversation with the Chinese Foreign Minister so he could handle the introductions.

"Gentlemen," he began, "let me introduce you to a remarkable woman. Had I not been snatched from my nursery at the age of five, this, undoubtedly, is the woman I would have married." He giggled, not unlike a five year old.

Helen shook hands with each of the Chinese before turning back to her old friend.

"Your holiness," she said, "you are very kind, but as I've told you before, I'm far too young for you." There was considerable laughter, with even Zhang, whom Helen thought to be sceptical about his government's volte face on Tibet, joining in.

Harry watched with fascination and more than a little envy. Not only did Helen George get to spend her working days with Daniel Barenboim, she was sharing a joke with his other great hero; somebody else he was destined never to meet. He wished he could work out what they were saying.

The coverage from within the conference venue came to an end. Harry took his reader out of its case and pulled up The Times. Almost immediately he noticed a shadow cast across its clear white screen. He looked around.

"Excuse me," said a tall slim man in a finely cut suit, "Mr Harry Noble?"

"Yes."

"Do you think I might have a few minutes of your time?"

"In connection with what?" Harry enquired, politely.

"In connection with the reasons for your current visit to Moscow," the man said.

Harry wasn't sure whether the cryptic nature of his answer was motivated by menace or was a function of the man's strong accent and heavily schooled English. He hoped for the latter.

"Please, sit down," he said, pointing to the chair opposite.

"Mr Noble," the Russian began. My name is Yuri Zaytzev. I'm a senior adviser to Gennady Kutuzov."

Twelve

Kutuzov was the Russian Foreign Minister. Harry was pleased the suspense was at an end, but less pleased to discover that the man worked for Kutuzov, an abrasive character known to have a difficult relationship with Kotov.

"What can I do for you Mr Zaytzev?"

"I think we have common cause, Mr Noble. We are both interested in bringing influence to bear upon President Kotov in respect of Russia's decision on the blueprint. As you may know, the President and the Foreign Minister have, how shall we say, a difficult relationship. Obviously they have a lot of respect for one another, but, well frankly, they don't really get along."

"That must make it rather difficult for your man to bring any influence to bear." Harry said, smiling.

"Indeed, which is where I hoped it might be possible to enlist your support. From his public statements we are aware that our President is sympathetic to the blueprint. Until recently, Mr Kutuzov was part of a consultative committee preparing for the Tbilisi summit. But the President now appears to have dispensed with his advisors, except, that is, for you, Mr Noble."

"I wouldn't exactly describe myself as an advisor. More a friend of a friend who happened to be in Moscow." Harry said.

"I think we both know that is not true," Zaytzev said, sounding slightly menacing once again.

"So what else do you know?" Harry asked bluntly.

"We know, for example, that you are very close to Helen George. We also know that you have friends in high places strongly opposed to the blueprint."

"It's no secret that I'm here to counsel your President against supporting the blueprint. But it doesn't sound like you are going to be able to help me much in that regard."

The Russian laughed. "You are probably right there. We just wanted you to know that there is considerable opposition to the blueprint within the Russian government. If you should need any help while you are here, I would be happy to arrange it."

"May I ask, how deep does that opposition run?"

"Alas, not sufficiently deep to countenance a move to oust the President by constitutional means."

Harry looked surprised.

"No, please Mr Noble, I didn't mean to suggest any kind of plot against the President. He is far too popular to risk such a move. What I would say is that if the blueprint is adopted, then its successful implementation will require calm and stability. We certainly have the power to cause a great deal of trouble, on a wide scale, across Russia. I assume the President realises this. Perhaps you could make sure he is fully aware of the political reality." The Russian stood up and handed Harry his card. "As I said, if there is anything I can do to help you, just give me a call. Don't get up Mr Noble, it was a pleasure to meet you."

Harry watched him walk across the hotel foyer. By the time he reached the revolving doors he was flanked by two heavy minders. This wasn't a game, he thought, as he got up and walked towards the elevator.

It was three weeks since the funeral of her grandmother. Antonella had made the long journey, an hour and a half on two buses, to the Jewish Cemetery at Butanan. She was determined to keep a weekly vigil at her grandmother's grave but doubted it would be possible given the distance involved and the many pressures on her time.

It was a warm day. She felt uncomfortable sitting beside the still fresh mound of earth. She was still angry, not about her grandmother's death, but about the condition of her life. Virtually everything she had done was motivated by concern for others. She asked for nothing for herself despite having suffered for decades the drudgery of a life lived in poverty. She had worked hard, she was intelligent, she had considerable talents that would, in a society that valued the right things, have helped her attain a better quality of life. But this had bought little in terms of material comforts or security. She was much poorer at the end of her life than her parents had been when she was born.

Surely Sophia Ascoli and the millions like her were entitled to a lucky break somewhere along the line. Antonella pulled herself up. No, that's wrong. People shouldn't have to depend on a lucky break for their wellbeing. Security should be the right of everyone who is prepared to work; and her grandmother had never stopped working. She frequently spoke of what she would have liked to have done with her life had circumstances been different. But opportunities had not presented themselves. They seemed always to fall into the laps of others, in many cases those of people who appeared to work less hard, be less good and therefore less deserving. There was something deeply unjust at the heart of society.

The only way to come to terms with this injustice, Antonella decided, was to do something about it. If there was evidence that each generation had a better experience of life than the one before, she could accept the idea that the suffering of one generation was necessary for the emancipation of the next. But there seemed no such direction to human advance. She struggled to see how her life would be any different from her grandmother's. She raised the solitary rose she had brought with her to her lips, and kissed its petals before laying it down on the mound of earth, and crying once more.

Harry was still not a hundred per cent. Unexpected visits from Kremlin thugs apart, he was at a loose end until Kotov returned. He decided to spend the morning in his hotel room before going out for lunch. He arranged the pillows so he could lie comfortably. He pointed the remote control at the TV and clicked through the channels until he found CNN. He landed on the latest in a series of round table discussions dissecting aspects of the blueprint. He'd seen a couple of these and they'd been quite good. He decided to watch.

This debate was entitled 'The end of speculation' – a title derived from the provisions of section eleven which legislated for the prohibition of speculative investment in the financial and commodity markets. The panel included an investment banker, a speculative investor who had made billions playing the markets, and an economist of whom Harry had heard, but who had no associations with the New Radical school which informed much of the economics in the blueprint. The final panellist was Richard Deane, who had served as Treasury Secretary in the Hendricks administration.

"According to the provisions of the blueprint," the presenter began in the faux-dramatic voice that Harry found so irritating, "speculative investment will be outlawed on May 1st next year. Richard Deane, can the global economy survive such an attack?"

"I think the first thing to note," he began, "is that if the blueprint gets approval and is implemented, the global economy will bear little comparison to what we've been used to. If speculation was outlawed today and no other measures were taken to reformulate the economy, then collapse would be inevitable. But as the blueprint stands, well, we are in uncharted territory. It will be a great experiment. Within the new context outlined in the blueprint, I think the global economy would survive, yes."

"Is that true, David Hellstrom?" the presenter asked, turning to the investment banker.

"Well, I guess Richard must have a better sense of how things are going to play out than the rest of us. I just can't imagine an economy without speculation. Speculative investment in financial and commodity markets is a fundamental aspect of the pricing mechanism: its impact is felt throughout the economy."

"That's certainly true," snorted the economist. "Unfortunately, the impact is nearly always negative. My friends here will doubtless argue that speculative investment plays a positive role in the provision of investment capital to the real economy. I see no evidence of this. Not only is speculation unnecessary for economic success, but for much of the last two centuries the activities of speculators have had a detrimental effect on the real economy. Speculation drives the boom-bust cycles that cause so much misery. And far from aiding the pricing mechanism, I would argue that it distorts it severely. In order to establish the correct price for given commodity, purchases of that commodity, or promises to buy that commodity at some point in the future, must be restricted to people who have a genuine use for the commodity in question. Those who speculate on changes in future prices are not simply taking advantage of fluctuations caused by changes in real supply and demand, they are creating the price volatility from which they seek to benefit, in the process denying the benefits of the pricing mechanism to genuine buyers and sellers."

"Marion Bolt, that's a pretty severe criticism of the way you make your living," the presenter said, turning to the billionaire speculator, "would you like to respond?"

"I sure would," she began, in a southern drawl that made Harry wince, "and I'm sorry, but I think Max is being a party pooper." The camera zoomed in on the economist, who remained impassive. "I think there's a great deal of jealousy out there. Somehow it's no longer okay to be successful. I've made my fortune through hard work. I have never broken any laws. I've simply done what millions of others have done, but with a little more success, is all."

"So you don't see any connection between the casino capitalism from which you make your living, and the desperate plight of millions worldwide for whom the economy is simply not working?" the presenter asked.

"No I don't. Look, the world ain't perfect. There are always going to be winners and losers, and I'm one of the winners.

Hell, am I supposed be feel guilty for engaging successfully in a legitimate business activity?"

"David. You are responsible for billions of dollars of client funds at Goldman Sachs. Do you think the activities and attitudes of people like Ms Bolt here give the financial markets a bad name?"

"I'm not sure I can answer that question, but what I can say is that the financial markets are essential to the wider economy. It is through the financial markets that the business community finds funds for investment. The distinction between the financial economy and the so-called real economy is a false one; they are part and parcel of the same thing."

"But, David," interrupted Max Jonas, the economist, "you know as well as I do that more than 99 per cent of trades in financial markets are purely speculative: less that one per cent of transactions involve money that will be used to finance investment in the production of goods and services, or to fund trade. The behaviour of speculators denies much needed investment to the real economy which is obliged to pay a premium to secure the funding it needs."

"Richard Deane, do I see you nodding your agreement with Max Jonas?"

"You do, Martha, and Max is right, in recent times the financial markets seem to have forgotten their principal purpose. Although I do have some sympathy with investors. If I had to make a choice between the potentially lucrative short-term gains to be made from speculative trading and the lower, long-term yields offered by traditional investment models, and if I was legally bound to work in my clients' best interests, it would be a tough call."

"Max Jonas?"

"It's all very well sympathising with a small group of people who derive huge incomes from playing the money markets, but let's not forget where the money to fund those incomes comes from: it's either created specifically for the purpose of speculation, or it's appropriated from others who create genuine wealth in the real economy."

"I'm afraid that's right," agreed the former Treasury Secretary. "Far from being an essential element of the mechanism through which businesses raise investment capital, the financial markets have become a millstone round the neck of genuine entrepreneurship. If speculative trading was banned tonight, then all that spare capital in Marion's offshore accounts would flood back into the real economy where it would earn a sustainable rate of return."

Harry was intrigued. Both Richard Deane and Max Jonas were taking strongly pro-blueprint positions. This would have been unthinkable just six months ago. He wondered whether they believed what they were saying, or if, having seen the writing on the wall, they were putting down markers for the future. Harry had a fair idea what they must be going through. While he had many reasons for opposing the blueprint, he had no argument with its provisions to rein in the financial markets. He had taken firmly against the obsequiousness of bankers and others who made fortunes from this legitimised gambling since the 2008 financial crisis.

"Perhaps," continued the presenter, "we could examine two other aspects of the blueprint's assault on speculative investments: proposed changes to the currency and land markets. Marion Bolt?"

"You know, Martha, assault is the right word. I think these changes are probably not even legal." Max Jonas laughed derisively, but Bolt was in full flow. "How can these idiots seriously think the global economy can be run on a single currency? People simply won't accept it."

"Come on, Marion," interrupted Jonas. "You've seen the opinion polls. People in every country have made it quite clear they are happy to have a single global currency just as long as they can keep the name of their own currency and maintain control over the design of notes and coins."

"Oh, and look what happened to the Euro back in 2014?"

"But Marion," Richard Deane interrupted her this time, "the Euro fell victim to the irresponsible behaviour of speculators intent on exploiting political divisions between member states. And people were glad to see the back of it because it was associated with troubled economic times. The proposed global currency will have a much better chance of success."

"David Hellstrom, what about the land question?"

"In my opinion, the proposals for changes to the way the land market works are perhaps the most worrying of the measures contained in this generally rather worrying document." He held up a copy of the blueprint and let it drop softly on to the table from a height of a few inches. "Private property in land, and the benefits it bestows on the landowner, have been a cornerstone of progress since the emergence of the earliest agrarian economies. The proposals for a universal tax on land values strike me as a recipe for disaster."

"But haven't speculative bubbles in the land market been a contributory factor in the damaging cycle of boom-bust that has blighted the economy since the Industrial Revolution?" The question was directed back at Hellstrom, but he was unprepared for it.

Max Jonas took his opportunity. "That is precisely the case, Martha. And the good thing about the blueprint's proposal is that the gradual and globally coordinated phasing in of LVT, in conjunction with other measures, will, over a period of a decade, allow us ample opportunity to evaluate its impact, and fine tune the policy where necessary."

"Okay, we need to take a commercial break, but before that we're going live to the news centre for a breaking story which I think we might be discussing on our return."

"Massive breaking news this hour." The announcer ramped up the dramatic tone. "Could the summit process be in danger following revelations concerning the private life of a key member of the committee?" Harry bounced to the end of the bed and turned up the volume.

"According to reports, committee member Jay Robertson took special advantage of opportunities for leisure during last weekend's Jakarta summit. It is alleged that Robertson, whose wife and young child live in Vancouver, struck up an intimate relationship with Citra Sianturi, the 26-year-old daughter of Indonesian Prime Minister, Anna Sianturi." At this point, footage of Citra taken from a modelling session was shown. "Reliable sources say they spent time together while the summit was in session, with Robertson seen entering the young woman's home very early in the morning and not leaving until several hours later.

Twelve

Harry couldn't believe his ears. This had to be a set-up, but then CNN wouldn't be reporting a groundless allegation. He was surprised by a pang of sympathy for Helen George, but quickly shook it off. This might be very distasteful, but the timing couldn't be better.

"We now cross live to our reporter outside the conference centre in Yokohama."

Thirteen

Helen's speech to the assembled delegates was well received. The atmosphere in the hall was relaxed and positive. But as the main doors were opened to let the delegates make their exit, a commotion could be heard in the lobby. Helen was anxious. The hall was a couple of metres below ground. Could there have been an explosion outside that nobody had heard? Her concern turned to near panic as she saw Mike come running through the now fully open doors. Saeed saw him too, and moved towards Helen who was standing beside the podium, introducing Rita to the Dalai Lama.

"Excuse me your holiness, Rita, could you find Daniel and bring him here. No, meet us back there," she said, pointing to a gap beside the platform that led to a small backstage area. Realising something was afoot, the Dalai Lama's minders spirited him away. Helen made her way behind the platform where she was joined by Mike and a rather breathless Saeed.

"What is it Mike?"

"It's Robertson: his fling with Citra is on all the news channels."

"Jesus."

"The media are going crazy. They're all in the lobby. Whose idea was it to give them access to the inner workings of the summit? There's no other way out of the hall you know?"

"Where's Jay?"

Rita had returned with Barenboim. "He's over there," she said, pointing to the other side of the platform. "I think he's talking to the Taiwanese President."

"I'll get him," Saeed said, clambering onto the platform because the small passageway had become congested.

"What the hell do we do now?" Helen's question was not directed at anyone in particular, which was just as well as no answer came. "Right," she continued, "Mike: sheep dog trials – we need to isolate the committee from the delegates and get the delegates out past the press and upstairs as calmly as possible."

"Local security is trying to get the press out of the building now," he said, as Saeed returned with Robertson who looked confused.

"Saeed, you brief the others. Nobody to talk to the press, okay? Presumably Jane is here somewhere?" Jane Abbot handled PR; she was about to be properly tested for the first time.

"She's out there now, holding them off," Mike said.

"Saeed, get hold of Jane and tell her there will be a press conference in twenty minutes."

"Who?" he asked.

"Me, Daniel and Jay." Panic spread across Robertson's face as he realised what was happening. "Daniel, Rita, stay with me."

"Helen, what's happening?" Rita sounded scared.

"While we were in Jakarta, Jay became romantically involved with the Prime Minister's daughter. We found out. We decided to keep it between the four of us and hoped it would blow over. It hasn't. Apparently it's all over the news channels."

Rita looked at Jay, first in disbelief, then with concern, as the colour drained from his face. Robertson wobbled. Rita thought he was going to faint.

"Oh my god. How could I have been so stupid?" he mumbled.

"We can all have a go at answering that one later," Helen said tersely. "For now, this is what's going to happen. In twenty minutes the three of us will face the media. I will make a short statement about what we knew and when. We will take questions. We will answer all questions briefly, but truthfully."

"What do you want me to do?" Barenboim asked.

"Just sit there and bring some credibility to proceedings. God knows we need it." She stopped and took out her phone. It was Jane.

"Helen," she said, "I've got three friendly reporters, but I'm working blind here. What do you want them to ask?"

Helen thought for a second. "Have you considered the possibility that Professor Robertson has been set up? Got that. And Jane, call me back with a name, somebody I'll recognise, please."

"Helen, I don't think I can do it," Jay said pathetically.

"I don't care what you think, Jay. There's too much hanging on this. You created this mess, you can help us clear it up."

Robertson looked close to tears. Rita moved towards him and took his arm. They moved away from the others.

"Jesus Daniel, why now, when the world's press is right outside?"

"The timing is no coincidence, Helen. This has been planned right down to the last detail. Don't be surprised if there are people out there who seem to know more than we do."

"Just tell me I'm doing the right thing."

"Helen," he took both her hands and held them together, "you are handling the situation perfectly." She thanked him before moving towards Rita and Jay and sitting down next to them.

"Jay," she said, her tone much softer now. "You can do this. You are going out there and you are going to apologise. Now I'm pretty sure you, and we, are being set up, but until we have proof, you have to take full responsibility for what has happened. You will apologise for the embarrassment you have caused to your colleagues, to the Japanese government and to the delegates to the summit. Is that clear?"

He tried to pull himself together, before breaking down again. "What about Julia?" he managed to squeeze out between sobs.

"Don't worry about Julia, it's the middle of the night in Vancouver. She won't have heard anything. You can phone her after the press conference." At this he became almost hysterical.

Helen stood up. She looked around the room which was almost empty. She saw Mike escorting the Japanese delegation out into the lobby. Things seemed a little quieter. The Dalai Lama had reappeared and was waiting to speak to her. She walked towards him.

"Ah my dear," he said, "the temptations of the flesh."

She couldn't help but smile. "This could bring the entire process down you know?"

"Not if you remain calm and continue to have faith in the justness of what you are doing," he replied. "Helen, you know, if there is anything I can do to help?"

"Perhaps there is. You get on well with President Horomito don't you?"

"Very well."

"We're holding a press conference in," she looked at her watch, "ten minutes. Do you think you could persuade him to do it with us. If you and he were there it could make a huge difference."

"Leave it with me. I'll see you in ten."

She watched the adorable man's bent frame scuttle towards the door. As she moved back towards the others, Jane called back.

"It's Henri Alliard of Le Monde. He has the beard?"

"Yes, okay," Helen replied impatiently. "Possible change of plan Jane. There may be others at the conference, but don't say anything just in case."

At least Robertson had stopped crying. Daniel and Rita were giving him a pep talk. Helen felt calmer; the adrenaline was subsiding.

Harry watched the coverage in disbelief. He suddenly realised he hadn't blinked for some time and that his mouth was hanging open. He was also happy to note that all symptoms of his hangover had gone. He couldn't believe Helen was going to hold a live press conference. She would have had no idea the story was about to break. And presumably she knew nothing of Robertson's alleged indiscretion in Jakarta. He got down on his hands and knees and opened the mini bar. He found some peanuts and a bottle of sparkling water. He was going to enjoy himself.

Coverage switched to the lobby of the conference centre. He turned the sound back on. A row of tables, bedecked with microphones, had been hurriedly assembled a short way in front of the door to the hall, behind which Helen and her colleagues were presumably imprisoned. A thickset woman with dark hair was standing in front of the still closed doors. A man he recognised as Mike Dixon moved into picture and whispered something in her ear. For a moment she looked startled before regaining her composure. The woman looked to her left, towards the stairs that the delegates had climbed a few minutes before. It looked like she was waiting for a signal. After about thirty seconds she turned and opened the double doors, stepping across the threshold and apparently gesturing to those inside. The cameras went mad, and the TV camera zoomed in to reveal Helen emerging with Barenboim and Robertson. He saw Rita Correia exit the room slightly behind them and move off towards the stairs. The others walked impassively towards the tables. As the camera panned back, Harry noticed that two seats had been added at either end. Behind one stood the Dalai Lama, behind the other, President Horomito of Japan. The five of them sat down together. Robertson next to the Dalai Lama, Barenboim next to Horomito; Helen in the middle.

Harry was flabbergasted. How could she have organised such a response so quickly?

The Dalai Lemen spoke first. "Ladies and gentlemen," he said. "I'd like to thank you for attending this press conference at such short notice." There was more laughter than could reasonably have been expected. "I'm very pleased that our host, President Horomito, has been able to join us. First, Helen George will make a brief statement. President Horomito will also address you. We will then invite questions."

"As you will know," Helen began, "allegations have today been made that Professor Jay Robertson engaged in an illicit affair with the daughter of the Indonesian Prime Minister during our recent visit to Jakarta. I can confirm these allegations are true. I can also confirm that I, along with my colleagues, President Barenboim and Dr Jamali, have known about the affair since last Saturday morning. No other member of the committee had any knowledge of the episode until a few minutes ago. Professor Robertson has expressed to me profound regret for his actions, for the implications it could have for the work of the committee, and especially for the embarrassment he has caused our hosts both here and in Indonesia. While we understand the media interest that will be generated by this news, we hope that once you've had the opportunity to ask questions we can put this unfortunate episode behind us and get on with our work."

She nodded towards the Japanese president who stood.

"Thank you, Helen." He paused while what seemed like a thousand flashes fired. "It is my earnest hope that these revelations do not distract us from the very serious work still to be done at this summit, and at the summits to come as we make our way to Berlin. Whatever may have happened in Jakarta, it should have no bearing on this process. It is a great privilege for my government to be chosen to host this crucial summit, and I look forward to beginning our work this afternoon."

"Right. Questions," Helen said, pointing first to a Japanese journalist with a kindly face standing near the front of the baying pack.

"Professor Robertson," the reporter began. "Perhaps you could begin by telling us your version of events?"

"There is only one version of events. I met Citra Sianturi at a private dinner hosted by her mother last Friday evening. We subsequently spent time together over the following two days. I now recognise that my behaviour was not only inappropriate but extremely stupid. I am deeply sorry for my actions. I would like to apologise to President Horomito, to Prime Minister Sianturi, to the delegates to this conference and, of course, to my colleagues whom I have let down badly." It was clear to everyone present that Robertson was sincere. The room became strangely quiet.

"Yes, Dennis," Helen said, pointing to the Far East correspondent of the New York Post.

"Jay, have you spoken with your wife yet?"

"No, I haven't." Robertson replied, his voice wavering. "I will be speaking to her shortly." He picked out the TV camera and stared at it. A tear ran down his cheek but his voice held. "I'm so sorry Julia," he said. "I love you."

Helen hadn't bargained for this, but didn't think it could do any harm. She had already spotted the Frenchman. "Monsieur Alliard, please."

"Ms George, have you considered the possibility that Professor Robertson may have been set up?"

"I haven't really had time to consider anything," she answered. "However, it does strike me as something of a coincidence that this story should break at precisely the moment we had allowed you all in to cover the inner workings of the summit."

"So you think there may be some conspiracy against the summit process in which Professor Robertson has been an unwitting victim?" Alliard followed up.

"I wouldn't call Professor Robertson a victim. He did what he did. He has apologised for his mistake. As for a conspiracy, I don't think it would be appropriate to speculate at this point." She had said enough; there was a different buzz around the place now.

"Next question?"

"If I may ask his holiness a question," asked a Chinese journalist. The Dalai Lama smiled at her. "Your Holiness, do you think Professor Robertson should resign from the committee?" Helen desperately wanted to answer but knew she couldn't.

"Absolutely not." The Dalai Lama was indignant. Helen feared his enthusiasm might get the better of him. "Professor Robertson has been very stupid. Extremely stupid." He paused. "But I take him at his word, and I see no reason why this incident should be a matter for resignation."

Helen took several further questions, none of which added much to what had gone before. She thanked everyone. The five panellists then stood and filed towards the stairs: Jane at the front, Mike bringing up the rear.

Harry watched the Dalai Lama's robe disappear from view. Helen had handled the situation very well, but he had little sense of how it would play out in the media. The sentimental stuff would go down well, no doubt. There had been several articles in the press suggesting the committee was rather short on the kind of human qualities which people liked. Now one of their number had been humiliated in public and forced to make a grovelling apology, it felt rather cathartic. Harry was concerned that Helen especially would come out of it very well, but there was something else. Every time he had dealings with this woman, whether in person, or across a distance of several thousand miles, he felt closer to her. Not in a romantic way, but he was impressed by her evident integrity and strength, and he was having to work harder at persuading himself that he was right and she was wrong.

Helen was almost running. She overtook Jane before realising she had no idea where she was going. Rita came out of a door further up the corridor. "You were brilliant," she said.

Helen was close to tears. "I just need a few minutes," she said to Saeed who had appeared from the same door. He nodded. The two women sat down in a small meeting room. The TV was still on. Rita grabbed the remote and switched it off.

"I knew there must have been things going on," Rita said, "I've hardly seen you, but I had no idea. You must be exhausted."

Helen nodded, and they sat in silence for a few moments before there was a knock on the door. Saeed came in. "Right," he said, as if to signal the crisis was over. "The first meetings are underway. You two are meeting the Chinese in half an hour. Funding health care provision is what they want to talk about." Helen looked at Rita, feigning hysteria.

"Don't worry, the Brazilian said. "While you've been fire fighting, I've been preparing. It'll be fine."

"You've got nothing tonight Helen," Saeed continued. "The private dinner with Horomito is scheduled for tomorrow evening. He's also invited Ann Margaret, apparently he's a fan. It'll be just the three of you. Mike had Robertson taken back to the hotel. Zhang has agreed to cover his meeting this afternoon. We're seeing Jay at five, but Daniel can't make it. Perhaps Rita would like to sit in on the meeting?" he suggested.

"I think that might help," Helen said.

Jane came in through the now open door. "I thought you might like an update."

"What are they saying?" Helen asked.

"It's going 50-50 at the moment. Predictable outrage in some quarters. How can we look to the committee for moral guidance when one of their number clearly has no integrity, that kind of thing. But elsewhere a strong strand arguing that this shouldn't be allowed to derail the process. And, you are coming out of it very well, Helen. It was a very smart move to have Horomito and the Dalai Lama up there with you."

Helen liked Jane. She was about ten years older than her, and knew her job very well. Nothing seemed to phase her. "Should we make any further statement?" she asked.

"I don't think so. Let's carry on with the summit and keep Robertson as far from the cameras as possible. You're flying to Stockholm on Saturday, aren't you?" she asked Helen.

"That's right. I was hoping to have a day off on Friday."

"Could you bear to do a recorded interview with CNN on Friday morning. I think it would be good to get you out there while you're at the top of your game, as it were."

"Okay, make it early. Thanks Jane." Abbot left the room.

Helen looked at the other two. "Jesus guys," she said. "Do you not think I've already done enough to get to heaven?"

Robertson was silent in the back of the car. He was distraught. Not only did he assume his career was at an end, but probably his marriage too. As they drove back to the hotel, he went over in his mind what he was going to say to his wife.

They soon arrived. Rick Spedman, who was under instructions not to let Robertson out of his sight, got out first, and opened the door. As Jay struggled to pull himself out of the car, Rick offered him his hand. Robertson took his wrist, and their eyes met as/was levered out of the back seat. Robertson barely knew Spedman; he wondered if the American was judging him.

They travelled up to the 24th floor in silence. Rick opened the door and entered first. He checked the room was clear and ushered Jay in.

"Would you like a drink?" Robertson asked.

"I'll have a juice, thanks."

Robertson poured himself a whisky.

"So, you going to phone your wife?" Spedman asked him.

"I guess so. What the hell am I going to say?"

"She'll know already. The press will be outside. She'll have switched on the news. She'll be hurt, and very angry. But it needn't be the end of your marriage."

"It sounds like you speak from experience."

"We all make mistakes Jay. You'll have to work damned hard, starting right now." Rick handed him his phone. Here, use this one, less chance of being hacked. Jay dialled the number and waited.

"Jay, is that you?" Julia answered.

"It is. Listen. I'm so sorry."

"Yeah. You just said that on TV. It would have been nice to hear it in person first."

Jay couldn't think of anything to say.

"And why didn't you call me yesterday?"

"Why would I have called you yesterday?" he asked, confused.

"Because you knew this was going to happen; you could have given me a slightly softer landing."

"Wait a minute. I found out the story was going to break literally 20 minutes before the press conference."

"Well somebody's been keeping things from you, buddy. I got a heads up yesterday."

"Who from?" Jay was bewildered.

"Ron, the security guy. He said he'd heard that something was going to come out today, and there might be a problem with the press. He suggested I send Nathalie away for a couple of days, so I had your folks collect her after school yesterday."

"Hang on a second. Rick, did we know this story was going to break in advance?"

"If we did, nobody told me," Spedman answered.

"Julia's saying she was tipped off yesterday by her security detail."

Rick looked surprised. He took out his spare phone and left the room.

"Sorry, darling. Jesus what a mess. I have been so stupid. I don't know what to say."

"I don't think here's anything you can say. Perhaps it's best left until you're here."

"I'll get out of the Stockholm meeting. I'll be home on Saturday." He wondered whether to tell her that he loved her, but decided against it.

"I'll see you then. If you call again, use my cell. They're going to move me later this morning, some hotel down town where they can keep the press away. Goodbye." She hung up. Jay felt awful. At least Nathalie was well out of it. He knew he should call her, but he couldn't face talking to his father.

Spedman came back into the room. "Well that's put the cat among the pigeons. Mike confirms he had no prior knowledge of the story breaking today; which means that Ron Krajicek is somehow better informed than we are."

"Isn't that a little worrying?" Jay asked.

"It depends how Krajicek got the information."

"Shouldn't he have told his superiors?"

"It's a difficult call. The guys on the ground get tip-offs all the time. Most of them prove to be groundless. Knowing Ron, I suspect he was just trying to do the best for your little girl. How did it go?" Rick pointed at the phone.

"Oh, she was quite calm actually. She said there was no point trying to discuss it over the phone."

"Think she's going to leave you?"

"God, I hope not. Mind you, if she did we would hardly see less of each other."

Saeed had been trying to protect Helen, but Mike Dixon wanted five minutes with them both before her meeting with the Chinese.

"Mike, sit down. Give me some good news, please." Helen said.

"Well, I might be able to oblige." He smiled. "I've just been talking to Ron Krajicek. He's covering security at Jay's home in Vancouver. He was tipped off yesterday that something was about to break. He had Julia send the little girl to her grandparents."

"Did he tell you his source?"

"Yes. Bob Stirling, middle-ranking intelligence officer at Langley. Krajicek and Stirling are old friends, they served together in Afghanistan. Looks as if Stirling was acting out of concern for a four year old girl."

"Anything else? Does he have any connection with Dawkins?" Saeed asked.

"Worked in the same building for the best part of a decade. Their paths may well have crossed."

"Wait a minute guys. Are you saying that Howard Dawkins might be behind this leak to the press?" Helen asked.

"I think we should consider the possibility."

"But if Dawkins was responsible for the leak, then he must have known about the affair." Helen's voice trailed off. She realised she was way behind them.

"We need to make a connection between Dawkins and Stirling. If we can prove a conspiracy, then perhaps something positive will emerge from the whole sorry episode."

Thirteen

The meeting with the Chinese proved a welcome distraction. On the way back to the hotel, Helen and Rita discussed how to handle Robertson. They agreed they could do without him in Stockholm. It wasn't a full-blown summit, and some of the others were taking the opportunity of a short break. He should go back to Canada to try to sort things out with Julia.

As they pulled into the forecourt of the hotel, Rita spotted Rick Spedman waiting for them.

"Hi Rick, how's it going?" Helen asked.

"So far so good. His wife seemed to let him down gently."

Helen hadn't had a minute to think about Julia. She was a strong woman, just the kind of partner someone liked Robertson needed. Helen felt some responsibility towards her.

"Mike and Saeed are with him now, I'll take you up."

Rick led them across the hotel lobby towards the elevator. As they approached the room where the others were waiting, Helen heard laughter. She was relieved; she couldn't cope with any more of Robertson's tears.

"Carry on," she said, as she entered the room, but they didn't. Rita asked Jay if he was alright, and he thanked her, saying he was feeling better.

"Mike," Helen asked, "any more news on Krajicek?"

"We've drawn a blank I'm afraid. To be honest, the way things run at Langley it would be difficult to prove a connection. We would need somebody who worked on a Dawkins-led operation in which Krajicek was involved, and was prepared to confirm the link. But given what we already know, the chances of Dawkins being behind this must be pretty high. He's out of the CIA now, but he would still have easy access to resources there, and most of his ex-colleagues would do anything he asked."

"Mike," Jay said, "tell Helen what you told me just now, about whether I could have been spotted in Jakarta."

"As I told you before, Helen. We tailed Jay all the way. Our guys would have known if someone else was doing the same."

"So it has to be an inside job, right?" said Jay.

"We certainly have to consider the possibility that someone inside the Prime Minister's residence was passing information to Dawkins."

"If it's true, then it's useful information to have. But it hardly let's you off the hook Jay."

Robertson looked defeated again. "No, I'm sorry," he said. "Helen, would it be okay if I skipped Stockholm? I really need to get home and try to sort things out with Julia."

"I think that would be a good idea, yes. How long do you think you'll need?"

"I really don't know."

Helen found his vagueness irritating. "I want you back in Houston on Wednesday 25th. That gives you nine days."

"Thank you Helen. I really am very sorry for all of this." She just about managed a sympathetic smile as he left the room.

The four of them sat in exhausted silence until Rita spoke: "Right," she said, "if you don't need me for anything else, I'm going to have a lovely long bath."

Helen looked at Saeed, she knew there was one further item on the agenda, but wasn't sure whether Saeed wanted Rita in the meeting.

"I don't think so," he said as she stood up, moved behind Helen and placed a hand on her shoulder.

Helen looked up at her. "Thanks for all your help today," she said. "And thank God we don't have too many days like this," she said, turning to the others. "I presume you want to talk about Lundberg?"

Saeed told her about the conversation in the car that morning. Helen felt considerable sympathy, but was worried. They couldn't afford another scandal.

"Let's put the two things together," she said after a moment. "We can't be sure, but we reckon Dawkins is behind the Robertson fiasco. He may even have someone close to the Prime Minister who was updating him from inside the residence. It also seems likely that someone is monitoring Veronica Abel's phone calls; someone who knows about her relationship with Lundberg."

"Hang on," Mike interrupted. "They certainly know now, they may not have known before they started monitoring her. Stefan said she has a bad relationship with Weiss. He has a reputation for being a control freak. Perhaps he's monitoring her calls anyway; may be he has a private investigator on her?"

"Possible," Helen agreed. "It would explain how quickly Lundberg's conversations with Abel are getting into the public domain."

"So," said Jamali, "we assume that Dawkins is running the Robertson sting, but we're not sure he has anything to do with Lundberg/Abel. I think we could make some political capital out of this and send a message to Victor Weiss that we know his game."

"Go on," Helen said.

"Okay. We persuade Lundberg to feed Abel some information that could only have come from the inside. Something salacious but rather absurd. We give a friendly news provider advance warning that the story is going to break. A couple of hours after the Journal runs the story, the friendly source follows up with evidence that it's a hoax."

"It's risky, but it might work. All we need is a authentic story. Any suggestions?" Helen asked.

"How about," Mike said, "Lundberg tells Abel that Helen George is a bully who runs the committee with a rod of iron, stifling all dissent and ruthlessly imposing her will on proceedings?" He smiled.

"Hang on, the story needs to be credible." She looked at them both.

"There's a big difference between something being credible and something being true." Saeed said. "We all know that you're a great diplomat and an inspiring leader. But there are a lot of people out there who don't understand how you've managed to hold this process together. It is a credible story."

"Let's get Jane in here. If she approves the idea, we'll do it."

Moments later, Jane Abbot came into the room with her wet hair wrapped in a towel. She looked a little annoyed. She sat and listened as they filled her in on the background and outlined their plan, at one point unwinding the towel to give her hair a quick dry.

"It's high risk, but we're in a high risk game now. Nobody else can know about it until comes out. We're sure this room is clean are we Mike?" He nodded. "And it does gives us an opportunity to score some big PR points. Gerald is good friends with Davina Harold at Slate. She'd love to get one over on Weiss. Once Slate runs its story, we'll make committee members available to tell the press what a great person Helen is, and how they all adore working for her."

"It's brilliant," Mike said, getting quite excited.

"There are downsides though," Helen said. "It might leave Veronica Abel exposed. Once Weiss realises we've got his number, who knows what he might do?"

"What's he going to do? Tell his wife he's had a private dick listening to her phone calls. He wouldn't dare," Jane said.

"Okay," Helen said. "I'm persuaded, and I'm happy to be exposed as the bitch from hell for a couple of hours. Jane, you talk to Gerald. Mike, make sure we have a super-secure line for Lundberg to talk to Abel. Where is Lundberg?"

"I'm meeting him in the bar at seven." Saeed said, looking at his watch. "Perfect timing, shall we go?"

Lundberg was looking apprehensive. Saeed explained the situation. The Swede was concerned for his lover, but keen on the idea of getting one over on Weiss. He clearly hated the man.

"So you want me to tell Veronica that you are a bully, and you run the committee with a rod of iron?"

"Yes," Helen said, "Jane will give you a script. It's crucial you use the right words. We need you to be quoted verbatim telling the same ridiculous lies that Slate will have prior notice of."

"I understand. Of course, you are making an big assumption here Helen. What if I've spent the last eighteen months telling Veronica what a pleasure it is to work with you and what a great job you are doing leading the committee?" He smiled at her. Saeed's phone beeped.

"It's Daniel, he's waiting for me in the lobby. I'll go and bring him up to speed and leave you with your drinks."

"Are you sure you're happy with this?" Helen asked Lundberg.

"Yes. I can't see it making things any worse for my prospects with Veronica. And it would be great to get one over on Weiss. Not just because of her, but because of everything he stands for."

"Nothing much changed after Murdoch, did it. The media still wields enormous power."

"It does. It's a shame we couldn't address that problem more directly in the blueprint."

"Perhaps, but there's plenty in there that will help reduce the power of people like Victor Weiss. In any case, if this plan works, his reputation will be in tatters."

"I'll drink to that." Stefan raised his glass.

Helen wondered about asking the next question. She had never imagined being so close to Lundberg. "Tell me, Stefan, what's she like?"

"Veronica, you mean?

"Yes."

Lundberg's face softened. For a moment he looked in the first flush of love. "She has a brilliant mind, she's strong, she's funny and she is an optimist. In so many ways, Helen, she's just like you. Now perhaps you understand a little the reasons for my coolness towards you. I'm quite a nice guy when you get to know me."

Helen was lost for words.

Fourteen

Rudolf Dreyfus was missing his wife. They had always known their respective careers would limit their time together. He didn't like it, but had learned to accept it. And he was sure that once Helen's work with the committee was over, she would make good on her promise to take a break. He was ready to give up most of his work-related travel as he wanted to spend more time composing. He worried for Helen though. He wasn't sure she'd be able to cope with virtual retirement. And he was worried for her now. He couldn't imagine going through the kind of day she had yesterday; he would have snapped.

He'd been lying in bed, not fully awake, for half an hour. His slumber was broken by a beep from his phone. It was a message from Helen: "Don't worry about the news, things are not what they seem." Rudolf suspected it would only fully make sense once he turned on the news, which he did, straight away.

"A quick catch up for anyone just joining us," said the presenter. "Could this be the end for Helen George and her committee of twelve wise people. According to an apparently impeccably sourced story in the Wall Street Journal, Helen George runs the committee, and I quote, "with a rod of iron. She brooks no opposition and stifles debate among the committee members." The text was beginning to make sense. Rudolph could hardly believe his ears: he knew the allegations were unfounded, but what could it possibly mean? Suddenly the newsreader stopped talking. An arm appeared from off camera and placed some papers in front of her. She had her hand to her ear, apparently taking instructions from her producer.

"Well," she continued after a moment, "further developments in the case of the Wall Street Journal versus Helen George. Slate Magazine has just published a piece claiming they had prior notice of the Wall Street Journal story. Slate also claims to have incontestable evidence which proves the Journal story is a hoax. We'll be right back."

For once, Rudolf was glad of the commercial break. He knew Helen must be behind it, but was surprised at her audacity. To set out to discredit one of the world's most influential media barons was surely more than even his extremely capable wife was capable. And it was looking like she'd pulled it off. He couldn't wait to find out the details, but he knew it wouldn't be a good time to phone. CNN was back.

"This incredible sequence of events follows a series of reports in the Wall Street Journal over the last few weeks clearly designed to damage the credibility of the committee and derail the summit process; stories that appeared to be sourced very close to the committee itself. So far, Victor Weiss, publisher of the Wall Street Journal has been unavailable for comment." Another pause for direction. "We now cross live to the White House where President Solis is about to make a statement."

"Ladies and Gentleman," began the president. "I have a short statement to make and I will not be taking questions." She paused. "Over the last two days, the Committee for the

Establishment of a Framework for Global Governance and Economic Reform, whose work I very much support, has come under intense public scrutiny. This morning's revelations point to the existence of a dishonest and anti-democratic campaign against the work of the committee by one of our, hitherto, more respected news organisations."

"While it is perfectly legitimate to take a position opposed to the blueprint, I call on its opponents to make their case openly and honestly. It is no exaggeration to say that the summit process is the most important diplomatic initiative in the history of humankind. It deserves better than the kind of gutter journalism we have seen this morning."

"I am proud to count Helen George as a friend. I have been in regular contact with members of the committee over the last year and a half, and if any further evidence was necessary, I can assure you that the claims made by the Wall Street Journal this morning are completely unfounded. Thank you very much."

"Yes, yes. Go Hilda" Rita shouted excitedly. It was early evening in Tokyo and after a productive if slightly surreal day, the committee had convened to watch the press coverage unfold.

"Did anyone brief Solis?" Helen asked, looking at Saeed.

"Not as far as I know. Jane?"

"Nothing to do with me. She's acting off her own bat."

"Hilda always hated Weiss, but she must be feeling very confident to do this," Helen said.

"This is working out better than we could have expected." Lundberg checked himself as he remembered the others didn't know of his pivotal role in events.

"Indeed it is," said Barenboim wistfully. "Almost too good to be true. Jane, what should we do now, in terms of the press, I mean?"

"Well, I guess we don't need to do quite so much." Helen, I assume you are still dining with Horomito tonight?"

"Yes, and I'm taking Ann Margaret."

"Okay, why don't you and Stefan talk to the press downstairs before you leave. I'll check with the President's office and see if he'll greet you on the steps outside the residence. I know it's a private dinner, but I'm sure he'll be happy to weigh in. That way we get you and Stefan in front of the press, and an hour later you are seen socialising not only with Horomito, but with another committee member. If anyone has lingering doubts about the story being a fabrication, that should put them all to bed."

"Sounds like a strategy," Helen said. "And it'll also send a message to Weiss, whichever hole he's hiding in."

"And to his wife," Lundberg said matter-of-factly. Those in the room not privy to the full story looked bemused. "Don't worry," he added, "it's a private joke between Helen and me." Confusion about Lundberg's first statement was compounded by the second. Everyone knew that he and George had a prickly relationship; they were intrigued by this apparent reconciliation.

Helen decided to take advantage of the opportunity. "One final thing," she said. "As you may know, I've been badgering Stefan to adopt a higher profile role with the media, and I'm pleased to say he has agreed to take on that role in the run up to Berlin." Rita once again led an impromptu round of applause.

"Okay," Helen said after a moment, "we're not out of the woods yet. We may be off the hook in respect of Jay, and we may have succeeded in silencing one of our most powerful critics, but there are still plenty of people out there who want to see this process fail. Be careful, and please report anything suspicious to Mike, Saeed or myself. Have a great evening everyone."

"Harry, it's Oscar. You still in Moscow,"

"Oscar, how are you? Yes, still in Moscow. Kotov's back in the morning, Hope to see him again then." Harry answered.

"Cut the chit-chat Harry, I'm not in the mood."

"Oh, sorry Oscar, what's up?" Harry knew perfectly well the cause of Silverman's foul temper.

"Are you for real Noble? Don't the fucking Soviets have TV?"

"Yes, lots of TVs, all over the place in fact, not too many Soviets these days though." Harry had decided to distance himself from Silverman and Dawkins. His old friend was becoming increasingly boorish. Now he was in with Kotov, his best chance of influencing the summit process was as his own master, not doing someone else's bidding.

"What do you think Harry? This whole Wall Street Journal business. You really think your friend Helen George has the balls to get one over on Weiss like this?"

"She's certainly very determined," Harry replied. "She also has some very good people on her team. I haven't spoken to her. I don't know what happened, but I certainly think it's possible that she set Weiss up. Although I'm not really sure why. I know he's been running negative stories, but this seems like excessive payback to me."

"I don't give a shit about Weiss."

"So you're not working with him?" Harry didn't think Weiss would be part of the Dawkins operation, but he wanted to pump Silverman for as much information as he could. The American had a habit of talking too much when he was drunk or angry. Harry sensed he was both.

"Nah. Dawkins approached him when he started running the stories, but Weiss is such an ego. Thinks he's bigger than everyone else. Didn't feel the need for any help."

"I don't understand, Oscar. I'd have thought you'd be pleased that Weiss has been shafted."

"Yeah I'm pleased, but in case you hadn't noticed, this whole thing has pushed the Robertson story off the front pages."

It all fell into place.

"And Robertson is part of Dawkins' operation?"

"Hell Harry, Robertson is Dawkins' operation. That's all he's got. If we don't make the Robertson thing stick, we have nothing. Well, nothing except your polite diplomatic efforts over there in Moscow."

"You're telling me that Dawkins has played all his cards?"

"I don't know. He keeps telling me not to worry, says he has it all in hand. May be he has. It's just not looking like a winning strategy right now."

"Listen, Oscar, " Harry softened his tone. "You know I am as committed to stopping this process as you are. I'm making good progress with Kotov. We still have two weeks until the Tbilisi summit and I plan to be a thorn in Kotov's side until he gets there."

"Okay Harry," Silverman sounded resigned. "Keep me in the loop, Dawkins wants regular updates."

Harry wasn't especially surprised that Howard Dawkins was behind the Robertson story. It's just the kind of thing he'd try. What puzzled him was how he'd pulled it off. Harry knew Indonesia well and Dawkins had no history there. He sat down on his bed and turned on the TV. There she was again. As he watched Helen standing on the steps outside the Emperor's palace with the Japanese President, he wondered quite how he'd got himself so centrally involved in the biggest news story on the planet.

It had taken Antonella some time to pluck up the courage. After finishing her shift, she had made her way to the Faculty of Education on the enormous university campus across the river from the Hilton. She didn't know this part of the campus at all, most of her classes were held on the other side of the site, a ten minute bus ride away. But this evening she was not attending lectures. She eventually found the room where the meeting was being held and pushed open the door. There was a man and two women standing by a table at the front of the room. As soon as they saw her, the man moved towards the door to greet her.

"You must be Antonella," he said. "David Moreira, we spoke on the phone."

"Yes. Pleased to meet you. I'm afraid I'm a little early."

"No problem. It's good to meet new members before everyone else turns up, we can brief you on the agenda, then hopefully you'll be able to take part in the discussion."

"Great." Antonella was already beginning to relax.

"Okay. Well this is Marcia, and this is Patricia. The three of us organise the meetings. We weren't formally elected, but we're reasonably democratic in our decision making, and we do have help from some of the others. Membership of the group is quite fluid. People come and go; a lot of members have jobs, obviously, and many students are reluctant to miss their lectures, however important the cause."

"And you started out as a 27 Club, is that right?"

"Yes, we were one of the first in Brazil. Then, like most 27 clubs, once the blueprint was published, and we realised that not only did it embody most of the 27 principles, but also provided a political mechanism for delivering the kind of change they demanded, then we became a blueprint club."

"And do you know how many blueprint clubs there are, in the world I mean?"

"It's difficult to know for sure. There's a website where organisers can register clubs; a directory if you like, so people can find their nearest one. And there are currently more than 40,000 registered worldwide."

"And do they all do the same thing?"

"No. There are no rules. Anyone can set up a club, and pursue whatever activities in support of the blueprint they like. There are education projects, lobbying groups which target governments and politicians, groups that organise marches and demos in support of the summit process, and others that focus primarily on discussion, like this one."

"But this club isn't just a talking shop?"

"No it's not. In fact tonight's meeting is about how best to mobilise visible support for the blueprint in the run up to the Berlin summit, and, assuming Berlin goes according to plan, to make sure support for the blueprint doesn't fade away during the transition period."

"I think that's going to be very important," Antonella said, growing in confidence. "There will be massive media coverage in the run up to Berlin, but once it's over, there's a danger that people will forget all about it. Six months is a long time; we're going to have to work very hard to keep up momentum."

"Exactly, and of course one of the ways we can do this is by preparing people for the changes they will face after 1st May next year. For most people it shouldn't mean too much upheaval, but things will change."

"Yes, of course, and it will be down to us to offer advice and support."

"So are you with us then?"

"I am."

Antonella enjoyed the meeting. Once it was over she hung around and talked to some of the other members. She was impressed by the enthusiasm and commitment of the people she met. Everybody seemed to share her belief in the blueprint and its potential to change things for the better. She was among the last to leave, and, as she made her way home, she felt that, in a small way at least, she was starting to make good on her promise to her grandmother.

Against his better judgment, Kersen Atunarang had been persuaded to join several of his colleagues for an evening of karaoke. Afraid that he would be the only man, Kersen had persuaded first Mike Dixon, with some difficulty, and then Wen Zhang, to tag along. Rita was determined that they should go to an authentic karaoke bar, and mix it with real Japanese. Mike arranged low-key security, and Rita booked a table at the Ishiko Club, a bar frequented by Japanese celebrities with a fierce no-media policy. Helen had cleared the adventure on condition that Mike was there.

Kersen was in two minds about it. He could sing. As a young man he had trained professionally for a couple of years, but none of his colleagues knew this, and he liked things that way. Tonight his cover would be blown and he would be forced into a closer relationship with them than he would otherwise have chosen.

He had to admit the venue was pleasant. Very comfortable, good food, and it stocked his favourite Japanese beer. Mike had made it a condition of attendance that he would not sing, but the others drew lots, and took their turn along with the other guests. Rita had chosen a reputable club. There was no drunkenness, and the quality of the singing was rather good, until Zhang's turn came. Safiya and Jemma sang Both Sides Now as a duet; they both had sweet voices. Kersen decided to play it safe, choosing Moon River, a song he had grown up listening to at his grandmother's house. He was very pleased with his performance on this occasion. He knew the words by heart, so didn't have to read them from the screen at his feet. As he finished, he looked through the lights towards his audience and saw several people standing to applaud. His colleagues were whooping in the far corner. He wouldn't be able to live this down.

He'd only just sat down when he felt his phone vibrate in his pocket. He took it out and was alarmed to see it was a call from the Indonesian Prime Minister's residence. He made his way out of the bar towards the cloakroom and took the call.

"Dr Atunarang?" a voice asked.

"This is he."

"Please hold for the Prime Minister."

"Kersen, how are you?"

"Very well, Prime Minister, and you?"

"I'm fine, I fear I have a problem though. It's my daughter. I think she's gone missing."

"What do you mean, missing?"

"Well, she flew to Paris on Monday evening, at least that's what she told me. She was going to meet some French professor she was interviewing for her thesis. She said she would call me as soon as she got there, but I've heard nothing. Now all this business about her stupid behaviour with Professor Robertson has come out, I am worried for her. As you can imagine, there's been a great deal of unfavourable press coverage here."

"Do you have any idea what might have happened?"

"I really don't know. At first I wondered if she was lying to me, and had flown to Japan to meet up with Robertson again. I had my people check the passenger lists and she definitely boarded the flight to Paris, but after that I know nothing."

"Try not to worry Prime Minister, I'm sure there's a perfectly innocent explanation. Perhaps when the story broke she found herself a hotel room somewhere and decided to lie low for a few days."

"I suppose it's possible, but if that's the case, why hasn't she contacted me?"

"I don't know. Prime Minister, allow me to make some enquiries this end. Obviously I'll be discreet."

"Thank you Kersen, I am very grateful. I am so angry with Citra, at the same time she is still my daughter, and I desperately want to know that she is safe. And Kersen, please send my best wishes to Helen. I think it's remarkable how she's dealt with everything over the last couple of days."

"I certainly will. Goodbye now."

Mike caught sight of his expression as he returned to his seat. "Is everything okay?" he asked, leaning over to make himself heard.

Kersen nodded. "I'll tell you in the car on the way back."

Helen was impressed at the extent of President Horomito's knowledge of Ann Margaret's work. He must have read each of her books several times. He had even arranged an official visit to London to coincide with Benjamin Webb's acclaimed production of Eckart's Renewal at the National Theatre a couple of year's ago.

It was twenty minutes before they were able to curtail Horomito's private homage, which Helen could tell Ann Margaret was beginning to find a little embarrassing. Eventually she posed him a direct question:

"One thing you haven't mentioned. Mr President, something that I think is central to much of Ann Margaret's work: the mechanics of individual psychological and collective social change and, of course, the link between the two."

Ann Margaret smiled approvingly at her.

"Ah," replied the President, "a very pertinent question, I think. Perhaps what you are really asking me is whether the blueprint really has, how do you say, a cat out of hells chance of being successfully implemented?"

"That's about it." Helen confirmed, smiling back at Ann Margaret.

"I think, if you look back through the history of all the great civilizations, you will detect a clear pattern: Occasional periods of rapid, often revolutionary change, usually in pursuit of progressive goals and a more inclusive society, punctuated by longer periods during which society struggles to come to terms with the changes to which it has, perhaps unwittingly, committed itself."

"So do you think people will struggle to come to terms with the changes outlined in the blueprint, assuming it is implemented?" asked Ann Margaret.

"Well that would depend on whether, this time, change was adopted unwittingly, or instead embraced by the majority of citizens in full conscious knowledge both of its objectives and its likely consequences. My reading of the situation is that a substantial majority are indeed committed to the principles outlined in the blueprint, but I'm not sure they're necessarily fully conscious of the implications. Whether this improves the prospects of success is a moot point." He stressed the last two words as if to advertise his command of English.

"So you think the blueprint might have more chance of success if people didn't really understand what they're getting into?" Helen asked.

"I think people will not care about the details as long as they begin to see some improvement in their lives. And that does not mean only their personal situation. People are tired of endless stories of hardship and struggle. Globalisation may not have done very much for the poorest, but it has at least brought the miserable reality of many people's lives into to the consciousness of those who are more fortunate. It has served to widen the scope of our moral concern to the point at which people have said enough is enough."

"I worry that when the impact of changes to economic structures and institutions becomes apparent, people will struggle to adjust their attitudes and behaviours. They may genuinely want change, but will they necessarily be able to deliver the required changes at the level of their individual interactions?" Ann Margaret prompted.

"Or will they simply revert to biological type, as most organisms do when they come under pressure?" added Helen.

"Well, there are two different questions there," President Horomito replied. "First we need accurately to determine the extent to which our biological inheritance influences behaviour. The second concerns the type of pressure that people are likely to face under the new order."

"I think the answer to your first question is less and less. As we have become more conscious of the influence of evolutionary factors on our behaviour, the more we have become masters of our own destiny," Ann Margaret said, to nods from the President.

"At the same time, culture has become more complex. Behaviours and attitudes that may be rooted in our genes are now mediated through ever-changing cultural forms," said Helen.

"That is all undoubtedly true," replied Horomito, "but interestingly, if we are considering the potential for moral progress, which I think we are, then our species has had greater success in producing morally aware individuals than it has in producing morally advanced communities, societies or cultures."

"Yes, yes, Mr President," Ann Margaret was almost excited. "Perhaps you know of the work of Reinhold Niebuhr in this regard. Almost a century ago he concluded that while there were many impressive examples of individuals with advanced levels of moral awareness, when people came together in groups, the collective moral level was reduced almost to the lowest common denominator."

"Indeed," replied the President, "but Niebuhr was perfectly aware that these shining examples of individual moral excellence were, despite their visibility, few and far between. Today the average level of moral awareness among the population is much higher; and that is very positive."

"And over the last decade, there has been an encouraging resurgence of interest in Lawrence Kohlberg's stage theory of moral development. Great progress has been made towards better understanding the factors that influence attainment of the higher stages," Helen said.

"And it must be true," Horomito said, "that improvement in the average level of moral awareness among the population can only help our cause."

"But is that average level sufficiently high to make for a successful implementation of the blueprint?" Helen asked.

"It's not simply a question of critical mass," said Horomito, "One of the crucial things will be the quality of leadership, especially political leadership, after May next year. And I have to say, Helen, it concerns me greatly that you have not yet committed to a formal role."

Helen sighed. "There are several reasons for that. First, though, is my firm belief that if the success of this project is dependent on a single individual, then it will be bound to fail, sooner or later."

Horomito looked at her. "I'm sorry for putting you on the spot. That was a good answer, and you are right of course. But I am still worried."

"What about your second question, Mr President," Ann Margaret asked. "What kind of pressures do you think people are likely to face once the blueprint is implemented?"

"I think," Horomito paused to consider his answer, "that will vary from individual to individual. Some people are stubbornly resistant to change, even when it is clearly in their best interest. Others thrive on it. I think one of the most interesting areas will be the workplace. It will take time for the impact of the blueprint to filter down to the day to day reality of people's lives. But it will certainly happen within a generation. People entering the workplace today have been educated and trained to operate in a quite different environment to the one envisaged in the blueprint. Some will fare better than others."

"But the reform of workplaces will be carefully managed. In the same way that workers receive training to operate new technology as it is introduced, they will receive support and guidance in adapting to a changed culture at work." said Ann Margaret.

"Yes indeed, " Horomito said, "and of course, everyone is in the same boat. It's not as if one section of society is being asked to make sacrifices while another remains untouched. Nobody will be getting preferential treatment. The beauty of the blueprint is that it really creates a genuine global community of citizens."

"Yes," Ann Margaret concurred, "and it creates an environment in which people will finally be able to identify with all other humans as being like themselves, rather than having their perceptions distorted by the opaque lens of cultural, religious or racial difference."

"Absolutely," Helen agreed, "we are all pretty much the same in terms of our needs and aspirations. When people are able to realise those aspirations under open and fair economic conditions this should become apparent to even the most die-hard sceptic."

"The only people likely to resist," responded Horomito, "are those who seek to distinguish themselves from others through the acquisition of disproportionate power or wealth."

"And even they may see the writing on the wall," Helen said. "The benefits of a society based on cooperation should quickly become apparent. In any case, the ruthless pursuit of power and wealth will be much more difficult under the new framework.

The President nodded in agreement. "I wonder," he asked, "what you think about the reasons for the overwhelming support for the process. Are people supportive because they are desperate for a way out of the crisis, or because they know it is the right thing to do?"

"I think," answered Helen, "that the initial motivation came out of necessity: the deepening crisis, the humiliation of Hendricks, the opportunity afforded by the publication of the 27 principles; all combined to give people a sense that change was not just necessary but also achievable. But since the committee was set up, and especially since the blueprint was published, I think growing numbers have come to understand the moral argument for change. Polls show that more than a half of people would support the blueprint even without the threat from climate change."

"What about the relentless focus on economics, Helen? Do you not think that may have cost you some support?"

"Possibly, yes, but when it comes to addressing poverty, and creating a fairer society, and putting measures in place to bring the causes of climate change under control, it's all about economics."

"I think it helps," added Ann Margaret, "to remember that changes to economic structures and institutions are not ends in themselves: they are the means to escaping the crisis and creating a platform from which we can take civilization to the next level."

The conversation continued for another hour. Helen had always assumed the blueprint would have President Horomito's support, but she hadn't bargained on him being such an eloquent defender of its principles.

Outside the Ishiko Club, there were two cars for the six of them. Mike managed to manoeuvre himself into the second with Kersen and Rita without it being too obvious. Kersen recounted the conversation with Mrs Sianturi. The three of them agreed that Citra had probably arrived in Paris just as the media storm about her affair with Robertson broke, and had decided to keep her head down. Perhaps it was strange that she had not been in touch, but she was an adult.

"I went through my twenties barely speaking to my mother," Rita said.

Nonetheless, Mike would make discreet enquiries. It would be disastrous, just as they had succeeded putting the story to bed, if Citra were to make some ill-judged media appearance in Europe where she was beyond anyone's control.

"What do you really think Mike? How did the story about Robertson get out?" Kersen was hoping that Mike might be a little less guarded in Helen's absence. For his part, Mike was fully aware that although Rita knew about the Dawkins operation, Kersen did not. And while he had no reason not to trust the Indonesian, he didn't feel able extend the circle of knowledge without Helen's say so.

"I don't know Kersen. Someone close to the Prime Minister must have tipped off someone who's plotting against us. But who, I really don't know."

On arrival at the hotel, Mike phoned up to Helen who had only just got back herself. "Have you got five minutes?" he asked her.

"Is it important?" she asked impatiently, "of course it is. I'll meet you in the bar."

They met Helen on her way out of the elevator. "So how was the karaoke?" she asked.

"Well," Rita answered, "there's no longer any question over who has the finest voice on the committee." She looked at Kersen.

"Really? There's a piano over in the corner, perhaps Daniel would accompany you."

Kersen decided it was best to play along. "I would love to sing for you Helen, but I'm afraid we have rather more pressing business."

"I'll hold you to that. Right, tell me latest."

Mike and Kersen described the phone conversation with the Indonesian Prime Minister. Helen was grateful, at least, for the personal message of support. She had been wondering whether the affair had queered her own pitch with Mrs Sianturi.

"I assume it's okay to bring Kersen up to speed?" Mike asked. "I haven't yet."

"Of course." Helen replied.

Mike told Kersen all they knew about the Dawkins-led operation to destabilise the summit process and how they were now able to conclude, with a reasonable degree of certainty, that, as Dawkins was not behind the Lundberg story, he probably was involved in the Robertson situation. Kersen listened carefully, and looked neither worried nor surprised. After Mike finished he was silent for a moment.

"You know, I have known Citra Sianturi since she was a young girl, and while I have no grounds to suspect her involvement, I do know that her mother runs a very tight ship. She has a very small staff; few of whom would have known about her dalliance with Robertson. I think, therefore, that we should not rule out the possibility of Citra being somehow involved in the plot you describe."

Rita, Mike and Helen looked at each other for a moment. None of them had considered this possibility.

"Helen, you remember the night we met Citra, the way she was towards Robertson. With hindsight it was hardly the behaviour of a young woman fawning over her favourite academic. You must admit the possibility that her seduction of Robertson was premeditated."

Helen's head was in her hands. "You're right. Why didn't we see this before? And now she's gone awol in Paris."

"I have good contacts in the French service. I'll get a heads-up if she boards another flight," said Mike.

"Okay," Helen said. "I could talk to Jay about our suspicions, but I suspect it would push him over the edge. Obviously we can't go public with this, for a start we have no evidence. I think we should sit tight. If Dawkins is going to use Citra to further his cause he's not going to do it yet, not after seeing what happened to Victor Weiss today. He may leave it a couple of weeks, by which time we will be a lot closer to our goal. In the meantime, Mike, we need to gather as much intelligence as we can."

"It's midday in Paris, I'll get to work right away."

"Thanks. I'll brief Saeed and Daniel, and I think, unless you have any objections Mike, we should probably involve Jane in everything going forward?"

"Agreed."

"Good. But that's it for now. The four of us, Jane, Saeed and Daniel. I don't want this going any further; our inner circle is big enough already."

Harry Noble was dining alone in his hotel. Under more normal circumstances he would have eaten out, but the day's events were playing on his mind. And he knew he was under surveillance. He had no idea whether the creepy Zaytzev had a plan, or if he was just trying to incentivize Harry not to let Kotov off the hook with his thinly-veiled threats. Nonetheless, he decided it would be sensible to keep his head down, especially given the raised media profile of the subject of his discussions with Kotov.

Harry had no intention of easing up on the President. His opposition to the blueprint remained unwavering, even if he did find the methods of his American allies distasteful. But he was struggling to get a handle on his growing admiration for Helen George. He had always known she would be a tough opponent, but hadn't expected her to get quite this far under his skin. He was struggling with something else: the realisation that all the decent people seemed to be on the other side. On his side he had the likes of Dawkins, Silverman, Zaytzev, and Victor Weiss.

As he finished a perfectly acceptable bottle of claret – all the Burgundy on the list was obscenely over-priced – he made a promise to himself not to let his head rule his heart. If the only way to stop the blueprint was for him to become complicit in activities that were beyond the pail, then he would have no part in it.

Fifteen

The final morning of the Yokohama summit was given over to a session open to all delegates at which the proposals for monetary reform were to be discussed. Wen Zhang was chairing. This was a diplomatic necessity, but it hadn't stopped Robertson from kicking up a fuss. Admittedly, Zhang had not been especially collegiate when the committee had discussed the subject. As discussions had gone on, however, he had once again proved to be far more radical than his reputation suggested.

As she ate breakfast in her room, Helen remembered a conversation she'd had with Robertson about Zhang's motivation.

"I just find him so difficult to deal with," the Canadian had complained after a heated discussion during which most members of the committee initially supported his position, but on the arguments offered by the two men, ended up leaning towards Zhang.

"Jay," Helen counselled. "I think you're struggling because your arguments are too pre-rehearsed. You're debating with him on the basis of what you assume he believes, rather than what he actually says."

"But it's obvious what he believes Helen. It's written in black and white in more than two hundred published papers and public statements. And believe me, I've read them all."

"Perhaps he's revised his opinion, or perhaps those papers were written for a different purpose."

"A leopard doesn't change its spots; not in the world of academic economics at any rate."

Helen was right though. In order to attain a position of influence within the Chinese hierarchy, Wen Zhang had played a long and difficult game. He'd always known his career lay in politics, not academia. He also knew that if he wanted to make a real difference on the world stage, then he had to set himself up as the most respected economist in a country fast becoming the world's largest economy. He'd been forced to make many compromises along the way, but helping deliver the blueprint was ample reward, and the culmination of all he had worked for.

Robertson might not understand, but Helen had very quickly realised that having Zhang on board could be the difference between success and failure. The Canadian thought it dishonest that someone should build an entire career by concealing his real views. But that wasn't the full story.

As a young man, Zhang had seen what many economists failed to see; that the discipline of economics falls into two distinct spheres: the mainstream, an institution which sets out to provide a theoretical underpinning to the efforts of politicians to manage economies in a context in which certain assumptions are unassailable, and an alternative sphere, which Zhang called real world economics. Here, the assumptions of the mainstream were laid bare and subjected to serious analysis and criticism. And real world economics had one overriding assumption of its own: that the assumptions of mainstream economics had to be overturned if progress towards a more inclusive and just society was to be made.

Unbeknown to Helen or Jay, prior to his winning a seat on the committee, this was the objective to which Zhang had devoted his entire career, while working assiduously to hide his true motives. Now, in the conducive environment of the committee, he was enjoying unprecedented freedom. At the slightest provocation, he would reel off a list of mainstream assumptions which held back progress: "the entitlements of land ownership, the absurd notion of taxing effort and enterprise, the right to speculative investment, allowing private banks to issue money, the belief that a competition-based economy best suits the character of most human beings, the belief that free-markets alone will necessarily maximise wealth creation and assure its optimal distribution, and the idea that those markets should determine the rate of resource depletion." If his questioner didn't immediately respond, he would continue: "Each of these assumptions goes to the heart of an economic system which, whether it be the intention of its proponents or not, inevitably favours the interests of a wealthy minority and condemns millions to inescapable poverty."

Because of his background and reputation within the mainstream, such statements had far greater impact. It also helped that there were no histrionics, no cynicism, and no vitriol against a supposed ruling class. Just the calm determination of a reasonable man giving the overwhelming impression that he knows his subject.

Robertson, by contrast, had made a career out of condemning the current order as unjust and inhumane, in the process making as many enemies as friends. Despite this, at least until the problems in Jakarta, Helen had had no regrets about co-opting Robertson onto the committee. Though they still had only a grudging respect for each other, from her point of view, the two economists complemented each other perfectly. For the other committee members, having two experts making similar arguments from different starting points was very helpful.

Helen knew Zhang was key to delivering the Chinese vote. He might reasonably be considered the most important member of the committee; no one else held sway over the decision of such a key nation. Helen was also aware how important Zhang was to the chances of success post-implementation, for she was prepared to bet that he would be the next President of China.

As she was finishing breakfast, her phone rang. It was Rudolf. She hadn't been able to speak to him the previous evening: by the time she'd finally got to her room, he was already in rehearsals for a concert that evening at Carnegie Hall. She had been worried because he would have been unable to avoid the saturation coverage of the Weiss story.

"Hello my love, how are you? You must be due on stage any time."

"Half an hour. I'm fine though. I just spent a delightful hour with John Adams. He was very keen to hear all about you. He is such a lovely man, and such an inspiration. We decided to try to get Batter My Heart on the programme for Berlin."

"Oh Jesus, that'll have my mascara running for the cameras." They both laughed.

"How are you? I can't believe what you've had to deal with over the last few days. You must be exhausted."

"I am, but I do feel we've begun to turn things round."

"It was a bit of a risk you took."

"It was. But we were pretty sure about it."

"Well, I think you are remarkable. And so does John. He was berating me for not having introduced you."

"Will he be in Berlin?"

"Hopefully, if we can get his piece on the programme."

"Good, I plan to spend a great deal more time with your friends over the next few years. What are you doing tonight?"

"Britten, Poulenc and Barber. It's a fundraising gala. Apparently the President might be coming, although we won't know for sure until she turns up."

"Well, if she does make it, and if you get to meet her, will you pass on my special gratitude?"

"Of course I will. Take care darling."

Wen Zhang opened the session by welcoming the delegates. He even made a joke: wondering if they had gathered in the right place, as media coverage on this final day of the summit didn't seem as intense as it had on the first.

He and Robertson co-presented the case for withdrawing from commercial banks the right to create money. They began by describing the concept of an optimal money supply: the idea that, at any given moment, the quantity of money in circulation should be linked to the quantity of real wealth existing in the economy.

As Robertson explained, "Money, whether in the form of notes and coins, the electronic balances held in back accounts, the value of loans on the books of banks, or the advances made by credit card companies, is a means of exchange and measure of value. It can also be used as a store of wealth, but of itself it does not constitute wealth. Wealth includes things that can be acquired with money, but money is not wealth. Wealth is properly defined as goods, services, resources or experiences that people either need or desire and which have an exchange value in the marketplace."

"It stands to reason, therefore, that for an economy to operate in equilibrium, changes in the quantity of money in circulation should shadow the quantity of wealth being created and consumed, plus an additional amount to enable a sustainable level of investment in new undertakings."

"At present," Zhang took over, "apart from the notes and coins issued by central banks, which make up just three per cent of the money supply, the rest is created as debt by privately owned banks when they make loans to their customers. These loans have to be repaid at interest. This places an immediate cost on economic activity and thus discourages entrepreneurship. With virtually all money currently created as debt, and only banks allowed to create it, debt has to be repaid out of other money loaned at interest. The cumulative effect is to impose a tax on entrepreneurship; to extract wealth from the economy before it has even been created, and channel it into the pockets of over-rewarded bank executives and their shareholders."

Zhang paused for a moment and surveyed the room. Persuaded he still had the attention of most of those present, he continued.

"Under current arrangements there is no free money. Even the notes and coins issued by the authorities are released into circulation through the banks. This gives privately owned banks an effective monopoly over money issue. It also affords them the opportunity to generate profits that are quite different from those made by other types of firm. And it means the economy exists in a state of constant disequilibrium as the amount of money in circulation is never optimal."

Helen looked around the room, she was concerned that the presentation might be a little dry. The topic was not the easiest to break down into bite-sized chunks, and there were many non-economists present. But everyone looked attentive, and nobody had dozed off.

President Horomito indicated his desire to speak. "Dr Zhang, you used the words 'free money'. Perhaps you could explain what you mean by this, and how the provision of free money would have a beneficial impact on the economy?"

"Certainly, Mr President. I think it helps to consider the economy as a huge, complex machine, with millions of different processes, some coordinated, some independent, with all manner of different inputs and outputs. The one thing this machine requires above all else to function effectively is a good lubricant in the right quantity, to keep the cogs turning and the gears in synch; to prevent the machine from seizing up. Money, or credit, is that lubricant. But money has no intrinsic value. Of itself, it is neither an input into, nor an output of, the great complex economic machine. It is simply the oil that keeps the machine running. Now, if that essential lubricant comes at an inflated cost, and if a only a tiny proportion of the population have an ownership stake in its provision, or easy access to it, then the economic machine is not only going struggle under a heavy burden before it gets going, but the minority of people that control its creation will be able to take for themselves a large quantity of supposed wealth, in the form of money, which has yet to be created. This is why money has to be free."

"And presumably," the Korean Finance Minister took the opportunity to ask a question, "this is why the blueprint argues for the abolition of bank interest. If interest is no longer to be charged as part of the mechanism by which money is issued into the economy then there is no reason why interest should be paid to those who place their surplus cash in bank savings accounts."

Zhang indicated to Robertson that he should answer the question.

"That is correct, Minister. However, in the blueprint we are careful to distinguish between traditional bank interest, that is interest charged and paid as part of the private bank based system of money issue, and returns payable to providers of surplus wealth for direct investment in tangible economic activity. The risk-free rewards currently enjoyed by those who place their savings in interest bearing bank accounts constitute a form of unearned income. The blueprint takes a strong position against all forms of unearned income."

"But could it not be argued that the dividends payable to those who invest directly in tangible economic activity are also unearned? After all, the investor expends very little of his labour beyond using his judgement to decide in which enterprise to invest?" asked President Horomito.

"It could be so argued, Mr President, but on this point we have taken a pragmatic view. It is a natural and desirable consequence of economic activity that surplus wealth accrue continuously. These surpluses, be they paid as wages to labour, or as dividends to investors, are the life blood of the economy. As long as they are invested in tangible economic activity, to which some risk is nearly always attached, there is no reason why investors should not earn a return."

"If these surplus funds are re-invested," asked the Mongolian Prime Minister, "why is there a need for a non-bank money issuing authority as suggested in the blueprint? Especially as elsewhere in the blueprint, you propose that the wealth that accumulates in land values, wealth that is currently lost to the economy as a source of investment, be recycled as public revenue. Surely there will be enough money to go around?"

"There may well be enough money to go round, Mr Prime Minister," Zhang replied, "but why limit economic expansion to the investment available in the form of returns from previous activity? A shortage of money should not prevent any viable business from getting the funding it requires. There is no cost to issuing free money for investment purposes as long as the loan is paid back in full."

"You say there is no cost attached to this method of money creation. But surely if no limit is placed on the amount of money that can be created, then inflation will result?" asked President Horomito.

"It is true that under the current system, inflation generally arises when there is too much money chasing too few goods and services: demand outstrips supply thus forcing up prices. But this need not be the case under the system of free money we propose. If money is issued only in support of genuine investment opportunities, and not in pursuit of bank profits or to fund consumption, and if that money is cancelled once it is repaid to the money issuing authority, then a balance between the supply of goods and services and quantity of money available to buy those goods and services should be maintained, and inflation should be avoided."

"But some investment opportunities do not provide any returns, sometimes even the efforts of the most creative entrepreneurs come to nought. What happens to this neat circular flow of money in such cases?" asked the Chinese Finance Minister.

"In such cases," answered Robertson, "the money would not be repaid to the money issuing authority. The loan would be written off, and in one sense the money would be lost. But it would, nonetheless, have been spent into the economy, either in the acquisition of capital goods or in the payment of wages prior to the enterprise failing."

Helen raised her hand and Zhang invited her to speak. "It's important to remember," she began, "that the factors influencing business failure would be quite different under the arrangements proposed in the blueprint: start-up costs for new businesses would be much lower. There would be no interest payments on loans, and no premium to be paid for over-priced premises once artificially inflated land values are brought under control. There will be fewer business failures as a result."

"Could talk a little more about the nature of the money / you issuing authority?" asked the Taiwanese prime minister.

Robertson took the question: "We propose a global statutory authority operating through decentralised agencies in each country. The distribution of money can still be carried out through a network of banks very similar to those we have at present. Those banks would be paid a flat fee for providing this service. The operating costs of the money issuing authority would be paid from the tax revenues of participating nations in proportion to the quantity of money issued in each country."

"But how would banks be able make a profit if they can no longer charge interest on their loans?"

"Banks provide a range of services to their customers beyond money issue. The profits earned through the process of debt-based money issue are not normal profits. They are super-profits only possible because banks are afforded this special privilege. Normal profits will still be available to any bank that is well managed and responsive to its customers demands for other banking services."

Helen's phone was buzzing in her pocket. She decided the session was going well enough to absent herself for a while. As the large doors swung closed behind her she saw Saeed waiting for her.

"Sorry Helen, I didn't want to come into the hall and disturb proceedings without first seeing if I could tempt you out by phone. How's it going in there?"

"Pretty well, I think. Zhang and Robertson make a good team. What can I do for you?"

"I have good news. I've just got off the phone with Kotov's office. He will meet us next Thursday. I know it's a bit tight, but it's only a short hop from Stockholm."

"That should be okay, I can still get to Vienna by Friday. It doesn't give us much time to prepare, though."

"I know, but we should have some time during the Stockholm summit. It's not as if we have a great deal of arm-twisting to do there, we're just going to say thank you really."

"Okay, I'll call Rudolf and make sure he's not going to divorce me if I turn up a day later."

Harry woke early. He never slept well in hotels, not city centre hotels at any rate. The sealed windows and air-conditioned heating played hell with his sinuses and made him feel groggy. He surprised himself by venturing down to the hotel's basement spa where he survived ten minutes in the sauna before completing a pleasing fifteen lengths of the empty swimming pool. Even then, he couldn't escape thoughts of Helen George, as he recalled turning up the fact that she had been a competitive swimmer in her youth.

He hadn't heard anything from Kotov, but as he tucked into scrambled eggs, he noticed a man dressed in government 'uniform' talking to the maitre d'. His heart sank as he realised Zaytzev's people wore the same clothes. He was relieved when the maitre d' came over and informed him that President Kotov's driver would be waiting for him outside when he had finished his breakfast.

He ate up quickly, and returned to his room where he brushed his teeth and picked up his coat before heading back down to the lobby. The spring was back in his step.

It was barely worth sending a car as The Kremlin was only ten minutes walk away. He was taken straight up to Kotov's office where the President greeted him warmly. Harry asked how the trip had gone; apparently very well. He was surprised there had been no press coverage for the last couple of days, and was intrigued to know what Kotov had been up to, but decided against asking a direct question.

"So, Harry, how have you been entertaining yourself?"

"To be honest, Mr President, I spent quite a lot of time in front of the television watching events unfold in Japan."

"Ah yes. Quite a spectacle wasn't it. I saw some of it on the plane. I was impressed with the way Helen George dealt with it all. There's a great deal of speculation about conspiracies to bring down the summit process and kill off the blueprint. Do you think there is any truth in the rumours?"

"I think it quite likely that certain elements, perhaps representing the interests of big business or even the intelligence services of certain countries, might have plans to derail the process."

"But you don't have any inside knowledge?" Kotov asked, smiling.

"No, Mr President. I do not wish to see the blueprint adopted, but I think the best way to achieve that objective is through diplomatic channels."

"Well said, Harry. Now, we need to spend some time working out a clear negotiating position. It seems I am to be the subject of an exceptional lobbying exercise. Your friend Helen George and my old friend Saeed Jamali are paying us a visit next week."

"Really?" Harry was unprepared for the news.

"Yes, I feel rather honoured," Kotov confirmed. Harry thought he was being sarcastic, but couldn't quite tell through Kotov's accent. "And I would be grateful if you would remain in Moscow for the next week to help me prepare for the meeting. In fact, it might be a good idea if you sat in. It would be good to have an advisor there, and I don't feel comfortable with my own people."

Harry was initially horrified at the prospect, and afraid his cover would be blown. But he quickly warmed to the idea. It would be Helen who would be caught off guard. In any case, they knew each other well enough for the kind of greeting Kotov would expect to see in such circumstances.

"It would be an honour to be there, Mr President," he replied.

"You don't think Ms George would be distracted by your presence then?"

"I'm sure she would. She has no idea I'm in Moscow. She knows my position on the blueprint. When she walks through that door and sees me sitting here, I'm sure it'll take the wind out of her sails."

"Good. Now, today I want to talk to you about what happens if I decide not to support the blueprint. Let's suppose we are agreed that although the world has many problems, the blueprint is not the solution. We will still be facing the same problems; we need an alternative strategy. We can't be responsible for scuppering two years of intense diplomatic efforts and have nothing to offer by way of an alternative."

"Absolutely, Mr President." Harry took off his jacket and sat down.

After a positive session on monetary reform, the debate continued over lunch. President Choi had invited Helen,

Zhang and Robertson to join him. Zhang had warned his colleagues that it would be a working lunch, and so it proved.

"It was a very interesting session," the President said as they set about their first course. "And I am largely persuaded by the arguments you put forward. I wonder, though, if you have considered resurrecting the tried and tested gold standard system for managing the money supply. I believe it has much to recommend it."

Zhang signalled to Robertson that he should answer.

"Mr President. We did indeed consider a return to the gold standard, but we rejected it on several grounds: First, although it implies steady annual growth in the quantity of money, it removes decisions about the optimal supply of money from human beings. Second, to be truly just, it would require the effective nationalisation of all gold still to be extracted, so that countries with large reserves of unmined gold, like your own, and South Africa, didn't have an unfair advantage. And third, we don't see any benefit to be gained by restricting the money supply by pegging it to a scarce resource like gold. The problem with the current system is that bankers were incentivised by the profit motive both to oversupply and undersupply money, at different times, driving the cycle of boom-bust. With commercial banks no longer able to create money, there will be no need for currencies to be tied to a commodity like gold."

President Choi seemed momentarily floored by the authority of Robertson's reply, so there was a pause before his next question.

"I see. Perhaps then, we need something to sell to the banks, to make them a little more comfortable with the changes we shall be demanding of them."

"Mr President," Zhang answered this time. "There is no reason why banks should not continue to fulfil the function of medium between those with surplus money and those seeking funds for investment. The important thing is that the rewards to investors be directly linked to the profit levels of the enterprises into which their money is invested. And also that banks share the risks associated with their investment decisions."

"Might there also be a possibility," asked Choi, "that banks, or other institutions, would devise unitised products which would allow investors to spread their risk across a range of investment opportunities?"

"Absolutely, and a secondary market in such unitised investment vehicles might also be desirable. Banks would be free to invest their clients' money in these markets, although their investment activities should, of course, be kept quite separate from their retail business."

"But wouldn't a secondary market necessarily lead to speculative trading?"

"That," Robertson took over, "is why the trading of such products would be subject to certain rules. There would be heavy penalties for selling early. If you committed to a five year investment, for example, and decided to sell after three, then you would receive back your original investment less any dividends already paid. There would be no incentive to sell. And these new arrangements would encourage the kind of long-term investment commitments that firms need."

The President took a large mouthful of crab meat and chewed thoughtfully. The others waited respectfully in anticipation of another question. "And what about the issue of money to fund public investments?" he asked, finally.

"Of course," Zhang answered, "while the principal means of money issue will be via the new money issuing authorities, and the principal source of public revenue will be non-distortionary taxes, we also make provision for the issue of money specifically for the purpose of state investment in infrastructure projects, and in essential public services which do not attract investment from the private sector."

"And how will these investments generate a return?" President Choi asked.

"They will generate a social return by providing the population with good public infrastructure: roads, railways, hospitals, parks and utilities for example, and by ensuring these are maintained and renewed in a timely fashion. They will generate a financial return by ensuring that private enterprise has access to the best possible economic infrastructure and can thus expand its activities, generate more wealth, and thus return more to the treasury via taxation."

"Some advocates of monetary reform argue that all new money should be spent into circulation via public expenditure. This way national economies can avoid falling victim to the politically-motivated antics of the financial markets." Robertson added.

"And there is nothing in the blueprint which prevents governments from prioritising this form of money issue over the issue of money direct into the private sector," Zhang clarified. "But we believe that a more dynamic and inclusive economy will emerge if state-controlled money issue is restricted to those investments which do not attract private investment."

"And what about the proposed single global currency?" Choi moved quickly on. "Presumably the existence of such a currency will make it possible for investors to place their money wherever they want in the world, without having to bear the cost of exchange charges or the risk or currency fluctuations?"

"Yes, indeed," Jay answered. "We anticipate the establishment of global, regional, national and even community focussed investment vehicles. Any citizen, in any country, will be able to invest anywhere in the global economy. However, we suspect that once a level economic playing field is established, most people will want to invest close to home where they can see the results of their investment, as well as receiving a share of any profits."

Choi looked satisfied with the answers to his questions. It was not clear whether he had finished, but he paused long enough for Helen to take her chance.

"On a general point, we have worked hard to ensure the blueprint is not too prescriptive. We have tried not to legislate in too much detail. As Professor Robertson said, we anticipate the establishment of certain types of investment vehicle, but the shape those vehicles might take is up to the market. We propose a set of principles, and outline a framework within which economic activity should be conducted. As long as those principles are observed, and that framework respected, then we believe a dynamic, sustainable, just and inclusive economy will emerge."

The rest of the afternoon was rather more relaxed. Helen had a private meeting with the Dalai Lama to which she was very much looking forward. She hadn't seen him since he intervened so helpfully at the press conference on the first morning. As it was a fine afternoon, the Dalai Lama proposed that they visit the Sankei Gardens, a couple of miles from the conference centre.

The driver pulled in near the public entrance to the park. Sarah, the agent accompanying them, opened the door for Helen, who walked quickly around the car so she could help the Dalai Lama out. He still had boundless energy though she had noticed he was a little unsteady on his legs at times.

He took Helen's arm and led her towards a crescent-shaped lake which he pointed out on a tourist map he had pulled from his pocket.

"Do you think we look like tourists?" he turned around to ask Sarah, who was walking a couple of paces behind them.

Being a weekday afternoon, the park was reasonably quiet. Helen hoped they wouldn't attract too much attention and was relieved when, having consulted his map once more, the Dalai Lama led them to a bench shaded by a pergola, in an area of beautifully manicured gardens.

"It's lovely not to have to worry about work for a couple of hours," Helen said as they sat down.

"My dear, don't expect me to let you off that lightly. I was hoping to speak to you about the lack of reference to spirituality in the blueprint."

"What do you mean? There's a whole section on the importance of freedom of religious expression?"

"Yes, yes, and that's all very good. But I'm thinking more of the spiritual dimension in life once the new economic and political order is in place."

"I'm not sure that's something we can give guidance on in the blueprint, your holiness. Surely that's your job?"

"Of course it is, but sometimes I could do with a little help you know. I've been fighting all my life. You make a very good moral case for the changes proposed in the blueprint, but you don't give credit to the spiritual or religious origins of those moral foundations."

"That's because I'm not sure the moral foundations necessarily are spiritual in origin, certainly not exclusively. And even if they were, I'm not sure a metaphysical argument for a new economic system would deliver the support we need."

The Dalai Lama thought for a moment.

"I just think it's a little disingenuous for secularists and atheists to take all the credit for the greatest moral leap forward in the history of humankind, when it is people of faith who have been holding the rest of society to account for so long."

"But you were invited to sit on the committee."

"I know, and you know my reasons for declining that flattering invitation. The thing is, I am worried about what happens next. Assuming the blueprint is adopted I think people are going to need faith more than ever to help them through what will inevitably be a time of great upheaval."

"That's why we wanted you on the committee. But perhaps you were right to keep out of the fray. Perhaps your opportunity will come once the blueprint is implemented."

"I'm glad you said that, because I have to confess I've been keeping something from you."

"Go on."

"Having studied the blueprint long and hard, and noted the recommendations for various bodies to oversee its implementation, I have decided to establish a separate body: a global council of faiths."

"That's great. How far progressed are you?"

I have received certain commitments. In fact I'm almost there, just one problem in fact."

"Don't tell me, the Vatican?" The Dalai Lama nodded. "I'm afraid that's one area where I can't help you," Helen said.

"Perhaps not directly, but I've got any idea that might just get the Vatican on board. What would you think about our launching the council in Berlin. If I can present the Vatican with a fait accompli, tell them that every other major faith leader is going to be there, then I don't think they'll want to be left out."

"Not that the Pope speaks even for a majority of Catholics these days," Helen muttered, "but the symbolism would be very strong."

"So I have your blessing then?"

"You don't need my blessing. But I think it would round off a successful Berlin Summit perfectly. I'll tell you one thing though, security won't like it."

Helen heard a phone ring. For a moment she was confused. It had never crossed her mind that the Dalai Lama carried his own phone. He looked almost as surprised as he struggled to liberate the device from beneath the creases of his robe. He looked at the screen before putting the phone to his ear.

"Madam President," he answered, "how lovely to hear from you." Helen racked her brains. Surely he wasn't taking a call from Hilda Solis.

"Really, that is interesting. Oh I see. That must have put you in a rather awkward position. Oh, you're not entirely sure. Yes, by a happy coincidence I'm with her now. Of course, I'll be sure to pass on the information. Oh you did? Yes, I hear he's a lovely man."

Helen was utterly confused. As the call came to an end she was desperate to hear the other side of the conversation, but the Dalai Lama took even longer to return his phone to his pocket.

"Sorry my dear," he said eventually. "I don't get many calls; in fact only a dozen or so people have my number. That was President Solis. She was phoning in the hope that I might be able to get a message to you, which of course I can."

"Go on," Helen said, impatiently.

"Well it's all rather intriguing. She's just returned from Reykjavik where she had to fly at short notice for a secret meeting with President Kotov of Russia"

"Presumably at Kotov's behest?"

"Yes, indeed. It seems he was keen to discuss contingency plans in the event of the blueprint not being adopted at Berlin."

"Jesus Christ," Helen blurted out. The Dalai Lama smiled. "What did she say to him?"

"She made it clear that the United States would be supporting the blueprint and that she was determined to do all in her power to ensure it was adopted, but" "she had to acknowledge the need for contingency planning in the event of failure." Helen completed the sentence.

"Exactly. Well she would have to say that wouldn't she? It remains a possibility after all. And it would be dreadful if no contingency were in place."

"Did she get the impression Kotov is likely to go against us?"

"She said she didn't know, but she thinks it must be a possibility."

Helen thought for a moment. "What was the bit about him being a lovely man, surely she doesn't have a soft spot for Kotov?"

"Oh no, no, no. She met your husband last evening. Apparently they really hit it off. She thought he was charming. Hopefully I may get to meet him in Berlin?"

"Everybody is going to meet everybody in Berlin."

Sixteen

Oscar Silverman had heard nothing for days. As far as he knew Harry Noble was still in Moscow, but he couldn't raise Howard Dawkins at all. It was two days since the end of the Yokohama summit, and Helen George and the blueprint had higher approval ratings than ever. He was beginning to think it was a done deal. Perhaps Noble would make progress with the Russians, but he doubted it. He was also unsure whether Dawkins cared enough to take the steps necessary to halt this seemingly unstoppable process.

It was a beautiful fall day. From his garden, which had coped with an unforgivingly hot summer remarkably well, Silverman looked out across the Blue Ridge Mountains in all their variegated glory. The leaves may be turning a good month earlier than they did when he was a boy, but what did that matter? They remained an absolute joy. At such moments he felt completely at one with the world.

He had come to the conclusion, not for the first time, that his drinking was out of hand. When he felt out of control he drank too much. And while alcohol helped him forget, it seriously affected his ability to exert influence over events. And right now events needed him sober. The previous evening he had poured away an obscene quantity of whiskey and locked the door to the wine cellar before mailing the key to his brother with strict instructions not to return it until after the Berlin summit. It was only a ten minute drive to the liquor store, but Silverman knew from past experience that such periods of self-imposed prohibition worked, as long as he had something to focus on.

He sat down with a coffee, a cigarette and a proper newspaper, one produced on newsprint, the pages of which he could turn with his hands. The subscription had cost him a small fortune. It was exactly four weeks until the Berlin summit. Twenty eight days to make a difference. With the exception of the Russians, who could still go either way, there was no indication that any other country or bloc would oppose the blueprint. The Europeans were already agreed. There was the Houston summit in a couple of weeks time, but the whole region would be slavishly following that bitch Solis. And then Tbilisi, where presumably the Russians would finally make their decision and his doubts about Harry Noble would be confirmed. Diplomatically, the Russians were the only hope. Howard Dawkins claimed to have something else up his sleeve but had made a poor job of things so far. Silverman was glad he was sober and intended to stay that way. If he needed to intervene directly, he would have to be at the top of his game.

It was Saturday afternoon in Stockholm. Despite the long flight from Tokyo, Helen felt rested. It helped that the summit pressure was off for a while. Although Europe's leaders were gathering in earnest, this meeting would be treated by most as an opportunity for backslapping and self-congratulation. But Helen wanted to talk about the world post-Berlin. She was unsure which scenario concerned her most: the blueprint being adopted and nobody being properly prepared to implement it; or there being no contingency plan in place in the event of the Russians bringing the whole process down.

The final evening in Yokohama had been quiet. The only fly in the ointment was a call from Prime Minister Sianturi who had contacted Helen directly to apologise again for her daughter's behaviour, and to alert her to the fact that Citra was still unaccounted for, presumably in Paris. Helen discussed with Mike the possibility of his going to Paris to track her down, but had been persuaded that all necessary steps were being taken by his contacts in the French capital.

On Friday morning, she had gone ahead with the hour long CNN interview that Jane had set up after the Robertson story broke. Originally planned as an opportunity to restore credibility before the Victor Weiss sting had largely achieved that objective, Helen took full advantage of the chance to talk in more general terms about the summit process and her hopes for the run up to Berlin.

She was unhappy that the interviewer had chosen to devote so much time to her personal role, and took every opportunity to emphasise the collegiate nature of the committee, and her immense debt to colleagues. Nevertheless, echoing President Horomito, the interviewer had asked about the implications of Helen's decision to withdraw from politics after Berlin.

Ahead of the interview, she had agreed with Jane and Saeed that she would lie if the questioning became too intense. She hated lying: she could remember few occasions when a forced lie had not come back to bite her, but the situation left her little alternative.

"Helen, I really must press you on this question," the interviewer had said. "You are on record as saying that, assuming that the blueprint is approved, you will retire from politics after the Berlin summit. Many people are now saying that Berlin is just the beginning and that the period between Berlin and full implementation on May 1st next year will be crucial. Surely the process cannot afford to lose its leader at such a crucial juncture?"

"Certainly it has always been my intention to stand down after the Berlin summit. However, that intention was expressed some time ago, and things change. If there is wide-spread support for my continuing in some role post-Berlin, then perhaps I will have to give it consideration."

"Several commentators have suggested that the logical conclusion of the process would be the election of a world president to oversee the proposed new institutions and structures. Might you be a candidate for that role?"

"Absolutely not. Nowhere in the blueprint do we argue for the establishment of such a post. I think it is both unnecessary and unworkable. There will be no world president."

Fortunately, Helen had been able to talk to Rudolf ahead of the broadcast and assure him that she had not changed her mind. He was back in Thonon for a couple of days before heading to Vienna for his daughter's wedding. He had forgiven Helen for delaying her own arrival in Austria, but had also taken the precaution of booking her on a second flight from Moscow to Vienna, just in case hers should be cancelled. Helen promised him that she would drive from Moscow if necessary. She was not going to miss Jenifer's wedding.

There was a reduced contingent in Stockholm: Mike and Jane were there, along with Saeed, Safiya, Rita, Ann Margaret and Jemma. Lundberg was also with them. Diplomatically, Lundberg's presence was vital: His successor as European President had failed to earn the respect of many member states, and had not been directly involved in the process by which the EU had pre-approved the blueprint. In many ways, Lundberg was still top dog in Europe; he would be in his element this week.

That evening he was joining Helen and Saeed for dinner, not just because he was the only one who knew his way around Stockholm's restaurants, but because they wanted his advice ahead of their meeting with Kotov. In the event, he delivered an excellent venue with an enticing menu and a quiet corner away from other diners.

"So who is this man advising Kotov?" Lundberg asked, as he poured the wine.

Helen looked at Saeed. She couldn't face telling the improbable story of Harry Noble again.

"Wait a minute," said Lundberg, as Jamali wound up. "So this character, who is a middle ranking intelligence officer, and whose only connection to the world of international diplomacy is as a fan of your husband's work, Helen, has assumed the role of principal advisor to the Russian president?"

"Yes, Stefan," Helen answered, determined to remain serious. "The problem is, Noble is not stupid. He's an articulate opponent of the blueprint, but not an extremist. He's been in Moscow a week now, and he's still there, apparently locked in private talks with Kotov."

"I see. Well, I suppose we're not engaged in a conventional process of diplomacy here. Why shouldn't any Tom, Dick or Harry for that matter be advising one of the most powerful men in the world?"

Helen tried to stifle a laugh. "Okay, however absurd it sounds," she said, "the last major hurdle to our getting the blueprint approved is the Russians. By all reports, that decision will be a personal one made by Kotov. We know he's fallen out with his own people. He has turned to Noble for counsel, presumably because Noble has sold himself as having connections to me. Saeed and I are meeting him on Thursday to persuade him to support the blueprint. We have the benefit of knowing about Noble's involvement, although he probably doesn't know we know. We also have the advantage of knowing his position. So we can probably have a pretty good stab at working out his strategy with Kotov."

"Go on," said Lundberg.

"Noble is a cultured man but rather old fashioned in his views. I suspect his world view has three main elements. First, he is naturally resistant to change: while he acknowledges problems with the world, he thinks things are pretty good compared to what they might be and therefore that the current order is worth defending. Second, although he's not strongly nationalist, he's interested in and open to influences from other countries and cultures but he believes the nation state model to be the only viable form of governance. Anything that impinges on what he perceives as the sovereign rights of nations, especially his own, is necessarily bad."

"And third?" Lundberg asked.

"He's a pessimist; he lacks moral ambition; he has no faith in the human race to rise to the challenges it faces and make a great leap forward. He opposes the blueprint not just because he's unsure of it's values, but because he doesn't think humans are ready for transformative change. In fact, I don't think he believes we ever will be."

"So," said Lundberg. "He's an intellectual, a thinker, and rather conservative in his views. Would you say he is passionate in his beliefs?"

"He's too rational to be passionate. He does show some emotion though. He has a good sense of humour. He comes over as a little superior and can be rather condescending, to women at least. He is sincere though, and I think he has integrity."

"Well, he sounds like a good match for Kotov. I would use several of the same adjectives to describe the Russian," Saeed said.

"Of course," Lundberg said, "you and Kotov go back along way."

"We first met thirty years ago. There was no indication then that he would go so far. He didn't have the ambition you find in most aspiring politicians. In fact he was scathing about the whole system."

"On that basis, would you not expect him to embrace the opportunity for change offered by the blueprint?" asked Lundberg.

"Thirty years is a long time," Helen said. "And the experience of Russian politics is, I should imagine, enough to dent anyone's idealism."

"So what will Noble's strategy be?" Lundberg asked. "Presumably he will play the nationalist card, and try to persuade Kotov that after the upheavals of the last century, his country needs stability, not more change."

"That'll certainly be part of his message, but the Russian economy is in such a state. They have more to gain from the blueprint than many countries." Helen said.

"Before we discuss the approach we take with Kotov," Jamali suggested, "perhaps we should be clear about the sequence of events should Kotov decide to vote against. Presumably he will make his intentions known at, or just before, the Tbilisi summit?"

The others nodded.

"Assuming Kotov decides not to give his support, that would give us a week before Berlin to coordinate a unified response. Kotov will be assuming, encouraged by Noble, that he can single-handedly bring the process down. Why don't we sound out key players and seek their agreement to go ahead without Russia in the event of Kotov deciding to veto the blueprint. Russia needs trade if it is to avoid meltdown. If it won't join the game under the rules that every other nation is prepared to accept, then why should it be allowed to play?"

"I agree," Lundberg said. "But I'm not sure how we have this conversation without the whole process unravelling. Our success has been built on the capacity to achieve consensus between nations with a long history of antagonism. Now we are asking everyone to gang up on a single dissenter, it rather goes against the grain."

"It does," Helen agreed, "but I'm not sure we have to involve everyone. Russia has nothing to offer in place of the blueprint, and desperately needs trade. At least sixty per cent of that trade is with Europe and China. We can sort out the Europeans while we are here, and I'll get Zhang to talk to the Chinese; he's back in Beijing now. I'll talk to Solis as well. Three phone calls should be sufficient to make Kotov back down."

"Okay," Saeed agreed. "But this is our final negotiating position. I wasn't proposing we threaten Kotov at our meeting on Thursday."

"Fine," said Helen, "no mention of this on Thursday. But I'll be more confident going into that meeting knowing we have a fall back position."

Harry was exhausted. He'd never had a great deal of time for politicians, but he admired them for their limitless energy. Kotov was no exception. After nearly ten hours of intense conversation, with just one short break, he was finally allowed to return to his hotel.

It had been a productive day, but Harry was concerned: Firstly, they hadn't discussed the blueprint, only the Russian strategy should Kotov decide not to support it. And he was giving nothing away on his decision. He seemed to have entered a long period of meditative deliberation. Harry was also concerned about Kotov's strategy. The Russian had told him about the secret meeting in Reykjavik with President Solis, and seemed certain that should he choose to veto the blueprint and thus bring the process down, the locus of power would shift quickly to an alliance between Russia and the United States which would fill the void left by the committee. While Harry didn't doubt that Solis had given

Kotov certain assurances, he felt sure the other side would also have a contingency plan, and she would almost certainly be involved in that too. He had to decide whether to let Kotov know of his concerns. It wasn't easy advising the President of Russia. How much should he assume that he would have worked out for himself? Kotov's decision over the blueprint would be influenced by his confidence in his own ability to offer the world a credible alternative post-Berlin. If all his eggs were in the Solis basket, and Solis was stringing him along, he could be left very embarrassed.

Harry wasn't sure what to do. He already felt some loyalty to Kotov. At the same time, his priority was to prevent adoption of the blueprint. Only now did he pause to consider the wider political consequences of the blueprint failing. The world, it gradually dawned on him, could be plunged into chaos. The weight of citizen expectations sat firmly on the shoulders of the committee and the blueprint. The process had come to dominate so completely that it's collapse threatened a political and diplomatic vacuum that Kotov would struggle to fill. Noble took a couple of aspirin and fell into bed.

The flight from Tokyo to Vancouver had given Robertson plenty of time to rehearse his apology, but the first meeting with his wife had not gone well. Despite the story being knocked off the front pages by the revelations about Victor Weiss, the Robertson's home was still under siege from the local media. He and Julia were holed up in a downtown hotel with low key security in the hope of not drawing attention to their presence. At least their daughter was well out of it, enjoying an extended holiday with Jay's parents, oblivious to the turmoil.

In the year and a half since Jay had become a public figure, Julia had worked hard to ensure that she did not. There were no photos of her in the public domain. By the time Jay woke, she had already gone out, leaving a note with the single word: shopping. She would be back before long, and Jay knew there was little he could do except apologise, profusely and continuously, in the hope that she would eventually let him off the hook.

He had slept badly and felt dreadful. He assumed he would have time for a shower before his wife's return, but as he dried himself he heard her let herself in. This meant having to retrieve his clothes from the bedroom dressed only in a towel. An otherwise ordinary act made excruciatingly awkward by the circumstances. She noticed his embarrassment.

"It's okay, we are still married you know," she had turned to look out of the window.

"I won't be a minute," Jay said, apologetically.

When he returned she was staring at him with the same look of controlled rage she had when they agreed to call a truce the previous evening.

"So," she said calmly, "where were we?"

"If I remember correctly I was apologising, and you were telling me that wasn't good enough," he replied, trying desperately not to antagonise her further.

"The thing I don't understand, is that we talked about this."

"About what?"

"About, being faithful, about loyalty, the terms and conditions of our relationship," she said, sarcastically. "We talked about it when we first got together, and again when we got engaged."

"I know, I know."

"Do you remember, we talked about open marriages, and you said that wasn't for you. You said that the worst thing I could do to you was to sleep with another man. You said that."

"Yes, I know I did," he couldn't look at her.

"And you have done to me precisely the thing that you said would hurt you most if I did it to you. Did you think I felt differently about it? Christ, it was one of the reasons I felt able to make a commitment to you: because you made out that fidelity was important."

"I'm sorry," he said. "I was weak and stupid. I made a terrible mistake. It'll haunt me for the rest of my life."

"It'll haunt you will it? My life will never be the same, because our relationship has changed forever, and you did it Jay. You had no right." She was shouting now.

"Do we still have a relationship?"

She turned away to the window again. "I don't know," she said, quietly. "We'll always have a relationship through Nathalie. God knows she's barely seen you in the last two years, and now this."

"Look, it's only another month. After that I'll be back here for good. We can start again."

"I don't know Jay. I just don't know. I'm 38 years old. I thought we might have another child, but why would I want another child with you after this? Perhaps I still have time to start over. Maybe I can choose better next time."

"I'm sure you can. I hope you won't though." Jay was desperate to say the right thing, and for Julia to soften a little. She was the only person in the world he really spoke to. And now he had no source of support or advice, or sympathy; not that he deserved any. He felt dreadfully guilty but he knew that wasn't enough. He looked up and saw her take a deep breath; preparing for another volley.

"How could you have been so stupid? It's not just our marriage, you could have brought the entire process down. In fact you still might. I mean, how attractive, how seductive can a twenty-six year old student really be?

"I told you last night, it wasn't planned. I had no idea I was going to meet her until the dinner. I had a few drinks, I was bewitched. Christ Julia, it's been dreadful seeing so little of you and Nathalie over the last two years."

"So you go and do the one thing that's likely to mean you'll see even less of us."

"No. I wasn't thinking straight. I've been tired. Actually, the last few months I've been rather depressed." He looked at her, but still saw no sign of softening.

"Depressed? If you were depressed why didn't you tell me. We could have flown out and spent some time with you between summits. Jesus, am I supposed to interpret this as the attention-seeking behaviour of someone with mild mental health symptoms?"

"No, I didn't mean that."

"The hell you didn't. I'll tell you how I interpret it Jay: You're just another man who can't keep his dick in his pants when he sees a pretty girl."

Jay didn't reply. Julia seemed to have come to a natural break.

"I think we should go and see Nathalie. She won't understand what's going on," Jay suggested.

"We can't. The security people say it's too risky. You'll have to get your Dad to bring her here. But not today. If I have to pretend that everything's okay between us, I need more time. You'd better phone him."

"Gunter? Hi, how are you? That's right, it's Oscar Silverman. Don't tell me you still have my number in your phone. You do, huh? How long has it been? Yeah, that's about what I reckon, five years. Yeah, summer of 2018. Yep, I'm retired, officially anyway. Unofficially I'm working on something rather important, which is why I called you. Are you still in Hamburg? Potsdam huh? Listen Gunter, are you busy next week? If I fly in Tuesday could we spend some time? I need to get your opinion on something. Great. Okay. I'll let you know what time my flight gets in. No, there's no need for you to meet me off the plane. In fact, it might be better if you didn't. Good to talk after so long. Bye now."

That evening, Lundberg had arranged an informal dinner with the British Prime Minister and the French President. The PM, Rachel Brightwell, was an old friend of Helen's, but she had never spent any time with the French President, who had a reputation for being brilliant but prickly. He was, however, a very good friend of Lundberg's.

On the way to the hotel where they were dining, Helen quizzed Lundberg about the likely content of the evening's conversation. She rather hoped it would be a mainly social affair, but knew that was unlikely.

"I know that Brightwell and Morel spent last evening together. They appear to have become rather close over the last year; which is interesting. I suspect they will want to talk economics, I'm afraid. Morel is keen on the economic justice elements of the blueprint, but last time I spoke to him, he said he was struggling to come up with a synthesis which he could use to sell the programme to colleagues and the electorate."

"Brightwell is pretty clued up on economics. I hope we're not exposed as illiterates."

"Yes, but she's one of your best mates, isn't she?" Lundberg smiled.

"And Morel is one of yours, so we should be fine."

Brightwell and Morel had something else in common. They were both 'new era' politicians; leaders of recently formed alliances who had come to power in what many saw as a seismic shift in European politics. After the collapse of the Euro, the centre-right axis which had driven the European project for the previous decade was forced from power across the continent.

Following the election of radical governments in France and Germany the previous year, at the 2015 election in Britain, the Labour party returned to power with a small working majority. But Labour proved no more adept at addressing the economic crisis than the previous government. In the meantime, the Lib-Dems, now freed from the yoke of coalition, and although a small force in parliament, had regrouped under Rachel Brightwell, a financial journalist of some repute, who only entered parliament at a by-election in 2014. Brightwell forged strong links with the Green Party which had managed to win three seats in 2015.

By the time the Labour Government fell to a no-confidence motion in 2018, the Lib-Dem/Green alliance was able to run on a platform of radical reform to which the Labour and Conservative parties were united in opposition. Brightwell entered Downing Street with a comfortable majority on a programme to work in partnership with other nations to reform international institutions, and so avoid the endemic economic crises of the previous decade. That progressive partnership inevitably excluded the Hendricks administration in the United States, but Brightwell worked tirelessly in support of reform with her European allies, and it was largely thanks to her efforts that the blueprint had been approved without the need for a formal summit.

As they pulled up outside the restaurant, Helen saw Rachel getting out of the car in front of them. She jumped out and ran to catch up with her leaving Lundberg to make his own way.

"Rachel, how are you?"

"Helen," they kissed, "great. And you."

"Oh you know. Exhausted. I feel about eighty. But having survived the last week, I reckon I'm probably indestructible."

"You've done really well, you know. I'm not sure I could have held it together."

"Well, I've had a lot of help. Hilda's press conference couldn't have been better timed."

"You might be surprised at how much work has been going on behind the scenes to make sure the process isn't brought down by wayward men."

"Talking of which, how's Morel? You know I still haven't met him properly?"

"He's fine actually. And don't worry, between you and me I think he's slightly in awe of you."

"Oh, not another one." They both laughed. "Stefan said he wants to talk economics tonight; something about developing a synthesis?"

"Yes, it's something we've talked about: He feels, and I agree, that it would be helpful to distil down some of the detail in the background papers into more easily digested briefings. How the changes to the economic system hang together, for example. Assuming we get that far, implementation is not going to be painless. It would be good if we can explain to people exactly how change is going to bring benefits in the longer term."

"Sounds reasonable," Helen said, just as Lundberg caught them up.

"Hello Rachel. Good to see you."

"You too," the Prime Minister replied. "Morel's car is just pulling up, so we may as well go through."

Helen found the French President to be charming and articulate. He was a historian, and fascinated at the thought of future historians looking back on the events of the last two years. He spoke as if implementation of the blueprint was a certainty. Helen felt the need to remind him that, although they were approaching the home straight, there were still many obstacles in their way. They talked briefly about the Russian problem. Brightwell and Morel were surprised to learn that Helen was going to Moscow, but she and Stefan had agreed not to mention their plan for dealing with a Kotov veto until they had separate meetings the following day.

Between courses they moved on to the main topic of the evening, Helen taking the initiative. "Monsieur President," she began. "The Prime Minister has been telling me of your idea for a synthesis of the economic proposals in the blueprint, perhaps you could elaborate?"

"Certainly," Morel replied in a rich accent. "I think it would be very helpful if we could produce a brief pamphlet, written in plain language, which would help explain to non-economists how the changes proposed in the blueprint will ultimately make possible a better life experience for everyone. I already have some people working on a version of this which will be distributed to every household in France. I have a meeting to discuss its contents tomorrow, so I thought I'd take this opportunity to get your thoughts on some of the economic provisions. As you know, I am not an economist." He smiled.

"I completely understand," Helen said, "as you will know, neither of us are economists either, but we have benefited from the very patient assistance of some of our colleagues on the committee. If I am reading you correctly, you would like a straightforward synopsis of the proposals for the reform of land tenure, the monetary system and the financial markets, focussing on how the three are linked?" Morel nodded.

Helen looked at Rachel for backup, which came in the form of a wink.

"Well, perhaps it would help if I described my understanding, as a layperson, and then Stefan and I could answer any questions." Again Morel nodded his approval.

"Okay. For me, the key is to put an end to all forms of unearned income. Unearned income is fundamental to the historical and ongoing concentration of wealth in the hands of a small minority. It is generally only available to people who already have surplus wealth, and while the blueprint accepts the need for those with surplus wealth to be rewarded for any risk-bearing investment they may make, this should not extend to income derived from activities that do not produce any additional tangible wealth."

"By tangible wealth I take it you mean goods, services or experiences that people need and want?" asked Brightwell.

"Exactly," Helen answered, "anything that adds to human wellbeing."

"Does the blueprint distinguish between needs and wants in terms of their economic importance?" asked President Morel.

"It does, though it steers clear of regulating for the production of essential needs before non-essentials. We hope that by creating conditions in which all citizens have equal and fair access to economic opportunities and resources, the market will better manage the distribution of investment so that essentials are prioritised. Once everyone has a stake in the economy, all will have some purchasing power, and they will use it first to secure the basics: housing, food and clothing. Markets only fail in this regard under the current system because many people are purposefully excluded by being denied sufficient purchasing power."

"But if tangible wealth also includes people's desires for luxuries, how do you persuade a billionaire that he really doesn't need to drink champagne with every meal, unless you regulate to favour the production of essentials?" asked Brightwell.

"Over time, as the new order delivers improved economic security across the board, billionaire status will no longer be something that people aspire too. We hope that people will be persuaded that accumulating exceptional personal wealth is neither necessary nor desirable."

"Ah," interrupted President Morel, "but what about the champagne industry? It employs thousands of people."

"The champagne industry will flourish, Monsieur President. Many more people will be able to afford champagne, perhaps not with every meal, but certainly as a regular treat. More people will buy it, and more people will acquire a taste for it. Demand can only increase."

Morel smiled.

"But let's get back to unearned income," Helen continued. "It occurs in three principle forms: the rent of land which is kept by the landowner despite not being the product of his effort; the gains on speculative investment in shares, bonds, currencies and all manner of financial devices, which make no real economic contribution but instead deprive the real economy of much needed investment; and the benefits enjoyed by a small elite of senior executives and shareholders in banks through the privilege of being able to create money. Not only does that privilege shower unearned wealth on those who own and run the banks, but the nature of the money-creation process places unnecessary constraints on entrepreneurship. It also, and this is key, feeds directly into the processes by which landowners and speculators derive the unearned income that allows them to maintain such a tight grip over the economy."

"Would not Marxists include a fourth source of unearned income," Morel asked, "in the form of the surplus value extracted by capitalists as profits; value that is, in reality, a product of the labour they employ?"

"Undoubtedly they would, Mr President, but we have opted to follow the line of the classical economists who argue that returns to capital are justified. We hope that by taxing land values, business owners will be prevented from inflating their profits by appropriating earnings that are really the product of other people's labour."

Morel smiled and took a sip of wine, seemingly satisfied with the answer. "So," he said, "by regulating against unearned income you ensure that more investment is available for genuine economic activity, and you remove the means by which a wealthy elite are able to set themselves apart from the rest of the population?"

"Exactly. And over time, you create an environment in which more people have access to economic resources and the opportunity to exploit them."

"We're talking about reversing the process of financialisation that has consumed virtually the entire economy over the last few decades," Lundberg said. "We have allowed a few clever people to turn the financial markets, which once served a useful purpose, into a huge casino in which they are able to make immense fortunes with scant regard for the consequences."

"You know, on several occasions I've challenged investment bankers to explain to me how their activities add value, or generate any real wealth." Brightwell said. "Of course, they are only able to answer in terms of conventional measures. They quote turnover and profit figures. And they tell me how much tax they pay, as if I'm supposed to be grateful. But they fail to understand that most of the wealth they are dealing in is imagined, and not tied to the creation of anything tangible."

By the time coffee was served, the conversation had moved away from economics. It turned out that President Morel had secured for himself a place on the small committee responsible for organising the post-summit Berlin concert.

When Lundberg queried whether the holder of such an important position had time to involve himself in the organisation of a cultural event, Morel had admonished him.

"Stefan, I'm setting an example to other world leaders. Culture has been neglected by politicians for far too long. This has to change: I'm sure your husband would agree, Helen?"

"Indeed he would. And I know he's determined to make the concert an event to remember."

"Excellent. I have just one more question, though." He looked at Lundberg.

"While I accept in principle the need for a new system of money issue, I am concerned that this is an area where we are struggling to take public opinion with us. Not because the majority of ordinary people are opposed to monetary reform, rather because they find it difficult to comprehend. The question I am most commonly asked is how can it be right to create money out of nothing?"

The Swede thought for a moment. "I think the best way to answer that question is to remind people that money is already created out of nothing under the current system. The key question is who should create money and who should benefit from the process by which it is created? The principal role of money should be to lubricate the wheels of economic activity: to facilitate exchange, to provide a universally accepted measure of value, and to enable people to store wealth temporarily, prior to using it for consumption or investment. Under current arrangements, control over money issue is granted to a handful of people who are then able to exercise control over the entire economy. Not only do banks charge for the privilege of providing the economy with money, they also decide to whom it will be issued. Wealthy individuals and large, successful corporations find it much easier to obtain credit than the less well off."

"So the means by which money is issued makes it inevitable that the gap between rich and poor will grow," Brightwell added.

"The means by which it is issued and the criteria for deciding to whom it is issued," agreed Lundberg. "From the point of view of private banks, the best candidates for the extension of credit, that is to say the issue of new money, are people who already have assets. Wealth begets wealth. The inequitable distribution of newly issued money is both a cause and a symptom of inequality."

"So the solution," suggested President Morel, "is to remove the privilege of money issue from vested interests, to place it in the hands of a money-issuing authority which is not driven by the need to generate profits, and to ensure that credit is extended to anyone who has a viable plan for generating real wealth."

"I think," Helen said, "you have the concluding paragraph of your pamphlet, Monsieur President."

Seventeen

"Daddy, you're here."

Nathalie Robertson was delighted to see her father. She ran into the hotel room and threw herself into his arms. Finally, somebody who wasn't angry with him. Jay struggled to hold back tears. He thought he saw Julia's face soften but it didn't last long. He swung his daughter around twice before bouncing her on the bed several times, each bounce bringing a squeal of delight.

When he looked up, he saw his parents standing a few feet away. His father looked severe, his mother, sympathetic.

"Hello Dad, Mom. How are you both?"

"Oh we're just fine darling," his mother said, moving towards him, "it's you we're worried about," she said, touching his arm. Julia exchanged glances with Jay's father: they had never spoken of it, but they shared a dislike of the way his mother indulged him. Jay handed Nathalie to Julia and, after hugging his mother, turned to his father. They shook hands formally; the older man nodded but said nothing.

"Right," Jay said, taking the initiative to avoid further awkwardness. "If we've only got a couple of hours, I would like to spend the first hour playing with my beautiful daughter, then I'll put on my disguise and perhaps you and I can go down to the bar for a drink, Dad?"

As nobody voiced any objections, Jay took Nathalie back and they headed down the wide steps that separated the sleeping area from the rest of the suite. Jay's mother followed them to the table where she took out a colouring book and some crayons. His father remained in the bedroom with Julia.

"Are you ok?" he asked.

"No," she replied, once again looking out of the window, "but thanks for asking."

"Is he in a real state?"

"Yep. All over the place. He can't stop apologising. I think he probably means it, but it's too soon for me. I need to be angry. He'll just have to wait."

"Is he stable? Do you think he can he go back to work?"

"Oh yes, he'll be okay. Never ceases to amaze me how men can compartmentalise things. His whole life is coming apart at the seams, but he'll still get up for work in the morning."

"I wonder where he gets that from." He hadn't meant it to be audible, but Julia turned around and raised both eyebrows. She wasn't going to turn on her father-in-law. He had a massive ego, just like Jay, but he was her only ally at the moment.

"What would you do?" she asked.

"I'd give him another chance. I'm not sure he deserves it, but I would. Tell him you want to sort things out, but that it's gonna take time. You don't want him flying off to Houston thinking he's lost you and Nathalie. Who knows what he might do if that happened."

"So I have to be reasonable. I have to go the extra mile to make him comfortable just so he doesn't go and screw another twenty year old?"

"If you think there's any chance of saving your marriage, then yes, I'm afraid you do."

Julia sat down beside him on the edge of the bed. Rather clumsily, he put his hand on her shoulder.

It was an unusually warm September morning in Moscow. On any other Sunday in one of his favourite cities, Harry would have spent breakfast planning an itinerary to take in a number of cultural and architectural treasures, but today he had to work. Kotov had little free time before their meeting with Helen George on Thursday. Moscow would have to wait.

He arrived early at Kotov's office in the Kremlin only to find the President had been delayed. He would be an hour at least, so Harry decided to take advantage of the weather. As he walked across Red Square towards The Historical Museum, he realised he was not alone.

"Good morning Mr Noble." Harry looked to his left, though he didn't need to. He recognised the almost comically threatening voice of Zayztev.

"Mr Zaytzev," he responded cheerily. "How lovely to see you. Surely you're not working on such a beautiful Sunday morning?" Zaytzev looked at him, irritated. Harry was pleased with the reaction. He looked to his right. "Perhaps you might introduce me to your companion?" He had pushed his luck a little too far: the unnamed companion moved closer and took a firm grip of his upper arm. As he did so, he pushed Harry to the left, following Zaytzev, who had changed direction a moment earlier. They were walking quickly towards a waiting car. Harry was being abducted. He decided it would be futile to resist.

"I would happily have accompanied you to your car without this show of force," he said, still calm, once he and Zaytzev were strapped into the back seat.

"As I'm sure you appreciate, Mr Noble, we don't like to take any unnecessary risks in our business."

"And what exactly is your business?" Harry asked tersely.

"I think I informed you of that at our last meeting, and I fail to see why your are so antagonistic towards me, Mr Noble. After all, we are on the same side."

"Indeed," Harry said, tiring quickly of the conversation. "Perhaps you might tell me what I can do for you?"

"Very well. You can tell me about your progress. Is your mission proving fruitful or is Kotov going to support the blueprint?"

"I believe I'm making progress, although President Kotov has yet to make up his mind."

Zaytzev gave him a withering look. "I knew you would make no difference. Kotov made up his mind a long time ago. Perhaps, Mr Noble, you need a different strategy." Harry said nothing. "Perhaps you should remind President Kotov that there is substantial opposition to the blueprint in Russia. While he seems to have taken it upon himself to exercise unilateral power over the lives of all Russians, he doesn't control everyone or everything. If he insists on committing this country to the blueprint then other measures will be taken to prevent it being implemented; and the effect of those measures will spread far beyond Russia's borders."

Harry looked at him, but again said nothing. The car pulled over, not far from the point at which they had begun their journey.

"Now, Mr Noble," Zaytzev concluded, "if you'd like to continue on your way, I am late for my game of tennis."

Harry got out and looked at his watch. He headed back towards the Kremlin. He decided to tell Kotov about Zaytzev. He didn't expect the news to have any impact on the President's decision, but if Kotov were to support the blueprint, he should do so in full knowledge of the possible consequences. Harry was in no doubt that Zaytzev was serious, nor that he had the means to carry out his threats.

Jay and his father decided to sit at the bar rather than perch on the lows stools dotted around even lower tables. Both ordered beer. Jay had no intention of trying to defend his behaviour; he was tired of arguing. He was pleased when his father spoke first.

"I made a mistake once. Biggest mistake of my life." Jay hadn't expected this. "It didn't cost me my marriage, your mother was too forgiving for that, but I wish the hell I hadn't done it. She suffered so much. I didn't deserve to keep her. She was young enough to start over, but for some reason she stood by me. I was younger than you, of course. You and your sister were still far in the future. But I'm not sure that makes so much difference. The thing is I betrayed her, and I shouldn't have. I know that now. And I'm very fortunate that she was able to forgive me. But it changes things Jay: it's never the same. And that's something you're gonna have to live with. But Julia is a damn fine woman, just like your mother was, and still is. You'll have to work hard to save your marriage, but it'll be worth it."

Jay was silent. His father leant forward so he could see his face. Jay sat back; for the first time in his life he felt able to let his father see his tears.

"However," suddenly the older man was his usual, overbearing self again. "You may be able to save your marriage, but you certainly seem to have screwed up this whole blueprint process? And that's a real crime against humanity."

Since being appointed to the committee Jay hadn't spoken to his father about his work. He knew the man's politics and supposed he would be broadly supportive, but was surprised to discover the extent of his enthusiasm.

"As you know," he said, "I've never had a great deal time for politicians and their endless triangulations, but I have to admit I've been mighty impressed by the tone and efficacy of the work you've all been doing. That Helen George must be some woman?"

"Oh she is. What with Helen and Julia, I'm not sure who I fear most."

"You'll be fine. But for God's sake Jay, don't do anything else to put your marriage, or the blueprint, at risk. Do you hear me?

Jay nodded.

It was a week since Mbonga had left Julius and his family. He had done so with a heavy heart. He couldn't imagine coping in his friend's situation. He had made his way into southern Kenya without much difficulty, and quickly onto Kisumu on the banks of Lake Victoria. Kisumu had once been a thriving port city, but now had little to recommend it. The government had stopped funding work to manage the spread of the water hyacinth that now covered much of the lake and forced the closure of trade routes. Trade was the lifeblood of Kisumu; without it the town had nothing.

Having heard this miserable story described by an old man in a bar within view of the vegetation-strangled lake, Mbonga remembered that he also had a problem: he had no idea how to proceed. He needed to go North, or at least North East, but that meant crossing huge tranches of desert. He knew there would be little transport across this inhospitable terrain. He told the old man of his predicament.

"You want to get to Europe?" he asked, no hint of surprise in his voice. Mbonga nodded. "I'm not sure you can get to Europe from here," he said, scratching his head. He looked at Mbonga for a reaction and then burst out laughing. "Of course you can get to Europe, but not overland. You'll be dead before you get across Sudan, and Ethiopia would be no better."

"So what then?"

"How are your sea legs?"

"Okay," Mbonga said, remembering his trip up Lake Malawi.

"Right then, you need to make your way to Mombassa and get on a boat." He signalled to Mbonga to lay out his map on the bar, and showed him the route.

Mbonga was dismayed to discover that Mombassa was well to the south of Kisumu, and a relatively short distance from the point where he had crossed the border from Tanzania.

Had he known of this maritime option, he could have saved himself much time.

"Now, there's not much commercial traffic between Mombassa and Europe, but there are regular trips by water tankers. There's a chronic shortage of water throughout most of Kenya. Thousands have died. Most of the rest are being kept alive by supplies of drinking water that are being shipped in from southern Europe. When I was in Mombassa six months ago, there were two or three tankers arriving and departing every week."

"And, do they take paying passengers," Mbonga asked.

"Not officially, but I'm sure if you made some enquiries you might be lucky. The men who crew these ships earn very little, if you understand me?"

Two days later, Mbonga was in a truck fifty miles from Mombassa. He and his new friend Abdul - who was smoking qat in quantities Mbonga suspected were not compatible with road safety - had not seen another soul for several hours. This part of Kenya had suffered dreadfully with the drought. For the last two seasons the rains had failed completely, and for several years prior they had been sporadic. The skeletons of dead cattle littered the roadside. Abdul reported having seen rotting human corpses along the route on more than one occasion.

It was something of surprise, therefore, to come upon two figures on foot, clearly struggling in the heat, a little way ahead of them. Abdul pulled over shortly before reaching them. They seemed not to have heard the truck approaching. Mbonga jumped down from the cab and walked after them. As soon as he called out they turned around. A man and a woman, both exhausted and badly dehydrated. As he approached them, the man collapsed, the woman trying unsuccessfully to break his fall.

"He's completely dehydrated," she explained. "He's been giving too much of his ration to me. I couldn't persuade him to drink more. He's so stubborn."

"How long have you been walking?" Mbonga asked.

"Ten days. We became lost on the second day, and only found our way back to the road a couple of hours ago. It's been hell: we ran out of food two days ago, and finished our water this morning."

Abdul had joined them at the side of the road, with a large bottle of water. "Just a little, don't let him have too much at once," he told the woman. After a couple of sips the man began to revive. "Let's move into the shade of the truck for a while. We have some food in the cab. I presume you're heading for Mombassa?" The woman nodded.

They sat in the shade for more than an hour while Alex and Malaika told their story. They were both doctors working at a refugee camp near the border with Tanzania. Ten days ago, the camp had been raided by an armed gang who stole everything of value, including the generator. This had left them with no means of communication, little water and virtually no food. Those refugees who were well enough left the camp, the others were abandoned to their fate. Alex and Malaika had no option but to set out for Mombassa on foot. Their own daughter was unwell, but as supply runs to the camp had become very sporadic, they had no idea when the next truck would arrive. They calculated they could make it to the main road within three days, and then find a lift to

Mombassa where they had friends who would take them in. Tragically, their three year old daughter, Zanzie, had become steadily more ill, and had died two days ago. Mbonga fought back tears as they talked of the little girl's last hours.

"We are both doctors," Alex concluded, "but there was nothing we could do to save the life of our beautiful little daughter."

All four of them climbed into the cab. After half an hour of silence, Alex asked Mbonga where he was from. Mbonga explained that he was from Swaziland, and the inevitable questions followed. Alex and Malaika seemed relieved to have something distract them, and they were able to confirm that Mombassa was the place to find water ships heading for Europe.

When they arrived, Alex directed them to their friend's house. Mbonga made sure there was someone to receive them before Abdul took him down to the port area, and wished him luck.

Security around the port was visible, but not especially tight. Mbonga headed straight for a bar inside the supposedly secure zone where he suspected ship's crew might be relaxing. Before long he had arranged passage to Marseilles, at a price, but with no questions asked. He would have to keep well away from the senior crew, and he would need to take all his own food. Water was no problem, as the crew had developed a rudimentary well-bucket system to get the remaining water out of the tanker's vast reservoirs. Whatever else might happen en route, Mbonga would not die of thirst. He arranged to meet his contact at 8pm, an hour before the ship was due to leave, and headed back into town to see what provisions he could find for the twelve day voyage.

Helen was feeling confident. There was a robust plan for dealing with the one remaining unknown – Kotov – and she was looking forward to renewing her acquaintance with Harry Noble. This morning she was meeting Sarah Bright-well to update her on the Kotov situation, but otherwise her schedule in Stockholm was light.

There was a knock at the door. Helen shouted across the fifteen metre width of the ridiculously large suite she had been given, "Come in," at which the British Prime Minister entered.

They looked at each other, Helen was perplexed and Sarah was laughing. "Well, I could have had someone call and confirm a time and venue for our meeting, but I'm four doors down the corridor and I guessed you'd be up by now."

"How exciting," Helen replied, "It's rather unusual to receive visitors unannounced. Should I assume you're still struggling with the formality of high office?"

"Honestly Helen, I can't stand it. 57 per cent of the British people elected me to lead them. I reckon that means I'm reasonably competent. But since becoming PM, I'm not allowed to do anything for myself. And don't tell me it's because of security. There's an army of hangers on, most of whom only exist to do things that I could do perfectly well for myself. I'm not the fucking queen."

Helen laughed.

"Sorry, rant over. It's worse when we travel, of course."

"One of the best things about the committee, and one of the key reasons for its success," Helen reached over and touched the wooden frame of the window, "is the fact that I was able to limit its staff. Okay, we've got a full roster of security people, but beyond the twelve committee members, we've done all this with two press people, one travel fixer, two researchers and a brilliant guy with a computer who makes sure everyone gets the meetings they request and nobody is double booked. Jane did all the drafting and re-drafting of the blueprint document herself. It's an object lesson in how to run a tight ship. I think I might write a book about it once it's all over."

"I guess you had the advantage of setting up your institution from scratch. Mine is centuries old, and has an uneasy relationship with the word 'change'."

"I know," Helen said excitedly, "let's strike a blow for self-help. I'll make you a cup of coffee with this natty little machine, okay?"

"Sounds great. Now, tell me about Kotov?"

Helen told Sarah what they had decided in the event of Kotov coming out against the blueprint. Sarah was impressed at the prospect of some diplomatic hardball. She understood that Kotov was under immense pressure at home, but reckoned that left to his own devices, he would strongly endorse the blueprint. They agreed that effectively blackmailing him to do something he really wanted to do anyway was legitimate.

Helen's phone rang. "Hi Stefan, how's it going. Yes, I'm with Sarah now. She's fine. What did Morel say? That's great. That just leaves the Germans. Yes, I'll sound her out. Thanks.

Bye now." She could see that Sarah was waiting to hear the *Rachel* other half of the conversation. "Stefan's spoken to Morel. He's given his full support and has agreed to speak to the Spanish PM this afternoon. That just leaves Chancellor Emmerich."

"He's very close to Kotov you know?"

"I know. Is it worth the risk of including the Germans when we don't even know if we are going to need this manoeuvre. If Kotov gets wind of plans to force his hand, it might push him in the other direction?"

"I'm not sure. You know them both better than I do."

"I'll talk to Ann Margaret. She'll know what to do. We are meeting Emmerich this afternoon anyway."

"Oh, he's not having a last minute change of mind is he?"

"No, I don't think so. Wants to talk about immigration."

"Ah yes, his pet topic."

It was already dark when Mbonga returned to the port, his rucksack stuffed with provisions. He was pleased to find his contact waiting for him outside an empty warehouse, not far from a rather rickety-looking gang plank towards the bow of the ship. He didn't know how big ships got, but this one was at least twenty times the length of the Illala. He wasn't sure whether that should make him more or less nervous.

The man, who had decided their relationship was now sufficiently established to introduce himself as Eric, led him up the gang plank and through a maze of corridors between the piles of metal containers on the ship's deck.

"Most of these are empty," he said, pointing at the wall of rusting yellow and blue painted boxes. "It's cheaper to leave them on the ship than to have them removed." After several turns, Mbonga began to lose his bearings. They descended a staircase onto another deck where Eric levered open a heavy metal door.

"Okay, this is where you stay. These are sleeping quarters for more crew, but we only have a skeleton, so they are not used. If anyone does come up here and find you just stay calm and tell them that you are a friend of Eric. They shouldn't give you any trouble. I'll come back in a couple of days and we can go and fill your water carrier." He pointed to a large jerry can full of water.

"And do I have to stay down here?"

"You can take a walk between the containers if you like, but stay forward of the stairwell, that way there's less chance of being spotted. You should be able to find your way to the bow. But be careful. If you fall overboard, nobody will ever know."

Mbonga shook his hand and thanked him. There was a light in the room, and a mattress with a blanket on the bed. Tomorrow he would explore the deck, but now he was ready to sleep. He locked the cabin door from the inside, unpacked the provisions he had bought, and laid them out under the small table beside his bed. He undressed, lay down and was asleep in seconds.

Chancellor Emmerich was a larger than life figure with the kind of moustache that went out of fashion with Flaubert. In public he was full of bluster, but in private he was a thoughtful, serious character. And this was the man across the table from whom Helen and Ann Margaret now sat.

"Helen," he began, "may I first take this opportunity to congratulate you on the blueprint, and the impressive progress you have made in persuading world leaders of the importance of implementing it."

"Thank you Sir, we really do feel that we are nearly there, after all these months of hard work."

"But I think there remains one area of concern, am I right?"

Helen looked at Ann Margaret. They were not sure what Emmerich was talking about. They had discussed whether to broach the subject of Kotov with the German but hadn't made a decision before the meeting began. Helen decided to be bullish.

"We are reasonably confident that any outstanding issues will be resolved by the time we reach Berlin," she answered.

"But I believe you are going to Moscow when you leave here?"

At least they knew that Emmerich and Kotov were in contact. "That is correct. Dr Jamali and I are meeting President Kotov on Thursday."

"And I'm sure you will have a very positive meeting." Emmerich's expression changed suddenly. He was no longer stringing them along. "Don't worry, I've made it absolutely clear to the old dog that he must support the blueprint. He knows as well as anyone the consequences of not doing so, especially for his own people."

"And you are confident that he will heed your advice?" Ann Margaret asked.

"What do I say? I am confident of the outcome, but I think that you should still make the trip to Moscow, if only to let Vladimir see that you take him seriously."

"Thank you for your advice, Sir. It is much appreciated."

Emmerich smiled; he clearly liked being appreciated. "Now, to the matter in hand," he said. "I wanted to talk to you about immigration, and the blueprint's provisions for international labour mobility. As you both know, Germany has struggled with the problem for many years. At times our efforts to integrate minorities have been successful; at other times, less so. But we are a little concerned about what will happen in the longer term, assuming, of course, that the blueprint is successfully implemented."

"But Mr President," Ann Margaret answered first, "as you will know, the blueprint cites research that suggests that as there is a gradual equalisation in wealth and economic opportunities between countries, far fewer people will be feel compelled to move to richer nations in search of work." She signalled to Helen to continue.

"There is considerable evidence that even among those migrants who have made successful lives, their preference would still be to have remained in their own country and contribute to the building of strong societies at home."

"Yes. We have conducted some research of our own among migrant populations in Germany, and the results give some cause for concern. You see, around 40 per cent of German citizens from ethnic minorities say they hope the blueprint will give their countries an economic boost so they can return home and make new lives for themselves; so they can reconnect with their roots, as it were."

"Yes," Helen said, "that is what we all hope for. The plight of many poor countries has been exacerbated by the loss of many capable people through migration."

"Exactly," said Emmerich, exasperated that they still hadn't taken his point. "What worries me is the impact on the German economy should there be a mass exodus of some of our most productive workers. Where are we going to find people with the skills to fill these jobs?"

Helen and Ann Margaret looked at each other.

"Well," Helen answered. "I really don't think you have to worry, Chancellor. There is unlikely to be a mass exodus immediately the blueprint is implemented. It will take time, possibly many years, for countries like Turkey or Bosnia to create economic opportunities comparable to those you have in Germany. By then, a new generation of Germans will be entering the labour market and you will have had ample time to invest in training and education to ensure your indigenous workforce is up to the job."

"Possibly," the Chancellor said slowly, "but what about all the jobs that Germans have become used to not having to do for themselves. In catering, for example, and cleaning."

"Well," said Helen again, "those jobs will have to pay whatever rate is necessary to persuade people to take them."

"And the market will work in the interests of all citizens, not just those with pre-existing wealth, or other arbitrarily-endowed privileges." Ann Margaret looked at Helen as she finished, as if seeking acknowledgment for a rather impressively crafted sentence.

The Chancellor played with the end of his moustache and nodded to himself. "As I said, ladies, the blueprint has my unwavering support. I shall think about what you have said this afternoon, and put my people to work on it. I'm sure this process is not going to be easy, but challenges are more easily risen to when there is at least some light at the end of the tunnel. Now if you'll excuse me, I have a hair appointment." Emmerich stood and followed his assistant out of the door.

Helen and Ann Margaret looked at each other again, and, after allowing sufficient time for the Chancellor to make his way out of earshot, burst out laughing.

"What an extraordinary man," Helen said.

"He is. As a German, I'm never sure whether to be embarrassed or honoured to be led by such an eccentric. But he is very clever Helen, and a man of his word."

"I like him, I think. Sometimes, though, when we are having these discussions about how things will turn out, I do wonder if I have the right to sound so confident. I mean, none of this has ever been tested in a laboratory."

"That's the problem, isn't it? We don't have a laboratory. Well we do I suppose; we have the laboratory of history and a long list of failed experiments."

"But might not the blueprint be another such experiment, doomed to failure at the hands of fragile and inadequate human beings?"

"I don't think so. For one thing, this experiment is quite unlike anything that has so far been tried. And for another, for the first time we are trying to establish a new moral order that encompasses the whole of humankind. Certainly, it's ambitious, but what else are we to do?"

Eighteen

Oscar Silverman's flight was three hours late, most of the delay being spent on the tarmac at JFK while a technical problem with the aircraft was rectified. By the time he landed in Berlin he was not in a good mood. He'd had too much time to think about what he was getting involved in. While he didn't doubt his mission was necessary and its success vital, he was uncomfortable with the company he had to keep. He knew Gunter well and had learned to trust him, but the German was not driven by principle. In fact he seemed to have no principles whatsoever. He had cut his teeth in the Stasi, working for the communists for more than a decade, presumably killing and otherwise denying basic freedoms to decent East Germans whose only crime was trying to escape the stifling oppression of the communist regime.

Quite how Gunter, almost uniquely among ex-Stasi officials, had managed to reinvent himself and become a trusted agent in Germany's intelligence service post-unification was a mystery, but Silverman had to put his doubts to one side. He needed the German for his knowledge of Berlin, and for his technical prowess.

He got through immigration and customs mercifully quickly and found a taxi, handing the driver the address of the café in Potsdam where they had arranged to meet.

He flicked on the TV in the back of the cab and found CNN. He'd become a bit of a news junkie since giving up alcohol and committing himself fully to this project. Helen George and her committee were in the news almost continuously now, and Silverman wanted to keep track of developments. The news from Stockholm was rather dull, however; the only newsworthy item concerned Kotov. There was 'mounting speculation' that the Russian was about to put a spanner in the works, but Silverman reckoned CNN knew no more about Kotov's intentions than he did.

The taxi pulled up outside the café five minutes before he was due to meet Gunter. He chose a table on the pavement and ordered a coffee. A few moments later he saw the German approaching and stood to greet him.

"Oscar, you look very well. It's good to see you."

"You too, Gunter. How are you?"

"Never been better. Thank you."

Silverman remembered this was Gunter's stock reply to any enquiry after his wellbeing. His English was not perfect, but he had practiced and memorised a vast array of stock responses. He was an intriguing character: charming but utterly devoid of empathy. Gunter must have killed many times. Silverman had, himself, conspired in many deaths, and personally given kill orders on more than one occasion, but he'd always kept at a distance from the execution of such orders. And his conscience was aided by the very real difference that he was motivated by principle, whereas the man now sat across the table from him was little more than a gun for hire. It both fascinated and concerned him that such a genial person could commit murder without any apparent impact on his mental health.

"I imagine," Silverman began, "that you have worked out why I am here?"

"Of course. You want to bring a halt to the summit process. You have exhausted diplomatic channels and your friend Howard Dawkins is struggling in his efforts to use the media to discredit certain committee members. You have therefore concluded that direct action is the only remaining option."

"You're very well informed."

"It always helps to be prepared." The German smiled.

"So can we take out the committee in Berlin?"

"Just the committee, or would you like to throw in a few of the summit delegates?"

"You have a plan then?"

"It won't be easy. The security cordon around the conference venue will be virtually impossible to penetrate, at least by conventional means."

"Is that why they've chosen Templehof, because it's easy to lock down?"

"I think so. Plus the fact that everything you could possibly need for such a meeting is on site. The runways are no longer in use of course, so they can't fly people straight in, but I suspect they'll run helicopter shuttles from Brandenberg. Unless we set up an anti-aircraft battery in Hasenheide Park, it'll be impossible to target delegates individually."

"So how do we do it?"

Gunter reached into his bag and pulled out a tatty map which he unfolded on the table.

"A relic from my days in the Stasi," he winked at Silverman, "but a very useful relic. Now, let me see."

The phone on the table next to Helen's bed rang. It was Mike.

"I've have President Solis for you. For some reason its proving impossible to patch her through to our network, but the hotel system is wired, and checks out secure."

"Thanks Mike." The line went dead for a moment.

"Helen, how are you?"

"Very well, Madam President, and you?"

"Pretty good. How are things there in Stockholm?"

"All fine. Even Emmerich is being helpful and cooperative"

"Any news of Kotov?"

"That's what I was hoping to discuss with you, Hilda. Saeed and I are meeting him on Thursday but our sense is that he could still go the wrong way. What do you think?"

"Well it's certainly a possibility. In Reykjavik, he seemed very upbeat about salvaging something positive from the ashes of a failed process."

"You were right to string him along. The last thing we want is for Kotov to feel isolated and plotted against."

"I guess so, but we can't let the Russians sabotage the blueprint if that really is Kotov's aim."

"No we can't," Helen paused. "which is why we've decided to isolate him, and plot."

"Go on."

"It's only a last resort, if and when Kotov comes out against the blueprint. We figure that if the key European powers, the Chinese and the US all let it be known that they will not trade with Russia outside the terms of the blueprint then he'll be forced to back down."

"It should work. Is everybody else onside?"

"The Europeans, yes. Zhang is talking to the Chinese today. And, er, I'm talking to you."

"On condition that the Chinese go for it, then count me in."

"Thanks Hilda."

"No problem. You're running this show. I just do what I'm told. I'm looking forward to seeing you in Houston."

"Me too. I think we're nearly there you know?"

"Uh huh."

Wen Zhang had mixed feelings about being back in China. He was pleased to be able to spend some time with his wife, but he enjoyed being part of the summit process and was slightly regretting his decision to skip the Stockholm summit in order to make the trip home. Showing his face in Beijing would do his future job prospects no harm, however. And, as it was turning out, the worrying business with Kotov made his presence particularly useful.

He had been sitting outside President Choi's office for twenty minutes before he was shown in.

"Zhang, good to see you again. I enjoyed lunch with you and your colleagues last week," the President said, walking around his enormous desk, grasping his former colleague's arm and shaking his hand vigorously.

"It's very good to be home, Mr President. It's almost a year since I was in China, you know?"

"And how we have missed you. Mind you, it feels like we've seen more of you in the last few months, what with all the media coverage, than we did when you were in government here. Tell me, how have you enjoyed it? Has it matched your expectations?"

"It has exceeded them by some way. It has been a privilege to work with so many accomplished people. As you might imagine, some were rather suspicious of me at the beginning, but I feel I have made some very good relationships from among my colleagues."

"And what about Robertson? What's he really like?"

"He is a passionate man, and sometimes he lets that passion get the better of his intellect, but I like him. It's good to be challenged occasionally and Robertson certainly knows his economics."

"I am sure the experience will stand you in good stead in the years to come."

"I think so, Mr President." The two men stared at each other. "I'm afraid I'm not just here on a social call. There is one rather urgent matter we need to discuss in respect of the committee's work, I'm afraid."

"Of course, go on."

"I imagine you are aware of the media speculation over the Russians and the possibility that they will decide not to support the blueprint."

"Yes. Kotov is such a cultured man. I can't believe he's playing this dangerous game."

"I imagine he has political difficulties at home which are influencing his decision, or rather his lack of one."

"I always thought that Russia was even less ready for the burden of democracy than we are here in China." Zhang smiled but said nothing. China's continuing lack of democratic reform was a point of tension between the two men.

"Do you want me to speak to him? I probably have as good a chance as anyone of making him see sense."

"That would be most helpful Mr President. However, before you do, perhaps I might appraise you of a contingency plan we are discussing in case President Kotov does come out against the blueprint at the Tbilisi summit."

Zhang was pretty sure that Choi would join with the Europeans and Americans in forcing Kotov's hands, but he knew better than to presume. He was thus relieved when, after thinking for a few moments, Choi gave his support.

"I'll speak to Kotov this afternoon," he said. "Obviously I'll mention nothing of this contingency plan. Let's hope we don't have to use it. It would be a shame if the blueprint could only be implemented after an act of diplomatic blackmail."

"I agree, Mr President. And with your help, I'm sure we can avoid that necessity."

He probably didn't need his disguise, but Gunter figured that the surveillance cameras around Berlin would be working overtime. By changing his appearance with each visit, he would ensure that once the operation was over, it would be impossible to trace it back to him. With the sum of money Oscar Silverman was promising, a very comfortable retirement in Switzerland was within reach.

His first port of call was Templehof itself. The summit was still three weeks away, nonetheless he was surprised to find only a small area – presumably the designated site of the security command centre – had so far been cordoned off. He would have free access to most of the complex, including the conference centre, the hotels, the leisure facilities and the concert hall. While his plan did not require access to any of these, he wanted to check out as much of the place as he could. He knew there had been considerable renovation in recent years; his old site plans would be out of date.

As he made his way around, attaching first to a group of Japanese tourists, and then offering himself as an informal guide to an American couple, he was able to take all the photographs he needed. He rather enjoyed chatting with the other visitors, and agreeing with them what an honour it was for Germany to be hosting the final summit.

Although the interior of the former terminal building had been transformed since Gunter had worked there secretly in the 1980s, the original superstructure was untouched. At that time, with Germany still divided, and with Templehof falling under American jurisdiction, the Stasi had found a way into the old airport. And as far as Gunter knew, they were never detected. All he needed to do now was ensure that the means of access he had used almost forty years earlier were still viable.

Apart from some conversations to finalise the plan for dealing with a Kotov veto, and others to remind people it was time to start thinking about the transitionary period, post-Berlin, Helen had done very little work in Stockholm. She'd spent lots of time with Sarah Brightwell and with Rita – the two of them had got on very well – but the three days had been mercifully uneventful.

Before flying to Moscow early the following morning, there was a yet another reception to negotiate. Helen and Sarah went down together to find a convivial buzz about the large ballroom. It was a relief to Helen to find her companion more in demand than she was, so at the first opportunity she made her excuses and went off to rescue Safiya who was looking bored with the company of a middle-ranking Norwegian diplomat. Having escorted Safiya to safety, they looked for somewhere to sit, eventually settling for a sofa within view of a table where Saeed and Jemma were engaged in animated conversation with the Portuguese Prime Minister and his wife.

"But really Dr Jamali," she heard the Prime Minister's wife say, "do you honestly think entrepreneurship will expand if competition ceases to be the key motivating factor in economic behaviour."

"I certainly do," Jamali replied. "It comes down to the nature and context of competition. Under current arrangements, the threat of insecurity forces people to compete with each other. We are told that there is a limit to the quantity of goods that can be produced, and that if we don't compete for our share, we will lose out to others."

"But surely," the Prime Minister joined in, "there is plenty of evidence for people losing out in the competition for scarce resources. I read only last week that a billion and half people in the world don't have enough food."

"I too read that report, and another that suggested a similar number are seriously overweight. The conclusion to be drawn from those figures is that far from there being a shortage of resources, in this case food, the world is producing enough for everyone."

"The problem," Jemma took up the argument, "is not one of scarcity, but with the systems of production and distribution, how they are funded and who controls them. And, of course, the underlying belief system which assumes that an economy based on competition is the best fit with human nature. With ownership and access to productive resources concentrated in the hands of a minority, competition serves to create resource scarcity which need not exist."

"And you think that by forcing people to cooperate, the problems with production will disappear?" asked the Prime Minister.

"It's not a question of forcing people. Certainly the blueprint places great emphasis on the need for cooperation within and between communities and nations, but it's also about creating conditions in which people can take responsibility for there own wellbeing, by giving them control over the factors that determine economic security."

"But doesn't democracy already give people a say in how things are run?" asked the Prime Minister's wife.

"To an extent, yes. But it hasn't made much difference to the balance of economic power over the last several decades," Saeed said.

"But what about the link between competition and efficiency?" the Prime Minister asked. "When firms have to compete for market share they are under an obligation to minimise their costs and make production as efficient as possible."

"Yes, but efficiency isn't the only criteria against which performance should be assessed," Jemma explained. "If two competing firms engage in a race to the bottom, constantly reducing costs to cut prices, they have to dispense with workers. They still control access to the land and materials used by the business, but they employ fewer people. Those people have no access to resources of their own. By constantly competing with others, firms come to control an ever greater share of resources while at the same time permitting fewer people a real stake in the economy. The logical conclusion is an economy in which a small number of people control all economic resources, while employing as few others as possible to produce goods and services for two classes of citizen: business owners and employees. In many countries, these two classes already constitute less than half the population, and the rich nations are heading in the same direction. How can the entire productive base of an economy be controlled only for the benefit of a minority?"

"And as for efficiency," Saeed weighed in, "there are many studies which document the waste and duplication of effort that arises in a competition-based economy, when several firms compete to bring a new product to the market, but only one succeeds."

"Okay. Let us accept your argument for a moment. What about motivation? How will people be motivated to work in a cooperative economy?"

Jemma looked at Saeed, he nodded that she should answer.

"Millions of people are already motivated to work outside the competitive economy: in the caring professions, in teaching, for charities. We hope to create an environment in which more people will be motivated by recognition of common interests, one which exploits the desire among people to cooperate rather than compete."

"Do you think the instincts of those individuals who do thrive on competition will be extinguished overnight?"

"Of course not," Saeed answered. "But we do believe that while those instincts may be innate, they only come to dominate because they are encouraged. My bet is that when they are not so encouraged, they will lie dormant, and a spirit of cooperation will emerge in their place."

"But you are talking about changing the psychology of billions of people," the Prime Minister's wife said, still unconvinced.

"Not changing psychologies so much, rather drawing out a part of the psyche that has been neglected and suppressed in many people." Jemma answered. "Certainly there will be some people unable to change, but the research points to their being in the minority. And in any case, the next generation is being born all the time. You shouldn't underestimate the power of the environment to help shape people's personalities, and especially their world view."

"Most people accept that if children grow up in a secure and loving environment, even today, with all the pressures of commercialisation that bear down on them, they usually grow into compassionate and caring human beings. Imagine what could be achieved if those sentiments were routinely encouraged." Jemma looked at the couple sat opposite them. She wondered if they were satisfied.

"And Ms Wiseman," asked the Prime Minister's wife, "will you be returning to New Zealand after the Berlin summit?"

Helen enjoyed the evening. No crisis to deal with, no argumentative heads of government to placate. Just before 11pm she decided to return to her room. She thought she might able to catch Rudolf, and she was in luck.

"Darling, how are you? How is Stockholm?"

"It's been great so far. No problems at all. Just one big European love in."

"Excellent. Have you been able to rest a little?"

"Yes, I feel very relaxed. How are things going there?"

"Considering my only daughter is getting married in four days time, very well I think."

"And how is Jenifer?"

"She's okay. And having finally got to see her and Dieter together, I'm beginning to understand what she sees in him."

"Would you rather she were marrying a musician?"

"Heavens no. A physician is just fine. I think he's a good man. I was relieved to discover he does have interests beyond medicine and my daughter; even if he can't tell the difference between Mozart and Beethoven."

Helen laughed. "Well I can't wait until Friday. I've missed you."

"Me too. I think it should be reasonably stress free. And at least we'll have some time together once the happy couple have departed."

"That will be good. Is Jenifer there? Can I have a quick word?"

"Of course, I'll hand you over. See you on Friday. Oh, and good luck in Moscow."

"Harry come in, sit down, I'll be two minutes."

Kotov returned to his chair and leant over some papers, reading. After a couple of minutes he looked in Harry's direction, as if his face might help him make whatever decision he had to make. He looked down again, picked up his pen and, with a flourish, signed the bottom of the document he'd been reading. He got up, and walked over to the large table, taking his usual seat opposite Harry.

"So Harry, your friend Helen George will be here tomorrow to persuade me to sign up to the blueprint. What do you think I should do?"

"I think you should listen to what she has to say, and think about it. You're under no obligation to make up your mind before the Tbilisi summit, so thank her for taking the time to visit you, and tell her you'll give her your decision in due course."

"Okay, Harry, that advice I will take. But you still believe my decision should be not to support the blueprint. Even if it throws the world into political turmoil?"

"I'm hardly going to change my position now, Mr President. But I will respect your decision, whatever it is."

"I'm sure you will, Harry. I'm sure you will. Now is there anything further we need to do by way of preparation?"

"I don't think so. But there is something I need to talk to you about."

"Go on."

"Does the name Zaytzev mean anything to you?"

"Yuri Zaytzev? Works for Kutuzov in the Foreign Ministry."

"Yes, that's the one."

"What about him?"

"He's paid me a couple of visits, once soon after I arrived, the second on Sunday morning, when he, well, abducted me, just outside here." Harry waved in the general direction of Red Square.

"Tell me everything, Harry."

"It's quite simple really, Zaytzev wants you to veto the blueprint, and he has been putting pressure on me to encourage you towards that decision."

"But you've been doing that anyway."

"That's true, but as I said, I will respect your decision, even if you support the blueprint. I rather get the impression that Mr Zaytzev will not."

"Who the hell does Zaytzev think he is? Or Kutuzov for that matter? I am President, and constitutionally I have the right to make this decision."

"I'm not sure Zaytzev necessarily limits himself to activities that fall within the constitution, or the law for that matter."

"Has he threatened you?"

"Well, no. He has threatened you, and indirectly the entire summit process."

"Fucking Zaytzev." Kotov used the expletive as if for the first time.

"I have to say he's not my cup of tea, either."

"But what can he do Harry? I have the full support of police and the armed forces."

"That's very good to hear Mr President. And the government has a firm grip on the state's military resources?"

"I have no reason to believe not." Kotov sounded confident, though Harry wasn't sure he was being completely honest.

Nineteen

"You are coming to the demo aren't you?" Antonella asked Tito, as they struggled to reconcile a pile of restaurant orders with a mounting backlog of dishes awaiting service.

"I don't really see the point. Why would you go on a demo to protest for something? It's not as if anyone is opposing the blueprint. The government is a hundred per cent behind it. So is everyone else."

"You don't get it, do you? This is the most important week of the entire summit process. The Russians still haven't announced their support, and if they decide not to, the whole thing is over."

"But what difference will a few thousand people demonstrating in São Paulo make to the President of Russia?"

"It's not just São Paulo; millions of people are turning out all over the world to put pressure on the Russians."

"Okay, I'll come. But first can we sort out this mess, or neither of us will have a job tomorrow. Here, take these two, table 24."

An hour later, having narrowly avoided a riot in the restaurant, they set off for Praça Arnaldo Martinelli, the starting point for the march. As they approached the square, they were consumed by a massive crowd; it was clearly going to be a huge event.

Antonella had arranged to meet some friends from the blueprint club by a statue at the south-eastern entrance to the square, but she quickly realised there was little chance of making it to their rendezvous point. They would just have to go with the flow.

The atmosphere was electric; tens of thousands of people waving banners, singing and, to the extent that the crush would allow, dancing their way slowly along the route. Many of the banners made direct appeals to the Russian leader.

It took three hours to cover five kilometres, back past the Hilton to the Parque Villa-Lobos where the vast crowd was addressed by several celebrities and politicians, culminating in an unannounced appearance by the President herself. She spoke only briefly, but her words struck a chord with Antonella.

"We have achieved much in this country over the last decade," she began. "Many other countries now cite Brazil as a shining example of the possibility of progress towards a more just and sustainable society. When I meet other world leaders, they frequently tell me how much they wish their country could replicate Brazil's successes."

"I usually reply by thanking them for their kind words, but reminding them of the other side of Brazil's success story: the millions whom we haven't been able to help out of poverty; and those whose lives continue to be blighted by the effects of climate change because other countries have been too slow to reduce their carbon emissions."

"The truth, I tell them, is that Brazil has hit an impenetrable wall. We cannot make further progress towards eradicating poverty or preserving the planet as a viable home for future generations until the rest of the world works with us, collectively, towards the same goal. The blueprint finally offers the world a chance to start cooperating. So today, I would like first to thank you, all of you, for turning out in such numbers, and for creating such a fantastic atmosphere. And I would urge President Kotov of Russia to give his unequivocal support to the blueprint. It is, without doubt, the most important political initiative in human history."

As President di Soto's final sentence echoed around the park, there was an explosion of cheering and shouting.

"You know we're breaking your golden rule, the two of us travelling together." It hadn't crossed Helen's mind until Saeed mentioned it, as they were sat in a queue at the end of the runway at Arlanda airport.

"Christ, I'd totally forgotten. It's too late now anyway," she shrugged as the plane started accelerating.

"You've been very relaxed the last few days. Do you think we've finally turned a corner?"

"Oh, I don't know Saeed. When I focus on the mechanics of the process and the progress we've made, I feel very positive. But when I think about what it's going to mean when it comes to implementation, well, then it's not all out there anymore is it? It's in here." She gestured in the general direction of her heart.

"How do you mean?"

"Well, there's quite a large part of me that wants to retire to France and live out the rest of my life in peace and quiet."

"That should still be possible."

"I suppose so. But who knows what's going to happen, really? Most of the stuff in the blueprint is completely untested? I worry about my own future too, you know."

312

"Of course you do. We all do. And I agree, there are no guarantees. But without change the one thing we can be certain of is an extremely uncertain future."

"I know. And don't worry, you won't catch me wobbling in public." She looked at him and smiled. "Now, tell me about Kotov. What's he like? What did he get up to as a young man?"

"He has a brilliant mind. One of those irritating people who sails through every academic challenge without effort. He had a strong anti-establishment streak; hated all forms of authority."

"Bit of an ego?"

"Yes he was, but then he was also incredibly generous and supportive of those he considered less fortunate."

"Did you take you under his wing then?"

"Oh no," he laughed, "Kotov considered me his intellectual equal, which of course I wasn't, so he set very high standards for me, and when I failed to meet his expectations, he would tear into me as if I had intentionally slighted him."

"And you never had any inkling that he would make a move into politics."

"Well, yes and no. He wanted to be top dog, intellectually. And in the three years we spent together, I never came across anyone able to challenge him on that score. But he detested conventional politics; especially those of his own country. As far as he was concerned, anyone who aspired to power through the democratic process was a megalomaniac. And if they claimed to be in politics to do good, then they were charlatans."

"Do you suppose he's modified his view in the meantime?"

"I doubt it. I suspect he decided to go into politics because he concluded that Russia couldn't be left in the hands of the Putinistas and others he considers incompetent or corrupt."

"So what's our strategy for the meeting?"

"I think we play it straight. We listen to his concerns and try to allay them in the same way we have with every other head of government over the last two years."

"And am I allowed to have a bit of fun with Harry Noble?"

"I don't see why not. Be careful though. Kotov respects loyalty, and has a soft spot for the underdog."

Robertson and his wife had managed to escape the Vancouver hotel where they'd been holed up for most of the last week. It was not the best environment in which to save a marriage. Now they could enjoy a couple of nights at a cabin in the mountains not far from Kamloops. Twenty-four hours in, things were going well.

The cabin was twenty miles from civilization. There were a number of others in the vicinity, mainly used at weekends for fishing and hunting trips. But the nearest was three miles away, so there was little likelihood of being disturbed. And as Jay's father had smuggled them out of Vancouver in the back of his obscenely large SUV, the media had no idea they were here.

Having demanded nothing but apology and explanation for three days, Julia now found it necessary to forbid Jay from using the word 'sorry'. She understood that he meant it. And he understood that his shame and guilt would never compensate for his cruel and idiotic behaviour.

"You know," she said, as Jay poured wine from a just-opened second bottle, "in another three weeks you'll be unemployed."

"What a pleasant thought," Jay sighed.

"Seriously? Are you looking forward to the process being over?"

"I'm looking forward to spending more time with you and Nathalie; in fact I'd be quite happy spending all my time with you and Nathalie."

"I really can't see you not working. You could have a little time off though. That would be nice. But you're really not going to miss the committee?"

"I'll miss some of them. Helen especially, she is truly inspirational. I'm sure I'll never work for anyone as good as her. But not the process; not the meetings and the endless diplomatic schmoozing. It really isn't my thing."

"So back to academia then?"

"I guess so, but where?"

"I imagine you have the pick of any research university in the world."

"Then perhaps we need to have that conversation about where we are going to live while Nathalie goes through school."

"You know what I think. I'd love to be near my folks; they don't get to see enough of her. And I don't think your parents would mind."

"I'm sure they wouldn't. They'd be glad for an excuse to travel, and I know McGill would have me back like a shot. And it's so much more relaxed than Yale."

"When would you start?"

"Next fall I guess. That would give us a year to move, settle in, and spend some time together."

Julia leant across the table towards him and they kissed. For the first time, Jay felt they might have a future together.

Immediately upon landing in Moscow, a flight attendant escorted Helen and Saeed to the front of the cabin. They were greeted at the top of the staircase by a good looking young man in a sharp suit who introduced himself as Vitaly. As they walked across the tarmac he explained that he was President Kotov's personal assistant, and would be taking them straight to the Kremlin.

They settled into the back seat of a very large limousine, with Vitaly next to the driver.

"And will anyone else be joining our meeting with the President?" Helen asked. She noticed the Russian's shoulders stiffen in front of her.

"Anyone else?" he asked, slightly flustered, "I'm not sure. Er, possibly."

Helen looked at Saeed who was smiling. They spent the rest of the rather fast journey in silence. At the Kremlin, a series of gates opened automatically allowing them deep inside the historic palace. Vitaly led them up a grand staircase and into a beautifully decorated anteroom. He suggested they might like to take advantage of the bathroom facilities through a door at its far end, and said he would return in a few minutes.

They were both in and out of the bathroom quickly and waiting to be collected when Kotov himself burst in.

"Jamali, how wonderful to see you," he boomed, giving Saeed a hug before turning to Helen. "And Ms George.

How have we managed not to meet before now? I really can't understand it. It is my great pleasure." He took her hand and kissed it.

"The honour is all mine Mr President," she said, impressed at the force of nature before her.

Vitaly appeared at the door, looking slightly embarrassed and even more irritated.

"Ah Vitaly, there you are. Right. Follow me. Oh, and Helen, it's alright to call you Helen is it? You must call me Vladimir. Jamali and I will address each other by our surnames. Why change the habits of a lifetime?"

They walked along a corridor decorated with acres of gold leaf before Vitaly, who had been walking ahead of them, pushed open a pair of heavy, leather-clad doors and stood aside so they could enter. As they did so, Harry Noble stood up from the table and moved towards them.

"Harry," Helen exclaimed, "what on earth are you doing here?" She said it in a way that would sound convincing to Kotov but make it abundantly clear to Noble that she knew about his involvement.

"I had thought about contacting you, but I know how much you like surprises," Harry played along. He was disturbed that Helen had rumbled him, but grateful she hadn't made things uncomfortable in front of Kotov.

"Perhaps you should introduce me to your colleague?" Harry suggested.

"Of course, Saeed Jamali, Harry Noble. Harry and I go back a long way, although I had no idea he was advising President Kotov." Saeed shook Noble's hand, smiled and nodded, but said nothing. He was struggling against a fit of giggles to keep up the charade.

/s "Right," Kotov said, let's get down to business." The President sat down next to Noble, with Helen and Saeed opposite. Vitaly took a seat at the far end of the oval table.

"First," began Kotov, I must congratulate you both on the progress you have made. It has been remarkable and inspiring to see nations cooperating so closely. It is a process of which I would very much like to be a part."

"Thank you, Mr President." Helen decided to let Kotov make the running.

"However, while I strongly support many of the principles outlined in the blueprint, as well as the overall thrust of the project, I am charged with making a decision on behalf of more than 100 million people. I have to be convinced that my decision is in the best interests of all, or at least the great majority, of Russians."

"Of course, Mr President. Many other heads of government have struggled with the same question," Helen said.

"I am sure, and in every case so far, you have managed to persuade them to support the blueprint. I suppose this is your opportunity to help me also to see the light."

"I would urge you to make a decision you are comfortable with. That said, as I am sure you know, it isn't just the Russian people who will be affected by your decision. It's difficult to see how the blueprint could be implemented without the participation of your great nation. It's also difficult to see how the world can escape its current problems without the blueprint."

"If I may say something, Mr President," Harry asked.

"Please, Harry."

"Helen, you present the decision as if President Kotov has no option but to support or reject the blueprint as it stands. But is not the point of these summits to negotiate on the detail of the blueprint and the timetable for implementation?"

"Of course. But so far, where delegate governments have had serious concerns we have tried to iron these out ahead of the summits."

"And, as you will know, a number of changes have been made to the blueprint as a result of those negotiations," added Jamali.

"Indeed, but most of those changes have been to the wording, have they not?"

"That's true. We haven't been challenged on substantive questions of policy, principle or vision. But that is what we are here for."

"Okay," Kotov cut in. "I have a proper challenge for you."

Helen looked at Saeed who was impassive, and then at Noble, who looked like he had no idea what Kotov was about to say.

"At the risk of upsetting our friend Harry here, I am going to be frank with you. If it were up to me, if I didn't have the complex minefield of Russian politics to navigate, then I would sign up to the blueprint today. But it is not that easy. Ordinary Russians have been suffering terribly for far too long. Those who are not drinking themselves to death are ripe for insurrection. And there are many influential people who are opposed to the potential loss of sovereignty, who would not hesitate to exploit the situation."

"But Mr President. Your position is not so weak. Your personal ratings are very high. Surely you can appeal to the better nature of Russians not to join any insurrection if it were to come to that."

It was exactly what Helen had wanted to say, except that the words came from Noble. There was silence for a moment while all five of them digested what Noble had said, and waited to see if he would try to extricate himself from the hole he had seemingly just dug.

"Well," Kotov said eventually. "You at least seem to have converted Mr Noble to your cause, Helen."

"I think, Mr President, that Harry was suggesting you should not let your decision be influenced by the threat of popular insurrection, whatever its motivation."

Harry nodded gratefully.

"No matter. You see my problem. I am the elected President. I have all of the responsibility, but I don't have all the power. I am afraid that by publicly announcing my support for the blueprint, I might unleash a chain of events which I cannot control."

"Kotov, do you think it would help if we gave you more time to make your announcement?" Saeed asked.

"But how long can you give me? Whether I announce at the beginning or the end of the Tbilisi summit, it won't make much difference. And we can't afford any uncertainty in the three days between Tbilisi and Berlin."

"I think we could give you until the Wednesday," Helen said. That really only leaves a day until Berlin by which time the media focus will be firmly on us."

"A good day to release bad news."

"But it won't be bad news to most Russians." Saeed said.

The President thought for a moment. "If we could delay my announcement until the Wednesday after the Tbilisi summit, it might help."

"Does that mean that you've already made your decision, Mr President?" Helen asked.

Kotov looked at Noble, who took a breath, as if about to say something.

"No," Kotov beat him to it. "You know what I want to do, but I haven't yet made a decision. I will decide by Wednesday 11 October at the latest, and I will give you as much notice of my decision as I can."

At dinner that evening Helen and Saeed decided not to talk about Kotov. In some respects they felt they had made progress, but Kotov's refusal to give a commitment was frustrating. Midway through the main course, the head waiter came over with a message. Mr Noble was outside. He would wait until they had finished dinner, unless he was welcome at their table. Helen looked at Saeed, who nodded.

As Harry approached the table, the waiter moved in behind him with a chair. "Helen, Dr Jamali. Thank you for seeing me."

"No problem, Harry. How did you track us down?"

"I managed to persuade Vitaly to release the sensitive information of your dining location." They laughed.

"And what can we do for you, Mr Noble?" Saeed asked.

"Please, call me Harry. I'm afraid there's something afoot that is of much more concern than President Kotov's decision over the blueprint." Harry said, almost in a whisper.

"Go on," Helen said.

"On my second day here, I was approached by a man named Zaytzev who works at the Foreign Ministry. Nasty fellow. Opposed to the blueprint. He wanted to apply pressure through me. On Sunday morning, along with one of his thugs, he abducted me for a short time and made it clear that if Kotov came out in support of the blueprint, he would take action himself to make sure it was never implemented."

"Have you told Kotov about this?"

"I have, but he reckons the Foreign Ministry doesn't have the power or resources to derail the process. I assume, however, that this is what he was referring to in our discussions today. He hasn't discussed it with me, but I wonder if he knows that the threat could be genuine."

"Do you have any idea what form this threat might take?" Saeed asked.

"I have no information, but if Zaytzev's people are anything like Zaytzev, it won't be a diplomatic initiative."

"Okay. Thanks Harry. I'll get Mike onto it as soon as we've finished here. Now, would you like to stay for desert and perhaps help us with this bottle of wine? I told Saeed we shouldn't order a second."

"Ooh, may I see?" Helen handed him the bottle. "Oh yes. Bonnes-Mares, 2005. Kotov didn't offer me anything this good."

Twenty

The traffic on the way to the airport was diabolical. Although Helen was travelling with a bodyguard, being on personal business meant no fast tracking through diplomatic channels, so she was very relieved when she arrived at check-in with just five minutes to spare.

She had left Saeed eating breakfast. He was flying to New York later in the day and would be briefing Hilda Solis on progress in Moscow before making his way to Houston to prepare for the next summit.

The thought of not making it to Jenifer's wedding was quite as stress-inducing as the possibility of Kotov vetoing the blueprint. Now she was airborne she could finally relax.

She had spoken to Mike Dixon the previous evening to alert him to Noble's news about Zaytzev and was slightly surprised not to have heard anything back. She called up his number.

"Hi Helen. Are you on the plane?"

"I am. Anything on our Russian friend?"

"Nothing specific but his character references are not good I'm afraid. Well connected and influential with all the wrong people, and a ruthless bastard by all accounts. I think Noble is probably right to be concerned."

"Thanks Mike, let me know if you come up with anything specific."

"Will do."

"Oh, Mike. Any news on Citra?"

"None at all. I'm starting to worry about that as well. She's disappeared.

"Okay. Keep me posted."

Helen was pleased to see Rudolf waiting alone for her as she pulled her case through customs and out into the arrivals hall. At least they would have half an hour together before being plunged into the sanity-threatening environment of a family wedding. It was mainly Rudolf's family, although she was looking forward to seeing her father, who had recovered sufficiently well from a course of chemotherapy to make the trip.

"How's it going?" she asked, as Rudolf released her from a long embrace.

"I would say the atmosphere is a little tense, but no tantrums yet. She wants it to be perfect, and we have this rather large elephant in the room."

"Have you heard anything from Agnes?"

"No. Nobody has. I do know that she received the invitation. I really hope she doesn't turn up. A wedding is not the right place to heal a severely fractured relationship between mother and daughter. Anyway, you've been more of a mother to her than that woman."

"That's kind of you to say, but I'm not her mother. How are you bearing up?"

"Oh pretty well. You know how much I dislike big family occasions, but I've been quite enjoying myself for the last couple of days. I've spent a lot of time with your father. He's seems very well."

"That is good news."

"And so proud of his daughter."

Helen put both arms around Rudolf's waist and walked sideways beside him.

"So what's the plan for Sunday?"

"Ah, you'll like this. I have a meeting in Paris on Monday. So I thought we could take the train, have dinner at Les Mauvais Garcons and spend the night at the Duc de Saint-Simon."

"Sounds perfect. What's your meeting about?"

"Working out the programme for some big shindig in Berlin in a couple of weeks time. Apparently the French President is chairing the committee."

"Don't worry. Morel likes me. You won't have any problems. I've missed you, you know. I hope we are going to get some time together before Paris"

"I'll do my best."

They sank into the back of a taxi. Helen looked into the rear view mirror to see the taxi driver looking uninterested, before running her hand up the inside of Rudolf's thigh.

Jenifer was thrilled that Helen had made it. After a host of introductions, mostly to people whom she had never met, and who were painfully in awe of her, Jenifer insisted that Helen go upstairs to see her dress. Helen promised she would be right up, but first she had to find her father.

Rudolf suggested she look outside on the terrace, and there he was, sat at a table with a pot of tea in front of him, looking into the distant countryside.

"How's the tea?"

"Oh you know, the standard stuff you get in hotels everywhere."

"Tell me about it."

"Have you not found a single hotel that serves decent tea on your travels?"

"Actually, the place in Jakarta wasn't too bad."

"I'm surprised you weren't drinking something stronger in Jakarta, what with all the shenanigans."

"Oh I was, believe me."

The old man turned to look at his daughter. "How are you my darling. It's been wonderful having you in the corner of my sitting room every evening, but I have been worried about you. On occasions you have seemed a little tired."

"I'm fine dad, honestly," she said, bending down to kiss him on the forehead. "How are you?"

"Well, it seems I'm better than anyone thought possible. I have another scan next week, and if that's clear then I'm officially in remission. And according to the literature my life expectancy, which as you know until very recently was just six months, will suddenly be extended by forty years."

"That'll make you a hundred and twenty three."

"I know. Marvellous, isn't it?"

"So you're going to be around to see the blueprint implemented then?"

"You bet I am. I rather enjoy telling people that my daughter has some involvement with the blueprint. Of course back in Donegal, nobody believes me."

"Well, it's good to keep your feet on the ground."

"Ah, that it is." He looked at up at her. "I am so very proud of you, you know."

Helen nodded. "I know."

"And so would your mother have been."

"Now steady on. If Ma was here she'd already have got wind of the problem with the Russians and would be taking me to task for not having it sorted yet."

He laughed. "She wasn't an easy woman, your mother. But then growing up with her was good preparation for what came after, was it not?"

"I guess so, although I've still to meet another woman like her."

Rudolf joined them on the terrace. "She's looking well, isn't she Brian?"

"She's beautiful."

Helen saw a tear in the corner of his eye. "Right," she said. "I have to go and find Jenifer. Something about a dress?"

The rest of the day passed very quickly. Jenifer looked lovely in her dress, and Helen had little trouble persuading her of the fact. The afternoon turned out to be rather like a summit, with Helen chatting to lots of people for the first time, most of them falling over themselves to tell her how wonderful she was. There was a formal dinner which began thankfully early. Helen didn't want a late night, but she still found herself alone in the bar with Jenifer after everyone else had gone to bed.

"So, are you all set?"

"I think so. He's the right guy for me. I should know. I've had so many relationships with wrong guys. And he's grown up a lot in the last two years."

"Your dad likes him you know?"

"I know he does. He's been really great. But then he never was the problem."

"I presume you are not hoping for any unannounced arrivals in the morning?"

"My mother you mean?"

Helen nodded.

"God I hope not. I'm not sure I could cope."

"Do you have any idea where she is?"

"Last heard of holed up on a yacht with a Saudi prince and an endless supply of champagne."

"It'll be cheap champagne. Saudi princes have lost a lot of value in the last few years." They both laughed.

"Seriously though, I do hope for some kind of reconciliation at some point."

"Don't give up. I came to an understanding with my mother before she died. I'm not saying it made up for all that went before. And your situation is different. With my mum it was a case of things never being good enough, and her vile temper. From what Rudolf has told me, you endured serious maternal neglect bordering on abuse."

"I still think it was my fault, though. I don't remember her drinking when dad was still at home."

"That's because you were in bed by the time things got serious. Your dad left because he wasn't going to let her drag you and him down with her. He probably saved your life."

"I'm not sure it was worth it."

"Hey, stop that. You've had more than your share of troubles, but you came out the other side. That's because you were strong, and because your father loved you. And look at you now. You're healthy, you're beautiful. You have the world at your feet."

"I don't want to have kids."

Helen was surprised at the apparent change of subject. "You don't have to have children, sweetheart. God knows there are enough born every day. The human race can cope with one more redundant womb you know? And I don't get the impression that Dieter is driven by the desire to procreate."

"Thanks Helen. I'm so glad you're here."

"Me too. Now I promised your father I'd only be ten minutes an hour ago, and you need a good night's sleep."

The following morning Helen was sitting in the bar trying to remain oblivious to the increasingly frenetic activity around her. She spotted Rudolf looking in her direction, somewhat bewildered.

"How's it going?" she mouthed across the crowded room.

He shrugged by way of reply. He was obviously not in control of events, but didn't seem overly concerned. As Helen smiled back at him, her phone rang. It was Mike.

"Hello Mike, I assume this is important. You know what day it is?"

"Sorry Helen. It's Citra. She's surfaced in DC, staying at a hotel used as a safe venue by the CIA. I'm trying to get more information, but I thought you should know as soon as possible." Mike paused, but before Helen could say anything, he continued. "You know this could connect her to Dawkins."

"That would seem a fair conclusion. Okay, let Saeed, Daniel and Jane know. I'll be out of contact for about three hours, but I'll check in once the party starts. And Mike, brief Kersen would you? Get him to phone Anna Sianturi, see if she's heard anything."

"Will do. What about Jay?"

"No. Leave Jay for now. Is Rick still with him?"

"Yes, apparently he and Julia are up in the mountains, and things are going well."

"Oh Jesus. Poor Julia. Thanks Mike. I'll call you when I can."

Rudolf had seen her take the call, and was hovering as she hung up. He looked at her with eyebrows raised.

"We agreed not to talk about work until after the wedding," she said.

"Don't worry. I'm feeling calm. What's the gossip?"

"Citra, in Washington, with Dawkins."

"Shit."

Harry was waiting in the lobby of his hotel for a car to arrive. It was his last evening in Moscow and he was dining with the Kotovs before flying back to London. There had been no further sign of Zaytzev since the excursion on Sunday, but Harry knew he might appear at any moment. He was nervous.

He saw Kotov's driver come through the revolving doors and walk towards him. "Hello again Mr Noble. Please follow me, Sir."

They were soon gliding through the light Moscow traffic towards Kroylatskoye. Harry had decided to tackle Kotov again over Zaytzev. He wasn't sure how far he should push, nor what Kotov's reaction would be if he overstepped the mark. But he had to make his point. He was convinced Zaytzev would stop at nothing to derail the process.

Miriam Kotov was delightful, though not at all interested in politics. She did, however, possess an impressively deep knowledge of art, especially that of her native Italy. This presented Harry with a problem: should he talk art with the lovely Miriam and thus exclude Kotov from the conversation; or talk politics with the President and have no excuse to stare deeply into his wife's beautiful eyes? Happily, Miriam made the decision for him, dominating the conversation until the main course was over when she abruptly announced she had some work to attend to and would leave the men to talk business.

"I am very grateful for your visit and your counsel Harry. And I'm sorry if I appeared to pull the rug from under you in our meeting with Helen and Jamali on Thursday. But you always knew I supported the blueprint in principle?"

"Of course I did Mr President, and I appreciate the magnitude of your decision. It's an extremely hard call. I'm glad I don't have to make it."

"But I can tell there is still something on your mind Harry. I suppose it's Zaytzev?"

"I'm afraid so."

"Harry, as you pointed out, I can't let my decision be influenced by threats of violence."

"I appreciate that, Sir. But I'd be more comfortable if I knew the extent of Zaytzev's power."

"You are right to be worried Harry. He could probably make happen anything he wanted. He could certainly have me killed, although I don't think he would."

"So what is his strategy likely to be?"

"I'm not sure. But I will talk to the Foreign Minister. Try to build some bridges, that sort of thing. Kutuzov is an honourable man, even if he is my sworn enemy."

"Thank you Mr President."

"And Harry, I hope you will keep in touch. In fact, why don't you accompany me to the Tbilisi summit?"

"That would be a great honour Mr President, Thank you."

The wedding ceremony passed without a hitch, the bride was radiant and the groom looked very much in love. To Helen's mild surprise, Rudolf had a tear in his eye as he returned to his seat having given his daughter away. And the reception was going well too. Helen was relieved at the timing: a 4 o'clock ceremony followed by champagne and dinner with dancing to follow. She could have phoned Mike back before now but she was enjoying herself, and, whatever her instructions, she knew he'd phone if there was anything serious to report. She'd lost sight of Rudolf for some time when he surprised her by putting his arms around her and pulling her onto the dance floor. After an energetic ten minutes, with her shoes giving trouble, they found a table. Within seconds of sitting down, her phone rang.

"Mike."

"Sorry Helen, I know I was supposed to wait for you to call me, but"

"It's okay. Go on."

"We've have a confirmed sighting of Howard Dawkins going into the hotel where Citra is staying. She's working with him."

"Great."

"We're trying to find out what they have planned. I'll let you know as soon as I have more."

"Okay. Thanks Mike."

Jenifer and Dieter left early the following morning for a honeymoon hiking in the Garfagnana north of Lucca. Helen was rather jealous; it was one of her favourite parts of Italy. As soon as the newlyweds had departed, she and Rudolf were in a taxi to the station to catch their train for Paris. It was a ten hour journey with a change in Strasbourg, but it would give them time together; and they both loved train travel.

It took almost two hours to bring Rudolf fully up to date with developments over the last couple of weeks. There was a great deal to digest, but it was the continuing role of Harry Noble that most interested him.

"He must have something about him, you know." he said.

"That's just it though. He's a very intelligent man, but there's nothing that marks him out."

"Do you trust him?"

"I certainly trust him to do the right thing, whatever that is."

"Don't tell me you're starting to have doubts about the blueprint?"

"No, I don't mean that. I'm not sure what I mean. I know he remains opposed to the blueprint, but he won't cross a line. I'm going to keep in touch with him. If there is a serious threat to the process, I think Harry will probably have a pretty good handle on it."

As the train sped through Munich and on towards Stuttgart, Helen looked out of the window?"

"Berlin's that way, right?" she asked, looking out of the window.

"Very good darling."

"How far?"

"About six hundred kilometres. Not so far."

"Six hundred kilometres. Isn't that a long way?" she said cryptically. Rudolf looked at her, trying to elicit some meaning from the question. "Three weeks, you know, it'll all be over. If we make it to Berlin."

"You'll make it. Seriously, the chances of the blueprint surviving to Berlin are far greater that agreement being reached on a programme for the gala concert."

"Are you having problems then?"

"Too many people with too many ideas."

"And Morel making the final decision?"

"Yes, do you think you could put in a good word for me?"

"I really don't need to."

"I've spoken to Daniel. He's agreed to play."

"I thought you might ask him. I'm glad he said yes. He hasn't performed in public for such a long time. What's he going to play?"

"He won't tell us; and that's another cause of tension."

"I'll see if I can tease it out of him on the plane."

"Of course, I forgot, you're flying out with him. What are you going to do during the day tomorrow?"

"I though I might stand outside the Élysée and lobby the members of your committee as they go in to choose the music."

Rudolf laughed. "Now that would be amusing. But seriously, what will you do?"

"I think I might visit my favourite museum, see if they've moved anything around."

"Ah, Monsieur Rodin."

Julia and Jay had risen early and gone for a walk to collect wood for the fire. It was a beautiful day; the night had brought the first, happily light, dusting of snow. As they returned to their cabin, they saw Rick Spedman sat on the porch waiting for them. It was still only eight. Jay's heart sank. Spedman had been keeping his distance, and they weren't due to leave for another 24 hours. If he was here now, something must be up.

"You two look well," he said as they approached.

"We are, thank you," Julia said as they climbed the steps of the porch. They went into the cabin.

"I'm afraid I have some news. Mike phoned this morning. Miss Sianturi has surfaced in Washington DC."

"Shit," Jay said.

Rick noticed Julia take his hand. "She's had meetings with Howard Dawkins. It seems she may be working for him."

"Who's Howard Dawkins?" Julia asked Jay.

"I don't know. Rick?"

"He's a former CIA Deputy Director. Powerful, well connected. He's been linked to a covert operation to derail the summit process. We've been keeping tabs on him for a while now."

Jay felt as if the progress of the last few days was immediately undone. He looked at Julia. The colour had drained from her face.

"What does it mean? I mean what's likely to happen next? I mean the story's already out there. It's old news. There isn't anything else." Jay was panicking.

"We don't know, although something must be brewing. I have to ask you to pack up. We'll head back to Vancouver this afternoon. Helen has asked that you fly to Houston a day early. Whatever's going on, they want to be prepared." Rick looked at Julia who was staring at the floor.

"Anyway, I'll come back about noon. Okay?" Spedman turned to leave.

Mbonga had been at sea for six days. There wasn't much to do, but he was content. He had only one objective and he was on his way to achieving it, currently with very little effort. Eric had found some books for him to read: ancient novels by Graham Greene, whom Mbonga hadn't heard of. He liked them though. The language was a little old-fashioned, but the stories were great, and contained so much history, which he found fascinating. It was marvellous to imagine himself in London during the Blitz, or Saigon in the 1950s. He wondered if he had it in him to one day write an account of his own adventure.

When he wasn't reading, he took exercise among the containers. He had mapped out a route that took him to the bow and back again. At the front of the ship he got a real sense of the speed of travel as the huge vessel cut through the water.

He was keeping careful track of the days. Today was Sunday. He had become bored with his established route, so decided to vary it. As he entered a new container corridor he heard a tapping noise. It was the sound of metal on metal, but strangely muffled. He soon realised it was coming from inside one of the containers he had just passed. As he looked at the outside of the container, the sound continued. He quickly worked out how the levered door system worked, and, as he lifted the opening mechanism, the heavy metal door slowly swung open. As it did, he was overcome by a dreadful stench. Looking into the gloom, he could see four faces, each with hands in front of their eyes to protect them from the light.

"Oh my god," he shouted. "How many of you are there?"

"We are eight." Mbonga couldn't identify the source of the voice, but it sounded like that of a teenage girl. He peered into the back of the container and saw her moving towards him. "I am the only one of us who speaks English."

Mbonga reckoned she was about fourteen. "How long have you been shut in here?" he asked.

"We were smuggled on board the day before the ship sailed. The man who helped us said he would come back, and bring us food and some water. We haven't even been able to empty our toilet buckets.

"Do you know his name?"

"He said his name was Omari. Do you know him?"

"No. I am also not supposed to be here, but the man who helped me was called Eric. And so far he has kept his promises. I will see him this evening. I'll ask him about Omari."

"Can you help us?" the girl asked.

"Of course. This part of the ship is quite safe; the crew don't come down here. Let's get everybody out in the fresh air, and we can clean out the container. Is everybody well?"

"There is one baby, who has been sick, but I don't think it's so serious."

As the stowaways came out of the container, each insisted on shaking hands with Mbonga. He thought this quite absurd, but greeted them all warmly. They lined up in the shade of the containers opposite. Mbonga and the girl went into the stinking container to recover three slop buckets. He struggled to avoid vomiting.

"Look," he said to the girl, "let's leave them over there for now. Once we have the container sorted out, I'll show you the quickest route to the side of the ship, and we can throw them overboard."

The girl nodded. A man in his fifties came forward. He said something to her. Although Mbonga was able to identify the language as Swahili, he still needed a translation.

"He is going to help us. He also wants to know if you can get us food and water. We have very little left."

"Water no problem. I can show you how to get that for yourselves. Food is a bit more tricky. I can share some with you. But I have very little. I'll have to talk to Eric."

The three of them spent the next hour cleaning out the container. Once the smell had gone, it wasn't too bad. They had bed rolls to sleep on, and had managed to keep the interior remarkably clean. When Mbonga and the girl returned with water, they sat down and she told him that they were all from the same village, not far from Mombassa. One of the women knew Omari, who had said he could arrange passage to Europe. They were desperate to escape the situation at home so had each paid a substantial sum of money to be smuggled onto the boat.

Before he left them, Mbonga suggested they set up the toilet buckets a little way from the container. They should leave the container doors unlocked. He would return later, once he had spoken to Eric, with some food. The girl, who's name was Sara, thanked him, and as he got up to leave, the others all lined up to shake his hand once again.

He wanted to find Eric, but it occurred to him that if he was caught, he wouldn't be much help to the Kenyans in the container. So he sat in his room and waited. Later, when he asked if there was a crew member named Omari, Eric gave him a puzzled look.

"There should have been. But he left the ship about four hours before we sailed and never came back. The captain was furious. We are already running a skeleton crew; that idiot not showing up has created more work for all of us."

Mbonga told him about the stowaways locked in the container. Eric was appalled. They agreed that they would have to pool resources to make sure these people did not starve before they reached Marseilles.

"Wait a minute," Mbonga asked, once they had a plan of action. "How are they going to get off the boat without being spotted?"

"I'll come with you tomorrow and check which container they're in. Some are due to be unloaded in Marseilles. Omari will have known which ones. I imagine he chose that container for a reason."

"Unless he only ever intended to take their money and leave them to die."

Twenty-One

After leaving the Rodin Museum, Helen took the metro to a café where she had arranged to meet Rudolf and Daniel. Their meeting had gone surprisingly well. Rudolf, at least, had been impressed at the way Morel had taken control. They had settled on a programme: Rudolf had got his John Adams piece, although he still didn't know what Daniel would be playing.

"You will tell me before we start rehearsals, won't you?" he asked again, exasperated.

"Why do you need to know beforehand. I'll tell you when we get into the room. I probably won't make up my mind until then anyway."

"Really Daniel, I must insist on knowing ahead of time. This is the most important concert of my career; I must be able to prepare properly."

Helen knew Daniel was winding him up, she had seen this happen several times before; at the same time, she knew her husband was genuinely stressed at the prospect of not being able to prepare for the concert as thoroughly as he would like. She needed to change the subject.

"So Daniel, are you ready to get back to the cut and thrust of international diplomacy?"

"Probably about as much as you are, Helen. Rudolf tells me there have been some interesting developments?"

"Well, we don't deal in mundane developments, do we?"

"Any news of Robertson?"

"Yes, actually. Good and bad. According to Rick Spedman, who's playing chaperone, he and Julia are patching things up. But yesterday we got word that Citra had surfaced in Washington and has been meeting with Howard Dawkins." Barenboim sighed. "And I had to get Rick to break the news."

"You don't think there's any more to come out do you?"

"I doubt it. But once again it'll deflect attention away from the success of the summit and onto the personal shortcomings of a member of the committee."

"That's true," Barenboim agreed. "But it'll blow over in a couple of days. And in any case, we are not expecting any problems with the summit itself, are we?"

"Not as far as I am aware, it's mainly a rubber-stamping exercise, not unlike Stockholm. I plan to let Hilda run things."

"Well I think we should continue with our current, successful strategy, and speak truth to the corrupt and malign power of the media, and of people like Howard Dawkins."

"That sounds like a plan." Helen smiled at him.

"Now, my wife is waiting for me at home, and I'm sure you two don't want to spend your last evening in Paris with an old fool like me, so I'll bid you farewell."

The following morning Mike was at Charles de Gaulle to greet them. Once they were through security and into the VIP lounge, he brought them up to speed.

"We don't know a great deal, but we do know enough to plan our response."

"Go on," Helen said.

"French security pulled out all the stops. Once we made the link between Citra and Dawkins, they were able to find out where she'd been staying in Paris, and piece together fragments of phone conversations."

"And," Helen was getting impatient.

"They're planning to put Citra on prime time TV, we think tonight."

"Just before the summit opens. Great." Helen thought for a moment. "Okay. I'll talk to Jane from the plane. How long have we got?"

"About twenty minutes to boarding."

"I'll make one call from here." Mike and Daniel stood up, assuming Helen wanted some privacy, but she waved them to sit down again. "Gerald, Helen. Not bad under the circumstances. Yes, all hell is going to break loose tomorrow evening. It's Citra Sianturi. We think she's going on TV in the States. Do you think you can find out which channel? Really? Okay, if you get confirmation let me know. My phone will be back on in an hour or so. Thanks Gerald."

"He reckons it'll be CNN."

"Tuesday night. It'll be Morgan," Mike said, sounding resigned.

"Fucking brilliant," Helen said.

Barenboim coughed.

It didn't take long for Gerald Small to get confirmation. There was to be no publicity until three hours before the show, but Piers Morgan Tonight would be running a prime time special: an hour-long live interview with Citra Sianturi.

In Houston they went straight into a meeting with Saeed, Jane and Kersen who were waiting at the airport. Kersen had spoken at length to Anna Sianturi who, while relieved to discover her daughter was safe and well, was appalled at the news.

"When does Jay's flight get in?" Helen asked.

"Not until seven this evening," Saeed answered.

"An hour before the programme," Jane added.

"We need to keep him away from the press," Daniel suggested.

"They could probably get on a flight to San Antonio, and we could pick them up from there. That way we could get Jay to the hotel before anyone realises he's here," Mike said.

"Where are they now?"

"They're in Seattle. Rick is reasonably confident they won't be spotted. Apparently Julia made Jay a very effective disguise." The situation was too serious for laughter.

"Okay. Mike, get them on a flight to San Antonio. I guess we need to wait and see what she says to Piers Morgan before we can formulate a response."

Oscar Silverman had been back from Berlin nearly a week and was beginning to think he'd heard the last of Howard Dawkins and his convoluted schemes to discredit the summit process, so he was surprised to see Dawkins' name on his phone as he pulled it from his pocket.

"Oscar, how are you."

"Good, thank you Howard. And you?"

"Very well."

"I was beginning to think you'd retired again."

"Oh no, I've been working very hard behind the scenes. In fact that's why I'm calling. I know you don't watch much

TV, Oscar, but I wanted to make sure you tune in to Piers Morgan this evening. I think you'll find it interesting."

"C'mon, Oscar, I can't stand the man. Why would I want to watch him."

"Just watch it Oscar, for me. You'll find it has some connection with the project we've been working on."

"Oh I see. Your last roll of the dice is it Howard?"

"Just wait until you've seen the show. I think you might revise your opinion of both me and Mr Morgan."

Silverman laughed. "I have an open mind as far as you're concerned Howard. But Morgan is a lost cause I'm afraid."

"Okay, Oscar, just make sure to watch. Say, Oscar. Are you on the wagon?"

"Couple of weeks now. You know I don't drink when I'm working."

"Working, eh?"

"Yup, still working on the same project, Howard. I wasn't sure you'd have a backup plan. Don't fret if Piers Morgan doesn't do the job, you can rely on your old pal Oscar."

"I'm sure I can Oscar. Sorry gotta go." Dawkins hung up.

Silverman thought about the conversation. Whatever Dawkins had cooked up with CNN, he felt sure there was no way the summit process would be derailed via another media expose.

Antonella had decided to tell someone about her meeting with Helen George, and how, ever since the death of her grandmother, she'd been unable to think of anything except the blueprint and the summit process. Tito had been intrigued by the story and had responded sympathetically.

She had initially thought him rather full of himself, but he'd turned out to be a good friend; handsome if not especially bright, and certainly not the man of her dreams. She hoped there would be no romantic interest on his part because she valued their friendship.

They were going off shift at the same time and had agreed to go for a coffee but their plans changed when they met in the staff room.

"Have you heard?" Tito asked her with his usual vagueness.

"Heard what?"

"That Indonesian model, the one who slept with the economist guy from the committee, she's live on TV tonight. We should stay here and watch it."

"You mean the Prime Minister's daughter? I thought she had disappeared."

"She had, but now she's re-appeared, and is doing a live interview."

"What time's it on?"

"Any time now."

They had the staff room to themselves, so they sat down in front of the TV just as the programme was starting.

"Good evening and welcome to the show. Tonight we have an exclusive live interview with Citra Sianturi, daughter of the Indonesian Prime Minister, who, just two weeks ago, dealt a major blow to the summit process when it was revealed that she had slept with one of the committee members, Jay Robertson. Citra, welcome to the show."

"Thank you Piers. It's a great pleasure to be here."

"Citra, it's now two weeks since you hit the headlines when news of your relationship with Professor Robertson became public. Where have you been, and why have you decided to give your first interview now?"

"Let me start by saying that it was never my intention that news of my brief relationship with Professor Robertson become public. I have no idea how that news got into the public domain."

"So when did you first learn that you had become the unwitting focus of the world's media?"

"I flew to Paris to interview a fellow academic in connection with my doctoral thesis. At the airport I saw my photograph on a giant TV screen in the terminal building. Then there was a picture of Professor Robertson. I knew immediately what must be happening. I hid my face and headed straight to the metro, then I checked into a quiet hotel. I remained there until one of your researchers tracked me down, and arranged for me to come here to do this interview."

"What a fascinating story. It must have been rather frightening for you, holed up in a Paris hotel, knowing the world's press was searching for you.

"It was rather uncomfortable. I didn't know how long I would have to remain in hiding."

Morgan looked at the camera. "After the break I'll be talking to Citra about the time she spent with Professor Robertson, and what, in the course of their affair, she learned about the summit process. Stay with us folks, believe me it's worth the wait."

"The whole thing is going to be a pack of lies." Helen was watching the live broadcast with Saeed, Kersen and Jane.

The others had been briefed, and Mike had driven to San Antonio to pick up Jay and Rick.

"It'll get much worse over the next hour," Jane said.

"Although if it is a tissue of lies, then presumably it will be easier to rebut." Saeed suggested.

"Doesn't always work that way I'm afraid. If she says something that the audience wants to believe, then no amount of spinning will persuade them otherwise."

"But we know the majority of people are with us," Saeed added.

"True, but that support is based on people's trust in our promise to deliver a different world based on a new set of values. Those values include integrity and honesty. Whether or not Citra lies through her teeth, it will remain the case that one of our number acted dishonestly," Jane answered.

"So an apology is never enough?"

"It rather depends how forgiving people are."

"I still don't understand how that man became one of the most influential journalists in the world," Helen said.

"I wouldn't call him a journalist," Jane answered. "He's an entertainer. Mind you, he does have a certain charm. And he's very good at getting people to open up."

"Welcome back to Piers Morgan Tonight. With me is Citra Sianturi, who recently made headlines when she was revealed as the secret lover of committee member Jay Robertson. Citra, perhaps you could tell us about the first time you met Professor Robertson?"

The next few questions and answers were rather mundane, describing, largely truthfully as far as Helen could tell, the mechanics of Citra's meetings with Jay. There was a collective cringe when Morgan asked her how well the Professor performed in bed. Her answer, that it wouldn't be appropriate to answer such a question on TV, was too much for Helen.

"Jesus, I hope her mother isn't watching this," she said.

From then on things got steadily worse. After her initial refusal, Citra went on to describe much of what she and Robertson had got up to during their secret meetings. But it was when Morgan asked about post-coital pillow talk, and if she'd learned anything interesting about the summit process or other members of the committee, that things became serious.

She had been very well briefed, for instead of going after Helen, or other high profile members of the committee, like Barenboim or Lundberg, she chose to slander some of their lesser know colleagues.

Robertson, Citra alleged, had described Jemma Wiseman as "possibly the least intelligent person he'd ever had the misfortune to work with. Not untypically among apparently successful people, she lacked both substance and character." Safiya was a hot-headed Marxist whose revolutionary objectives caused many a debate to disintegrate into chaos, severely testing Helen's ability to hold things together. Ajala Subramanium was a climate change obsessive whose influence derived only from political patronage driven by the caste system in her native India. Rita was a 'manipulative bitch' who seemed to be able to twist Helen around her little finger. Robertson had speculated, according to Citra, that she and Helen were having a lesbian affair.

"It sounds like Professor Robertson has a particular problem with the female members of the committee. Would you describe him as a misogynist?" Morgan asked.

"Well, he certainly didn't have any trouble with me as a woman. But then he and I see eye to eye on a great many issues. That was part of the attraction between us. Perhaps no such attraction exists between Professor Robertson and these other women. I certainly wouldn't call him a misogynist."

"I don't believe a word of it." Antonella said, as the show went to another commercial break.

"I know it sounds unbelievable," Tito said, "but you don't know Helen George that well, do you? And you've never met Jay Robertson. These powerful people, they have big egos you know. They often think they can get away with anything."

"But why would this stupid woman go on TV to say these things, even if it was true. And what she said about the TV researcher tracking her down in Paris. I don't believe it. The story was old news. No, at the very least, she got in touch with them to sell her story. And I bet all that stuff is made up. Jay Robertson might have been unable to resist a beautiful woman, but he wouldn't have said these things, not unless he's really stupid."

"It makes good television, though." The conversation had become a little deep for Tito, but Antonella's fascination with the process had been further fuelled. She wondered if Helen George was watching.

"That's enough for me." Helen said. "I'll go and speak to Rita and the others. Saeed, call me as soon as Mike gets back?"

As she waited for the elevator, Helen took a moment to consider her reaction. She felt confident that within a couple of days they would have put this hiccup behind them. She knew Citra was lying: Robertson had always got on exceptionally well with Jemma and Rita, and had enormous respect for Ajala. And while he'd had differences of opinion with Safiya, these had always been expressed calmly and constructively. Besides, on two separate occasions having had too much to drink, he had given her the distinct impression that he found the Eritrean rather attractive.

Dawkins' strategy was very clever; the words he'd put into Citra's mouth were designed to have maximum impact, but they couldn't be less true. All that was required now was an effective means to prove their falsity to the half a billion or so people who will have tuned in to the programme.

She got to Rita's room and knocked on the door. It opened almost immediately and Rita took her by the hand and dragged her into the room, wrapping her arm around Helen's waist and, in best Brazilian soap-opera fashion, imploring her to "kiss me, passionately, on the lips, and let me tear off your clothes you delicious creature."

Helen was caught momentarily off guard until she saw Jemma and Safiya sitting on the bed laughing hysterically.

"I'm glad to see you three aren't upset at having your names dragged through the mud on prime time television."

"Don't worry Helen," Jemma said. "It's too preposterous for words. And anyway we have a plan. Call a press conference right away, and we'll say that Jay tried to seduce each of us at different summits and we all rejected his advances.

That's why he hates us so much." It was some time before they stopped laughing.

"Seriously though. Where's Ajala? I'm not sure she's as thick-skinned as you lot. And she has a reputation to protect."

"Don't worry Helen, I spoke to her already. She's cool. She's coming down, so all four of us victimised females can share some solidarity."

There was a knock on the door and Ajala came in.

"Are you alright," Helen asked, concerned.

"I'm fine, thank you Helen. A little shaken, but I'll be okay," she replied before herself bursting into laughter.

"They are such fools. They only had to google me to find out that my family is low caste. How could they be so stupid?"

Jay was able to confirm much of what Citra had said about their time together, but the stuff about his colleagues was complete fabrication. They had not even talked about the committee or its work. That's why he had been so surprised when the story broke. She had given no indication that it was anything other than a fling.

"Well," Helen asked, "are we agreed that our best approach is to refute the allegations in the strongest possible terms?"

"Yes," Jane said, "but we don't want to sound too defensive, and we need a way to disprove the allegations."

"We could hold a press conference tomorrow morning, and put Jay on the platform with the four women he is supposed to have slandered."

"Wait," Jay said. "I think this needs more. Jane, could you get me an interview with Piers Morgan so I can answer the allegations directly?"

"I'm sure they'd jump at the chance. But are we sure we want to expose Jay to a no-holds-barred interview with Morgan?" she looked at Helen.

"I'm not sure. I'm not saying no, Jay. Perhaps we should sleep on it. Jane, you sound them out. Not tomorrow. I want the summit to be the top story tomorrow. Perhaps Thursday evening?"

Helen's mind was racing. The idea of putting Jay on TV was appealing. What she really wanted to do was implicate Howard Dawkins, but she knew the evidence against him was only circumstantial. As she kicked off her shoes and sat down on the edge of her bed, her phone rang. It was Harry Noble.

"Hello Harry, this is a nice surprise."

"And this time one you weren't expecting, I assume?"

"It's always good to talk to you, whether or not one has advanced warning. What can I do for you?"

"I've just been watching that dreadful man Piers Morgan interview Citra Sianturi. I imagine you have too."

"Yes," she answered guardedly.

"Presumably you don't believe she's acting alone."

"I know damn well she's not, but I can't do much about it without some evidence."

I can't give you proof Helen, but I can confirm the man's identity. You understand that in order to protect myself, I must ask you to give me the name first."

Helen thought for a second. She couldn't believe Noble was working for the other side, not after all that had passed between them.

"Howard Dawkins." It was a statement not a question.

"Yes." Noble replied, equally assertively.

"Thanks Harry. It's good to have you on our side."

"I assure you I haven't changed sides. But I'm not having anything to do with Dawkins and his methods. Better to lose with integrity than stoop that low."

Harry wasn't much looking forward to returning to work after two weeks at the centre of diplomatic events. He decided to go in early, the stress of a rush hour commute would only worsen his mood, and he was cheered by a gorgeous sunrise as he waited on the platform at Henley for the 06.36 to Paddington.

He noticed a handwritten note on his desk as he unlocked the door to his office. It was from his section head requesting a meeting the moment he returned. Harry knew his boss wouldn't be in yet, so he settled down with his coffee to catch up on emails before heading along the corridor.

Andrew Burton had done very well for himself. Not yet forty, Harry remembered with fondness the day he joined the service. Harry had been his mentor for the first year. He was proud that his protégé had done so well, and had no problem having the younger man as his boss.

"Hello Harry, come in, have a seat. How was Moscow?"

"So you know about my little jaunt then?"

"It's part of my job to know what my staff are up to. In fact, I think it may have been you who taught me that." They both smiled.

"You know I've been with Kotov then."

"We suspected as much. You have now confirmed it, so that helps. But your personal dealings with Kotov are not our immediate concern, assuming that protocols were followed."

Harry nodded.

"No, we have intelligence about contacts between your chum Oscar Silverman and an ex-Stasi thug who goes by the name of Gunter."

"Gunter Schmidt?" The surprise in Harry's voice was apparent.

"You know him?"

"I know of him. I can't believe Silverman is having dealings with him though. Thug is far too mild a word."

"Well he is, Harry. And it's set off one or two alarm bells upstairs."

Burton was suddenly serious. Harry realised that this was no longer a cosy chat between friends. Surely he was not suspected of involvement in whatever Silverman was cooking up with Gunter. It quickly occurred to him that he would have drawn the same conclusion given the evidence Burton was faced with.

"Well that's never good news. I must apologise if my involvement in the summit process has made life difficult for you with your superiors."

"It's nothing I can't handle, Harry. But you should be aware that questions have been asked about your role. A few years ago, opposing the blueprint would have won you many friends in the service, but not now. Given the esteem in which you're held here, nobody's going to worry about you engaging in a little private diplomacy. But that needs to be the extent of it. Am I clear?"

Harry had never seen Burton so serious. He decided nothing would be gained by defending himself against non-specific accusations. He chose instead to eat humble pie.

"Very clear. Thank you."

"Be careful, Harry. Close eyes are being kept."

Harry nodded.

"Now, tell me about Kotov. How the hell did you get so close to him?"

Jay was unable to switch off the endless coverage of the interview which had, by 3am, snowballed into the biggest news story of the year. Not only were the usual suspects of the punditry world lining up have to have their say; there were also psychologists and even an expert in sexual dysfunction, all invited to interpret the meaning of Jay's infidelity in the context of both his marriage and the summit process. Much was made of the idea that he may subconsciously have been driven into the arms of this beautiful and intelligent young woman because of the trauma of having been separated from his family and being forced to spend so much time with a cabal of strong, successful females. The more Jay heard, the more angry he became, with himself for allowing the situation to develop in the first place, but also with the media for the tawdriness of it all.

As the night went on, a clear take on the story began to emerge: while Citra might be a gold digger, Jay was the real wrongdoer. Pundit after pundit opined, in increasingly strident terms, that Robertson would have to resign from the committee and that Helen would probably also have to go, for supporting him when the story first broke.

Jay was surprised by his reaction. Instead of drinking himself to sleep – his tolerance of alcohol had never been great – the longer he watched, the more focussed he became. It was all so preposterous. He'd had sex with someone he shouldn't have gone near. As a result, according to some of the most influential talking heads on the planet, this meant the end of a process that most people believed was humankind's best chance of averting disaster. He wasn't going to be the fall guy for the end of civilization. He would persuade Helen to let him go on Piers Morgan, and he would save the process, his own reputation, and, most importantly, his marriage.

He made a mental note to ask Helen about Howard Dawkins and whether they had any evidence to connect him to Citra. Eventually, he switched off the television and then the light. He turned onto his front, and hoped he would sleep.

Helen had a 7am breakfast meeting with Hilda Solis, ostensibly to run through arrangements for the summit and flag up any potential problems. But talk soon moved to the events of the previous evening.

"Why do we fight to defend a free press when all it does is give them licence to tell lies and slander people?" Solis asked, once Helen had finished running through the list of accusations.

"We can't blame the media for this, Hilda. Robertson brought it upon himself. We have to fight lies with truth, and, given that the truth is somewhat less interesting than the lies, find a way to persuade the media to engage with it."

"Somewhat less interesting? Do you have something that might help to turn the tables?"

"I do, but I'm not sure we can use it," she looked at the President who immediately realised Helen was seeking counsel.

"Go on girl, let it out."

"Jay wants to go live with Piers Morgan to rebut the story."

"That's brave."

"It is, but we can't just put him up there without a story to bury the current one."

"I guess liar, liar, pants on fire probably won't cut it."

"No, but we do have a story to counter with. In fact, if we can prove it, it will blow Citra Sianturi out of the water."

"Go on."

"Citra is part of a conspiracy to derail the summit process."

"You sound very confident. Who's running it?"

"Howard Dawkins."

"And you can prove it?"

"I have no physical evidence, but I know it to be true."

"Well, your word is good enough for me, but we're going to need evidence before we send Robertson into the lion's den."

"Mike's working on it, but I think he's struggling. Dawkins seems to have half of DC in his pay."

"That's true enough, but I have most of the other half. I'll make some calls. When were you planning to put Robertson up?"

"Tomorrow evening."

"That'll mean forty-eight hours of radio silence. You sure you can survive that?"

"I think so. As long as CNN starts trailing the follow-up as soon as its confirmed. In the meantime we have to make sure this summit is sufficiently newsworthy."

By the time Helen returned from breakfast with the President, Jane, Saeed, Daniel and Jay were waiting for her on the balcony of a meeting room which, bizarrely, looked out onto the hotel pool. Only Saeed was dressed for the occasion, in white shorts and sunglasses.

"Hi Helen, would you like some coffee?" Jay stood up and brought the pot over to where she had sat down.

"Thanks. So where are we?"

"We've not started actually," Saeed said. "Jay asked us to wait until you got here."

"Fine. Jay?"

"I have to ask you a question Helen. If I'm putting you on the spot by asking in front of colleagues, I apologise."

"Go on," Helen said, impressed at the way Jay was handling himself.

"Rick mentioned to me that you thought Citra was working for this guy Howard Dawkins? And that you suspected a conspiracy."

"Yes, we do." Before Jay could say anything further she continued, "The reason we didn't tell you was that until last night, the evidence was entirely circumstantial." It was immediately obvious to Jay that although the others knew of the conspiracy, they didn't know that Helen now had proof.

"But you now have evidence?" he asked, before anyone else could.

"Probably not enough to put you on TV tomorrow tonight. But that gives us a day and a half to find it."

Helen saw Mike run into the meeting room. He was rather out of breath. As he recovered, he looked at Helen and smiled.

"Hello Mike, do you have news for us?"

"Er, yes. I just had a call from Percy Stephens."

"National Security Advisor," Saeed said, in case anyone had forgotten who Stephens was.

"He has CCTV footage of Dawkins meeting Citra on three separate occasions in the last week. He said he would have passed it to us sooner but none of the people monitoring the tapes recognised her until she went on TV last night."

"So we've got him." Daniel said.

"They've also given me a list of people still in the service known to be in regular contact with Dawkins, some very senior, who might also be implicated."

Vladimir Kotov was alone in his office watching the opening of the Houston summit. It felt odd to be so far away from a process in which he was a key player. He had never quite got used to being at the centre of world affairs, and while he wouldn't admit it to anyone, he frequently shuddered at the thought of the immense power he held. Harry Noble had been right: democracy was a sham. Unlike Noble, however, Kotov hadn't given up all hope in its power to fix society.

He listened to Hilda Solis's opening address with interest. He was surprised at her apparent confidence. Her demeanour suggested she had received very good news only moments before climbing onto the platform. Beside and just behind her sat Helen George. She also looked more relaxed than he would have expected given the events of the last twenty-four hours. As far as the world's media was concerned, the summit process was in its death throes. Yet here were two people with everything invested in it, looking almost serene. As Solis's speech came to and end, the broadcast cut away to a trailer. It was Piers Morgan.

"Last night we brought you the most explosive story of the year so far. As a result, the summit process now rests on a knife edge. But could there be more to this incredible story? Join me live tomorrow at 7pm eastern, when the next chapter in this extraordinary saga will be unveiled."

Twenty-Two

Jay was excused duties at the summit to prepare for his TV appearance, and to fly to New York with Jane in good time for the interview. She was determined that they have every angle covered, and was pleased to find Robertson to be a focussed and hardworking student.

It had been a weird couple of days. After CNN had agreed to trail the show heavily, no other information had been made available to the press and there had been no leaks. It was all rather surreal: everybody knew there must be a huge story about to break, but nobody knew what it was, and no media organisation was prepared to go out on a limb. The situation had taken on the quality of a soap opera cliff-hanger. The world was waiting for a moment of supreme catharsis after which the summit process would be back on track.

Citra had gone to ground again and Howard Dawkins seemed to have got wind that something was up. Inexplicably, he had taken a flight to Los Angeles the previous evening where, under President Solis's orders, he was being kept under surveillance.

By 7pm, Jay was as prepared as he could be. The show's producers had been provided with proof of the conspiracy ahead of time and were happy to make this the focus.

"Sixty seconds", someone called out from behind the bank of cameras. Piers Morgan was still putting his tie on. Jay was impressed at how calm he looked.

"Twenty seconds. Clear the set please." As the lights came up and the music faded, Jay's nerves suddenly left him.

"Welcome to the show, Ladies and Gentlemen." Morgan spoke without his usual swagger. "Many of you will have been watching Tuesday's show, when Citra Sianturi made allegations against Professor Jay Robertson, allegations which, for a while, looked like they might bring the summit process crashing down. I'm delighted to be able to welcome Professor Robertson on to the show to rebut those allegations."

Jay nodded into the camera facing him, but said nothing.

"But not only is Professor Robertson here to rebut the allegations against him, he brings with him allegations of his own. Is that correct, Jay?"

"Yes, thank you Piers. Perhaps it will be helpful if I deal first, and briefly, with the allegations made against me. As I have admitted, I had a brief affair with Citra Sianturi while the committee was in Indonesia for the Jakarta summit. I deeply regret my behaviour, and, as I have already said, I apologise unreservedly, to my colleagues on the committee, to Mrs Sianturi, the Indonesian prime Minister, and, of course, to my wife." There was no emotion in his voice.

"Since these allegations originally surfaced, however, evidence has emerged that Ms Sianturi is part of a high-level conspiracy to derail the summit process,"

"When you say high-level, how high does it go? And do you have proof?" Morgan interrupted him.

"Well," he answered, holding up a piece of paper. "I have here a list of people, all former or current employees of the United States intelligence services, who we believe were involved in a conspiracy to recruit Citra Sianturi, to have her entrap me, to hide Ms Sianturi in Paris while the story rumbled on, before flying her to Washington, and then here to New York to appear on your show on Tuesday evening."

"And are you able to tell us who headed this conspiracy?"

"I am. The conspiracy was planned and executed by former Deputy Director of the CIA, Howard Dawkins."

"And you have conclusive evidence to back up your claim?"

"Absolutely. I don't have it with me. It's been passed to the FBI. I believe agents will be moving in shortly to detain the key players now that the conspiracy has been made public."

"And so all the allegations made against you by Ms Sianturi are untrue?"

"No. We had sex, on two occasions; a fact I deeply regret. Her claims in respect of what I am alleged to have said about some of my colleagues are completely fictitious though."

Morgan was about to ask another question, but looked distracted. He was getting instructions from his producer.

"Okay, we are not going to a commercial break. Instead we can go live to Los Angeles where our local affiliate has a news crew outside a downtown hotel." The screen filled with live coverage of a middle-aged man being led away in handcuffs, his head bowed.

Harry watched in fascination. He couldn't believe that someone as experienced and well-connected as Dawkins could be left so exposed. This would have been unthinkable a couple of years ago. It was clear evidence that the balance of power had shifted firmly behind the blueprint. Nevertheless, he was astounded at the speed with which evidence had been gathered against Dawkins. And enough to arrest him. He suddenly felt slightly uneasy over his own position, though he was not sorry to see the back of Dawkins, and quite happy with his own, small, role in breaking the conspiracy. His phone rang. It was Kotov.

"Mr President, how are you?"

"I'm not sure, Harry. Tell me, are you involved in this conspiracy? Am I going to have to disown you in order to avoid becoming tarred with the same brush as this Howard Dawkins character?"

"I can assure you, Mr President. I have not been involved in any conspiracy, although I have known about this particular plan for some days now."

"So you are in the clear?"

"I am Mr President. I promise you there will be no come back." He thought for a moment. "I might as well tell you, Mr President. I gave them Dawkins."

"You are playing a rather high-risk game Harry."

"It does seem to have turned out that way."

"And are there any other conspiracies against the process of which you are aware?"

"Mr President. It may be helpful if I were to make a short visit to Moscow to brief you."

Kotov sighed.

Mbonga and his friends in the container were up at the crack of dawn. Eric had come by the previous evening to confirm that they would be docking in Marseilles at around 10am. The coast of France had been visible for the last couple of days, but their entrance into Marseilles had been delayed.

Eric had been able to establish that the Kenyans' container would indeed be unloaded, and was headed for somewhere in eastern France, although he couldn't be more specific. He had also managed to secure additional supplies. The plan was for Mbonga and the refugees to lock themselves inside the container, and make their own judgement as to when to escape. The container was listed as empty, so was unlikely to be opened by customs, but they were prepared for that eventuality. Mbonga knew that in the event of being discovered, his special mission would make no difference to the outcome: like the others he would be put on one of the daily repatriation ships and have to take his chances in Morocco, Libya or Tunisia. It was the only option though. Eric had tried before to smuggle off stowaways; it was fraught with difficulty. He convinced Mbonga that hiding in the container was his best chance of making it to Berlin.

They were surprised how quickly the unloading process began. Within an hour of the engines shutting down, they heard footsteps on top of their container and what Mbonga assumed to be a giant magnet being positioned in the middle of its roof. There was a strange, almost weightless, feeling as the huge metal box first moved quickly skyward, before being swung out on a wide arc where it remained suspended for about twenty minutes. Eventually they were lowered, apparently straight onto a trailer. They were soon accelerating downhill on what felt like a slip road onto a motorway. Eric had been right. Their escape to dry land could not have been easier.

As the day went on, the temperature inside the container began to rise. They could have opened the doors for ventilation, but decided not to as they weren't sure they would be able to close them again travelling at speed. As Mbonga's travelling companions slept, he looked at them and wondered what their future held. Despite the language barrier, he had enjoyed their company for the past two weeks. He couldn't imagine how they could possibly start new lives in Europe. Their only hope, he speculated, was for the blueprint to be adopted and that they remain hidden until the new order ushered in a more compassionate immigration policy in countries like France. He knew it was a long shot, though.

After eventually dozing off himself he was woken by a heavy jolt. It sounded as if the container and the trailer onto which it had been loaded had been detached from the truck. He could make out several voices. They seemed to meet at a point a few feet away from the container, and then fade into the distance. Mbonga woke his companions. They decided that if they heard no more noise for five minutes, they would open the door.

Mbonga jumped down first. It was dark, and much colder than he had been used to. They seemed to be in a makeshift lorry park. There was a petrol station and a café in the distance. Beyond that he could see traffic on a main road. There was no sign of their driver, or of anyone else.

They had already decided that once they were in France, they would go their separate ways. In any case, the Kenyans had no desire to go to Germany. They said their goodbyes quickly. Mbonga was fighting back tears as he kissed each of the children on the forehead. He turned and started jogging towards the road.

Harry had managed to get on a flight to Moscow early on Friday morning. He had a return ticket the same evening which he hoped he would be able to use. It was his nephew's birthday the following day and he'd promised his sister he would try to make the trip up to Warwick.

He still hadn't decided whether to tell Kotov everything. He had no reason to doubt Andrew Burton's information about the meeting between Silverman and Gunter, but felt uneasy about letting Kotov know. While the idea of Silverman and Gunter working together was perplexing, Harry's principal concern was still Zaytzev. There were too many unknowns. He decided to call Silverman, who answered immediately, despite the late hour.

"Harry, how are you? Good to hear from you."

Noble was immediately suspicious when he heard that Silverman was both sober and focused. "Well, thank you Oscar. I thought I'd touch base with you about this Dawkins business."

"Harry, the guy's an idiot. First, did he really think he could bring the process down by recycling old news, and second, what the hell was he doing to get himself caught?"

"I must say I was surprised they arrested him."

"That was all for TV. Word is he'll be out in 48 hours. They've got nothing to charge him with. He hasn't committed any crime in the United States, and you can't commit treason against a damn committee."

"If he gets out, is he still in the game?"

"Hell no, he's a busted flush. He won't find anyone on the inside prepared to work with him, ever."

"And what about you Oscar? You never had much faith in Dawkins. I can't believe you don't have one last trick up your sleeve?"

"To be honest, if Dawkins can't make it stick with all the resources at his disposal, there ain't much I can do."

"So you're throwing in the towel?"

"I wouldn't say that. I'm just sitting tight, watching how things unfold. I still think it could be an interesting couple of weeks. Are you still working with Kotov."

"Yes. In fact I'm on my way to Moscow to see him now."

"I wish you luck in your mission, Harry. Good to speak to you."

"You too Oscar. Keep in touch. Bye now."

Harry's suspicions were confirmed. Silverman was far too relaxed for there not to be something big in the pipeline. He decided to let Kotov know about Silverman and Gunter. But he would also give him a hard time about Zaytzev. What did it matter if Kotov thought him paranoid?

Helen spent most of Friday morning doing follow-up interviews after Jay's appearance on Piers Morgan. She'd had to work frustratingly hard to get the focus back onto the summit process. She took the opportunity to stress that the last remaining obstacle to adoption of the blueprint was the anti-democratic activities of people like Howard Dawkins. She warned that the biggest threat could come in the days after the Berlin summit, at the beginning of the transition period. She urged people to show their support for the blueprint by taking to the streets to celebrate the historic achievement, and to make clear its overwhelming democratic credentials.

After a hurried lunch, she and Ajala had a meeting with the Nicaraguan and El Salvadorian delegations. These two countries were strong supporters of the blueprint but had concerns about the practicalities of resurrecting their shattered economies.

"The biggest worry for both our countries," began the Salvadorian President, "is that upwards of seventy per cent of the population are unable to meet their basic needs for food, clothing, housing and healthcare. Improving this situation is our first priority. And while we recognise how the blueprint will help create a better context in which to do this, the fact remains that the lions share of economic output is from sectors that have nothing to do with basic needs provision."

"And of course, this successful economic activity is controlled by a small number of corporations, and an even smaller number of individuals," the Nicaraguan Prime Minister continued. "And this is the part of the economy we rely on almost exclusively for state revenues; the only source of funds we have to keep our populations from destitution."

"It's a difficult question," Helen agreed. "How do you redirect economic activity towards supporting the needs of the majority of the population without crippling the state services on which most people currently depend? First, I think you must be clear that change is not about turning the clock back to a time when the economy was exclusively agricultural. Your manufacturing and service sectors might need to re-evaluate their priorities, but they must not be run down. Supporters of the current order have long argued that wealth generation at the top is the best way to create improvements in wellbeing at the bottom. The blueprint aims to make that myth a reality by addressing the structural inequities that cause wealth to trickle up to the better off, rather than down to those most in need."

Helen was conscious of sounding like she was making a speech, but she had their attention, and they showed no signs of wanting to interrupt. "In countries like yours," she continued, "two things have to happen. Firstly, the poor have to get access to land to grow food, and to build homes. In time the agricultural sector may well develop, and become more dependent on technology and less dependent on manual labour. But for now, it is the surest way of enabling people to engage economically and take responsibility for their own wellbeing."

"And the second prerequisite?" the Nicaraguan President prompted.

"Credit must be made available, both to small scale farmers for the purchase of tools and seeds, but also to people working in other sectors." She looked to Ajala to continue.

"The blueprint has clear prescriptions as to how these objectives can be quickly achieved. As a result of the long-term economic crisis, much land that was formerly given over to cash crops now stands idle. The imposition of a land value tax on all landholdings above a certain size will force large landowners to vacate unused plots. These can then be claimed by smallholders. Title can pass temporarily to the state until such time that new landowners are able to generate sufficient surpluses to cover the tax liability. Whoever pays the land tax gains title to the land. As for the credit required to kick start other enterprises, by May next year, the new currency will be in circulation, and regional and national money-issuing authorities will be up and running. For the first year, the criteria for providing credit will be relaxed in recognition of the dire state of many nations' economies, especially smaller ones."

"My finance minister is still not comfortable with the idea of money being dished out willy-nilly to anyone who wants to start a business. And isn't it true that cheap credit has contributed to the economic crises of recent decades?" asked the Nicaraguan President.

"That is true," Helen replied, "but there is a fundamental difference between money lent for consumption and credit offered for investment. The problem with cheap credit was that everyone borrowed unsustainably to fund consumption, while lending to businesses for investment dried up. But in any case, credit will not be granted without conditions. Certainly the criteria will be relaxed, but there will still be simple assessments; and of course all loans will have to repaid over a fixed term, albeit without punitive interest."

"I like to think of it like this," Ajala picked up the thread. "Most people need to work and most people want to work. In most places there is sufficient land and resources to provide viable work opportunities for everyone. The only things stopping people from taking full responsibility for themselves and their dependents is their being denied access to land, and the fact that they are refused credit because they have nothing to offer as collateral. The blueprint addresses each of these problems, but it makes no prescriptions about what kind of economy each nation should seek to create, beyond establishing a framework which encourages full participation in the economy by all those of working age."

"And don't forget," Helen added. "You won't be alone: every government in the world, rich and poor, will be struggling with the same questions. Not only will you be able to share experiences with other countries, but the Blueprint Transition Authority will be on hand to provide advice."

"Do you anticipate things getting worse before they get better?" asked the Salvadorian president.

"I think that depends on the circumstances in different countries. For the last several years, things have been getting steadily worse for most people in nearly every country. Our short-term goal is to reverse that trend, but for many people signs of progress will not be evident for a couple of years."

By Saturday afternoon, the main business of the summit was complete and the press had pretty much forgotten about the Robertson story. Helen had allowed Jay to return to Vancouver to complete the repair job on his marriage. That evening, President Solis was hosting a private dinner at the White House, to which the six women on the committee were invited. With the exception of Helen, none had previously spent time socially with the President, and all were excited. As they sat down to dinner, Solis stood up and proposed a toast:

"To the role of six exceptional women in bringing the blueprint to the point of implementation," she said. "And to women all over the world who will make it work." There was much laughter amid the clinking of glasses.

"Seriously though," the President continued, "I know that one or two men – good men – have made important contributions to this process, but I am convinced that it is your input, as women, that has made it a success. In nearly forty years I have never been as excited as I am today. I went into politics because of a belief in the possibility of creating a world in which the life experience of the majority of human beings can match the life experience of the most fortunate. I have to admit, this is a day I thought I would never see."

The large double doors at the end of the room swung open, and Solis looked round. "Good," she said, the food's here. Time for me to shut up."

"I wonder, Madame President, if I may ask an impertinent question," Ann Margaret enquired, as they settled down to the first course.

"On condition that you call me Hilda, you may," the President replied.

"It's an issue that's come up from time to time during our deliberations, although the blueprint doesn't have a position on it. But I wonder what you think about the possibility of a return to isolationism, as an unintended consequence of moving to smaller-scale, more localised economies? I guess my question is: what will happen to international trade, and indeed cultural exchange, if we succeed in creating a more inclusive economy with greater local and regional self-reliance?"

"It's a good question, though I hope it's not directed at me because of my country's periodic flirtation with isolationism?"

"Of course not. But would you agree the prospect is a real one, and that it would best be avoided."

"I would, especially here in the United States, where we have the capacity to become self sufficient in many respects.

That would be a bad thing. Even if we succeed in cracking the economic and environmental problems, cooperation between nations, both political and economic, will be crucial as we tackle the next set of problems."

"Trade need not be exploitative if it is conducted on fair terms," said Safiya, "and it's the oldest basis for relations between nations. It would be dreadful if we retreated to a world where countries failed to take advantage of the opportunities offered by trade."

"I agree," Solis said. "Although we must accept that the benefits of trade are not always as great as economists claim."

"Trade should only occur if it clearly benefits both parties, and if both parties perceive it to be so." Ajala took her turn. "But I see a great deal of potential for such mutually beneficial trade once artificially created resource scarcity ceases to be a driver of economic activity, and once indebted countries are no longer driven to trade on unfair terms simply to earn sufficient foreign currency to repay their debts."

"I agree we must encourage trade between nations for all its many potential benefits, but I would say a word for the concept of necessary trade, Solis replied. "Some things, especially raw materials, are not available in certain countries and have to be imported. Other things, which could be produced almost anywhere, are sometimes transported half way around the world, for no good reason."

"Butter," Rita said to laughter. "When I was studying in London the shops were full of butter from New Zealand. It could not have come from further away. There are thousands of cows in Britain. The country has a proud tradition of dairy production. How can it make sense to produce butter in New Zealand and ship it half way round the world?"

"I guess it makes sense under the current system because of the distortions we have allowed into the economy," Solis replied. "It's cheaper to import butter from New Zealand as to source it locally, but I agree it doesn't make sense."

"And we shouldn't forget," said Ajala, " that the transportation of basic foodstuffs around the globe has been one of the main sources of carbon emissions. Once we change the economic basis for trade, and once more basic products are produced closer to the markets into which they are sold, then not only will more people be engaged in the production of the things they need to survive, but there will also be a natural reduction in activities that drive climate change."

"Yes," Helen agreed, "if we want to feed, clothe and house all human beings, then the economy should be structured to give us the best chance of achieving that aim. Once that has been achieved, we can devise new and sustainable ways of trade between nations in order to further raise quality of life, and to improve diversity in consumption and experience. That is why trade and cultural exchange is a good thing, and it's why I think countries like the United States are unlikely to retreat into isolationism." She looked at Hilda.

"Right then," said the President, "I think we've all earned dessert."

Twenty-Three

Helen was happy to be back in London. It was the city in which she felt most at home, even if she would rather be relaxing in Thonon. Rudolf would be arriving in a matter of hours; a fact that improved her mood immeasurably. She had checked into Brown's Hotel after making her way there from Heathrow. The long flight from Houston had allowed her a few hours sleep, and now she was enjoying the hospitality of what had been one of her favourite hotels ever since Rudolf had treated her to a night there, long before he could afford it, nearly twenty years ago.

She had ventured out for breakfast, and tried to enjoy a walk through Green and St James's Parks before returning via St James's Square and Jermyn Street. But it was a depressingly grey day, and the fine drizzle showed no sign of abating. So she returned to the hotel to do some work and await her husband's arrival.

She'd not long been back in her room when the phone rang. It was Harry Noble.

"And how did you know I was here? she asked.

"You forget, I work in that lovely building overlooking Lambeth Bridge. We know everything. And right now our strict instructions are to ensure that you come to no harm."

"I don't believe you've been assigned to protect me Harry?"

"I haven't. But I know the man who has."

"I see. And what can I do for you?"

"I think it might be good if we could meet up. Are you free tomorrow morning?"

"Yes, where, what time?"

"How about Postman's Park, 10.30am?"

"Perfect. See you then."

Confounding Helen's expectations, by the time Rudolf arrived the London sky had cleared. They decided to skip lunch and take a trip to Greenwich.

"Why don't we do something normal," Helen had said, prompting Rudolf to look up the train times. They stayed on the train until Maze Hill and walked up One Tree Hill to take in the view, before continuing on to the Royal Observatory. The improving weather had brought out dog walkers and tourists in equal number. Little had changed about the place since the last time they had visited, so long ago that neither of them could remember. They walked down the hill and past the Cutty Sark to the river, before making their way east to the 17th century pub which, at some point since the 1950s, had been renamed in honour of the famous tea clipper they had passed ten minutes earlier. They sat by the river, each with a pint of what Helen insisted on calling 'proper beer', slightly to Rudolf's irritation.

"It'll all be over in two weeks, you know?" she said.

"Will it though? Are you sure that's what you really want? I can't imagine what you will do with yourself. It'll take a great deal of getting used to."

"I know. I've been trying not to think about it too much. Until about a month ago I would imagine this perfect post-Berlin time when we would be together without a care in the world"

"We could be. But I'm not sure it would work. I think you would go mad. You need a little more in your life than a good novel and a perfect view of Lac Leman, don't you think?"

"Perhaps. But we agreed all this along time ago."

"We did, but a great deal has changed over the last couple of years. If I'm honest, I never thought the process would get this far. Now it has, perhaps you need to rethink. I know that nobody is indispensable, but I think the chances of a successful transition would be greater if you remained involved, in some capacity at least."

Helen looked at him, confused and not entirely taking in what he was saying.

"What I mean is that if you want to continue in some role, I don't mind. I will support you."

"Thank you darling. But, oh I don't know. I could do with a break you know."

"I'm sure they'll let you have a couple of days off after Berlin." She laughed. "I'm just saying; if, as I suspect, you get a formal offer in the next couple of weeks, I will understand completely if you decide not to retire quite yet."

"Retire? I guess I'm not old enough to retire."

"Absolutely not. I am of course. But I'll wait until you're ready."

Oscar Silverman stood up from the trunk of his car into which he had arranged two neatly packed travel bags. He put the road atlas on the roof and took one final look to confirm his route. It would be a straightforward drive to Buffalo were he to follow the interstate, but he was determined to make the most of the time of year: it would take longer, but the scenery along the way would more than compensate.

He'd been surprised when Gunter had offered to come to him for their next meeting. The German had been worried that if Silverman made the trip to Berlin twice in a month, unwelcome attention might be drawn. Gunter had a number of tried and tested identities; he would have no problem getting into the United States as a returning resident. And apparently he had a fondness for Buffalo, which Silverman failed to understand.

Antonella was searching the torn lining of her jacket for coins to pay her bus fare home. Having gathered together the assorted contents she discovered the lottery ticket she'd bought a couple of weeks previously. She went into the newsagent where she'd brought the ticket and asked the shopkeeper to check it for her. He put the ticket into the terminal. It popped out at once, but he didn't look up for several seconds.

"That's strange," he said finally.

"Have I won something?" Antonella asked.

"No. But it says to inform the ticket holder to call this telephone number, and quote this code. Oh, and I have to give you back your ticket and you mustn't lose it."

He wrote down the telephone number and the code at the bottom of the ticket, and handed it back to her.

"Good luck," he said.

"Thanks. But what do you think it means?"

"Perhaps you've won a big prize. I'd make that call if I were you."

Antonella didn't know what to think. She had no credit left on her phone, so she turned down the alleyway towards the kitchen entrance, and went into the staff lobby where there was a phone from which staff were allowed to make local calls.

"Hello," she said when the call was quickly answered. "I went to have my ticket checked and I was given a special code." She was asked to give her name and the code, and to confirm that she had bought the ticket herself.

"Well Miss Soares, I am very pleased to inform you that you are the winner of a special prize courtesy of one of our sponsors, Galaxy Travel."

"Galaxy Travel. Have I won a holiday then?"

"It's a bit more than that. You've won an all-expenses-paid trip to Germany for the Berlin summit next week. It's a good job you called as we need to confirm the booking today. Let me see. Ah yes: you will be travelling first class and staying in a luxury hotel in central Berlin, you will be attending the gala concert at the end of the summit with an opportunity to meet some of the dignitaries. Oh, and you will be provided with two thousand US dollars worth of spending money."

"Two thousand dollars? That's fantastic. When do I leave?"

"Next Monday. In fact I think you had better come into our office so we can sort everything out, rather than try to do it over the phone."

"Okay. I'm on the late shift tomorrow. I'll come in first thing. Is that okay?"

"Of course. Please ask for me at reception. My name is Maria Henriquez."

"I will. Thank you. Goodbye."

Antonella was stunned. She was going to the Berlin summit. She might even get to meet Helen George again. She couldn't believe it.

As she turned the corner into Postman's Park, Helen saw Harry standing by the wall reading the tiles. She crept quietly up behind him.

"Ah Mr Noble," she said in her best Russian accent.

As Harry turned around he looked startled, before recognising Helen and laughing.

"Shall we sit?" he asked, pointing to the bench on which they had talked a month earlier.

"I have to say, when we were last here I hadn't expected you to throw yourself into the summit process with such enthusiasm, Harry."

"Neither did I, believe me. It's all been rather surreal."

"So what's Kotov going to do?"

"I'm honestly not sure. I think the diplomatic pressure might get to him and he'll give the answer you want. When I was with him on Friday he took a call from President Choi. I don't know what passed between them but for the rest of our meeting he was rather grumpy."

"I hope you're right. And I hope that if you are right, there'll be no hard feelings?"

"Of course not, Helen. I've made friends of Rudolf Dreyfuss and his wife. Whatever the outcome, it's been thoroughly worthwhile."

"You'll be disappointed though?"

"On one level yes, but if I've been reminded of one thing in the last month, it's that things are rarely black and white.

My preference would have been to avoid the world getting into this state of crisis in the first place, and so avoid the need for your blueprint. But it did."

"Yes. It did. What did you want to talk to me about Harry?"

"I am concerned that there are more conspiracies out there Helen; conspiracies that will make Howard Dawkins' little escapade seem like child's play."

"Go on."

"You may have heard of an ex-CIA officer called Oscar Silverman?"

"Only through intelligence reports that he has connections to you." She decided to reciprocate Noble's candidness.

"Thought as much. It's true, Silverman and I go back a long way. Until quite recently I would have described him as a friend. He was involved, peripherally, with Dawkins. Although he thought, correctly as it turns out, that Dawkins was too soft to have any impact. So he's running his own operation to derail the process, and has enlisted the help of a former German intelligence officer by the name of Gunter Schmidt."

"He hasn't come up on our radar."

"Ah, finally a victory for MI5. It's all rather embarrassing actually. I've been hauled over the coals because my superiors suspect I'm involved with Silverman and Gunter."

"And you're not?"

"Absolutely not. Gunter is ex-Stasi; and a very nasty piece of work. I can't believe Silverman's working with him. He lives in Potsdam. We have to assume that Silverman has engaged him to help plan an attack on the Berlin summit itself."

"Jesus, just when I thought we were on top of things."

"And I still think Zaytzev is planning something."

"So, we're being targeted by two ruthless killers, both with access to considerable resources, but acting independently of each other."

"That's about the size of it."

"Mike Dixon is going to have a breakdown when I tell him. Thanks Harry. Look I'd better get going. But keep in touch, won't you?"

"Of course."

Helen was almost at St Paul's when her phone rang. It was Kotov.

"Mr President. How are you?"

"Very well, and you Helen, how are you?"

"Fine, thank you sir," she lied.

"I have made my decision," he said calmly.

"Oh, really?" she said, unsure how to react.

"Yes. I'm going to support the blueprint, though I'd be grateful if we could make the announcement together on Thursday evening at the start of the Tbilisi summit?"

"Of course, Mr President. Thank you for letting me know. I look forward to our next meeting."

"Me too. Goodbye Helen."

She threw her phone into the air, far higher than she had meant to, but just about managed to catch it. She wondered if she should call Harry, but decided against.

Gunter had booked them into an impressively refurbished 1950s-built motel on the outskirts of Buffalo. It was relatively cheap due to its location and its lack of the bland facilities that are expected of every hotel, anywhere in the world. Silverman really liked it. A piece of classic Americana from a time when the world was more straightforward.

Once he had taken a shower, they crossed the road to a restaurant, ordered quickly and got down to business.

"So, my friend," asked Silverman, "what progress have you made?"

"I've established the means to access the conference venue, but we need to discuss options. Are we looking to maximise physical damage to property and cause widespread chaos forcing the abandonment of the summit, or do we want a more strategic operation targeting key individuals and so preventing the summit from reconvening elsewhere at some point in the future?"

"Can we not have both?"

"Certainly, if we can get hold of a big enough bomb."

Silverman smiled. "And where are you going to source this weapon. I know you have connections to all the wrong people, Gunter, but still."

"I have been making some discreet enquiries. My approach to such operations is to seek out like-minded people who might have similar goals and access to resources which I don't.

"And who have you found?"

"It's still early days, Oscar. I have nothing confirmed. But I do know that there is someone who shares our objectives. I'm just not sure he will want to work with us. On the other hand, once he discovers that I have a way into Templehof, I think he might, what is it you Americans say, play ball?"

"So what's the problem?"

"I can't get him to return my calls. Most of the time my reputation open doors to all the right people, but just occasionally it scares them off. I have a close colleague doing some PR work on our behalf. I've had to mention your name in order to lend some credibility to the project."

"To whom?"

"Sorry, I can't tell you."

Silverman looked at him low across the table. "Listen, Gunter. Did you see what happened to Howard Dawkins the other day? If my name is linked to a conspiracy against the summit, I'll have to leave the United States. That is not going to happen. Do you understand me?"

"Relax Oscar. All my people are very careful. The risk to you is negligible."

Gunter's phoned beeped. He picked it up, keyed in the code and read the message. He looked irritated and dropped the phone onto the table, not realising that Silverman would be able to read the message: 'Tolstoy still won't talk to you.'

"Who the hell is Tolstoy?"

"Just a contact."

"Are you putting together a deal with the Russians?"

"Maybe. Why not? The cold war ended more than thirty years ago, Oscar. What do you want. A tin-pot operation with little chance of success, or to make your mark on history?"

Silverman was not happy. "Listen, I want this sorted before you go back to Germany."

It had taken Mbonga sometime to work out where he was. He had left the container just outside Grenoble, which, according to his map, meant he had to cover around eight hundred miles in eight days if he wanted to be in Berlin for the start of the summit. Walking was out of the question.

His first lift had taken him all the way to Geneva, but then he started getting some very unfriendly looks from Swiss drivers. It had taken a further two days to get first to Yverdon and then onto Neuchatel, from where nobody seemed to be going north.

After two hours of fruitless hitching, he dropped down onto the lakeshore where he spotted what appeared to be an abandoned bicycle. He was reluctant to take the bike, both for reasons of conscience, and consideration of the consequences of being caught, but after establishing that there was no one anywhere nearby, he picked it up and headed back to the road. If nobody would give him a lift, he would cycle the remaining six hundred miles to Berlin.

Jay and Julia had spent six days together but would soon be separated once again. She was driving him to the airport to begin what would be a marathon journey, requiring two changes of aircraft, to the Tbilisi summit.

Things had been difficult at the beginning. While nothing had materially changed, seeing her husband's ex-lover talking about their relationship on live television, and hearing a battery of so-called relationship experts discuss her marriage, had affected Julia badly. But at least they could now draw a line under the whole thing. Julia knew that while things would never be the same, her experience had been shared by many women. Not that this excused Jay's behaviour; but it helped to know she wasn't alone. And while she did still have the option to walk away, an option she would definitely take if he strayed again, she was still very fond of him. He was an exceptional man, and most of the time he cared deeply about her, and it showed in his behaviour. In many ways she couldn't be luckier, except, of course, that her husband had engaged in the most publicised adulterous affair the world had ever known.

She wasn't happy at the prospect of losing him for another two weeks. She knew he wouldn't do anything stupid, but she would miss him. She wasn't able to talk to him as she would have liked because Ron Krajicek was in the back seat. But she couldn't stand the silence.

"Ron," she asked, looking at him in the rear-view mirror, "have you any idea how long after the Berlin summit committee members and their families will continue to have protection?"

"I don't officially, but I can tell you that I have a new assignment beginning two weeks after Berlin ends. Do you know if I'm gonna be replaced, Jay?"

"I suspect not. I guess it'll depend on which, if any, of the committee members move over to the transition body. But I shan't be, so I suspect once you go, we'll be on our own"

"Well I'm sure you'll both be glad to see the back of me."

"Not at all," Julia said. "What I mean is, yes of course it will be great to have our lives back. But I can't imagine anyone having done a better job over the last year."

They arrived at the airport and parked. After checking in, they headed towards security with Ron a few steps behind.

When they reached the point at which they had to part, he hung back a little further.

"I've made a decision," Julia said seriously. "Don't worry. It's good."

"Really?"

"Yes. I know I said I wouldn't, but I've decided that I will come to Germany for the summit."

"That's fantastic."

"Well, I've never been to Berlin, I've never met any of your colleagues except Helen. And, well, it's a historic moment. I think I should be there. I've already spoken to your parents, they're happy to have Nathalie for a few days."

He held both her hands. "Thank you, darling. I don't know what to say."

Silverman had given Gunter twenty-four hours to make progress with Tolstoy. When they met at the same restaurant the following evening, the German had something positive to report.

"Have you spoken to your contact in Moscow?"

"I have. And he had some very interesting news."

"Really?"

"Yes, he reckons that Kotov has decided to support the blueprint. The source is someone inside Kotov's office. There has been no public announcement."

"Well, that doesn't surprise me one little bit." Silverman sighed.

"The good news is that Tolstoy now seems ready to work with us."

"Before I agree, I need to know who Tolstoy is."

"I'm not sure I can give you that information."

"Gunter. I am your employer. You used my name in order to get to Tolstoy. You can damn well tell me his name."

"Okay Oscar, calm down. It's Yuri Zaytzev, Foreign Ministry."

"Zaytzev? And is the operation sanctioned by Kutuzov?"

"That I don't know, and I won't be able to find out, so don't ask. Zaytzev has a great deal of influence in Russia. I can't think of anyone better to have on our side."

"I'm pleased you're pleased," Silverman said sarcastically. "It makes things more complicated though. What if Zaytzev's objectives are not quite the same as ours. We need to establish a proper chain of command."

"I don't know about that. Zaytzev won't be used to playing a subordinate role. I'm afraid if I make it a condition of our partnership that he answers to you, he will walk away." Silverman thought for a moment.

"Okay. We don't have to tell Zaytzev that I'm running the operation, but I'll come to Berlin so I can be a little closer to things. Russian involvement could create a whole host of problems. You'll need me around to troubleshoot."

"You really don't need to be there Oscar. You being in Berlin could put the operation at increased risk of detection. I would advise strongly against it."

"And I will consider your advice, before I make my decision."

Helen's flight to Tbilisi, which involved a change in Berlin that made her feel rather uncomfortable, arrived nearly four hours late. The press conference with Kotov to announce his decision was scheduled for 7pm which gave her about 40 minutes. Saeed was waiting as she dragged her case into the arrivals hall as quickly as she could. The security man grabbed the bag, and all three ran across the terminal towards the exit.

The driver immediately recognised Helen and, when Saeed told him they were late for an important press conference, promised he would get them there in time. After a whirlwind tour of Tbilisi's back streets, they pulled into the rear entrance of the conference centre. Helen saw Kotov standing under an awning for protection from the rain, smoking a cigarette. He looked nervous.

"Mr President, I'm sorry to have kept you waiting," she said as she got out of the car.

"Ah Helen, you're here. That is a relief. When I heard your flight had been delayed, I presumed you were flying Aeroflot, but they told me you were on Lufthansa, so I felt a little better." He laughed, slightly more heartily than the joke warranted.

"Well I'm here now. Would you like to spend ten minutes going over what we are going to say?"

"That would be very useful, but are you sure you don't want to go to your room first?"

"Don't worry. I've been sat on my backside for the last six hours. I'm ready for work. Is Harry Noble here?"

"No. After I made my decision, I thought it would be a little awkward to invite him."

"But you did let him know, about your decision, I mean."

"I didn't, no. Have you spoken to him?" He could tell from her expression that she hadn't. "Oh well," he said. "Noble's a good man. He'll take it on the chin."

Harry was preparing to leave for the evening when Andrew Burton put his head round the door. "I'd put the TV on if I were you. Live press conference coming up."

Harry felt sick. He knew Kotov had decided to support the blueprint, that much was evident when his invitation to the Tbilisi Summit was not confirmed by Kotov's office. He was surprised that neither Kotov nor Helen, who presumably had been given advance notice, had bothered to contact him. It looked as if his involvement in the summit process was at an end. He picked up the remote and pointed it at the TV in the corner of his office.

There was clapping from the assembled journalists as first Helen, then Kotov and finally President Kakhidze of Georgia stepped onto the platform. The Georgian president spoke first.

"It is my great pleasure," she began, "to welcome to Tbilisi my good friend President Kotov of Russia, and of course Helen George, chair of the Committee for the Establishment of a Framework for Global Governance and Economic Reform. I am doubly excited as President Kotov has chosen the Tbilisi summit to make a special announcement. President Kotov."

Kotov immediately confirmed Harry's fears, before speaking warmly and at length about the work of the committee and its singular achievement in bringing the blueprint to the verge of implementation. He apologised for having taken so long over his decision and thanked 'all those' whose advice he had sought on his way to making up his mind. At this point he looked straight to camera; Harry knew he was looking at him.

He picked up his phone, pulled up Helen's number and tapped in a message. "Congratulations to you both. I hope we get to work together again at some point." He pressed send and looked back at the TV.

A few seconds later Helen picked up her phone, which she had placed on the table in front of her. She read the message and then passed the phone to Kotov who read it and smiled. Although he had failed in his objective, Harry was not upset. In fact he felt a degree of satisfaction at a job, if not well done, then at least done properly. Seconds later his phone rang.

"Hello Oscar," he answered, determined to sound upbeat. "How are you?"

"I'm good, but I'm surprised you're sounding so chipper. Don't you have TV in England?"

"What can I say? I gave it my best shot. I couldn't have done more."

"You might have accepted from the start that you didn't have a cat in hell's chance with Kotov."

"I'm not sure that's entirely true, but you might be right." Harry remained calm.

"The hell I'm right. Dawkins failed miserably and you've done no better. Unless somebody does something pretty damn quick, it'll be a done deal."

"I think we've exhausted all avenues, don't you? Perhaps it's time for us old-timers finally to accept the inevitable. The blueprint is the democratic will of the world's people, after all."

"Democratic will my ass."

"So you're not giving up then?"

"I'll tell you one thing Harry. It ain't over until the fat lady sings." With that, Silverman hung up.

Harry needed no more convincing that he was involved in a plot with Gunter to target the Berlin summit. He walked along the corridor to Andrew Burton's office.

"Is he free?" he asked his PA, who nodded.

"Harry, come in."

"Thanks Andrew. I just got off the phone with Silverman. Although he didn't admit to it directly, I'm now sure he's working with Gunter on a plan to attack the Berlin summit. I think we should make formal contact with Mike Dixon and offer our support. The committee is going to have to beef up its intelligence operation and its security arrangements, and quickly."

"Okay. I'll give Mike a call. You don't know him do you?"

"Only by reputation: Helen George speaks very highly of him."

"He's exceptional. You'd like him."

"Hopefully I'll get chance to meet him one of these days."

"Anything else?"

"There is actually. I have reason to believe there is another, quite independent, conspiracy against the summit. When I was in Moscow I was leant on rather heavily by Yuri Zaytzev. He told me that if Kotov supported the blueprint then he would take steps to prevent it being implemented."

"Zaytzev is the kind of person who would stop at nothing from what I've heard."

"You're right. And in terms of power and access to resources, he's much better placed than Gunter and Silverman."

"Does Mike know about Zaytzev?"

"He will do by now. I briefed Helen on Tuesday. I'm sorry not to have come to you first."

"Don't worry. Things are moving very quickly. By the way, I'm sorry your efforts with Kotov came to nought." Harry smiled at him but said nothing. "Well, I'm not sorry, obviously. But you must have been disappointed?"

"I think the most important thing now is to do everything possible to avoid any loss of life in Berlin."

In Tbilisi, as expected, all the nations close to Moscow fell quickly into line once Kotov announced his decision. The following evening, Helen, Mike and Saeed went to dinner with the President at the Russian Embassy. Ostensibly a celebration, Kotov had worked out from Mike Dixon's presence that the main topic of conversation would be security, and he assumed that Noble would have briefed Helen on the threats made by Zaytzev.

"What kind of guy is he?" Mike asked Kotov once Saeed had steered conversation around to the topic.

"Rational, brilliant, determined, unprincipled and without scruple is how I would describe him." Kotov answered, almost as if he'd prepared his reply in advance.

"And how much power does he have?"

"Technically, he's a special adviser to Foreign Minister Kutuzov. Practically, he manages a fiefdom that extends way beyond the Foreign Ministry. He's very good at getting people to listen to him, and to take him seriously. He's a natural leader, someone people choose to follow without necessarily thinking very hard about why. And he appears to command exceptional loyalty; a trick I never learned."

"And we know he's opposed to the blueprint?" Saeed asked.

"Obsessively so, as far as I can work out. I don't think it would be an exaggeration to call him a sociopath. And when you mix a serious psychological disorder with an interest in politics and power, the prospects are not normally good."

"So his motivation for opposing the blueprint is not driven by principle. He thinks we're forcing Russia to give up some of its sovereign power; power which he personally covets." Helen said.

"That is a good assessment, yes." Kotov agreed.

"Okay," said Mike. "So this guy could and would do anything to bring the process down, and he has access to the people and resources that would enable him to do it. But presumably there are some people who are loyal to you and would obstruct Zaytzev if they suspected him of plotting against the summit?"

"Of course there are. But large sections of the security services are not under my control. Although Zaytzev has no formal position within the FSB, he pretty much runs it. I wouldn't describe it as a rogue organisation, but I can't imagine it's a very comfortable place for supporters of the blueprint."

"We need to get all the intelligence we can on Zaytzev and his people," Helen said. The others mumbled their agreement. "There's another side to this problem," she continued. "Assuming Berlin passes trouble-free and we enter the transition period, according to Noble, Zaytzev claims the ability to stage a coup against you, Mr President."

Kotov took a deep breath. "I have to say that's a distinct possibility. I have the support of the army for now, but once news of my decision is fully digested back home, I suspect that some senior people in the military will start agitating."

"There is only way to stop a coup," Saeed said. "That is to pre-empt it with people power. Over the next week we will be running a high profile campaign, urging people all over the world to celebrate the Berlin summit with huge demonstrations. When the Russian people see millions taking to the streets from New York to Tokyo, surely they will also want to be part of that celebration?"

"I very much hope that will be the case. I have a great deal of confidence in the Russian people to do the right thing. But perhaps all we can do is hope." Kotov took a large mouthful of wine.

As soon as Mike had received the call from Andrew Burton, Helen agreed that he fly to London. It was six years since he had been inside Thames House, but his memories of the place were warm, and he looked forward to catching up with Burton. And he was rather excited at finally getting to meet Harry Noble; the man had attained almost legendary status over the last few weeks.

They met in Burton's office, and after introductions, got quickly to the crux. Burton had spoken to Steven Mayer, Deputy Director of the CIA with responsibility for Europe, and a close ally of Hilda Solis. He had agreed to give all necessary support. The three of them quickly agreed that the existence of two independent threats to the summit made this an almost unique challenge. They needed quickly to establish a fully staffed intelligence gathering body on the ground in Berlin ahead of the summit. Security provision would also need to be raised to the highest level.

Mike had spoken to Chancellor Emmerich from Tbilisi, and received assurances that German special forces would be put at their disposal. Also that the army would flood the area around the summit venue several days ahead of time. They all agreed that the choice of Templehof as the venue had been inspired; it would make the task of keeping the summit secure much easier.

"Mike," Burton asked, "will you have time to head up the intelligence operation on the ground, or do we need to draft someone in?"

"I'd like to think I could do it, but I'm not sure Helen would let me. It would be good to have some help; ideally from somebody who knows Berlin, and has had dealings with some of the key players."

"I could do it," Harry said quickly. The others were silent. "Well, I spent three years in Berlin when I was seconded to six. I know Zaytzev and Silverman personally; I've had dealings with Gunter in the distant past, and I've also had some involvement, albeit peripheral, with the summit process."

"I have to say, you do appear to be remarkably well qualified for the role, Harry." Burton looked at Mike.

"That may be true, but I don't need to remind you that your 'peripheral' role in the summit process involved you doing all in your power to undermine it by trying to persuade Kotov not to support the blueprint. Are we to believe that having failed in that task, you've decided to switch sides?"

"My world view has certainly been altered somewhat by the events of the last few weeks," Harry said assertively. "And remember, I did you give you Dawkins."

"I think it understandable that Mike has some reservations, Harry. On the other hand, no other viable candidate comes to mind. When's your flight, Mike?"

"Six."

"Right, we need a decision by four o'clock. Let's think about our options and reconvene here at two. Okay?" They both nodded their agreement. Harry left the room quickly.

Helen and Rita had a couple of hours between meetings, so decided on a bit of pampering in the hotel's impressive but virtually empty spa. After a sauna, a swim and five minutes in the Jacuzzi, both were exhausted, so collapsed into recliners beside the pool. Their attempt at conversation was soon interrupted by Helen's phone.

"I'd better take this. It's Harry Noble." Rita raised her eyebrows. "Hi Harry. How's it going?"

"So far, so good. But I need to ask a favour, Helen." He explained the outcome of the meeting, and while he stopped short of begging her, he made it quite clear he really wanted the job. Helen was torn. She liked the idea of having Harry on the team but couldn't help but agree with Mike. She had no concerns that Harry would use the position to undermine the summit. But still she felt uncomfortable.

"Harry. I'll have to get back to you. Leave it with me. What time is your next meeting?"

"Just under two hours."

"I'll be in touch."

She told Rita of her dilemma, and of her gut instinct to bring Noble on board.

"Then go for it," Rita counselled. "It's not as if he's going to be working on his own. You could put Rick or someone in to shadow him if you have any concerns."

"Okay. I need to speak to Saeed and Daniel, then I'll give Mike a call." She hauled herself from the comfort of the recliner, and looked down at Rita. "You coming?" Rita knew Helen well enough to know when a question wasn't really a question.

Harry hadn't heard back. It was 2pm, so he went back to Burton's office.

"Come in Harry. Mike just called. He's going to be a couple of minutes late."

Harry sat down and said nothing. After a few second he started drumming his fingers on the polished oak table.

"You okay?" Burton asked.

"Yes, fine."

After what seemed like an age, Mike came in. "Harry," he said, "Helen asked me to apologise for not getting back to you herself." Noble braced himself. "She's just had to go into a meeting with the Moldovan President, but she asked me to pass on a message." Mike looked at Burton and smiled, before looking back at Noble. "You'd better go home and pack. We need you in Berlin on Sunday."

Twenty-Four

Helen called a meeting for 9am on Sunday morning, an hour before the start of summit business. She wanted to brief everyone on the latest security developments. All were present when she and Saeed entered the room. It occurred to her that this would probably be their last formal meeting. None was scheduled for the rest of this summit, nor in Berlin. She looked at each of them, and got a few quizzical looks in return.

"Okay," she began, "we are very nearly there. A week from now the Berlin summit will be over. And with the Russians in the bag," she was interrupted by applause, "and with the Russians in the bag, I think we can afford to relax just a little, on the diplomatic front at least."

"But we now face possibly the most dangerous week of the entire process. Some of you already know of what I'm about to speak. To the rest it will come as a shock." She paused. "We have good intelligence to suggest there are two independent but credible threats to disrupt the Berlin summit using violence."

"You mean terrorist attacks?" Robertson asked.

"Yes." A chilly silence fell on the room. "All possible measures are being taken to ensure the safety of those attending the summit, including us of course. Mike has been liaising with the German authorities for several weeks anyway, and he's now in Berlin setting up an advance intelligence and security operation at the conference venue. He's being supported by a senior British intelligence officer. They are working closely with MI5, the CIA and German intelligence. The German Army has been mobilised and all German special forces have been moved to Berlin."

"Should we not consider postponing the summit, or holding it elsewhere?" Jemma asked.

"We have until Tuesday evening to make that decision. If no firm evidence of an attack emerges by then, we will proceed with the summit as planned."

"And if evidence emerges while we're having breakfast on Wednesday morning?" Robertson asked.

"We will tackle the threat and proceed with the summit." There was a steeliness to Helen's voice that her colleagues had not heard before. "It'll be too late to move it by then."

"How much do we know about these conspiracies?" Lundberg asked.

"We know who's behind them. We don't have much detail about what's being planned. That's why we've set up security earlier than we otherwise would have."

"I think you are absolutely right, Helen," Ajala said. "For all we know these conspiracies may be hoaxes, threats circulated by opponents of the blueprint to test our resolve. We must not let these people intimidate us after coming so far. I'm sure everything will be just fine."

"Thank you Ajala." Helen said, slightly surprised.

"Okay, any other questions?" There were none. "Right then. It may not have occurred to any of you, but this is probably our last formal meeting as a group. I'd like, therefore, to take this opportunity to thank you for your hard work over the last two years. What we have achieved together is remarkable. I have no doubt that future historians will look back at this process, and at each of you, with fascination and gratitude."

It seemed not to have occurred to anyone that this would be their last meeting, for the atmosphere changed again. Rita was talking animatedly to Saeed; Jemma said something to Zhang. The others stared at the table, as if contemplating news they thought they would never hear. The realisation that this was their last meeting had a greater impact than learning that their lives may be in imminent danger.

"Come on, cheer up. We can all have our lives back now." Helen said. There was muted laughter before Wen Zhang rose to his feet.

"Helen," he began, very seriously. "I think I can speak for all of us when I say that without your leadership, your support and your inspiration we would not be here today. It has been a great honour to work with you. And for my part, it has been an equally great honour to work with each of you," he said, looking around the room.

Suddenly everyone was on their feet. There was much hugging and shaking of hands. Helen watched, and prayed that they would make it through the next week in one piece.

Harry had spent the flight from London immersed in copious briefing documents. There were reams of useful material on both Gunter and Zaytzev. And he had discovered several things about Silverman that would have altered their relationship had he known about them earlier. He was looking forward to the next week; the thought that he might be exposing himself to physical danger hadn't crossed his mind.

He didn't want to waste time waiting for his luggage, so he stayed in his seat until nearly everyone was off the plane, then packed his briefcase. He got to the carousel in time to see his bag slide down the conveyor and grabbed it in a single, pleasingly smooth, movement. He got his bearings and headed for customs. The exit was at the far end of the hall past several other carousels. Of these, only the last one was in use, and, as he surveyed the tired-looking people gathered round it, he couldn't believe his eyes. There, not thirty feet away, was Oscar Silverman. The American hadn't seen him, so Harry quickly changed direction to ensure that he wouldn't.

It was the perfect start to have established that Silverman was in Berlin before even leaving the airport. But Harry wanted to know more. He made his way to airport security and identified himself. He knew from the sign above the carousel that Silverman had flown American Airlines from Charlotte. He had someone print out the passenger list for the flight. He knew Silverman wouldn't be travelling under his own name. And, although it was a long shot, he fancied his chances of identifying his *nome de guerre*.

It didn't take long. The American appeared to be travelling under the name of John Tyler. Relatively unknown, Tyler had been the tenth president of United States. He recalled Silverman once saying that, as the man who brought Texas into the Union, Tyler had been unfairly neglected by historians. None of the other names on the passenger list came close. He headed for the exit and got into a taxi. He asked the driver to take him straight to Templehof.

Six days after Antonella had received news of her trip to Berlin, she was standing in a queue at Guarulhos Airport with her mother. Both were nervous. Neither had been to an airport before, let alone on a plane. This would be Antonella's first time outside Brazil. Her mother hated the thought of her daughter flying all that way, and while Antonella had no fear of flying, she was starting to get a little fraught because of her mother's endless worrying.

When she had visited the offices of the lottery company, the airline tickets were waiting for her along with details of her hotel reservation, and the name of the person who would meet her at the airport in Berlin and take her to the hotel. She had arranged to pick up the spending money on her way to the airport, rather than keeping such a large amount of cash at home. The money, in German Marks, was now secured in a fabric money belt strapped tightly beneath her T-shirt.

She would have to change planes in Paris where she had eight hours between flights; long enough, she had calculated, to catch the metro into town, do some sightseeing and have lunch, and still get back to the airport in time for the connection to Berlin. As she handed over her passport, she remembered how she came to have one in the first place.

"You never know when you might need to travel at short notice," her grandmother had said when she turned 18. At the time Antonella had thought it a peculiar thing to say, but for some reason she had decided to apply for a passport.

It didn't take long to check in. She said goodbye to her mother as quickly as she could, but as she placed her bag on the conveyer belt of the x-ray machine, she could still hear her wailing outside.

Mbonga was almost there. It had taken him six days to travel from Neuchatel to Beeliz, a small town about 20 miles southwest of Berlin. He'd covered about a third of that distance on his trusty bike, which he still had, thanks to a couple of drivers who let him strap it to the back of their trucks. He was tired, but the closer he got the more alive he felt.

He had crossed into Germany at Weidach. The truck driver who had given him a lift from Zurich to Munich had thought it too risky for Mbonga to stow away in his trailer, so he dropped him five miles shy of the border and drew him a map showing where to cross via a less-travelled route where there were unlikely to be any border officials. The plan had worked, and Mbonga was able to rendezvous with his lift at a truck stop about ten miles inside Germany a couple of hours later.

"Well, you're in Germany now. All you need to do is keep your head down and you'll make it to the Berlin summit." Rudi, the truck driver, said.

He was one of the most interesting people Mbonga had met along the way. An Irishman who, while he still had a home not far from a place called Limerick, had never been able to settle, and now made a good living for himself driving huge trucks around Europe. Mbonga had never met anyone who knew so much about so many things.

"Well you see," Rudi had explained, "I have a bit of an addiction to books. I read anything and everything. "

"I read quite a lot too," Mbonga protested, "but I'm not able to recall plot lines or facts like you are."

"No? Maybe not. I suppose I have a pretty good memory for stuff."

Rudi had been following the summit process more closely than Mbonga, although he had no interest in going to Berlin, and told Mbonga he must be mad for trying. He could quote several of the committee members from memory and was able to give Mbonga a brief character portrait of each.

"Anyway, why do you want to know all this stuff? It's not as if you're going to meet these people, are you?"

"I suppose not. But it helps me to build up a picture of what's going on."

"Shall I tell you the thing I find most interesting about the blueprint," Rudi asked, after an unusually long silence.

"Go on," Mbonga said.

"The way it talks about reconciling individual freedom and social justice. Now, as you might imagine, I've got a bit of a thing for freedom. It's why I drive this truck. I'm my own boss, I can work when I like and I don't have to spend time with other people, if I don't want to."

"You don't like company then?" Mbonga asked.

"Not really, no. You're alright though." Rudi replied, matter of factly.

"Anyway, freedom and justice. If you ask me, it's always defined the argument between left and right. Lefties argue that social justice should be society's overriding objective, but right-wingers reckon the cost is too great because you have to trample over the individual freedoms of too many people. And that's not on because for them individual freedom is the most important thing." Mbonga listened attentively. "But the blueprint correctly identifies what it is about the current set up that makes freedom and justice mutually exclusive. And it shows how, if you address the underlying causes of that conflict, you can have an economy that enables both at the same time."

"I agree," Mbonga said. "In my country the government is always talking about how they have given us freedom. We are all free to vote, free to discuss, free to express ourselves, free to think what we like, yet most of us have no jobs, and many of us are starving. What is the point of all this freedom? It's completely meaningless if we are denied the means to economic security; if we can't feed, clothe and house our families, or afford to send our children to school."

"That's exactly right. It's the same for many poor people here, and especially back home in Ireland. And it's why many people in eastern Europe still defend the old communist system. God knows it was dreadful in many respects, but at least most people had their basic needs met. Now don't get me wrong, I don't think we should go back down that road. But there has to be an alternative to the options currently on offer."

"Of course there's is an alternative." Mbonga said. "It's all written down here, in this little book." He picked up his copy of the blueprint which he had put on the dashboard.

"I tell you what. If that thing is successfully implemented, it'll be the greatest leap forward ever taken by human beings. If you do run into Helen George be sure to tell her that Rudi's rooting for her."

After they parted, Mbonga had got back on his bike. Now he was almost in Berlin, but he needed to sort himself out before checking into a hotel. He hadn't washed properly, or shaved at all, since leaving the ship nearly a week ago, and he didn't want to draw attention to himself. After an hour of cycling, he noticed a long driveway beyond a gate that had been securely chained. Next to the gate was a board that, although he didn't recognise the words printed on it, looked like a 'For Sale' sign.

He looked up and down the road, threw his bike over the gate, and then vaulted it himself. He cycled down the overgrown track eventually coming to a cottage, which judging from the weeds growing on the window sills had been vacant for several years. He pushed on the front door. It was locked. All the windows were intact and seemed to be locked from the inside. He walked around the back where he found the door into the kitchen wide open. There was some damage to the door and the frame; it had been forced. As Mbonga entered, he called out. The place was empty, save for a table and two chairs in the kitchen. He tried the kitchen tap. There was water: it was cold, but it would do. He checked the rest of the house to make sure he really was alone, before jamming one of the chairs under the kitchen door and stripping off.

After washing and shaving, he emptied the contents of his rucksack onto the table. Neatly folded, and exceptionally well-pressed, in a plastic bag at the bottom he found the change of clothes he had packed specifically to wear in Berlin. Once dressed, he found a full length mirror at the top of the stairs. For someone who had travelled six thousand miles by land and sea, he looked remarkably tidy. He set off on the final leg of his journey with renewed confidence.

Harry and Mike spent most of Sunday going over everything they each knew about the conspirators. They had nothing on the whereabouts of Gunter. He wasn't at his home in Potsdam, though he had been until three days ago. They'd been able to establish that Zaytzev was still in Moscow, and had tracked Silverman to a hotel near the Brandenberg Gate, where he'd checked in as John Tyler. They were sure Gunter would turn up soon; they just needed to sit on Silverman. They assumed Zaytzev would not be putting in a personal appearance, preferring to run things from Moscow. But they had worryingly little to go on.

"I could go to Moscow and talk to him," Harry suggested.

"It's a bit risky," Mike replied. "He's already taken a close interest in you. He may know that you're working for us now. Besides, from what you've said, you weren't on especially good terms even when you were on the same side."

"You're right. But we need something tangible in respect of Zaytzev."

"Well, we have every possible resource at our disposal. If we can't stop him, nobody can."

The closing session of the Tbilisi summit had something of a carnival atmosphere about it. There was no formal dinner or reception. The schedule in the run up to Berlin was too tight to permit another party. Once the formalities were done with, delegates crossed the road to the ballroom of the neighbouring hotel for drinks.

Helen had given Rita strict instructions to rescue her in the event of getting stuck with anyone of lesser rank than President or Prime Minister. In the event, she needn't have worried, as President Kotov monopolised her for the first hour.

"I think it has all gone rather well, don't you Helen?"

"Thanks to you, it's gone very well."

"I feel guilty now. Perhaps I should apologise for having given you so much trouble."

"Well that depends. Were you just stringing us along, or was there a real possibility that you might not have given your support."

"Oh no. The possibility was real enough. I made up my mind last Monday evening, and I phoned you the following morning."

"And are you happy that you made the right decision?"

"I am happy that I made the only decision I could possibly make. That is not to say I'm not worried about what happens next. But I am persuaded that the blueprint is our only hope. Honestly Helen, you should see the state of my country; it makes me ashamed. The only way to save Russia is to be a part of this project to save all of humankind. Of this, I am now convinced."

"Well, it's a great relief to have you on board Mr President. Of the major nations, I think Russia possibly has the most to gain. I read last week that unemployment has passed forty per cent"

"I suspect that's an underestimate. It is indeed terrible, but I don't think Russia's plight is simply a consequence of its past. The same could happen to any industrialised nation. If the blueprint can help us reverse the trend towards a two-tier economy, perhaps we can persuade people not to give up on their lives and on their communities. I'm not surprised so many people seek refuge in the vodka bottle when they see what is going on: a few people making a killing out of an economy which offers nothing to the majority of ordinary people."

"We certainly have to win the moral argument. It can't be right that a small minority are able to secure for themselves control over nearly all economic opportunities and resources."

"I agree, Helen. Everybody should feel under a moral obligation at least not to act in ways that deny the means to earn a living to other people."

"I think we've identified the structures and institutions that make this possible. If they can be dismantled, then everybody should be able to take responsibility for their own security and wellbeing."

"And the state will wither away?" Kotov had a glint in his eye.

"I know all about your anarchist leanings, Mr President."

"We're all anarchists here aren't we. In the true sense of the word, I mean?"

"I suppose we are. But if you quote me I'll deny it. I'm not sure the world is ready for a debate about the real meaning of anarchism. But I suppose you could see the blueprint as the first step in a progression towards a global society run along lines of cooperation and the mutual recognition of common interests. A network of strong local and regional economies, connected through sustainable and mutually beneficial trade, operating within a neutral global framework. The dream of small government realised, and an end to poverty."

"I knew you were one of the good guys, Helen."

"Let's just say we hold a similar world view."

"Talking about good guys. Have you spoken to Harry Noble? I hope he's forgiven us."

"Actually I have. He's got a new job. He's coordinating our intelligence gathering operation in Berlin." Kotov smiled.

Mbonga made his way to Treptow, a suburb of Berlin four kilometres from Templehof. He leant his bike against a railing and walked away as inconspicuously as he could. He tracked back a few hundred metres to a motel he had just cycled past. This was a good place to be. There were tram links to Templehof and to the centre of Berlin.

The motel looked perfect. He brushed down his coat and walked in. In his best rehearsed German he told the receptionist he'd like to book a room for one week. She immediately offered to speak in English and was very friendly. He had decided to use his credit card to pay for the room. He and Temily had acquired the card on a trip to South Africa several years earlier. They used it very occasionally, and only when they were certain they would be able to pay it off without running up interest. By using it now he would be able to make his remaining cash go further.

He handed over his passport and answered several routine questions, telling the receptionist that the purpose of his stay in Berlin was a holiday.

"Have you come for the summit?" she asked.

"I have," he decided to tell the truth. "For me this is the trip of a lifetime. I just wanted to be here to see history being made."

"Welcome to Germany, Mr Siphosa," she said as she handed him his key.

He found his room which was on the ground floor of the three story block, with a door straight out onto the car park. It was perfect. There was a television with an internet connection, and a machine for making tea and coffee.

He lay on the bed. He couldn't believe he'd made it. And while he was in the country illegally, his experience at reception suggested he was unlikely to be discovered. If he kept his head down he would be able to enjoy Berlin, and the summit, just like any other visitor.

He did wonder how he was going to pay off the credit card on his return home, but quickly buried that thought when he remembered he had no idea how he was going to get home anyway. He switched on the TV and logged onto the internet service. He sent Temily a long email, letting her know he had made it to Berlin, and describing his adventure. He longed to hear back from her. But after enjoying his first hot shower since the abandoned hotel in Tanzania, and waiting a further thirty minutes for a reply, he set off for the tram stop.

Helen had established a formal security committee to meet as often as required. She had asked Ann Margaret to join Saeed and Daniel on the team. Mike and Harry would usually be included, but for the first meeting would participate via video link from Berlin.

Mike gave them an update. Security arrangements were proceeding well with good cooperation from the German authorities. They had already established a wider-than-planned secure zone around Templehof. But beyond the venue, things were a little more difficult. The German's were reporting a surge in visitors, both from within Germany and beyond. Hotels were filling up fast. Nothing could be done to prevent people travelling to Berlin. In any case, as they were counting on massive street celebrations in support of the blueprint before and during the summit, they wanted people to come to Berlin.

There was less progress on the intelligence front. "It is extremely difficult to see how an attack could be launched against delegates inside the venue," Mike said. "Getting them to Templehof securely once they arrive at Branden-burg Airport should not be difficult. As there are so many of them, we are planning to run a convoy every two hours or so, when we'll close the roads. There will be disruption, but it shouldn't be too bad."

"And what about the two specific threats?" Helen asked.

"We don't have much more I'm afraid. But they have to put their heads above the parapet at some point. We will get to Gunter via Silverman. Harry's working on the Russians."

"I wonder if I might ask Harry a question?" Barenboim asked.

Harry's heart missed a beat. He couldn't believe he was about to be addressed by his hero. "Of course," he replied, moving into the frame.

"Hello Harry. Now, I don't know much about these things, but is there a possibility that the Russians know about Silverman, and vice versa? These people are all spies after all. Should we consider the possibility that they might pool their resources."

"We have considered that possibility, Sir," he answered rather awkwardly, "but we've found no evidence to suggest such a connection. I doubt that Silverman would sign up to a joint operation with the Russians, but then I was wrong about Gunter. We are still trying to make a connection."

"Mike," Helen asked, "do we have an update on the number of heads of government attending?"

"We have provisional yeses from all of them. A couple may be thwarted by weather-related travel problems, but there's a good chance they'll all be here."

Both of Antonella's flights were on time, and great fun. She didn't sleep much on the overnight from São Paulo to Paris; she was too excited, and there was so much to do on the plane. She'd walked miles around the French capital and was pretty exhausted by the time she arrived in Berlin, where she encountered a problem. The person who was supposed to meet her hadn't turned up. She waited about half an hour, but it was getting late, so she decided to pay for a taxi to the hotel.

Thankfully, the hotel knew all about her reservation: fully paid in advance until the following Monday, with breakfast included. She just needed to prove her identity to get her key.

She unpacked quickly and emailed Tito, asking him to contact the lottery company to find out what had happened to her contact. She was worried that if the contact had disappeared, she would have no way of getting into the end of summit gala concert. But she wasn't going to let this minor setback spoil things. She was in Berlin on the eve of the summit and with more money to spend than she had ever seen in her life. She decided to go out for something to eat. She walked west towards Alexaderplatz and after a few minutes found a nice looking café, about a third full.

There were five tables in the window. The three in the middle were unoccupied. She had taken the one by the wall furthest from the door. At the one nearest to the door she noticed a man reading the blueprint. From time to time he would look up; when the waitress came to take Antonella's order, and again when she brought her drink over. Both times she accidentally caught his eye, but the second time, neither looked quickly away. He was older than she was, late thirties, she thought, and had a kind face.

She suddenly felt rather alone. How was she was going to manage for six days without company? She wondered if her own interest in the blueprint was sufficient cause to talk to the man opposite, but decided not to risk it. This was her first evening in a strange town after all, and everybody had a copy of the blueprint – he could be a madman for all she knew.

On the other hand if he's not mad, then perhaps they'd have something in common; he may even be good company. She tried to put the thought out of her mind. She would do nothing to encourage the stranger, but if he chose to speak to her, she would respond positively.

She was about half way through an enormous plate of chicken and chips when she noticed that he'd put down his book and was looking in her direction.

"That looks good," he said.

"Mmm," she said, wiping her lips with her napkin. It's delicious, but too much for me. Would you like some chips?"

He got up and walked towards her. "Thank you," he said. "Um, may I join you, or should I take a handful back to my table?"

Antonella laughed. "Of course you may join me. Please sit down. My name's Antonella."

She held out her hand before realising it was covered in grease and withdrawing it.

"That's an interesting name. Where's it from? Mine is Mbonga, by the way."

"I think your name is more interesting than mine. I think you should tell me where you are from first," she smiled at him.

"Fair enough," he replied, swallowing his second forkful of chips.

"I'm from Swaziland, and you."

"Brazil."

"Ah, so you speak Portuguese?"

"That's right. Do you know any?"

"A little. I've been to Mozambique several times, in fact I passed through on my way here, just a few weeks ago."

"Could you not get a flight from Swaziland then?"

"I didn't fly. Far too expensive. I travelled by road and by sea."

"Wow. How long did it take you?"

"About six weeks."

For the next hour Antonella and Mbonga swapped accounts of how they each came to be in Berlin for the summit. Each detected in the other's story a sense of not quite being in control of events.

"I don't know if I believe in fate," Antonella said, "but you have to say it is pretty strange that we both ended up in this café at the same time."

"It is very strange. I'm glad I came here though. It would have been a shame to have missed you. What are your plans for the next few days?"

"I don't know. What do people do when they visit a city like Berlin at such an important time?"

Before catching a tram back to Treptow, Mbonga walked Antonella back to her hotel. They arranged to meet in the same café for breakfast the following morning.

Twenty-Five

Hilda Solis was making a stopover in London on her way to Berlin. Now that the problem with Kotov had been dealt with, there was only one item on the agenda for her meeting with the Prime Minister, Sarah Brightwell: how to ensure a seamless transition from the summit process to the transition period; and how to persuade Helen George to continue in a senior role.

"The problem we have is this: while every member of the committee is highly competent and widely respected, Helen is the face and voice of this entire process. As far as the world is concerned, she made it happen. I can't see how we get a successful transition if Helen's not involved."

"You're right Hilda. I saw one poll that suggested a majority would support the creation of a post of world president as long as it was filled by Helen."

"Well, I guess that's democracy for you."

"I'm just not sure she can be persuaded."

"I think you have to tell it like it is, Sarah. As it stands, even the best case scenario has everybody going home from Berlin and nothing happening for a couple of weeks while the diplomatic machinery lumbers into action to find a consensus candidate to chair the transition council. And if we can't nominate Helen, I can't see who we can nominate."

"I know. Jamali is the only other candidate. He's great behind the scenes, but he's not a leader."

"It could be weeks before transition can begin. We have a little over six months to deliver the whole thing. I'm sorry Sarah, it has to be Helen."

"Okay. I'll phone her tonight and arrange a meeting as soon as we land in Berlin. I'll also talk to Morel. Perhaps you could get a meeting with Kotov and Choi once they arrive. Helen will have no choice if we all go knocking on her door."

"Okay. Let me know how you get on. I can't believe we haven't sorted this before." She shook her head.

"Well, we've all been working pretty hard just to get this far."

Although Helen had changed planes in Berlin on her way to Tbilisi, when the wheels touched on her return it was a quite different feeling. She was travelling, once again, with Rita, Jay and Stefan. None spoke as they taxied towards the terminal, but each knew what the others were thinking. Mike was at the top of the ramp to meet them. He explained that they would not be entering the terminal building, rather they would exit the aircraft via a movable staircase and get on a bus that would take them across the airport to a helicopter which would take them to Templehof.

"Welcome to security, Berlin style."

"Are all the delegates going to be flown in by helicopter?" Stefan asked.

"We're not sure yet. To be honest this is a bit of an experiment." Helen looked at him, slightly concerned. "I don't mean the helicopter, no that's fine. We've closed a corridor of airspace between here and Templehof up to three thousand metres, and we've been doing extensive airborne surveillance.

There's no sign of any rogue anti-aircraft capability within range of the corridor."

"So when you say experiment," Helen said, "you're sending us up in a helicopter to make sure your surveillance operation is up to scratch."

"Look, I'll be on the helicopter with you," he said, slightly agitated. "Does that put your mind at ease?" She was tempted to tease Mike further, but it occurred to her that he might be as worried about being on this 'test' flight as she was, so she said nothing. In the event, the ten minute hop to Templehof passed without incident.

Helen was first out, and was delighted to see Rudolf waiting beyond the bluster of the rotors. She introduced him to the others. He'd met Robertson before and they had got on. She thought it very gracious of him to give the Canadian a hug. Rita also noticed the gesture. For her part she peppered Rudolf's cheeks with kisses, all the time repeating how excited she was finally to be meeting a man she'd heard so much about.

The helipad at Templehof was quite some way from the old terminal building which, for several decades after its construction, had been the largest permanent structure in the world. Helen had only seen pictures; it certainly was a sight to behold, even from a kilometre away. They boarded another airport bus and raced across the tarmac.

"We thought you might like an hour to yourselves before meeting up for a tour of the venue?" Mike suggested. "Saeed, Jemma, Ann Margaret and Kersen are already here. The others won't be landing for another couple of hours, so they'll have to get the tour tomorrow morning. I hope you like it. This is home for the next six days. Nobody is allowed out."

Helen and Rudolf decided to take the stairs to their room while the others waited for the lift. It had been a joke between them since the first time they had met secretly in a hotel, and Helen had delighted her new lover by racing up the stairs ahead of him. Just like the first time, he had a bottle of champagne on ice.

"I know you're working. If you don't want to drink, I'll understand."

"I do fancy a glass. Do you have that clever little stopper that works in champagne bottles? We could have the rest later."

Rudolf reached into his pocket and brought out the stopper.

"You're so clever," she said, kissing him.

"Well, even at times like this one must pay attention to the small details." He poured her a glass and she took a sip.

"Listen," she said. "there's something we need to talk about."

"Go on."

"Sarah called a little while ago. I'm seeing her and Hilda as soon as they get in." She sighed. "You were right: they're not going to let me off the hook. They want me to head up the Transitionary Council. There are no other qualified candidates, and they're worried about losing momentum."

"They're right."

"I know," she was almost shouting. "I'm sorry. I know we've prepared for this, but I'm tired. I need a break."

"You should make that a condition of taking the job."

"I will, but they'll only give me a week."

"I can't remember when we last spent a whole week together. It'll be the equivalent of a three month break for any normal couple. And tell them you insist on being based in Geneva. That way you can come home in the evening."

"I'll have to commit for at least six months."

"Six months is nothing darling. It'll fly by."

"Okay. I'm sorry. Now it's actually happening, I just need a little time to get used to the idea."

"It's alright, honestly"

"Good. Now, give me some more champagne please."

Mbonga hadn't slept so well in weeks. He woke early and refreshed, and bounced off the bed and into the bathroom for his second hot shower in as many days. The bathroom window, which was unfrosted but guarded by a blind, looked out onto a piece of derelict land behind the hotel. From the thickness of the vegetation covering the plot, and the scatterings of rubble about the place, Mbonga reckoned that whatever building had previously stood there had been demolished several years ago. He thought it strange that the site had not been redeveloped. He was about to pull the blind down when an unmarked white Mercedes van drove through a gate on its far side. He watched as two men got out of the cab. One must have opened a sliding door on the far side of the van for two other men then appeared. They were hidden from view for a few minutes, until the van drove off. The three men who remained had changed into white overalls of the kind worn by officials dealing with an industrial accident.

One of the men began hacking at the weeds with a scythe which, after a couple minutes, he let drop to the floor. One of the others then bent down over the area that had been cleared. Mbonga couldn't see what they were doing. Were they burying something, or perhaps, digging something up. Then, all of a sudden, first one, then a second man disappeared from view, as if they had jumped into a hole. The third man then looked around, lifted what Mbonga could now see was a large manhole cover, and with some effort, manoeuvred it into place. He then walked off in the direction that the van had departed.

Mbonga thought for a moment. It all looked a little suspicious. Neither the van nor the overalls suggested the men were working for a utility company. By the time he finished his shower his mind was racing. He stood in front of the mirror and slapped himself. "Get a grip," he said. But he couldn't get a grip, and by the time he got off the tram near Alexanderplatz, he was itching to tell Antonella about it.

"So you think these men were going underground into some kind of tunnel?"

"That's what it looked like."

"And they didn't come out?"

"I don't know. After half an hour I had to come here to meet you. But when I left the hotel, there was no sign of the white van or the man who replaced the manhole cover."

"Here, look at this". Antonella had taken a book out her bag. It was a Berlin tourist guide. "I was reading this last night." She found the page she was looking for, turned the book around and placed it in front of Mbonga.

"It's in Portuguese. I can't read Portuguese I'm afraid," he said.

"Sorry. I forgot."

"What does it say?"

"It's about a network of tunnels under Berlin that Hitler had built before the Second World War. About twenty years ago there was a plan to open them to the public but it was too expensive. Apparently they run all over the place but they've been sealed off."

"Perhaps they haven't all been sealed off. Maybe the one behind my hotel was left accessible for some reason?"

"So what do you think those men were doing?"

"Maybe they are something to do with security for the summit. That would explain why they weren't wearing any uniforms."

"Probably. But perhaps you should keep watch. See if they do something really suspicious."

The first full meeting of the security committee had convened in the command centre in a comparatively new building close to the main terminal. Daniel was late, but Helen suggested that Harry start anyway. By the time he arrived, Harry was already two minutes into his briefing. Daniel signalled his apology and indicated that there was no reason to stop, as he found a seat.

Harry rather nervously reported that they were still struggling to connect Silverman and Gunter. In fact Gunter was nowhere to be found. There had been similarly little progress in respect of Zaytzev. Mike took over.

"We need to do something to move things on," he began. "Harry wants to contact Zaytzev. I think it's risky as we don't know if Zaytzev knows that Harry is working for us. But if he does, at least he'll get the message that we're onto him."

"At this late stage I think we have to do everything we can," Saeed said. "In any case, what's the worse that can happen? Zaytzev accuses Harry of being a traitor and threatens to blow him up with the rest of us. We wouldn't be any worse off." Helen struggled to stifle a laugh.

Mike scowled at her. "So are we agreed then?" he asked. Harry was pleased to see there were no dissenters.

"Thanks guys," Helen said. "We also need to discuss who we are going to tell about these threats. My feeling is that it needs to stay within this group. Others to be informed strictly on a need to know basis."

"I agree Helen, broadly speaking," Daniel said, "but you haven't forgotten that every head of government in the world is due to arrive here over the next couple of days. Are you going to keep them all in the dark?"

"I think it's the best strategy. I would like to. Does anyone know if I have the authority to make such a decision?"

After several seconds Harry decided to speak. "It's your summit Helen. I think it's your decision. If we need to involve anyone else we can discuss it at these meetings and widen the circle if necessary."

"I think," Ann Margaret said, "it would be politic to appraise Chancellor Emmerich of the situation. It is his country after all. I'm slightly surprised he's not been in touch to ask why we're requesting so much assistance from the German military."

"Good idea. Will you talk to him? In fact, perhaps you could handle liaison with Emmerich's office, Ann Margaret?"

"Of course."

"Otherwise it's strictly need to know, and that includes other committee members."

After a morning spent sightseeing, Mbonga and Antonella returned to the motel to see if there had been any developments. Just after 5pm, the white van returned. They watched as the driver got out and removed the manhole cover. Three men, only two of whom Mbonga recognised from earlier, emerged. Their overalls were dirty and all three looked exhausted. The driver took some heavy pieces of metal out of the van. One of the others took out a gas canister and some other equipment, which they took some time to assemble. Soon there was a bright blue flame. They were welding the metal together. Some of the surrounding vegetation caught fire and two of the men stamped out the flames. It was still difficult to see exactly what was going on, but Mbonga was convinced they were securing the manhole cover so it couldn't be opened again. Ten minutes later, they loaded all the equipment back into the van and drove off.

"I thought you said only two men went into the tunnel this morning."

"I did. It was only two. I have never seen that third man before. He wasn't there this morning."

"So where did he come from?"

"Either he was already down there. Or, he went down there while we were out. Or he got into the tunnel from somewhere else and they met up underground."

"It all seems very suspicious. But I don't think we have enough evidence to go to the authorities. Do you?"

"No," Mbonga said, "but I am worried."

Harry had been trying for nearly three hours to get hold of Zaytzev. He had established that he was in Moscow, but couldn't work out whether his failure to get through was down to incompetence, technical problems or Zaytzev's disdain for him. Finally he recognised the voice on the other end of the line.

"Mr Noble, I'm really very busy. What can I do for you?"

Harry began by apologising for his failure to get Kotov to do the right thing, before explaining that he was in Berlin, and well positioned to help with any plan Zaytzev might have to prevent the summit from proceeding smoothly."

"So you think I have a plan to disrupt the Berlin summit, Mr Noble?"

"It had occurred to me that, given your opposition to the blueprint, you might decide to pursue that option."

"I see your logic, but I hadn't really thought about it." The line went quiet for a few seconds. "And even if I did have such a plan, what makes you think that I would want to enlist your support? You've not exactly proved your worth up to now."

"We're still on the same side, and you will remember I have contacts inside the committee."

"You had your chance Mr Noble. If you were really committed to stopping the process, and if you were really as close to Helen George as you claim, then you would have removed her from the picture by now. I don't think I need your help. Thank you Mr Noble. And goodbye."

Mike had been listening in. "He sounds too confident," he said.

"Just like Silverman," Harry concurred.

"Okay. I think we should assume that Silverman/Gunter and Zaytzev are working on the same scheme. I can just about accept the existence of one conspiracy evading our efforts to uncover it. But not two."

"I agree, although whether we're fighting on two fronts or one, we still have very little to aim at."

"Something will come up. We have everything covered. Unless someone has an ICBM targeted on Berlin, we'll find them."

"I think it's time I had a word with Silverman, don't you?"

"I guess so. What are you going to do?"

"I'll arrange an accidental meeting. If he reacts badly, I'll bring him in. I doubt we'll get anything out of him, but at least we take him out of the game. The last two afternoons he's been followed to a café in Alexanderplatz. I'll wait for him there and see what happens."

Mbonga spent most of the following day in his room hoping to discover more. By mid-afternoon there had been no further activity so he went into town to meet Antonella. She had found an upmarket restaurant not far from her hotel, and had promised to treat him to a meal. Before going out to eat, they went to the hotel's lounge to research a little deeper into the tunnels under the city.

It didn't take long for them turn up some information that shocked them both. On the website of a retired American airforceman, they unearthed an archived story entitled 'Tunnels under Templehof' in which the veteran described a successful attempt to locate tunnels that were rumoured to run under Templehof airport, where he had been stationed in the 1980s.

"You know what this means?" Antonella said.

"I know. Those men could be using the tunnels to access the summit venue. They could have been planting a bomb."

"Do you really think so? It's a long way from your hotel to Templehof."

"But you saw how tired and filthy they looked when they came out. They could easily have walked several kilometres there and back in that time."

At dinner they discussed what to do. Mbonga felt strongly that they should report what they had discovered to the authorities, but they were concerned that nobody would take them seriously: A young Brazilian woman in Berlin because she won a competition, and a Swazi, in Germany illegally, who travelled overland because he really wanted to go to the summit. They would sound like a pair of nutcases.

"Okay," Antonella said. "If we can't go to the police then we will have to get a message to Helen George directly."

Mbonga looked at her. "Do you happen to have her phone number then?" he asked, smiling.

"No, but I have met her."

"What? When? Why didn't you tell me?"

"Well, I've only just met you." She told Mbonga about the meeting with Helen, and the impression it had left on her.

"So you think she would recognise you?" he asked.

"I'm sure she would. I was with her for at least ten minutes, and after I'd sorted her out she asked me lots of questions about my life."

"Okay. I have an idea. Tomorrow there is a big demonstration in support of the blueprint in Alexanderplatz."

"Yes, we should go."

"Lots of people will be carrying placards." Antonella didn't follow. "We will take a placard with a message for Helen George. We just need to make sure we get in front of the TV cameras and hope she watches the coverage."

"I'll be amazed if it works, but it's worth a try."

"If it doesn't work, we go to the authorities. They'll probably throw me out, but you're here legally. You'll be alright."

Delegates to the conference were starting to arrive in Berlin. So far, all had been successfully transported from Brandenberg Airport to Templehof. Among them were Hilda Solis and Sarah Brightwell. They were dining with Helen in one of the several restaurants inside the Templehof complex. Helen had other things on her mind. Harry's attempt to pick up Silverman had failed. He'd fallen off the radar for a period during the afternoon, and hadn't turned up in the café where Harry had been waiting for him. There had been huge sigh of relief when he returned to his hotel. But she knew she couldn't put off this meeting.

It was proposed that Helen take charge of the Blueprint Transitionary Council for a period of eight months, covering the six months proposed transitionary period, and a further two months while the council was wound up, during which period she would continue to have an informal supervisory role, and troubleshoot problems with the new institutions established during the transition period.

Helen had three conditions: First, that the council be based in Geneva, so she could commute from home. Second, that travel would be kept to a minimum. Helen would make a maximum of one long-haul flight each month; otherwise, people would have to come to her. Third, she would like to take Jane, Jemma, Ann Margaret and Saeed to Geneva to work with her. Finally, while she was happy for an announcement to made at Berlin, and for preparatory work to begin /be immediately, she was having a week off after the summit. During that week she would only take calls from Saeed. Solis and Brightwell accepted the conditions without demur. For a moment Helen thought that perhaps she should have asked for more. But there wasn't anything else, except perhaps another week off, and she knew that wasn't practical.

It was the first time the three of them had met privately together, so once the business part of the evening was complete, they made the most of the excellent food on offer.

"So you're not expecting any surprises while we're here then?" Solis asked Helen matter of factly.

"I think we've had enough surprises over the last couple of weeks don't you?" She deflected the question successfully, but felt guilty about lying to the President of the United States about a plot that could, for all she knew, take out most of the delegates to the summit. For now she would be bound by the agreement made with her colleagues, but she wondered how long, if they got confirmation of a planned attack, it would be possible to keep it from these two. Helen felt as if she were playing dice with several hundred rather important lives.

Oscar Silverman was waiting in his hotel room for the call that would send him home. As promised, at exactly 9am his phone rang.

"Mr Tyler?"

"Yes. Have you been able to complete the work?"

"The item we discussed has been collected and installed. It will be commissioned tomorrow morning at 11am. Is there anything else I can do for you, Sir?

"Nothing. Thank you for your help. Goodbye."

It was a beautifully sunny Thursday morning. Not that Mike and Harry were aware of it, holed up in the windowless command centre where they had been since 5am. They were getting desperate. Silverman was still in his hotel and there was no sign of Gunter or any suspicious looking Russians who might be working for Zaytzev.

"Hell, Harry. We can't just sit here."

"I agree. We have to bring Silverman in. I'll go and get him."

Mike nodded his agreement as Rick Spedman came into the room. "Silverman's on the move," he said, "just got into a taxi. Looks like he's heading for the airport. Do we take him?"

"Yes. Take Harry with you."

Harry grabbed his jacket and the two men ran out of the room. On the way to the airport, they were able to establish that there were no direct flights to the United States for several hours.

"Where else might he be going?" Rick asked.

"He'll be going to the States. If he has to change he'll take the route least likely to suffer disruption. I bet it's London."

"There's a BA flight leaving in 90 minutes." Harry phoned airport security who were able to confirm that a John Tyler was booked on the London flight.

"Terminal 3, quick as you can," Rick said to the driver.

As they approached the BA check-in, they could see the American standing in line, three from the front. Harry joined the back of the queue. There were four people between him and Silverman. He would wait until Rick had his agents in position in case Silverman made a run for it. He was a big man; Harry wouldn't be able to take him alone.

The queue shuffled forward and then stopped. Harry kept going until he was standing beside Silverman. "Hello Oscar," he said calmly.

Silverman turned slowly to look at him. For a moment he looked confused. "What the fuck are you doing here Noble?" The penny quickly dropped. "You shit, you've been working for the other side all along."

"Actually no. Only since Sunday. Let's just say I saw the error of my ways, or rather yours, Oscar."

For a moment Silverman looked resigned. Then he picked up his case and shoved it in Harry's chest, causing him to fall backwards over a luggage trolley. As Harry struggled to his feet, he saw Silverman being handcuffed by two of Spedman's team. He was screaming and kicking out violently. Spedman walked calmly over to him, and, dodging the flailing feet, punched him once, very hard, in the solar plexus. Silverman was winded, his resistance at an end.

Helen had no appointments in the morning and was working in her room when Rita knocked on the door, announced herself, and came in. "Have you been watching the coverage?"

"Coverage?" Helen asked, her mind still on her papers.

"Yes, of the demonstration in Alexanderplatz. They reckon more than 100,000 people, and that's just in the square. They're all chanting your name you know?"

"Really? Jesus." Helen took off her glasses and looked at Rita. She could tell there was something else, but that Rita was waiting for her full attention, which she gave.

"What was the name of that chambermaid you met in São Paulo, the one who rescued you when banged your head?"

"Antonella?"

"That's right. You know a really funny thing just happened."

"Go on."

"I was watching the demo on TV, and the camera was panning the crowd. Everybody was shouting and singing. And there was a woman holding a placard, pointing it at the camera. It said 'Helen I must speak to you. Very Important. Antonella.'"

A shiver ran down Helen's spine. "Are you sure?

"Yes, clear as the day. What can it mean?"

"I have no idea. What would she be doing here? She was an ordinary hotel employee. It doesn't make sense."

"What should we do?"

"I don't know. But I do know there was something about that young woman that stayed with me." She picked up her phone. "Mike, I need you to find out where a Brazilian called Antonella Soares is staying and bring her in. At the moment it's just a hunch. Yes, thanks. Let me know when she's here. Oh and Mike, she's not a suspect."

"Is there something else going on, Helen?"

"Walk with me."

"Where are we going?"

"To see Harry and Mike."

"What's going on?"

"There's a plot, possibly two plots, to target the summit, and right now we have virtually no leads."

"Is that why Harry came on board?"

"Pretty much."

"Who knows?"

"Saeed, Daniel, Ann Margaret and now you."

"And you think Antonella might have information about these plots?"

"Frankly, we're clutching at straws."

In the five minutes it took them to reach the command centre, Mike had managed to find Antonella. "She's in a hotel half a mile from Alexanderplatz. Two female agents are on their way. Who is she?" Helen explained about their meeting in Brazil, and how Rita just spotted her on TV. Mike wasn't convinced. "Well, I suppose we need to follow up all leads, however tenuous. By the way, if your Brazilian friend doesn't have anything, Harry's just picked up Silverman."

"That must have been interesting," Helen said.

"Do you think that camera got a good shot of the placard?" Mbonga asked as they tried to make their way through the huge crowd in Alexanderplatz.

"I don't know. Even if it did, who knows if Helen saw us. I can't imagine she has much time to watch TV."

"I suppose not. But if she did, they'll be able to track you down in no time."

They got back to the hotel and waited. It was only twenty minutes before there was a knock on the door. Antonella jumped up and opened it. There were two women, in their thirties she thought, dressed informally, but in a way that suggested a uniform. The taller of the two, who spoke with an American accent, introduced herself as Donna Galen and asked if she could come in.

"Yes, please," she said.

"Are you Antonella Soares?"

"I am."

"We have instructions to escort you to the Templehof Conference Centre."

Antonella looked at Mbonga and smiled.

"It worked," he said.

"This is my friend, Mbonga Siphosa. He must come with us. He has important information."

"We were only asked to collect you, Miss Soares."

"But really, he must come too."

"Wait a minute, please." Donna Galen raised her wrist to her mouth. "Mike, there's two of them. The target is insisting her friend come along?" There was a pause. "Okay. Thanks." She looked at Antonella and smiled. "He said yes. Come on, quickly."

Silverman was in shock. He was still seething at the treachery of someone he considered a friend, but it was beginning to dawn on him what this meant. They wouldn't have arrested him unless they had evidence of his involvement in the plot. He was facing the prospect of spending the rest of his life in jail. Through the darkened windows of the police van, he could see they were driving through the security cordon at Templehof. Five minutes later the van stopped. Shortly afterwards the rear door opened and he was told to get out. He looked around. There was no sign of Noble; he must have travelled separately. He could see that they were inside a heavily fortified compound in which stood a modern building, not part of the old airport terminal.

He was led through a heavy metal door which opened automatically, along a corridor and then downstairs into a basement that housed four sound-proofed cells. The door to the first of these was opened, and one of the guards indicated to him to step inside. Once he had done so, the door shut heavily behind him, a series of automatic locks clicking into place.

He thought about what he would say to Noble. Obviously he would deny all knowledge of whatever they accused him of. He would give nothing away, even if they tortured him. But he wasn't going to let Noble off the hook. What can have happened to the man to make him switch sides? He knew Noble had always been a bit flaky, but among British colleagues he'd been a genuine ally. He just didn't understand.

Minutes later Antonella and Mbonga were sat in the back of what Mbonga decided was a bullet-proof car speeding towards Templehof.

"There must be something serious going on. They came to find us pretty quickly," Antonella said.

"I think so. Although it might not have anything to do with the tunnels."

"But what if it is? What if those men you saw were planting a bomb right under the summit?"

"If that's the case, then I suppose it's a very good job we were here: me to see it, and you to provide a way of getting a message to Helen George. You couldn't make it up though."

Harry was talking to Helen about Silverman. He had decided to let him sweat for a short while. The door opened and Mike came in, out of breath and looking white.

"I've just had Kotov on the phone," he said, "a portable nuclear device has gone missing from a secret military installation outside Moscow."

"How long?" Harry asked.

"They're not sure, but it could be as long as four days."

"Jesus," Helen said under her breath.

"Kotov has just landed at Brandenburg. The scientist who designed the device is also on his way, but he's currently in Finland, so won't be here until later tonight. I've asked for Kotov to be brought straight here."

"How big is this device?" Helen asked. "I mean how easy would it be to smuggle it into the country, into Berlin?"

"Despite immigration controls, there are very few secure border crossings between here and Moscow. If it's reasonably small, a courier would just need to evade random spot checks, or to pick a route than avoided major border crossings." Mike said.

"You mean anyone could smuggle a nuclear weapon from Moscow to Berlin without being detected?" Helen was incredulous.

"It's certainly possible," Harry confirmed, "And Zaytzev would have access to diplomatic passports."

"Listen," Mike said. "Berlin is one thing. This place is another. They won't get within a mile of the summit."

"It's a fucking atom bomb, Mike. They don't need to get within a mile. Every world leader will have died of radiation poisoning by the weekend."

"Right," Harry said. "We need to find it. I'll go in with Silverman now. I need to establish for certain whether he and Gunter are working with the Russians."

"Okay, but I want a report back in half an hour. Mike, get Ann Margaret and Rita in here. I'll call Daniel."

Twenty-Six

In the cavernous Templehof Arena, Daniel and Rudolf were catching up during a break from rehearsals. "I suppose you've heard: I'm not getting my wife back quite yet."

"I did. I was rather surprised. Helen has been so adamant about ending her involvement. I do think it's a good thing though."

"I hope she can get the right people and structures in place before May. Actually making something happen is always more difficult than deciding what to do in the first place. I mean look at this programme."

"The concert will be fine Rudolf. Stop fretting. As for the blueprint, at least there is a clear framework to which all countries will hopefully sign up to tomorrow. I think the only sticking points may be who gets the plum jobs."

"But there should be no advantage to be gained for a country by having its representative running one or other of the new bodies, should there?"

"That's the theory. It will be interesting to see how it works out in practice."

"And what about you Daniel. Does this really mark the end of your involvement?"

"Absolutely, my friend. I'm on the first train to Paris on Sunday morning, I plan to disappear from the public eye forever."

"From politics you mean?"

"No. I think that's it. Which means you get to conduct my last performance."

"You're not serious?"

"I'm afraid I am. I've been playing in public for 73 years. I think that's enough for one lifetime."

"But what will you do with yourself. Music and politics have been your entire life."

"I'll do what other people do when they retire. Spend time with my grandchildren, of whom I have seen far too little. Read books. Listen to music. I believe you have a new recording of the Brahms Violin Concerto out soon?" Rudolf nodded. "Well there you are. I'll finally be able to devote a proper amount of time to new releases."

"You will be terribly missed you know."

"After a couple of years people will assume I'm dead." Barenboim's laughter was interrupted by a phone call. "I'd better take it, it's your wife. Hello Helen. Yes, he's about to rehearse something else. I can give you half an hour. Okay, on my way."

He turned to look at Rudolf. "Major development on the security front. Got to go."

Harry had Silverman brought to a small interrogation room at the end of the cell corridor. Once he was seated, he signalled to the guard to wait outside.

"Hello Oscar. Sorry about the scene at the airport, but you could have come quietly you know?" Silverman looked at him but said nothing.

"Okay. We know you are involved in a plot, with Gunter Schmidt, to attack the summit. We have all the evidence we need to ensure you never see the Blue Ridge Mountains again. The only way you can avoid that outcome is to give us information to help prevent the attack."

"I'm not going to tell you anything." Silverman spoke calmly.

"I think you will, Oscar, eventually. You may have done some dodgy things in your life, but you're not a terrorist. What are you doing working with Gunter?"

"He's just the means to an end."

"And what exactly is that end Oscar?"

"You should know Harry. Until a few days ago, we were both working toward it, remember? Or were you working for other side all along?"

"To be honest with you Oscar, I've been struggling to remember exactly what we were fighting for. It's all very well working to ensure that power remains in the hands of an elite, especially if one counts oneself as a member of that elite. But when the world is collapsing around your ears?"

"There are two ways the world can be Harry: elite power or anarchy. What the opponents of elite power fail to understand is that there is no viable alternative."

"I accept there hasn't been up to now. But the blueprint offered the world an alternative. The world considered it and said yes in overwhelming numbers."

"You don't seriously think ordinary people understand the blueprint? You don't really think they can imagine the impact it'll have on their lives?"

"I do, Oscar. For many people, anything would be better than what they suffer at present. And frankly, there are many better-qualified people than you who have come out in support. It's not a lunatic fringe that's managed to brainwash millions of people."

"They're all idiots. It'll never get off the ground."

"The world's changing Oscar. The balance of power has shifted. We are all about to learn the true meaning of the democracy."

"Excuse me if I don't hold my breath."

"What do you hope to achieve by bombing the summit?"

"Well, at least it'll buy some time."

"For whom, Oscar? Do you have an alternative strategy, a plan b ready to implement? Don't you read the papers? Every government in the world is going to sign up to the blueprint, right here. Tomorrow."

Silverman laughed. "I wouldn't bet on it."

As soon as they arrived at Templehof, Antonella and Mbonga were taken up some stairs and into a room with lots of screens and strange looking equipment. Antonella immediately recognised Helen.

"Hello again," Helen said, holding out her hand.

"Hello," the Brazilian replied, more nervously than at their previous meeting.

"So, you needed to see me?" Helen looked at Mike, fully aware of how bizarre it must appear.

"Yes. Sorry. Please, first I must introduce my friend Mbonga. He is from Swaziland." Helen shook Mbonga's hand.

"Don't be nervous," she said, "Look, let's sit down over here and you can both tell me why you're here."

Mbonga began by telling of his suspicions at what he had seen outside his hotel room. Mike immediately joined them at the table. Antonella took up the story, explaining how they had discovered the existence of Nazi-built tunnels on the internet, and the fact that some of these tunnels ran under Templehof airport. At this point, Mike got up and made a phone call. As they finished their story, he returned to the table.

"It checks out," he said. "German security confirms the existence of the tunnels, although they thought all access points were sealed off more than a decade ago. Some of the tunnels under Templehof were swept a week ago, just before the security cordon was established. But they don't have up to date maps, so they didn't go all the way in. Some tunnels had been blocked with concrete, others were dead ends."

Helen tried to remain calm for the sake of her guests. "Well, it seems we owe you two a big debt of gratitude. Mike?"

"Yes. Absolutely. I'll head out to Treptow. Mbonga, you'd better come with me. I'll get German security to meet us there. Perhaps you could talk to Kotov as soon as he gets here?" Helen nodded.

"Antonella, why don't you stay here with me for a while?"

"I'll update Harry on the way out." Mike stood up and indicated to Mbonga to go with him.

Harry was getting nowhere with Silverman. He was standing outside the door to the cell wishing he hadn't given up smoking when Mike came round the corner.

"So who are these two people," he asked as Mike finished the story.

"One is a chambermaid Helen met when we were in São Paulo, the other is a Swazi who travelled overland to be here for the summit on a whim, and happened to meet the Brazilian in a café. It's almost as crazy as having you on the team."

"I'm not sure I'm helping much with Silverman."

"Have you told him we know about the device?"

"That's next. I'll also tell him we've found the tunnels. That might break his resolve."

"Good luck."

Harry went back into the room and sat down opposite Silverman. "We know about the bomb Oscar, and the tunnels." Silverman stared at him, his expression unchanged. Harry leant back.

"Do you know how many people would die if a nuclear device were detonated under this building?" It was immediately obvious to Harry that Silverman had no idea of the nature of the weapon. "Oh don't look so surprised, Oscar. We've known for sometime that you've been working not only with Gunter but also with Zaytzev. And we know Zaytzev was behind the disappearance of a portable nuclear device from a facility outside Moscow a few days ago. We also know about the ventilation shaft in Treptow used by your operatives to gain access to the tunnel network."

"If you know all this, why do you need me?"

"I suppose in the hope that you might see sense and help us find the device."

"Come on Harry. You know me. I don't get my hands dirty. I don't know where the bomb is. I don't even know how Gunter got into the tunnels."

"Where is Gunter now?"

"Long gone. You won't find him."

"So the device is in place, then?"

"No comment."

"How long have we got Oscar?"

Silverman looked at his watch.

"About 30 hours, I'd say."

That was enough for Harry. He headed upstairs to brief Helen and see if there was any news from Treptow. As he walked along the corridor he saw one of the female security staff escorting an attractive young woman out of the command centre. Inside the room, Helen had been joined by Daniel, Saeed, Ann Margaret and Rita.

"Harry. Good. Sit down. I'm was going to brief the others, but if you'd like to do it, you can bring us all up to date."

"Okay. I'll keep this short. In the last few hours we've made a great deal of progress. We have detained Oscar Silverman, ex-CIA and one of the suspected conspirators. I'm now convinced he was working with both Gunter and Zaytzev: there is only one plot against the summit. But that plot involves the detonation of a nuclear device in tunnels underneath the main Templehof building. I believe the device is already in place and is scheduled to go off sometime tomorrow afternoon or evening." He paused. Everyone remained remarkably calm. He assumed they were in shock.

"We believe we have identified the means by which the bombers accessed the tunnel system that runs under the city. Mike is on his way there with German security personnel. The task now is to find the device and disable it." As he finished, Helen's phone rang.

"Hi Mike, I'm putting you on speaker. Go ahead."

"Helen. I'm at the tunnel entrance. It's been used recently and sealed in the last couple of days. We are waiting for logistical support before we head down. Oh, Helen, what shall I do with Mbonga?"

"Have him brought back here."

"Who is Mbonga?" Daniel asked.

Helen quickly told the story of how they came upon the information about the tunnels, and how Kotov had revealed the possibility of a nuclear device being involved. She looked around the table. Everyone looked very uncomfortable.

"I know this is pretty disturbing news. Sorry to have to break it to you like this. Does anyone have any immediate questions?"

"Yes." Daniel said. "Harry, is Silverman likely to give us any help finding the bomb."

"I don't think so. He's the paymaster, but he doesn't know where the device is located. In fact, I don't think he knew that a nuclear device was being used until I told him just now."

"But he didn't deny it?" Helen asked.

"He couldn't. And he pretty much confirmed he was working with Zaytzev."

"Okay. Once again. I have to ask you to keep this information to yourselves. This can't get out."

"Should I tell Emmerich?" Ann Margaret asked.

Helen thought for a moment. "Yes," she answered.

"And what about a contingency plan? What if they can't find the device, or if they find it but can't make it safe? We will have to evacuate Berlin," Daniel said.

"We can't," Harry said softly. "Four million people, a million of whom live within a mile radius of Templehof. It's impossible without sparking mass panic."

"The scientist who put the device together will be here later this evening," Helen said. "President Kotov is in contact with him. He advises that if it can be found, disabling it should not be difficult."

"But Helen, he'll have less than twenty four hours."

"I know. But we're way ahead of where we were even three hours ago. We will find the bomb and deal with it. And the summit will proceed as planned." Helen sounded like she believed what she was saying. She did believe it. She had to.

"I have to go," Saeed said. "I'm meeting Kotov downstairs. He needs security clearance. Are you happy to have him in the room Helen?" She nodded.

"And I'll go and find Emmerich," Ann Margaret got up to leave with Saeed.

"What are you going to do with Antonella and her friend?" Harry asked.

"Give them a bloody medal. Rita, perhaps you could take care of them?"

"Of course I will Helen." She also left the room.

"Jesus guys. Is this the right thing to do?"

"It's the only thing we can do." Harry said. "I'll put together a plan for evacuating the delegates in case we haven't made the device safe by the time the summit starts."

"What will you do with them?" Daniel asked.

"Put them on a fleet of buses. Send them to Hamburg. Less likely to draw attention than ferrying them out by helicopter."

"Daniel, I'd better stay here. Will you tell Rudolf?"

"Of course I will."

"And tell him that I love him?" He left Helen alone in the room.

Harry went down and asked the guard to return Silverman to his cell. As he watched him being led down he felt guilty about the company he'd kept all these years. On his way back upstairs he met Saeed and Kotov.

"Harry," the Russian boomed. "I heard you were here. How marvellous that we have both ended up on the same side."

"I suppose it is Mr President. Now, are you going to be able to help us fix this latest problem?"

"I sincerely hope so," Kotov answered solemnly.

Mike's first foray into the tunnel lasted about thirty minutes. In the absence of anyone else, he had assumed control over the operation and wanted to see for himself what it was like underground so he could get an idea of how long it would take to find the device. He was accompanied by a German special forces officer called Rulein who explained that, as their maps were so poor, they would have to rely on compasses and measuring wheels to systematically navigate their way to the area underneath Templehof."

"It never occurred to me that a compass would work underground," Mike said.

"Marble," the German replied.

"I'm sorry?"

"Navigating underground tunnels was one of the first uses to which early compasses were put. Back in the thirteenth century in the marble mines in Carrara they used them to find their way around under the mountains."

German troops had already begun the laborious task of pushing towards Templehof by trying out every side tunnel, and marking the entrance to those which were dead ends, or which seemed to lead in the wrong direction, with a cross of red paint. Other troops were fixing lights to the sides of the tunnels, which were helpfully covered with pipes and cables.

By the time Mike and Rulein returned to the surface, the area of waste ground next to Mbonga's motel had been transformed into something resembling a fairground. There were lights everywhere. Several mobile cranes were winching generators into position, and assorted items of heavy plant and machinery were being driven onto the site. Mike couldn't imagine how half of the stuff could be used, but was pleased to see that every eventuality was being catered for. He was less pleased to see television crews setting up on the roof of Mbonga's hotel. He gave instructions for them to be removed to a designated press area some distance away. It had already beeen agreed that if the media tried to link the summit and the operation in Treptow, they would issue a firm denial; there was little else they could do.

It was exactly three weeks since Helen, Saeed, Harry and Kotov had met in The Kremlin. The atmosphere at this second meeting was rather more urgent.

"I take it you knew about the existence of this device?" Helen demanded of Kotov.

"I ordered the destruction of all such weapons the day after I took office, Helen. I was assured that my instructions had been carried out." Kotov looked distraught.

"What about this expert who's flying in? Can he be trusted?"

"I don't know the man personally, but his record is impeccable. There is no indication of any dealings with the FSB or with the Foreign Ministry, and no connection to Zaytzev. And he's been out of the country for the last three weeks. It is inconceivable that he was involved in the theft of the device. In any case, what option do we have Helen?"

"It feels like we're having to trust a number of people that none of us are very close to."

"Mike is keeping an eye on the Germans, not that they are a problem," Harry said. "Perhaps President Kotov could keep an eye on the scientist, sorry, what's his name?"

"Speranksy," Kotov replied. "And yes, that's an excellent idea. When he arrives I'll accompany him to the tunnel so I can supervise his work."

Jay Robertson had been making the most of Templehof's leisure facilities. If he had to be cooped up anywhere for security reasons, he could think of no better place. After an excellent game of squash with Jemma – he couldn't quite rid himself of the thought that she'd let him win, motivated by some perverse form of reverse sexism – he had returned to his room to shower ahead of Julia's arrival. Her flight had already landed at Brandenberg, but due to the rather random transport policy, until she arrived at Templehof, he wouldn't know whether she was being transferred by road or by air.

As he dried his hair he heard a helicopter fly overhead. Two minutes later, his phone beeped. 'Just landed'. He dressed quickly and headed downstairs to the entrance where the shuttle from the helipad deposited its passengers. He arrived in time to see Julia walking through the heavy glass doors in animated conversation with a man he thought he recognised. She saw him, quickly bade farewell to her travelling companion and walked towards him. She kissed him softly on the lips.

"Hello," she said

"Hello, thanks for coming. I've missed you."

"Me too."

"Who was that you were talking to. I'm sure I've met him."

"Of course you've met him, you idiot." Jay looked perplexed. "Labombard. The Canadian Prime Minister?"

"Of course, I really have been away too long."

"You're telling me. He's very nice you know. He invited us to dinner next time we're in Ottawa."

"Do we have plans to go to Ottawa, ever?"

Julia laughed. "So what's it like here?"

"It's great. Lots to do. I haven't done any work yet. And apart from the grand signing ceremony tomorrow, there's not much to be done, unless I'm called on for escorting duties, which is possible."

"And there's a party tonight?"

"Yes. Committee members and staff and their partners."

"Sounds great. And everything going well with the summit?"

"As far as I know. I think nearly all the delegates are here. The media is being very positive. I haven't seen much of

Helen. She's probably having a well-earned rest after everything she's been through the last couple of weeks."

"She'll be there tonight though, won't she?"

"Yes, I'm sure she will."

"Good. It'll be nice to see her again. And to meet some of your colleagues. Now, take me to our room. I'm going to need at least two hours to get ready."

Mbonga and Antonella were enjoying the hospitality. Rita had found them adjacent rooms on the same floor as most of the committee members. Mbonga took the opportunity to phone Temily. He hadn't spoken to her since he left, and she hadn't replied to the two emails he had sent. He calculated that she might still be at school, it being a Thursday, the evening she supervised netball practice. He was in luck.

Edmund, one of other teachers, answered the phone. "Mbonga, is it you? I can't believe it? Where are you?"

"I'm in Berlin."

"You made it then. Everyone has been wondering if you would get there."

"Is Temily there?"

"She is outside, I'll go and get her."

Thirty seconds later he heard his wife's voice. "Mbonga, are you alright?"

"I'm fine, how are you? How are the boys?"

"We're all fine. We've been worried about you."

"I sent you a couple of emails. Did you not receive them?"

"We've had no internet more or less since you left."

"Oh, I'm sorry. It hasn't been possible to phone until now."

"So where are you?"

"I'm in Berlin. I am actually at the summit."

"What do you mean you're at the summit?"

"In the hotel, at the conference centre. I've even met Helen George. I can't go into the details, but I'll tell you all about it when I get home."

Temily didn't sound convinced. "So when do you think you will be home? We need you back here."

"I'm not sure. Next week I hope."

"Well get a move on. Your brother heard there might be a job going at the garage, as a mechanic. Walter said he would keep it for you, as long as you're back next week."

"That would be very good. Tell Walter I definitely want the job. Take care my love."

"And you. I love you."

As he put the phone down there was a knock on the door. He rolled across the bed and opened it. He had expected to see Antonella, but Helen George was with her.

"Come in, please," he said. "Sit down."

"I just wanted to say thank you, properly, for what you did today. Through your action you may well have saved the summit."

Mbonga looked at Antonella, both smiled. "Well, we seem to make a good team," Mbonga said. "We still don't understand how we both came to be in Berlin. And if we hadn't met, I probably wouldn't have been able to report what I had seen to you. It was only because Antonella had met you, and you happened to be watching the television."

"Actually, it was Rita who spotted you on TV. I had told her about meeting Antonella when we were in São Paulo.

Luckily she remembered your name. But it is a remarkable series of coincidences."

"How are they getting on down in the tunnels. Do you think it's a bomb."

Helen knew she couldn't tell them everything, at the same time she didn't want to pull the wool over their eyes. "That seems most likely. You were right, the tunnels do run under this building. We have an evacuation plan in case we are unable to find it. But I am sure we will. You have nothing to worry about." They both relaxed visibly; she must have sounded convincing.

"Tomorrow evening, after the ceremony, there's a gala concert and I'd like to invite you both, assuming you don't have other plans?" They looked at each other, shrugged and nodded enthusiastically.

"There's one other thing, if I may?" Mbonga asked.

"Of course."

"I've just been talking to my wife on the phone. She wants to know when I'll be home. As you know I travelled here over land. It might not be easy for me to get back."

"Don't worry. I'll have someone sort out a flight for you" There was another knock on the door.

"Come in," Antonella called. It was Rita.

"Hi Helen, I thought you might be here. It's six-thirty. We have to be downstairs in half an hour."

"Thanks. I'd lost track of time. I'll get changed, then I'll drop in on Harry on the way down."

"Will you two be okay?" Antonella and Mbonga nodded again. "Okay. I'll let you know if there's any news."

"How much have you told them?" Rita asked as they left the room.

"I've told them we suspect a bomb, but not that it might be nuclear. I also told them that thanks to their efforts everything is under control. They seem remarkably calm under the circumstances. I'm going to put a guard on the door, just in case."

She found Harry and Kotov in the control room. "Any news of Speransky?" she asked them.

"Not yet. His flight was delayed. There's a helicopter waiting for him at Brandenberg," Harry answered. "And I've found out some more about him. People I trust tell me he that he is totally reliable. We don't have anything to fear."

"I just hope he gets here in time."

"We still have eighteen hours," Harry said, trying to be encouraging. "And the tunnel team are now within the airport perimeter. It won't be long until they find it." Harry's phone rang. "Speransky's here," he said, after a conversation to which he contributed just two words. "They're flying him straight to Treptow. There's a car waiting downstairs for you," he said to Kotov.

"I'll let Mike know not to let Speranksy into the tunnel until you get there."

"Thanks Harry." Kotov was gone.

By the time Helen got down to the restaurant, everyone else was there. She was looking forward to meeting her colleague's other halves, most of whom she hadn't met before. But first she needed to talk to her own. She could see Rudolf standing near the bar with Saeed.

"Hello stranger. How are you?" she said gently elbowing him in the ribs so he would make room for her.

"Darling. I'm fine. You?"

"Not too bad, all things considered. Daniel informed you of our news, I assume?"

"Yes. I have to say it did put me off my stride for a short while, but I understand the matter is being dealt with."

"Yes. And key personnel have just arrived on site, so with luck there will be news before too long."

They looked at each other; each knew that the other was scared, but neither could let it show.

"So, how are rehearsals going?" Helen asked, signalling an end to the requirement to speak in code.

"Well, I'm glad we have tomorrow. But so far, not too bad."

"I think it'll be marvellous, don't you Saeed?"

"I think I've attended six of your husband's concerts over the years, and I have to say that each one has left me in awe. But of course I shall be expecting something extra special from this one." Rudolf looked pained.

"Right I'd better go and talk to some of these spouses and partners," Helen said, kissing him again. As she headed towards the main part of the room where most of the guests were gathered, she bumped into Julia, alone, apparently on her way to the bathroom.

"Helen, how lovely to see you," she said.

"You too. How are you?" She hoped the question didn't sound too loaded.

"Actually okay. Obviously I wish I'd never let you take my husband from me; that might have avoided a great deal of heartache. I do hope he's been of some use over the last two years."

"We couldn't have done it without him."

"Thanks. I'll be glad to have him back though. And I'm only sorry he's given you so much trouble."

"You are the last person who needs to apologise. Are you heading straight back to Canada?"

"No, he's planned a surprise for me. We're going back on Thursday. I'd like to stay longer. I love Europe as you know, but Nathalie is with Jay's parents and she's been through enough in the last few weeks. She could do with some normal, boring family life; she's never really had that."

"And Jay tells me you're moving back to Montreal?"

"That's the plan. He has an offer to start at McGill next fall. So we've got a year to move, get Nathalie settled into school and, well, to start over I guess."

"He's a good man, you'll be okay. Now, I probably need to speak to everyone here before we go through to dinner, but we'll catch up later, okay?"

Dinner was good. The time passed very quickly. Helen and Saeed each had to field a couple of questions from colleagues about the ongoing security situation. Both gave the official line that there was no longer anything to be worried about.

Coffee was served in the reception area, and after spending a few minutes with Kersen and his wife, Helen spotted Stefan alone near the window. He wasn't the only partner-less colleague: Ajala was unmarried and Zhang's wife had not been able to make the trip from China; but she suspected Stefan would be finding the party hard.

"How are you doing?" she asked, as she stood beside him, looking out of the window across the vast expanse of the old airfield.

"Pretty well, actually."

"Can't be much fun seeing everyone with their partners."

"No. But I've had some rather good news."

"Really?"

"Yes. Weiss has agreed to give Veronica a divorce."

"That's fantastic."

"Thank you." He turned and smiled at her. He looked about twenty years younger.

"When are you going to see her?"

"She's sorting out the legal stuff at the moment, but she's hoping to come to Sweden in a couple of weeks time. You know Helen, it'll be the first time we've been able to spend more than a night together since we were students."

"I'm really pleased for you."

He smiled again, but his expression quickly turned serious. "Helen, is something going on? I get the impression that certain people are not as relaxed as they might be."

"There's a bomb. An operation is underway to find it and make it safe. But we may have to evacuate. A decision will be made at 8am."

"I see. Presumably few people know?"

"We thought the fewer the better, under the circumstances."

"Let me know if there's anything I can do."

Twenty-Seven

The search was in its ninth hour, and while they had to be getting closer, Mike was worried. Kotov and Speransky were waiting on the surface. German engineers had enlarged the shaft to the tunnel to make it big enough to drop quad bikes in. As soon as the device was found, they could be driven to the location in minutes. Cables had been laid so that Mike was able to talk to the lead party in the tunnel. He wondered whether they should trust Silverman's word. He had suggested the device was timed to go off just as everyone was gathering for the gala concert. But what if he'd been lying; the thing could blow at anytime.

He was about to call Helen to suggest she bring forward the evacuation, but before he could, the radio came to life.

"Mike, it's Rulein. We've got it. We'll send details of the exact position up the line."

"Is it accessible?"

"There are several booby traps. Conventional, not difficult to neutralise. We've taken out two of them already. Your Russian technician should be able to start work in about 30 minutes."

"Thanks. We're on our way." Kotov and Speransky were already climbing into the tunnel. Mike called Helen.

"Hi Mike," she answered expectantly.

"Helen, we've found it. Kotov and Speransky have just gone down. Speransky reckons it could take several hours, but he does seem confident. The Germans have rigged up communications relays. I should be able to call from inside the tunnel. I'll keep you posted."

"Thanks."

"She turned around and looked back into the room. She spotted Rudolf and walked towards him. She leant over to kiss him on his left check and whispered in his ear, "They've found it."

It was already past eleven and the party was coming to a natural end as many of the guests, conscious that tomorrow was a momentous day, drifted off. Helen returned to the command centre where she and Harry were joined by Saeed, Daniel, Rita and Ann Margaret.

"Harry, can you give us the latest?"

"Of course. The device has been found. Mike, President Kotov and Dr Speransky, the Russian scientist who designed it, are there. Several booby traps that had been laid around the device have been removed. Speransky is getting to work. Mike is going to check in every 20 minutes or so."

"How long is it likely to take?' Daniel asked

"We don't know, it could be several hours."

"And where exactly is the bomb?"

"It's about two hundred metres south-east of the main conference hall, under the old north runway. Not that its precise location makes much difference with this kind of weapon."

"Can we relax?" Helen asked.

"Speransky told Kotov that his wife gave birth to their third child this week. He hasn't seen the little boy yet. He plans to see him on Sunday."

"And what do you think Harry?" Daniel asked.

"I think such exercises always carry a degree of risk."

"Well," Helen said, "I'm not going to bed. Anyone for a game of cards?"

Ann Margaret and Daniel politely declined.

"That only leaves three of us. We need four," Saeed said as the others left the room.

"I'd love to join you, but I should probably stay here," Harry said.

"I know. I'll get Stefan," Helen said. "Don't worry, I told him, well not everything. Anyway he needs to know we've found it, even if he doesn't need to know what type it is. Your room?" Saeed nodded.

Within minutes of arriving at the location of the device, it was clear that Speransky didn't need anyone to keep an eye on him. He was calm and professional. He told Mike that his personal commitment to the blueprint was total, and, with a surprising dramatic flourish exaggerated by halting English, announced that this was "the most important assignment of my lifetime." He didn't seem concerned that his efforts were being nominally supervised by his country's President. Kotov's role was reduced to that of interpreter, though Mike was glad he was there.

The device had been placed on a pallet in the corner of a large chamber, about ten metres long and seven metres wide. The ceiling was a little higher than in the tunnel, at about three metres. They supposed the featureless concrete cell was built as a storage area. Floodlights had been installed in the three corners that were not occupied by a nuclear weapon, and the effect, as the light fell on the pale grey walls, was to create an environment almost too bright for unshaded eyes. Speransky was happy though. He declared the lighting to be perfect before retrieving a camera from his case and taking several photos of the device from different angles. Mike and Kotov looked at each other, but said nothing.

After making his initial assessment, Speransky asked Kotov to translate for Mike.

"The objective is to detach the warhead from the detonator. It appears that the device has not been assembled according to my design specification. This is probably because whoever put it together had some knowledge of it, but no access to the technical manuals. This will make it a little harder to disassemble, but it is still perfectly possible." Kotov translated.

Speranksy paused, and looked at them over very small spectacles which he wore in style of pince-nez. As he continued, so did Kotov. "There is virtually no possibility of the device detonating as a result of my efforts to neutralize it. Vibration is not a problem. Even if I were accidentally to drop it on the floor, it is unlikely to detonate. Nonetheless I shall take no risks. Please don't become impatient if my actions appear rather more deliberate than seems necessary."

"Is there any way of confirming when the bomb is scheduled to go off?" Kotov asked, in Russian, and then in English for Mike's benefit.

Speransky shook his head. "What I can say with certainty is that the only method of detonation is the onboard timing device. Remote detonation would be impossible inside this chamber, even from elsewhere in the tunnel system. I won't be able to access the interface to the timing device until I have separated the detonator from the warhead. So, we won't know how long we have, or had, until the device has been made safe."

"Perhaps that's for the best," Mike said, managing a smile.

The Russian understood him and replied in English. "I think so too."

"And if it does go off," Kotov asked, "will we know anything about it?"

"You might hear me swear, Mr President. But otherwise, no."

Helen, Saeed, Rita and Stefan were on their third hand of poker when Saeed threw down his cards. "It's no good. I need to talk about this. Helen, do you mind if I tell Stefan the bit he doesn't know. Then at least we are all equal."

"Okay. Go ahead," Helen said. Stefan looked confused.

"The bomb. It's nuclear. We are sitting here playing poker while the President of Russia and a technician he's never met are working to defuse an atomic bomb about a thirty metres below us?"

"It's in the tunnels?" Stefan asked calmly.

"You know about the tunnels?" Rita asked.

"Yes, there was an article about them, in the Wall Street Journal funnily enough. I read it when we were in Tbilisi. Don't tell me German security didn't think to check them?"

"They were checked, and all the entrances were sealed." Helen said. "But somebody knew their way around them rather better than we did. They planted the device after the security sweep was completed, probably on Tuesday."

"And do we know how long we've got?" Stefan asked.

"We think it's timed to go off as everyone gathers for the concert tomorrow evening."

"Well, let's hope the Russians know what they're doing. Now, whose bet is it?" Lundberg smiled reassuringly. Helen was finding it all increasingly surreal.

Harry had been alone in the command centre for nearly three hours. Mike hadn't reported in for some time. He thought about Silverman, who had been transferred to a maximum security prison on the outskirts of Berlin. It was ironic, he thought, that if the bomb blew now, Silverman would probably be unaffected, while Harry would be toast.

At 1am he had called down for a bottle of wine. There was no exceptional Burgundy on the list, but a very helpful German with no idea about wine but who was determined to give good service, eventually came up with a pleasant Givry.

Harry remembered his last visit to Givry when he'd spent most of a perfect spring morning with Monsieur du Closel on a tour of the family vineyards before tasting and buying a case of the latest vintage Premier Cru.

He drank slowly, partly because he needed to remain sober, but also because, if this was to be his last night on earth, he was determined to savour his final bottle of Burgundy.

Assuming Speransky was able to complete his task, Noble wondered what he would do next. He now felt positive about the post-summit world, and wondered if he might be able to find some kind of role in assisting with the implementation process. He didn't think he could ask Helen for another job, but after this little escapade he felt sure opportunities might open up in the Civil Service back in London. On the other hand, his sixtieth birthday was not far off. Perhaps he should enjoy the dawn of this brave new world from the privileged vantage point of an ordinary citizen.

The phone rang. He looked at the clock. It was 3.30am.

"Harry, it's Kotov," he could hear emotion in the Russian's voice.

"He's done it Harry. He's disabled the device. The warhead is being removed from the tunnel now, and will be transported to a secure facility near Leipzig. Speransky assures me that unless someone hijacks the truck and is able to wire up a new detonator, there is no further danger."

"Thank God. I'll call Helen."

"Harry?" Helen answered.

"The device has been made safe. You can go to bed now," he said. He heard only sobs before the line went dead.

Through a haze of tears, Helen told the others.

"Right," Saeed said, taking control. I'll go and tell Daniel. Rita, perhaps you could tell Ann Margaret? She'd better call Emmerich. I can't imagine he'll be sleeping."

"Thank you, all of you." Helen said, wiping away tears.

Various meetings had taken place since the delegates had begun arriving on Wednesday morning, but the business of the summit itself was largely ceremonial and celebratory. By midday, all had gathered in the main conference hall. The session was divided into two halves. A welcome speech from Chancellor Emmerich was followed by a formal signing ceremony at which each head of government would sign the Blueprint Implementation Plan, committing their country to work towards full implementation by 1st May 2024, just over six months away.

They had been keen to avoid the event too closely resembling the Eurovision Song Contest, so it was agreed that each signatory would be announced in German, while the name of the country they represented would be called in that country's native tongue. It took a bit of getting used to, but as the ceremony progressed, Helen thought it sounded better than the alternative, which would have involved translating titles and country names into several languages, and turned an already lengthy ceremony into something quite unbearable. Premierminister Larson of Sverige sounded okay and was understood by most, as was Präsident Solis of the United States.

They had decided that with nearly two hundred signatures to be collected, a conventional table arrangement would not be practical. So, rather like the Oscars, Helen and Saeed stood either side of a lectern. As each signatory was announced onto the stage, they moved forward, engaged in whatever combination of kissing, bowing, hand shaking and hugging seemed appropriate, before lining up behind the lectern while the signature was added.

With the exception of Daniel, who had been excused three hours on his feet, the other committee members were acting as ushers, arranging an orderly line of world leaders backstage. They were alphabetical by country name. As each name was called, the ushers would wave, and in one or two cases push, the next President or Prime Minister onto the stage. It was not an easy task, and while there were no major spats, it was apparent that most were quite unable to cope in an environment bordering on the chaotic with little protocol to guide proceedings.

There was only one noticeable hiccup, when Rita's grasp of the alphabet let her down, and she tried to send the President of Bahrain out ahead of the Prime Minister of the Bahamas. The two statesmen sorted it out amongst themselves, deciding to make an impromptu statement of cross-cultural cooperation by taking to the stage together. The announcer somehow managed to call both their names as if the whole thing had been planned in advance, though Helen and Saeed were unable to conceal their bemusement.

Virtually all the delegates – each country had been allowed four attendees and there were various representatives of UN and other multilateral bodies present – acceded to the request to remain in their seats for the duration of the ceremony. When it was over, there was a pause for refreshments before the second half. When they returned, eleven members of the committee were seated on the stage to the left, while Helen remained at the opposite side. A second lectern had been positioned in the middle of the stage, and it was here that each of ten speakers would deliver their addresses.

The ten had been selected by the drawing of lots. Each was expected to speak for no more than five minutes. They included Presidents Kotov and Horomito, and the Dalai Lama, whom Helen was delighted to introduce. As well as being typically fulsome in his praise of the committee, he took the opportunity to announce the establishment of the World Council of Faiths which would be holding its first meeting at the Rykestrasse Synagogue in Berlin the following morning.

Each speech was received with a standing ovation. Helen was impressed by all of them: there was clear evidence of regional cooperation in the drafting of texts. The Prime Minister of Nepal announced an agreement between his country and India, Pakistan, Bangladesh, Bhutan and Sri Lanka to work together on an accelerated regional implementation of the blueprint, which they hoped would be complete by 1st March. On hearing this, Helen looked over at Ajala who smiled, and winked back at her.

After the President of Namibia, who was the last to speak, wound up his address, he moved along the line shaking hands with each committee member before thanking Helen and leaving the stage to return to his seat in the front row.

Then it was her turn. She had barely slept, and had been working non-stop since 7am, but she'd never felt more alive. She hadn't prepared a speech. Instead she thanked each of the committee members by name, adding a short sentence highlighting their individual contribution. She saved Saeed until last. She then thanked Mike and Jane for their immense efforts. She expressed her gratitude to all of the delegates, thanking each of the ten speakers for their contributions. She then paused for such a long time that several of her colleagues began to look at each other.

"We must not," she eventually continued, "forget what this process is really about. It is not about saving the planet for some abstract notion of civilization, much as we hold that concept close to our hearts. It is about creating a world in which all human beings have a reasonable chance in life, and can take full responsibility for their own wellbeing in an environment that allows room, and provides opportunities, for everyone. It would not have succeeded without the vocal support of billions of so-called ordinary people who found the courage and strength to hold us to account, and to tell us that things had to change."

"When the history of this process comes to be written, the names of two such ordinary people will feature large in its pages. I would like to invite them on to the stage now to say a few words." Rita, who had left the podium at the beginning of Helen's speech, led Antonella and Mbonga onto the stage.

"Oh my God," Antonella's mother cried. She was at her neighbours house with her two sons. A few hours earlier Tito had called round with a message from Antonella.

"She is having a wonderful time," he had told her, "but she wanted me to remind you to watch the ceremony. Especially the bit with the speeches, and you must watch to the end."

"She said I must watch to the end? What a strange thing to say."

"I know. It was a bit of a strange conversation. She wouldn't tell me any more. She didn't seem quite herself, but said she was okay. She just made me promise to give you the message and to watch the ceremony myself."

Sra Simao, on whose sofa Antonella's mother was now sitting, could not contain herself. "It's her. It's Antonella. It's your daughter. What's she doing there?"

"I don't know, I don't know," her mother screamed, tears streaming down her face.

Antonella had agreed with Mbonga that she would go first, but now she was petrified. The auditorium was well lit, and in the first row she saw many faces she recognised. There was President Solis sat a few seats along from the President of China. A few seats further along sat the Brazilian President. This made her even more nervous.

"Ladies and gentleman," she had decided to speak in English. "A few weeks ago I had the great pleasure of meeting Helen George. I was working at my job in the hotel in São Paulo where the second summit was held. Helen was very kind to me. I had always been interested in the blueprint, but after meeting her I became even more interested. So it is a great honour to be able to speak to you today."

"A week before I met Helen, my grandmother died. She was 90 years old and had been ill for some time. It was a very sad day for me. I was very close to my grandmother. I loved her very much. Her name was Sophia Ascoli. She was born in Italy in 1943. But shortly afterwards, her parents, who, like me, were Jewish, had to flee the advancing German army. Eventually, thanks to the courage of a Brazilian diplomat who broke his country's laws and risked his own life to save people like my grandmother; along with her parents, she made her way to Brazil. My grandmother never had a chance to thank that brave man, but she always said that perhaps one day the courage and principle of people like him would help us to create a better world, a world in which all human beings can live without fear of persecution."

"My grandmother escaped persecution, but like many Brazilians she remained poor all her life. Today Brazil is considered a success story, a country that has pulled itself out of poverty. It has not. It has succeeded in pulling some of its people out of poverty, but life has barely improved for many. I know that in many countries the situation is even worse."

"Before she died, I promised my grandmother that my children would have a better life. Thanks to your commitment to the blueprint, I think I may now be able to make good on my promise."

She looked down into the front row. She saw tears running down the cheeks of President di Soto. She looked at Helen who nodded and smiled, before turning back to the auditorium.

"Thank you."

It was more than five minutes before the applause died down sufficiently for Helen to introduce the next speaker.

"My name is Mbonga Siphosa and I am from Swaziland," he began. He recounted the story of his journey to be at the summit, and the people he had met along the way: the emaciated children scavenging for food in Tete; the captain of the Illala which had by now sailed its last voyage; his friend Julius and his four children who had lost their mother to AIDS; Alex and Malaika, doctors who had been unable to save the life of their young daughter because of the drought and attendant civil breakdown in Kenya; and the container stowaways with whom he'd travelled from Mombassa to Marseilles. He read out their names and expressed the hope that if they had fallen into the hands of the French authorities, they would be treated mercifully.

"They are very good people," he concluded. "Just like you and me, they deserve a chance in life."

If anything, Mbonga's ovation outlasted that received by Antonella. After several minutes, Helen led them from the stage before returning. Unexpectedly, the other committee members were now on their feet standing at the front of the stage applauding the delegates. Helen joined them. She caught sight of Sarah Brightwell in the front row. The British Prime Minister was smiling broadly.

Helen managed to get an hour with Rudolf before he went into last minute rehearsals for the gala concert. She was exhausted but elated and thoroughly looking forward to the evening. Rudolf was a little on edge; preparations had not gone as well as he had hoped; thus the additional rehearsal, but Helen managed to extract an admission that he'd rather be rehearsing until the last minute, than having to sit around waiting for curtain up.

The first half went very well. The orchestra played effortlessly, as if lifted by the occasion. Helen could tell Rudolf was enjoying himself. Each time he turned to face the audience between pieces he looked straight at her. He only did this if he was satisfied with a performance. In no time at all he was thanking the audience, joking that it was one of the best behaved he had ever played in front of, and announcing a forty minute interval.

Members of the committee were invited backstage along with some friends of President Morel, who had put a few backs up by taking a bigger role in the organisation of the concert than was strictly necessary. Rudolf was delighted, however.

"It's so refreshing," he told Helen and Ann Margaret, "to have a promoter with absolute authority, someone who doesn't have to negotiate with anyone."

The Dalai Lama came over. Helen thanked him for the wonderful speech he'd given earlier, and promised that she would put in an appearance at the launch event for the World Council of Faiths the next morning.

"I'd like to meet Antonella and Mbonga, to congratulate them on their speeches. Are they here?" he asked.

"Yes. They're over there with Rita. Go and introduce yourself." As she spoke, she spotted Harry, standing not far away with Mike and Saeed. "But before you do, may I introduce you to someone else?"

"Of course you may."

She took his arm and guided him towards the group. Saeed saw them coming, stopped talking and signalled to Harry to turn around.

"Your holiness, I'd like to introduce an especially valued colleague of mine, Mr Harry Noble."

"What a very great pleasure it is to meet you Mr Noble." Harry was lost for words.

Minutes later they were all seated for the second half. As Helen sat down, it struck her that notwithstanding her new job, this was the final act in an epic drama played out over two years. She looked along the curve of the front row. At the end she saw Antonella and Mbonga; she thought of his remarkable pilgrimage and wondered what had guided him to make it, and so ultimately to save the summit, and thousands of lives.

Looking back at the stage, she saw Rudolf make his way to the podium. Daniel followed. As he took his seat at the piano, it occurred to her that she still didn't know what he'd chosen to play. In the silence, she watched as Rudolf raised his baton. Daniel held his hands above the keyboard, the right raised slightly higher than the left. Helen took a deep breath and closed her eyes.

If you'd like to join in the conversation about the issues raised
in this book, you might like to visit the author's website:

www.markbraund.com

or visit the Renegade Economist website:

www.renegadeeconomist.com

Also from Motherlode:

Four Horsemen:
The Survival Manual
by Braund and Ashcroft

Four Horsemen
The acclaimed film by Ross
Ashcroft. Available on DVD

CPSIA information can be obtained at www.ICGtesting.com
Printed in the USA
BVOW012309190213

313725BV00022B/804/P

9 780956 398529